FEARLESS

MMA SPORT & RUSSIAN MAFIA ROMANCE

AMARIE AVANT

D1520832

PROLOGUE

Vassili Karo Resnov
Mixed Martial Arts Arena, Brazil

"You good?" Vadim, my coach, asks in Russian. He applies pressure to the gash on my forehead. Blood is smeared all over the canvas beneath my feet. It drips from the incision at my temple. The medic already cleared me to continue. Although the sticky stream left me with only one working eye.

"Dah," I respond. My gaze is dead as I glare through my enemy, Tiago, seated across from me in the corner. Ten years ago, I would've laughed at the hothead. I was cocky then, too. Backing my shit up had always come easily. Now, my entire body is on fire. Killing Tiago in the cage is my fuel.

"How's your knee?" coach questions.

The death trance I've been in for two rounds fades the second Vadim mentions my knee. A vivid image of my wife, Zariah, permeates my mind. Her mahogany skin has lost its glow. Her deep, brown eyes were full of disdain, as the physician injected cortisone in my left knee not an hour ago.

Marriage to an attorney means I've got to fucking *defend myself* whenever she's worried about me. Don't get me wrong. There are broads in this world that want nothing more than to hang on my arm and get a piece of me. There's nothing like having a real woman, who loves you regardless of your faults. Truth is, she isn't all debates and arguments. I should've held off my return, but I was born for the octagon. All I have ever loved is my wife, our baby, Natasha, and pounding flesh.

"You aren't ready to return, Vassili," Zariah had said. She loves to bust my fucking balls, though. This time, she wasn't too far off from the truth. Every time I step into the cage, man, her heart breaks a little bit more. I'm a damned occupational hazard. She's too good for this shit…too good for *me*. So, how did someone like me get such an innocent treasure? One, I'm not a quitter. I've loved Zariah since long before she ever gave *me* a chance. Two, I did it with patience. It was seven whole damn years before she finally offered me the key to her heart in return.

Vadim's bushy, white eyebrows rise.

"Vassili, you good?"

I shake the daze from my brain.

"Khorosho. Khorosho—Good. Good. Just a little blood." *A lot of fucking blood.*

Nestor hands me a cup of water. He sniffs. "A little blood never hurt anyone, eh? Karo, knock 'em the fuck out."

"No, Karo is going to lay Tiago to rest."

Vadim has a hungry glare in his eyes, as he preps me with more Vaseline.

"Keep him moving. He'll tire. You're doing good, Karo. Don't let him get to your *knee.* Bring that *mudak* down. Kill 'em, Karo, kill 'em."

I nod, rising to my feet. Tiago and I come together, once more. I lock his arms and pin him against the fence. My *good knee* jabs into his abs. With each forceful hit, I annihilate his liver. Tiago goes back to the clinch. A hook punch lands right behind my ear, and then we're back to the middle of the cage. Back and forth we go, fists like bricks, as if one of us pissed on the other's mother's grave. I've got power, but this motherfucker is just as dominating.

Tire him out. Bring him down for the kill.

A kick against my left knee forces venom into my veins. White noise buzzes in my ears. Instantly, my mind is on *her* and her disappointment.

Kill. Kill. Kill. Should be the only thought in my mind. But, Zariah's arguing has bull-rushed back into my headspace. *Shit, don't think about Zariah now, I'm not going to bitch out!* She's sitting in the front row. Though a professional at taking hits, I'm not stupid enough to glance her way. My stats: 25 knockouts, 9 submissions, and 2 losses. The first 'L' was as an amateur. The second left me with a fractured patella 217 days ago. I've been ready to get my ass in the octagon ever since.

It's as if Zariah's heart is beating through mine when Tiago realizes my knee isn't as "good" as I let on during our promotions. With each blow, I counter, knowing she's right there, unable to breathe. Tiago alternates from targeting my knee to the gash on my head. The cortisone high my left knee was on has ended. A phantom serrated knife, burning like fire from being left on hot coals, has sliced through my knee.

"Karo, do you want to continue?" The ref asks, holding up a steady hand for Tiago to keep his distance.

This is where Zariah and I always chatted about putting our baby girl, Natasha, first. Though the crowd is egging me on—one fucking eye and all—Zariah's disappointment is palpable. Breathing jagged, my heart crumbles. I nod vigorously to continue. It's me or this motherfucker before me. One of us is going down tonight.

There has to be less than a precious minute left. And I can't take a loss by decision.

"Vassili, baby, stop. We have a good life! We have a beautiful baby girl, who your doctor hasn't cleared you to hold without you having to be in a seated position!" Zariah had said some odd months ago. That was after I lost the welterweight belt—my belt. It was my second professional loss.

Jumping to my dominant leg, I force my left leg forward. The kick dislocated my toe as my foot slams against Tiago's mouth. He's brought to his knees.

Total knock out or submission. The easy route would be another swift kick to his mouth and lodge that fucking mouthguard down his throat. Nah, let's go for overkill! Jaw tensed, I clamber behind him onto his back and pull my right arm around his neck. My bicep sinking into his carotid artery while my forearm curls around his spine. Gripping my fists together, I begin squeezing him in a rear-naked choke.

"Vassili, it's Natasha and me or the cage. You choose."

"Zariah, really, sweetheart? Don't do that. Don't fucking do that. Natasha is my princess. You're my queen, so you know that the answer will always be—"

Tap! Tiago gets in one tap. His hand pauses mid-second tap. His body then softens into a limp position in my arms.

The referee is calling the fight as the Brazilian slips to the floor. I jump up. My entire body is on fire now. The pain engulfs me as if I leaped headfirst into a volcano. Every muscle screams, every tendon haggard. I climb up the side of the fence, favoring my right knee. I straddle it and place my fists into the air.

"This is it! Killer Karo is back!" I hear through the loud-speakers. The announcer's already predicting that *my* belt will soon return to my grasp. The welterweight belt I lost seven months ago was always meant to be mine. The feel of it is so tangible. I breathe in the victory, glancing toward Zariah's chair.

It's *empty*.

The only time my wife left during the middle of a bout, she'd gone into labor with Natasha. Nestor said she'd squirmed in her seat almost the entire time waiting for my victory. Though I'd won that fight, my body had felt like shit. I'd still grabbed the keys to his motorcycle, speeding my ass off, to get to her.

She. Left. That high, that triumphant high, so much better than cocaine, crashes down around me. *My wife is gone.*

1

VASSILI

Venice Beach, California
Nine Years Ago

op! A cross hook whips through the air. The hit packs enough force to pop my jaw out of place. Every once in a while, my opponent gains the upper hand. It's a wake-up call that all the attempts of my crew to puff up my head are just that, puffs of smoke up my ass. I play into the invincibility crap on stage. That shit sells tickets, just as much as knocking a *mudak* out. Don't get me started on submissions. Sending my enemy to sleep is king.

The entire room falls quiet. The small crowd has forgotten how to speak. My opponent is one of the biggest shit talkers at Vadim's Gym. He's a major boxing *fan.* He always has something to say about MMA. He said boxing is a slow burn, but in the mixed martial arts world, the dynamics are much quicker. So this morning, I demanded that he come see me. He chose the old boxing stage, which is upstairs, lost

within the clutter of dusty equipment and offices. No sparring gear. The glossy look in his eyes tells me he is surprised
by making contact, as well. Now, here we are. As I readjust
my jaw, the wanna-be boxer brags,

"I told you, Vassili," he says, poising his right arm for a
hook.

For a split second, they all wonder if the 185 pounds of all
muscle, Killer Karo, is no longer untouchable. Is the dude
who got one in on me the next best thing?

Fuck no.

Not a moment later, I step back on my hind leg and lead
in with a power jab. My glove connects with his nose. Blood
projects outward as the cartilage snaps. The blow sends that
mudak to the opposite side of the ring. His body goes
between the ropes, slamming him against the floor.

Vadim's coaching assistant and the few people allowed up
here, are now rooting for me. They mutter about how lucky
the guy *was* three seconds ago.

His cross hook hadn't caught me off guard. A loud bitch
downstairs got the best of me, and she doesn't even know it.
The broad has a set of lungs on her. I swear, her mouth must
be wide enough for me to lodge my cock down her throat.
She's still screaming to high heaven about blowing Vadim's
Gym to the ground. Not the first broad to come in here
shouting about this, that and the other. She's the reason I had
to reach up and click my jaw back into place.

"What the fuck?" I ask in Russian, spitting blood on the
floor. I push the rope down and jump from the ring. I step
over the unconscious heap, eyes narrowed as I glare at all
these other idiots.

"We sent down Nestor the second it started," the assistant
says.

I bark, "You telling me that nobody can shut that bitch
up? Does she sound familiar to any of you?"

Everyone shakes their head 'no' in bewilderment.

While coming up the steps, my trainer, Nestor explains,

"Nobody down there knows who the broad is. She keeps asking for Sergy."

I rub my chin. "What did Sergy say or do to her? Not pay his fucking child support? He's down there working the weights, getting pretty ain't he?"

"Yeah, but he wasn't claiming the girl and she confirmed that he wasn't *her* Sergy." Nestor sighs. "She's a kid…a boner. She's very shapely but I swear, I think she's a kid."

Nestor licks his lips, thinking of the girl. I mumble under my breath, "We only have *one* Sergy."

"Should I go handle it?" asks Yuri, my fat cousin.

"Why are you asking now, *kuzen*? You could have handled the situation before *I took one to the fucking chin.*"

I start toward the stairs to handle the shit myself. Sweat drips from my muscles. I shuffle down the stairs to the sound of more threats about what's in the woman's purse.

When I make it to the first floor, there are a bunch of beef heads at the weight machines around the perimeter. Sergy, the three-headed monster, is the biggest one. Could be a heavyweight, but with two left feet, nobody's playing the fool.

I make my way through Vadim's men who are trying to sweet-talk the truth into her.

The instant my eyes land on her, I lose my ability to charm. God hasn't invented a word to describe how beautiful she is. Gorgeous has nothing on her. She's in a form-fitting black dress that stops mid-calf. There's nothing particularly sexy about the dress. Like she could wear it to the club and turn more heads than the women whose tits and asses are falling out. The allure is all her. Though projecting power and elegance, the silky fabric grips more curves than should be legal. Pointy heels that I love, grace her tiny feet. I can see myself gripping the long, thick braid slinked over her shoulder while her ass claps back against my cock.

She's a deep dark chocolate, with pink full lips. If I hadn't heard her cuss, I'd have to force my gaze away to search for the true culprit. But there are no other women and I can't take my gaze off her.

I gulp down the lump in my throat. *Am I fucking speechless?* Before I can tell myself not to bitch out, she starts in on another round.

"Where the hell is—"

"Miss, excuse me," I call out over her next threat.

Her fury turns my direction. Something in me wants to take every ounce of aggression she's willing to throw. Shit, I'll throw it right back at her in the sack. There's a spark of interest in her eyes, as they sweep up and down my sweaty muscles. She places a hand on her hips, dark eyes zeroing in on me, with the intention of eating me alive.

"Yes, excuse you. I want to see Sergio, *nowwww!*"

The left side of my mouth tips up. She stepped all over the rest of these fucks and thinks I'm next. *Nyet,* I won't be bested by a female. The shouting that caught me off guard doesn't count. Cussing doesn't come naturally for her. I'm betting the shouting masks her fear, as does her holding tight to her leather purse like she's carrying heat. Underneath the attitude, I sense her fear of me.

I tell her, "I can help you, Miss. I'm Vassili *Resnov.*"

Her pupils dilate further. More fear seeps in, taking away from the rapture of looking into her chocolate gaze. I know terror when I see it, even if her breasts are jutted out; hips, too. She's trying hard to appear confident, but she's scared. See, my last name *always* gets a reaction from the pussy.

Running a gloved hand over my Mohawk, I inquire, "You're looking for Sergy?"

. . .

The woman is taken back, just as I was upon first sight of her. She finds her voice, it's muted at first.

"Sergio, *Sergio*," she corrects. "And I'm going to bash his face in. See how he likes that. You all think you can go around hitting women. Well, I've got something for his ass." She taps her leather purse.

I've got something even harder for your ass. "I see. Come with me to my office."

Those stilettos don't budge an inch. "Where's Sergio?"

"He isn't here today." My statement is somewhere between the truth and a lie.

"C'mon, beautiful. You're making a scene, scaring those thick-necked pussies." I nudge my jaw toward the weight section.

The lady clasps the diamond butterfly necklace around her neck, her worry and fear increasing by the second.

"Humph, I know the name Resnov. You won't help me. Hell no, you'll *escort* me out back, *knock* me off and *drop* me into a Venice canal."

"There's never been blood on my hands."

Okay well, not the last breath kinda blood. I glance down at my hands and then hold them up. Nestor pulls off the boxing gloves one at a time. Next, I extend my hand.

"Clearly, Sergio has disrespected you. Please allow me to rectify that."

The girl's gaze falls from mine, as she shakes my hand. Her fingers are silky, so tiny I doubt they've ever even been in a catfight. Those sexy lips of hers almost relax. When I let her hand go, the rage returns to her eyes.

As we start up the stairs I share, "The owner, Vadim, is at a funeral today. Otherwise, the situation would've been handled by him."

She's quiet, simmering in anger, as my opponents usually

do. On the second floor, the guy I TKO'd is starting to awaken. The girl's steps falter.

"I offered the cage, but he preferred the ring. He also signed a disclaimer." I hold out my palms in a peaceful gesture. "And I've never hit a lady. So, you have nothing to fear. You're in good hands."

"I don't care about him," she retorts.

"Well, that makes two of us." I open the door to Vadim's office, gesturing for her to enter. My eyes rake over the small of her back and how it juts out. It's an ass begging for my kind of submission.

The heavenly view causes a pep in my step, as I walk in after her. There're MMA memorabilia on the walls. The trophies are so big that they stand equal to my 5 foot 11 stature. Champion belts dominate the walls along with a picture of Vadim's best fighters from the last 15 years.

"Please," I gesture toward a seat for her before I step around to Vadim's leather chair. For a moment, I'm mesmerized by the way she licks her lips apprehensively. For such an angry one, she has an innocent aura surrounding her.

"So, this Sergio, what does he look like?"

"You said you knew him."

"By nightfall, I'll know all about him."

Though I rarely smile, I offer the one that the ladies love. Shit, not this one.

"I give you my word. What does he look like?"

She bites her lip for a second. "Okay, he's at least a few inches taller than you, with more muscles than you," she sneers. "So stop eye-fucking me."

"Oh, I see it now. You have a beast of a boyfriend who likes to hit you. No matter how sexy your juicy ass is, I don't think running after 'The Incredible Hulk' is a good idea."

"Ha! Not my man. I'd never let a man like that touch me," she smirks.

I can pretty much read between the lines. She'd never let *me* touch her. Super expensive digs, rich girl attitude, when not shouting. I bet this black girl lives on the respectable side of Los Angeles. I consider the confusion with the name Sergy and Sergio.

"He's Italian?"

"Yeah."

"You're at the wrong gym, then." *But you're not leaving until I figure out more about you.* "Now we're getting somewhere, sweetheart. He got any tats?"

"Uh-uhn, I'm not your *sweetheart*," she corrects me. "To answer your question, yes, he does have tats. Not nearly as many as you do."

Her gaze scans up and down my muscular arms and upper body. There's not a single vacant spot left.

"Ironically, that asshole only has a pair of hands held together in a symbolic prayer sign on his bicep." Her mouth tenses in disgust, and then she licks her lips in consideration.

"Um, what's the name of the gym you think Sergio might be a member of?"

I grunt. "Why should I tell you? You don't have any business stepping into the gym like the one he's at. We're Russians here. Good people. Those Italians. *Mudaks.* You threaten them with what's in your purse, they're too stupid to call your bluff. They'll…" I form my hand in the shape of a gun and point it at her.

"Bang, beautiful. That's the end of your mouth. You're in safe hands with me, okay?"

"I'm not afraid of that piece of crap. He would already be dead had he touched one hair on *my* head."

I sink back in my chair. "Sergio didn't beat you. Who did that mudak beat?"

"My friend, Ronisha."

"Your friend? You came into a Russian gym for a *friend*." I rub my chin. "Not blood?"

She shakes her head. "No."

What kind of person places their life in danger over someone who isn't even family? There's no such thing as a black mafia. Trust me. I would know. So, no blood family and not part of *the* family.

"You swing both ways?"

"Listen, asshole, my friend is at the community hospital right now. Hit so hard she went into a seizure." A dam of tears flood down her high cheekbones.

Although she's beautiful when she cries, I have no sympathy. For all I know, she made up Ronisha and Sergio. Is this a setup? She's too young to be a federal agent. I assess the girl's digs. She's wearing too many name brands to have a friend that would be at the community hospital. People have died there with only a cough while waiting in the lobby. One measly exit wound and a motherfucker wouldn't make it. This chick is much too rich for Community, or to have any association with a person who has to receive treatment at that hospital. I steeple my fingers and wait for the crying fest to end. More than tears are needed to persuade me of her story.

Between sniffles, she opens her purse and pulls out a cell phone.

"Here's Ronisha. Th-this… this is how b-bad…badly Sergio hurt her," she stutters in devastation.

Her hand shakes violently as she gives the iPhone to me. My jaw clenches. The black girl on the photo is unrecognizable. One eye is swollen shut. The other is blood red from broken vessels. That's as much as I can make out from her black and blue face. After seeing this, if there is a damn Sergio, my mind is calculating the hours of torture he will endure at my hands.

"I'm going to kill him," the girl murmurs.

Her tone was so low that I have to look up. Damn, I never operate on emotion. Never placed myself in a position to give a damn about anyone besides my cousins and those closest to me.

That drive, which caused her to step inside of Vadim's talking shit, is back. Her gorgeous face is clouded in anger, fed by the love she has for her friend. Her emotion parallels the rage that storms through me when in the cage.

Either she deserves an Academy Award, or this isn't a game. I'm sold.

Rivers of tears begin to stream down her flawless mahogany skin again. Damn, I thought she blew me away on sight. Frowning at the cell phone screen, I hand it back over.

"Let me."

"L-let...let you what? Why?" She stammers, rubbing the back of her hand across her face to clear away the tears.

Because I need a reason to see you again. Though my fists are balled and I'm preparing for a fight, all I can think about is when I can see her again. I've seen her cry. Only I am capable of taking her tears away. Sergio's death will cease her crying.

"Why, Mr. Resnov?"

Because I have to see her smile if it's the last thing I do. I sit back in the chair with my usual nonchalant façade.

"Three reasons, doll. For one, you're all talk. Two, emotion is a sign of not having your head in the game. Don't open that pretty mouth to deny it either. And third, if he kills you instead—which I have no doubt will happen if you go— he and his entire family are dead. Now, you understand the Resnov way, eh?" I probe, making sure she gets it.

"Yes, I'm aware. 'Touch what's mine and the funeral home becomes rich'," she recites the motto perfectly.

It was a joke, but not really. My grandfather had said it, right after blowing away the entire remainder of a single

15

family's line. He was drunk off vodka and hadn't thought the saying would stick. Not sure why, but after that, our family never just took out the motherfucker that crossed us. We wipe out the person's entire lineage. Someone's great-grandson can become a loose end. Then came the next family that had to go, taken out by one of my uncles. Drenched in blood, he declared the same as my grandfather. There you have it. The Resnov way.

"I'll take care of everything." There's no mistake in my voice that she would never have to worry about Sergio.

"Excuse me, Vassili, but no thank you. I'm not afraid of Sergio. Any man who can hit a woman isn't a man at all. But with what I know of the Resnov name, I'm smart enough to apologize for stepping into your gym and causing a scene. Nevertheless, let's not mistake wisdom for fear. I am not afraid of you, either."

I lean back in the chair, rubbing the scar along my jaw. "Not my gym, but you'd like to apologize for cussing out everyone? I suggest you try it again. That was a statement of intent. Not an actual apology."

"I *apologize*. Like I said, I have more brains than to place myself at the mercy of a Resnov. I'll do the job myself. Me explaining the situation a minute ago was a form of apology. So, you'd understand why I arrived very distraught and angry. To be clear, you can't touch me either. Allowing me to walk out of here untouched would be the smartest thing you ever did," she concludes, on a hesitant note. Yet, the fire in her eyes tells me she believes the crap she dished out. When all I desire is to place my hands all over her body.

I can see my cock grazing against those dark pink lips.

"I accept the apology. We are far from done here, though. What's this aura of invincibility you have?" *This fake fearlessness?*

She smiles for the first time, digging back into her purse.

She pulls out a business card. My fingers brushed against hers purposefully. Instead of taking the card from her, I clasp her hand in mine.

Our eyes connect. "I can make you fear me in all the delicious ways you've only ever dreamed of. Would you like me to do that for you?" I ask, clutching her hand. The card is crumpled between us.

"The only pain I'd offer would come from you begging me for more, okay, beautiful?"

"Please stop," she murmurs.

I let her hand go and cock a grin, reading the card.

"Maxwell Washington. Chief of Police."

"My father," she adds smugly.

I nod. So this is where her logic of invincibility comes from. Even in the cage, I'm not that fucking cocky. My time will come. Washington's will too in the streets.

"I'm not stupid enough to traipse into any gym threatening a life without some kind of an insurance policy."

I flick the card back over. The mannerism lets it be known that her statement is weak shit.

"Why not have your pop handle it?"

Ms. Washington grumbles, "My father isn't the biggest fan of my best friend. Besides, I don't want Sergio out and ready to abuse another woman. God forbid, Ronisha allows him to use her as a punching bag again. She's let him back too many times as it is."

"So you'd risk your freedom if you're caught?"

"*She is my best friend,*" she belts out, through gritted teeth. "Ronisha's had a hard life. When we were kids, her father was on the force. Our fathers were partners on the beat in South L.A. Ronisha's father died when she was seven. By that time, she and I were thick as thieves. Anyway, she and her mom had to move to the projects. But I don't throw away my friend because of where they live. She had an aneurysm back when she was nine and I was eight. That stuck with me. I've always felt so bad for her. She would have been an amazing ballerina. Before that, I argued with my father to pay for ballet classes for both of us. Her mom didn't have the funds and I knew he wouldn't just pay for her. In my father's eyes, he justified the expense because it looked good to his friends that I was a ballerina. Sheesh, Ronisha *lived* to dance. After the aneurysm, though, she had no balance." Ms. Washington stops to breathe deeply, speaking to me as if we're old friends. I'm stuck on her every word.

"Ronisha is beautiful. May not look it from the picture. Mentally, she's still nine. Still, that nine-year-old girl who had an aneurysm that ended her dancing. Sergio and other boys like him enjoy sweet, naïve girls like her."

My body stiffens. I blink away images of another young girl who never had a chance to be a teenager. *I should have saved her.*

Unaware of the sudden discomfort I'm feeling, Ms. Washington wipes the tears from her eyes.

"Look, I came to the wrong place. Disrespected the wrong gym. You say it isn't yours. I say anytime a Resnov likes a business, you respect that place. I only came back to this room because you and your goons are more than capable of force. Also, telling you the truth might cushion how crazy I was being out there. Now I've told you too much," she said while rising from her chair. "But I don't believe you'll snitch on me."

"No snitch here," I say, standing before her. Her sweet floral scent infuses my nostrils. There's no way in hell I'll let any of those Italians fucks hurt her.

"Give me 'til evening and Sergio will be dealt with."

"Why are you insisting on helping me? I showed you my father's card. It was pretty much to get out of here alive. That is all."

I laugh. "Nobody will touch a hair on your head."

"Don't play me," Ms. Washington demands, raising her index finger.

"Let's sit," I insist, taking a seat in the chair next to her.

She doesn't sit. My glare is hard enough for her to change her mind and plop down again beside me. I rub my jaw.

"Sergio doesn't have much longer to breathe. You have my word. Now, let's talk about my compensation." *All I want to do is see you again.* By force or not, I will see Ms. Washington. Whatever happens after that is all up to her.

2

ZARIAH WASHINGTON

D amn, I thought I *was* handling myself well when I arrived. The Russians in Vadim's Gym had gladly offered Sergy up on a silver platter. But he wasn't the guy who needed his neck wrung.

My actions were comparable to loading a .9 millimeter and pressing it to my skull. Or rather, I've pressed it to my chest.

For a Russian mobster, Vassili is super-hot. I've always mocked the Russian accent. His sinks into my bones, turning them to putty. His voice was slow, deliberate, dripping in sex and heavy with strength. Maybe I'm going crazy? Can a voice sound like power?

Even with his body covered in tattoos, I can tell that each muscle is precisely defined. Vassili's shorts rode low, highlighting an impeccable V shape and his never-ending abs.

His jawline is likened to one of those drawings that an artist spends a lifetime sketching. Not an amateur, but rather one who is meticulous; gifted. It's perfectly squared and bristled. I lost my mind during those first few seconds. For instance, I imagined running my fingers along the jagged scar that's given the beast a somewhat distinguished character.

After he introduced himself, my legs were jelly, as we spoke downstairs.

Now, he's sitting next to me. He's offered me the deal of a lifetime. Ronisha is my heart. All the hurt she's endured because of a man is enough to be committed. Yet, I'm not quite ready to shake hands with the devil.

"Vassili, I will not spend the night with you." My tone is soothing, yet certain. If he weren't a Resnov and I was easy, yes, of course, I would jump on it! But he's part of the Russian syndicate and my parents have invested too much into me: education and virtue.

"Ms. Washington, all I can offer you is one night." Vassili turns back and forth, ever so slowly, in the leather swivel chair.

Stacks and stacks of abdominal muscles continue to beckon my eyes to take a look. I'm so damn tired. Today should've consisted of copious amounts of stiletto shoe purchases on Rodeo Drive before I head off to college. But Ronisha's mom called me at 4 o'clock this morning while she was hopping onto an ambulance.

I can't stop myself from staring at the bold tattoo across his chest. KILLER KARO. Nothing short of selling my soul will allow me to leave this office.

"All right, Mr. Resnov," I cave, looking just to the left of his eyes. The sides of his hair are cut low and the rest of his chocolate waves seem to fall near those eyes. Damn his eyes! Eyes so dark it should be a sin looking at them.

"*Vassili*," he says, in an accent that reminds me of satin; rough yet with an underlying soothing ring to it. "Call me, Vassili," he repeats.

"Well, Vassili, I'll do whatever I have to leave this gym." I smile. As a future lawyer, lying is in my genes. *I have no intention of seeing you again,* I contemplate.

His wide mouth spreads in a killer straight, white-toothed smile. So far, the wolf only flashed a grin when coaxing me to follow him. Obviously, I survived. This smile is different, though. It's expectant and it makes him all the more beautiful. Like shiny wrapping paper is shielding me from something dark and sinister. My grip is firm against the rough padding of his murderous hands still holding mine. He adds just enough strength to send a tremor shooting through my body. Dread and lust clash inside of me, causing the lips of my pussy to swell. Yet my instincts kick in at the same time.

I t's almost six in the evening. Eyes swollen with tears, I walk toward the exit of Los Angeles Community Hospital. I stop to rub the complementary antibacterial gel over my manicured hands. Ronisha has yet to awaken. I have spent all afternoon seated by her side playing music; alternating from an uplifting Tamela Mann to Beyoncé on my iPhone. The nurse said that Ronisha should be able to hear it. I'd asked the doctor so many questions until he reminded me that we've been here before. Sergio beating Ronisha's ass is nothing new.

Swoosh. The sliding glass doors part. The warm sun hits my skin and the helplessness fades away. Rather, it's replaced with an even greater feeling, anxiousness.

Vassili Resnov. His name roams through my mind as I pull the keys from my purse.

Why did I show him my father's business card? At that moment, it had seemed like my "get out of jail free" card.

More like not getting a cap in the ass and tossed into the LA River. Damn, if I didn't almost get myself murdered.

With shaky legs, I hold the door handle of my car while sliding onto the leather seat. I crossed paths with a Russian mobster and I'm still alive. Apparently, I've agreed to give myself to him for one night, yet he never asked for my name. I'm sure he can look up my dad's information and find me.

Maybe he was bluffing. He had *shit talk* down to an art. Perhaps I slithered through his defenses. My mind is delirious as I recall him standing before me. His hard body slick with sweat.

"Zar, he's full of testosterone," I tell myself while heading onto the freeway overpass. *Hell, he spends his days boxing and beating down pussy.* I've never had a bad boy. Never had any man, really. I do have an idiot ex-boyfriend who still thinks there's a spark, but that's neither here nor there.

I almost jump out of my skin when the automated voice on the radio tells me a call is coming in from my mom.

"Hey, Mom," I answer.

"Zariah, what's going on? I've called you repeatedly. Are you okay?"

Shoving Vassili and those delicious, dark thoughts from my mind, I reply,

"It's Ronisha again. Sorry, I had my phone on do not disturb. I didn't want any calls or texts to interfere with all of those machines in her hospital room. Her stupid boyfriend..." I try to tell her, my voice breaking.

"Oh, God, that poor baby. I wish *a certain someone* had some balls. Instead of ramming *his* pecker into easy—"

"Yeah, well, I'm with you on that," I cut in. "However, Mom, please be so kind as to refrain from referencing my father and his pecker in the same sentence."

Her and that damn word, *'easy'*. Her sentences always

default to 'easy bimbos'. Although there's only *one* woman my father is currently romancing. The secretary he left my mother for. I don't know what's harder for a black woman; being cheated on in general or losing your man to a white woman.

I've never been in love and cannot imagine either situation. But I try to sympathize with my mom.

"Zariah, I should come out there. No, wait. I *am* coming out there. I'll cash in on those frequent flier miles I haven't used since...in two years. Tell *that man* to cancel your plane ticket. I'll come get you. We'll see about Ronisha. We can drive back to the ATL together in your car. It will be a nice little road trip before you beginning college. I'll show you the new items I have for your dorm unless you'd like to move in with me. How does that sound?"

Hmmm, does she mean how does it sound for me to move in with her or is she referring to the road trip? I know she's lonely and I'm partially the reason to blame. No matter how it's perceived, I technically chose to live with my dad instead of her two years ago during the divorce. It was my mother's idea since she had to return to work. Even worse? Mom wasn't over my father and I could play snitch. We tell each other everything. So, Mom used me as a device to torment herself. She's still in love with my dad.

Concern for Ronisha is at the forefront of my mind as I attempt to persuade her. "Mom, what if I attend UCLA for the first semester..." I tried to say before she cut me off.

"Girl, no you will not! Your father applied to his alma mater without your knowledge. Besides, those good intentions of yours will only hold you back. Sweetheart, you're not Ronisha's mother. You can't continue to look out for her to your own detriment. Spelman is your dream."

3

VASSILI

"Vassili, you crazy?" Yuri grumbles, with one hand on the wheel of his SUV. He's driving to his father, Malich's estate. The choppy, gray Venice Beach water disappears from sight, as he navigates Neilson Way.

He's right, I'm crazy. I don't deserve to breathe the same air as her. I'm cut from a bad cloth, and she's pure goodness. Something told me that deep down underneath the anger was innocence. I'm searching for information on her on my phone while we ride. I've found out her full name is *Zariah* Washington. I like it. She's eighteen to my twenty-one. Her birthday passed this March. Good, I don't fuck jailbait. But I'd be lying through my teeth if I claimed that I would wait.

"This bitch's pop is the chief of police. You want to carry out a hit for her? Malich would be elated about your first hit, but for a bitch...*that* bitch? Washington isn't on..."

Yuri's voice trails off as soon as I stopped looking at her graduation photo to shoot him a glare. With my one look, I don't have to tell him to stop disrespecting and calling Zariah out of her name.

He treads lightly, eyes squinting somewhat, as he gathers his train of thought.

"Uh, Washington isn't on payroll, Vassili. And you've already told Malich that you aren't interested in the family business. This is bullshit." He shakes his head again. "Think about your pop, Vassili, *think!*"

I'm the oldest of a football team's worth of siblings. My father, Anatoly, is old school in his ways. The throne is passed to the oldest. The birthright is mine. Anatoly preferred one of my younger brothers to visit the U.S. to watch his kid brother. Malich is his West Coast connection and he hardly trusts him.

Anatoly wanted me by his side, preparing me to rule our own country one day. Fuck that. My father is too paranoid. Anatoly only agreed to my terms of living in California because he thought it would somehow soften me enough to return to the Resnov syndicate. I'd put two slugs into my father's forehead before I would return to the family business. Damn, thinking about how much I hate my father reminds me of Zariah's words.

"Sergio and other boys like him enjoy sweet, naïve girls like her."

Sweet, naïve girls are easy to manipulate. My hands claw into fists. Defending Ronisha isn't even a drop in the bucket to what I should've done to my father, for *her*.

But regarding my uncle, Malich, I respect him. So far, he hasn't crossed my father. His pockets are only as heavy as Anatoly allows. Malich isn't set in his ways, though. Old ways mean that business is first. Malich is a fan of MMA because their father, my grandfather, was a boxer and won a title. He held the title for years before heading the Resnov mob family. He had a hand in both while my father only believes in one or the other.

A few years ago, Anatoly learned about my interest in

MMA. He's still in my ear about the octagon all the way from Russia. He believes that if I had stayed in Russia, I would've assisted with the production of illegal imports of Russian vodka, illegal arts, and guns dealing. But that shit isn't me. And anything Anatoly has a hand in, I want no part of.

"Vassili, you're playing with fire." Yuri's tone is laced with caution while he stops at the wrought iron gates before his father's mansion.

"I know, Yuri. Now, find Sergio with the prayer hands on his bicep. I want him in Malich's basement by dark."

My boots step over piss, water and vomit, as my eyes adjust to the darkness of the room. Sergio's arms are tied above his head to a beam along the ceiling. One of Malich's goons thought that water torture would be a good starter. His stomach is extremely bloated. There are weights strapped to his dangling feet, stretching his body further. The guys did just enough to break his spirit, leaving the big motherfucker in tears.

I take a drag from my cigarette and release the smoke through my nose.

"I've been told you enjoy hitting women. Big *piz'da* like you can't find someone your own size to fight?"

"Please! Please!"

He starts to beg God, yet my heart hardens further. I rub a hand over the side of my neck where, conveniently, there's a tattoo of an eye inside a triangle. It's the symbol of God's omniscience, His ability to see everything. Yet, I don't feel convicted.

He speaks rapidly in Italian. He's praying to the Almighty God. I know his every word because Anatoly made learning the language a requirement when I was a child. Every bit of his training was to prepare me for the syndicate. Though I'll probably never get the chance to one-up an Italian who speaks ill of me unaware or negotiate an arms deal off of a port in Sicily.

"Listen." I clasp my hand against the back of his neck, bringing his tear-swollen gaze to mine. Time to cut in before he pleads to the Holy Spirit, again.

"I believe in God, too. Maybe I'll pray for your soul later. But tonight, you'll either go..." My cigarette points up and then down. "I can't see further than your death, but your death is inevitable."

I tune out his cries, burning the cigarette into his chest. Shit, I have prayers, too. Like bargaining with God that if nothing happens with Zariah tonight, I won't continue to pursue her. I hold my hands out so they can be weighed down with gloves. I glance at my knuckles, recalling how swollen and bloody they were the first time I had to fight. In an instant, I'm transported back to Russia. What a fucking dynasty the Resnovs are. The men are revered. There's no space for females.

Anatoly believes women serve two purposes. One, they can be used on their backs or their knees. Two, servants to cook and clean. My sister, his blood, meant nothing to him. She was like Ronisha. She was dealt a bad hand. Stuck in a story that would only end in tragedy. The Resnov name never protected a female who wasn't respected by a male counterpart. So, the first time I ever fought was for Sasha.

4

ZARIAH

This evening, I've washed away the grime of the hospital. The salted tears on my cheeks, from all my crying today, have been cleansed with expensive French soap. Hot torrents of water bring images of Vassili Resnov's hard body before my eyes. Damn, I breathe heavily, wondering how God made him so fine. Why? Why make a murdering criminal look like the epitome of sex? All rugged hard angles, muscles stacked for days and a thick-corded neck. In a daze, I place the loofah down. I grab the liquid soap and pour the creaminess into my hands. Moaning, I revel in thoughts of his hot, never-ending cum.

I hesitantly distribute the soap onto my skin, rubbing over my achy nipples and large breasts as the thick folds of my pussy tremble. Damn, my eyelids flutter shut as I touch myself. A whimper escapes my lips at the thought of how much more enticing it would be if it were his rough hands grazing over my flesh. I can still hear his voice in my ears. I reach lower, gliding the soap along my flat stomach; lower and lower still with an insatiable desire.

My fingertips skim past silky curls, causing my heart to

drum so loud in my ears that it drowned out the sound of the rain. I chicken out by slathering my curvy hip instead. Damn, what am I doing? I was already clean and haven't even been touched *there*. Not in a romantic or sexual way. Not yet.

With a huff, I turn off the waterspouts.

"Zariah, stop being an idiot. He is a *Resnov*."

Shit, even when I say the name out loud, an eerie chill still seeps deep into my bones. Hot, foggy steam surrounds me, but the name Resnov is chillingly potent.

"You have obligations, Zar."

I usually talk to myself whenever I'm overwhelmed or there is a report due in Dr. Frankston's class. Obtaining a classical high school diploma from Pressley Prep was hard enough, but Dr. Frankston always went harder on me. My black teachers always seemed to push their black students harder, but *he* took the damn cake for outrageous expectations.

Tonight, I do have obligations. And not that crazy statement Vassili said about us spending the night together. Though he made no stipulations, he doesn't know where I live. I'll never see him again. This evening, my father has decided to do what he knows best. Entertaining.

I've donned a designer champagne-colored mini dress and equally expensive stilettos. I take a deep breath, looking in the floor-to-ceiling mirror by my canopy bed. I could go for a pair of sneakers and sweats right now. I'd much rather be by Ronisha's side at this moment. But my father can be callous and controlling. He sprung this last-minute dinner on me without so much as a warning.

My thick hair has been straightened and styled into a bun. There's enough makeup on my face to paint me as an equal in high society this evening. Just enough to overlook the sadness in my eyes.

Holding my chin higher, I remind myself aloud, "I've crossed paths with a Resnov. I was bold enough to show him my father's business card and I survived."

My father's business card has come in handy on a few occasions. Even though I attend Pressley Preparatory Academy, I'm still a black chick. The majority of my white friends snort premium cocaine. They steal their parents' aged whiskey to drink and own the roads in their BMW convertibles. But let me be in Ronisha's neck of the woods. Mind you, her friends prefer kickbacks and weed, which is nothing extreme. Still, to most of them, I'm nothing but a bougie sellout. That's when Maxwell Washington's name is a saving grace.

As I step out of my room and head to the extravagant staircase, I begin to hear voices. Shit, it's Phillip Everly V, my ex-boyfriend. *Just my luck*, I grumble inwardly while descending the staircase.

His clear blue eyes brighten when I step into the dining room. In Tom Ford digs, he arises from his seat as does his district attorney father, Phillip Everly IV. His trophy mother, who always seems to be waxier by the second, nods toward me.

Where is the rest of the party? Or am I the token sacrifice? My father has offered me up on a silver platter before. Phil has always made for the token boyfriend position. The maid hasn't set the rest of the vast dining table for any other of my father's friends or political associates. I now realize I am, in fact, the sacrificial lamb being led to the slaughter. Dad never gave me as much attention as the day I started dating Phil. Let Maxwell tell it, he'd say we were perfect. Shit, we *were* until I pulled the pleasant, soft wool from my eyes. These days, my father offers me attention to remind me how much Phil loves me and how we make an impeccable couple.

"Zariah…" Mr. Everly smells of my father's most prized brandy as he hugs me. "You look as gorgeous as ever."

"Thank you, sir." My plastic grin is in place as I pull away from his embrace. I hug my father, as well. Mr. Everly receives so much *love* because he wrote an impeccable letter of recommendation for my college admission. I only offer a cordial nod to Phil and his mother before sitting. *Yeah, sucker, no hug for you.*

"When are you leaving for Spelman College?" Mr. Everly inquires. "We must have a toast."

"An HBCU," my dad almost spits the words.

Mrs. Everly's eyebrows merge. She isn't aware of the acronyms for the Historically Black College and University. I force my eyelashes not to flutter.

"Max, it's a grand idea. One of the administrative assistants on my team attended Spelman," Mr. Everly cuts in. His attempt to side with me about attending a black college falls short. He realizes his mistake in the mentioning of administrative assistants.

My pupils dilate with anger. Dad had ruined my mother over a damn administrative assistant. Maxwell doesn't catch his friend's flush of embarrassment for bringing up the taboo subject.

The DA cleans up his blunder by saying, "Spelman is filled with morals and rich in history."

"Only wish I could follow you," Phil jokes.

"Ha," I fake laugh. I broke up with him months ago. Phil was more like our fellow students at the Preparatory school than I thought. Most of the rich guys are, but he'd been deceptively charming. It took a while for me to figure out how addicted to coke he was.

The dinner is uneventful, besides my father's attempt to

interest me in attending Harvard University with Phillip. He'd gone behind my back and had one of his assistants apply for that university as well as his alma mater.

"No thanks, Dad." Ever the smartass, I elaborate, "I read a recent article *Bound by History: Harvard, Slavery, and Arc—*"

BOOM. Maxwell slams his fist down onto the table. "We will not discuss slavery over veal, Zariah." He chuckles tersely. "That is vastly inappropriate."

"Is it?" I arch an eyebrow.

"She's just like her mother." My dad chuckles again before sipping his snifter of bourbon.

Biting my bottom lip, I stare at the shiny gold charger and china plates before me. The Everlys laugh halfheartedly at my father's comparison of me to my mother. I can just about see her embarrassed face reflecting at me on my plate. When my parents were married, Dad had this awful way about him. Let my mom say something contrary to his beliefs and Maxwell would redirect my mother in a heart attack. I have yet to be reprimanded to the same level that my father did with my mom. Most of the time, my dad is with his girlfriend on the weekends. Before my graduation last week, I was too busy studying or partying away the end of high school.

Now, my mouth tenses. Dad is like Sergio. I'm sure Vassili is. Just. Like. My. Dad.

Where did my courage come from, as I wreaked havoc in Vadim's Gym? *Oh, yeah, I had just spoken with Ronisha's doctor.* The sun hadn't even risen in the sky this morning when the doctor had provided the rundown of her newest injuries. Reset nose, fractured collarbone, broken jaw…

I snapped.

Usually, I am too reserved for an argument, unless it's in preparation for the courtroom. But today is not screw with Zariah Washington day.

"Dad, may I be excused from the table?"

I'm already rising when he says no. The old anger momentarily reared in his eyes. With it, I'm reminded of seeing him backhanding my mother across the room. My father has never so much as spanked me. Not even a smack on the back of the hand. He beat the shit out of my older brother, Martin. Though it was on the occasion Martin had decided that there'd be no more beating our mom like she was a little kid.

Dad smiles and backs off. "Teenagers..."

There's another round of faux laughter as I continue out of the room. I hear footsteps behind me and turn around. Phil is rounding the corner. His blond hair combed over perfectly, everything about him is a beautiful illusion.

"Go eat dinner, please." I sigh. Shit, I can't look into his eyes without seeing powder dusted beneath his nose.

His blue eyes are filled with concern.

"Babe..."

My gaze becomes instantly emotionless.

"We've been over for months, Phil."

I shuffle up the stairs and slam the door behind me. *I'm never falling in love! I'd be a fucking idiot too.* I kick one shoe off, my foot instantly chilled by the marble floor. Cussing as I go, I kick off the other shoe at the same time I pull the dress over my head.

It doesn't thud. Not against the wall or the floor. My senses begin to prickle as my dress falls to the floor next to me. My arms wrap around my large chest as I stand about, naked as I've ever been in front of the opposite sex.

"Vassili," I whisper, alternating between covering my breasts to the tiny triangle of silk shielding my innocence.

He moves out of the shadows, placing my left stiletto onto the dresser. A long-sleeve thermal strains against his incredibly broad chest and thick biceps. He drags a hand through his hair that was lazily lying on his forehead like a shaggy dog.

"I came to collect my payment."

"Did you mu...mu... has it been done?"

Damn, I can't even say the word. Murder. Ice. *Kill.* The guy's boxing name is Killer Karo, for Christ's sake. Vassili Karo Resnov, Killer Karo, has almost 57K likes on Facebook. I found that out right after leaving Vadim's Gym.

"Yes, Zariah. It has been done."

I start for my silk robe at the foot of the bed.

He blocks my path, planting himself in front of my queen size canopy.

"I can't even dress?" I snap. "I'm cold," I murmured, weakly.

"Of course. What kind of monster would I be to leave you freezing?" He gestures toward the bed, but I'm not foolish enough to walk past him.

"I enjoyed the little ritual you went through after shower-ing. Cocoa butter, perfume against your wrists, then the pulse point at your neck."

He steps closer to me breathing me in. His breath tickles my neck. He clasps his hands around my wrists before bringing them up to his nose for another inhale. Did he feel that spark, or was it me?

My throat is heavy, it's a feat to murmur, "You've been here this entire time?"

"You were in the shower, you stopped too soon." He licked his lips.

"I could finish it for you, though."

My mouth is silenced with lust. I had to glance away from his dark gaze before gulping it all down enough to speak. I can't seem to wrap my head around the fact he's here, in the flesh. I say again, "You were here, in my room, this entire time."

My voice freezes over a little more with each word.

"Are you aware that the damn district attorney is downstairs?"

"That *mudak*, Phillip Everly, can stay downstairs all he'd like. I'm here for *you*," he replied.

His voice is playful, yet the hard look on his face sends another tremor of fear sparking down my spine. It lands as lust between my thighs. Vassili's tone hardens as he reminds me, "You shook my hand, Miss Washington."

"I sure did, asshole. Anything to get the fuck away from you. I also didn't think you'd kill the guy!" My bones are shaking, but I place a hand on my hip. "Where's my proof?"

He grabs the DirecTV remote from the dresser.

"There's a television in here somewhere, eh?"

I grumble, taking the remote from him. I press a button. The flat-screen descends from the ceiling and in front of a canvas of Paris that I completed at paint night.

"Turn to the news."

"Okay," I growl, turning the television onto FOX News. The newscaster advises, "In a gruesome turn of events, the body of a male has been found along the bank of the L.A. River below. The police have yet to release the man's name..."

An aerial view is plastered across the screen. The reporter in a helicopter mentions how tattered the body appears. There's drumming in my ears. I realize it's blood coursing through my veins.

"There are no leads."

With those words ringing in my ear, I press the OFF button. My knees weaken and before I know it, Vassili's warm hands are wrapped around my bare waist.

"You're a murderer. Don't touch me," I almost screech. The remote in my hand bounces off his hard chest, as I throw it at him with force.

36

"You asked for this, Zariah," he says, shaking my shoulders.

There's an underlying hurt in his voice. I've seen pain like this when my mom disappointed my father or couldn't meet his expectations. Then Ronisha learned that rubbing around two Barbie dolls doesn't compare to the real deal. She also learned how sex can leave you void since it doesn't equate to love. Add the young girls at my school into the equation who are suicidal because they have too many assets.

I stop tugging away from him. Against my better judgment, his hard body more than comforts me. His hard frame becomes my haven. His muscles cushion me from the overwhelming feeling that I'm drowning in. Moments pass as my breathing returns to normal. *I killed a man. I'm as much at fault as Vassili is. I caused this!* I gulp, working the muscles in my throat, preparing myself to speak. Yet Vassili's lips meet mine instead. It's a kiss that softens my heart and clouds my brain.

"You belong to me now, Zariah," he tells me. His lips seek mine. Our tongues twirl only a short while before he stops.

"I'd kill anyone who caused a tear to drop down your cheek." He rubs a thumb over my skin, collecting the tears that have fallen.

"Tell me the name of any motherfucker who has ever crossed you from birth. I will tear them apart."

His hoarse voice is an astonishing comfort to me. Before I can tell him that I don't need any more justice, Vassili kisses me again.

"I won't hurt you, Zariah. I won't touch anywhere along your sexy body or do anything that you aren't in agreement with tonight. You got that?"

I nod, tasting his mouth.

Maybe thirty minutes has passed. An hour, possibly two even. The tears have left salted streaks on my skin, yet I'm no longer sad. I'm content with Vassili. He said he wanted to show me how beautiful I am. Something life-altering has transferred between Vassili and me. He's murdered for me. Although I was acting in pure rage when making the request, the two of us are now connected. We're tethered to each other in ways I couldn't fathom at the time.

He had me unclasp my bra and slip out of my panties. In nothing, save for my soft brown skin, I'm seated on the floor. The silver-trimmed floor-length mirror is across from me. We are reflected in light and darkness.

Vassili is seated behind me. His jeans brush against my hips. His legs form around me as my toes press against the cool, silver lacquered frame. Legs wide open. The image before us is all delicate, my lady parts and the softness of the inside of my thighs. The look in Vassili's eyes tells me that my sex makes for a gorgeous focal point.

"Look how beautiful you are, Zariah," he says. "You were afraid to touch it in the shower. Can I touch this pretty pussy, eh?"

My nod is hesitant, not because I don't want him to. Damn, I want him to. I'm stuck on how he looks at me through the mirror. He's huge and scary. Yet his dark gaze is seared, riveted and entranced by *me*. I want everything to go slow, I want to cherish tonight.

Heat sweeps across my cheeks and neck as I glance at my honeyed walls reflected in the mirror before me.

Vassili picks up his bottle of vodka he'd brought into my room from the balcony and brings it up to his mouth. He sets the bottle back down then licks his middle finger before reaching around me. His golden hand is much lighter against my skin as he gropes one of my breasts.

"Keep looking at that pretty pussy, Zariah."

His tone slow, his gaze sliding from mine in the mirror back to my fully exposed sex.

"Beautiful. I don't deserve you, but you've given me the gift of touching it. Nobody else will love this pussy. Look, it's wet for me, begging for my cock."

His hand skims down my flat abdomen. His palm is abrasive and calloused but pleasantly soothing as it goes. His index finger plays with my intimate coils.

My lungs crash.

"It's fucking begging me." His vodka-peppered breath is pleasing against my cheek. "No matter what type of bad motherfucker we both *know* that I am, your body still calls to me."

"You're stabbing me in the back," I joke, voice barely found. I can't tell him that he does deserve me because I'm not a judge. Perhaps the words squeaked out. But the victory of getting them to pass the threshold of my lips causes a small grin to plaster across my face.

"Yeah, my cock is jealous," he glances down between us. "This motherfucker has never been harder."

Finally, his index and ring fingers spread my lips. There's a sweet succulent coating against the inside of them from his touch. My inner and outer folds are throbbing like never before. Sensations that seem past impossible cling to me. A craving so deep it hurts. *Please,* my brain screams. *Please touch me.* But I'm too afraid to say those words. I'm too afraid to hear the sound of my voice again. The letters, words, phrases might not string together correctly.

My heart drums in my ears. So far, I'm still innocent and quietly begging him to take me. Licking my lips, I watch the mirror's reflection of him as his middle finger rolls inside my juices. It skims across my valley. My hands zip out to grab ahold of Vassili's forearms, eyes wide in shock. Through the mirror, his gaze is filled with devious thoughts. Dark lust, delighted by my fear.

"I got you, Zariah," he says, lips skimming across my earlobe.

Nodding my head and chewing my lips, my hand stops bracing so hard around his forearm.

Vassili's finger continues to gloss around my juices, drawing more of a flood to my sex. Then he tastes the gloss from his finger.

His thick eyebrows furrowed in thought while my lungs are depleted of oxygen. I wait for him to say something. All the fear in me seems to evaporate at this moment. My mind is a whirlwind, waiting for his response

"Mmmm…" His voice is as primitive as a lion's growl. "I would say sweet. Fuck sweet. It's water, Zariah. Your pussy tastes like water."

"Vassili!" I seethe. My eyes dart toward my bedroom door. It's locked, it was locked before we came to the floor, but damn, I'm antsy.

"What?" Vassili's thick Russian accent is as sexy as it is rugged. "Water is my favorite drink."

"You are crazy," I grumble.

"Patience."

His other hand clamps ever so softly around my neck, fingers skimming my jaw. He tilts my neck. My eyes tear away from the reflection of my pussy, my gorgeous pussy— his words, not mine.

Our tongues twine as he reaches around my shoulder, deepening the kiss. Then his middle finger slams into my core. Delightful pain causes my ass to arch, cock spearing into my back. Again and again, his finger pumps into me as his tongue screws my mouth.

"Now two," he says.

Two what? There's no way I can speak. *Two what?*

"Look, Zariah," he nudged his square jaw to the mirror again. He pulls his middle finger out, rubbing his index around the liquid lust of it. Then those *two fingers* press their way inside, feeling some tight resistance.

"Shhh…" Vassili soothes. "You're tight as fuck, Zariah."

Oh, I was whimpering. Again my cheeks flame.

"Don't be embarrassed."

He nips at my earlobe, the pain masking that of my core as my body widens for his knuckles. I'm in a trance. I can't take my eyes off his white fingers, how they work their way in. Breaking me, freeing me a little more so I can take the fighter.

"Imagine my cock," he instructs. "Grind down, baby. Get your pussy ready for me."

"Mmmm…" I lick my lips, gaze locked onto the mirror. His two fingers submerge into me. My hips grind as told. With his hard body enveloped around my frame, I twirl downward. I imagine his cock, my hands grip onto his forearms. They're made of steel. His cock is made of steel. All of him is. I love this and I will welcome the fighter stretching me out, filling me with his strength.

"That's right. Get yourself off. Make my pussy wetter."

"Oh, oh… Vassili," I can't stop looking at me, him looking at *me*. The way his eyes consume me, tells me how beautiful I am. Does that sound crazy? No, I'm aware that I am pretty. I've always had confidence in that department. My gorgeous mother raised me to know that beauty is on the inside. So, I'm doubly beautiful. But, Vassili's gaze measures how beautiful I am. Infinitely beautiful. Damn, how damn gorgeous we are together, light and dark in the reflection of the mirror. I ride the waves of my orgasm. First one ever.

"Damn it, if you don't have the prettiest fuck face." He finally offers a grin for the first time tonight. It's to die for.

5

ZARIAH

Seven years later

That night will forever play through my mind. Maybe I was in a trance. Vassili had consent to roam over my entire body and do me any which way he wanted. I'll never forget how beautiful he made me feel as he looked at me, touched me and kissed me. Or having his arms wrapped around me as we sat on the veranda outside my bedroom. We drank Resnov vodka, ate chocolates he brought me and talked about everything under the stars. Vassili didn't do much smiling but I learned to look past his hard demeanor. After the attentive foreplay in front of the mirror, there was no denying that beneath the ruggedness, he was a good man. Can a man make you feel like the only person in the world and not have a soul?

Or was it all a game? It couldn't possibly have been a game. Every word I spoke about my plans and dreams, he clung to. Well, until we were both tipsy. I cuddled into his arms. I fell asleep, only to wake up to the sun beaming against our warm skin.

For the first three years of college, Vassili became what you'd call a millennial pen pal. I'd text him. He'd *sext* me back. Either Vassili had the most magnificent, gorgeous cock ever or he Googled the world's sexiest dick and texted a picture of that. I even joked about it. Sometimes Vassili would be my first reason to laugh in an entire 24-hour period. He was my slice of "normal" in a hectic college world. That, plus we connected over our shared secret. A deadly one.

While working on my undergrad, I became inundated with my core focus. Though our times on the phone or texting were my world, I began slowly giving up on the man I could see no future in. For all the encouragement he provided via a text message, somewhere in the back of my mind, I knew one thing was true.

Vassili was a Resnov.

After three years, our calls and texts were suddenly no more. I graduated on the accelerated track, due to hustling my ass off and a wealth of college courses I'd already taken at Presley Prep. Vassili was all the more invincible in the cage.

For graduate school, I attended a law school up north, in my home state of California. And here I am now, twenty-five years old, with an aspiring future.

"Congratulations, Zariah," my two old prep friends say as they crowd around me at Lulu's, a chic restaurant in Hollywood. We once tipped the servers a Benjamin just to allow us to purchase martinis when we were too damn young.

There's a cake in the center of the table. It's in the shape of a stiletto in my favorite color, silver.

"Oh, shit, the baker added the red bottom heel? Righteous!" Taryn giggles.

She's a wealthy mix of Asian and Somali. With tight eyes and a slick, long ponytail, Taryn embodies badass.

Glancing at the brown stick wedged from the top of the shoe, I consider, "And is this a cigarette or a ..."

"Gavel." They laugh in unison.

"The lawyer cakes were nowhere as pretty," Rhonda admits. She's a super curvy, platinum blonde with porcelain skin that pales against her sheer red dress. Her baby blues glance me up and down. I'm no longer the token black chick in an über rich society. I've traded in wearing name brands for bargain shopping.

Taryn shrugs. "So we decided to go with what we know. The stiletto and … dang, the baker said the gavel might look weird."

Grinning, I hold up my dry martini. "Well, I love it!"

Later on, Taryn picks up the tab and we head to the exit. I'm thankful she did because it was way out of my budget.

"You aren't headed home, are you?" Taryn says. "When you said you were coming home to attend law school three years ago, we thought you'd be around the corner. Not through the woods and over the bridge."

"I said *upstate* but I moved back in with my dad this morning. So…" I sigh, trying not to look down at my ensemble. "I'm home now."

"With your father? Yuck!" Rhonda's nose crinkles. "You can stay with me."

I smile. Ronisha had offered her one-bedroom apartment when I mentioned the move. She was working a shift at Shakey's Pizza this evening. We have plans to get together tomorrow afternoon.

"It's only temporary. I should have a place by the beginning of the month."

"Well, okay, but no going home." Taryn declares, "The night is still young."

Rhonda chimes in, "We're going to watch a boy fight! My money's on Karo. Zariah, you'd be wise to bet on him. You could pay off all those student loans or at the very least, move the heck out of your dad's."

"Karo?" I mumble, heart drumming as Rhonda sifts through her iPhone apps for the Lyft.

"He is everything in and out of the ring, if you know what I mean." Rhonda grins, eyes so tight, they almost seem to close.

I squirm in my seat. Vassili had a throng of women after him when we used to chat. One time, I believe it was my sophomore year, I'd called to tell him how I'd aced my first political debate. A female answered his phone. Jealousy burned over my skin when the bitch hung up the instant she heard my voice. Not a second later, Vassili called back. He'd made her apologize.

"In and out of the ring, humph?" Taryn smirks, "Or so Rhonda's been told."

As they snigger, leaning against each other, my pace falters. I glance down at myself freely for the first time. My dress skims down to mid-thigh but it's more preppy than sexy. Black leather kitten booties and minimal jewelry by way of silver hoops finish off my look.

I lucked out this evening when finding my old leather bomber jacket that never goes out of style. Still, I radiate 'girl next door,' and not the vixen that came and cussed Vassili to high heavens. Nor the sexy chick who had time to salt her texts with raunchy wit. Seven entire years have passed since that fateful night in my room. He didn't even fuck me when he had the chance! Did I bore him that night? Vassili had said he saw me almost get myself off in the shower. Was he humoring me?

"Zariah, hello! You in?" Rhonda asks.

"You're coming with us, Zar, regardless." Taryn back-tracks, placing an arm around me.

"Zar, the Lyft app says we're riding in a Prius. If there's a sunroof, you're sticking your head out of it. Hell, spread it wide! Show everyone your damn coochie for all I care. Tonight, we live it up."

The bright lights are on the stage. I grip my folded leather jacket to my lower abdominals during each hit. The crowd is wild, cheering on a featherweight match between a Latino and an Italian guy. This is raw. So much edgier than straight boxing. It's faster. Harder. There's much more blood involved.

The stage is painted in blood. The Latino pens the Italian to the ground, alternating between punches and forearm hits. With each smack, I hug myself.

When it's all over, I've damn near squirmed out of my seat. The Latin looks link meat tenderized enough for a screaming hot grill. And he won! His left eye is sealed shut. Too tired to jump and shout with victory, he falls to his knees. His arms stretch to the sky and the crowd goes wild.

"Ladies, it's about that time. I'm heading out." I start to arise. Though much time has passed, I've felt a connection to Vassili like I've never felt with any other. Regardless of his decision not to screw me years ago, I cannot watch him fight —win or lose.

"We haven't even seen the main event." Rhonda huffs.

In the background, the Latin commends his defeated opponent in a brief interview on the stage.

"Oh, no, ya don't." Taryn laces her arm through mine and yanks me back into place. Just then the announcer begins to hype up the place once more.

"Look, look, it's The Damager!" Taryn shouts over rap music. "He's fighting for Karo's belt."

On the large screen before us, statistics scroll for The Damager. Middleweight. 178 pounds, of pure muscle. He has 11 TKO's, 3 Submissions and 1 loss. My eyebrow arches. *What do they mean by submission?*

As soon as I begin to concentrate, my entire body unravels as Russian rap blares through the speakers. My eyes track Vassili from across the room as he steps out. If I thought his body was cut and ripped before, he is out-of-this-world stacked with muscles now. His arms exceed the circumference of my thighs. He's wearing a tight black shirt that reads KARO sport. Some of the audience sport his brand. Vassili rips the shirt down the middle of his chest. I gasp for air.

His hands are raised, head held high. The sound of people hyping him up matches the bravado of the rap music pounding through the speakers.

He steps into the cage and the roaring gets louder. The churning in my stomach due to the fear of blood has subsided. In its wake is all-consuming lust. A desire to see him conquer his opponent fearlessly.

I sit at the edge of my seat in the front row. He's less than twenty yards away. I can smell him. The scent brings back the memory of musk and strength I desired to taste on him while at Vadim's gym. Then I conjure how deliciously clean and good he smelled at my home that night, long ago.

His eyes narrow somewhat. Through a raging crowd, he sees me. The death mask across his face almost falters. That jagged scar that my fingers had trembled to touch, looked less menacing for all of a second. Damn, how was I so afraid to touch it?

I nod subtly in his direction. Why? Because my entire body has shut down.

He nods back and then the referee blares through the speaker.

The opening bell rings. The fighters touch gloves as a sign of respect. Once complete, they migrate to the opposite sides of the cage, getting a quick feel for each other. Before I have a chance to blink, Vassili is all over The Damager. He pounces with a right hook so hard, the wind rushes in my direction. The Damager tosses out a low kick of his own. On the defense, Vassili blocks his attempt. Vassili lunges and over-powers The Damager. Down on the ground, he climbs fast on top of The Damager's chest, slamming down quick fists as heavy as iron weights. The Damager tries to work his arm around Vassili's leg. He only succeeds in forcing himself up against the fence. Now, he's right where Vassili wanted him.

With one hand tugging the cage for leverage, Vassili slams his knee into his opponent's stomach. I jump out of my seat, as does everyone else. Hooting and hollering for him. A rush of adrenaline streams through my veins.

Killer Karo is declared the winner. Vassili climbs up the cage wall, straddling it. He pounds a fist against his powerful bronze chest.

In a whirlwind interview, he explains his strategy. His cocky ass is flippant while saying The Damager was a "wor-thy" opponent. The truth is in his eyes; this was no sweat off his back. Then, in the blink of an eye, the man I broke my heart by pushing away, is gone again.

I'd stopped accepting Vassili's calls and text messages. The image of a brighter future as a prime litigator didn't include a Russian mobster in my life, screwing me at nights. Although he hadn't tried to. Damn, the way my brain is set up, I'll drive myself insane one day with all this wondering why.

"You're in shock, aren't you?" Taryn asks, trying to dig into my thoughts.

Face still blank, I offer a nod. *I've seen him. Now, time to go.* The thought echoes in my ears as if someone else is steering my life. I don't want to go! My high school friends haven't made a move to get up yet.

The crowd slowly quiets down, but the closest people to me are hyped. There's mention of some sort of party in The Hills. Taryn chimes into the conversation. My gaze continues to be transfixed to the cage, where the man I never should've seen again left. He left his mark here. Somehow, on a stage bathed in blood and sweat, Vassili Resnov's presence reigns supreme.

My cell phone vibrates against my thigh. I aimlessly take the phone out of my leather jacket pocket, which is now draped over my lap. The phone number is as familiar to me as the reflection of my face. Though I deleted the 323-number long ago, it belongs to none other than Vassili Karo Resnov.

Him: Wait for me.

I smile. Then I glance at the last correspondence he sent. During my last year at Spelman, Vassili had a competition in Georgia. He'd offered me tickets. Then the next message from him was saying he would come to me if I was too afraid.

I never responded.

6

VASSILI

O ut of the blue, Zariah stopped calling and stopped replying to my messages. I ordered Yuri to visit her college. Check for her at the dorm, the part-time job she held in the registrar's office, fucking search for her in her classes. His orders were not to return until he'd confirmed she was A-fucking-Okay. Yuri reported that he saw her at the Spelman library, head in a book, studying. No marks. No bruises. No problems.

Tonight, after hitting the shower, I glance at my phone to see if she'd responded. My mouth hitches to the left. She said 'okay'.

I hurry and grab my things from the locker. I dressed in faded jeans, a thermal shirt, and boots. Yuri and Nestor sent the usual females away from me. Those *mudaks* were all too happy to share an extra round of pussy. Tonight is for me and Zariah.

When I step back into the arena, the cage is gone. The stage is halfway deconstructed. I glance around at the sea of chairs, one portion folded. The other is in the process of being folded by a handful of workers. An image of Zariah, cuddled in my arms, eighteen and fast asleep crosses my mind. I never knew such peace existed in the world. The next morning, she shattered it all with her desire to leave for college.

Guess that's what happens when you bargain with God after taking your first life? After murdering Sergio, I prayed. I told God I wouldn't fuck her on the first night unless she gave the go-ahead. The next morning, the Lord gave me the sign. I wouldn't get to have this innocent beauty, anyway. She was moving far away.

Now, it's been years since I've seen her in the flesh. The feel of her body is still ingrained in my brain. My gaze sweeps across the room again. Where is she? My usual frown is deep-set as I turn around. And then the air expels from my lungs as my gaze lands on her big, mahogany, innocent eyes.

She's hugging a leather jacket to her chest. It's blocking her sweet, succulent pussy that I never got to stretch and mold against my cock. The memory of her wearing panties and a bra that night is still fresh in my mind, as are those thick hips and toned thighs. There's no makeup on her face, allowing me to view her in all her natural glory. Not a single flaw is to be found on her dark-brown skin.

Shit. I've never liked a color more than when I first laid eyes on her in Vadim's Gym.

Thick pink lips frame a bright white smile when she asks, "You thought I left?"

"Thought I'd have to come get you." I shrug.

"Oh, you thought you'd have to *come to get me?*" She smirks. "Hmm, damn, you were always confused as to what belongs and doesn't belong to you, Vassili. You still trying to boss me around?"

"Depends," I tell her, closing in the space between us. She doesn't tremble in my arms as she once did. I'm not sure if this is a good or bad thing.

"Depends on what?" Her mouth is lush, waiting for me to dominate those lips.

"Did you wait for me?"

Zariah's gaze darkens in confusion. "I'm here, aren't I?"

"You know what I meant."

I could take her here, now. But I step back some, instead. When she only bites her lip in response, I have my answer. No one else has touched her. Now I can finally breathe. Why didn't I stop by in Georgia, all those years ago? Fuck that! Why didn't I mark her that first night I promised myself she was mine? *The prayer.* Never bargain with God.

Zariah places her hands on her hips.

"Vassili, I did not *wait* for you. Have some chill. Anyway, why'd you want me to stay behind this evening?"

I cock my head toward the closest exit.

"Because it was either those friends of yours bring you to me or I come to get you after the fight. You just returned from Berkley, Zariah. Seeing you tonight was inevitable."

She stops walking. "W-what? You know about my friends and the university I attended?"

"I know everything about you, Miss Washington. What sort of man would I be if I didn't keep tabs on my property?"

Her gaze cuts at me. "Your *property?*"

I almost smile, aware that my choice of words would make her angry. Fuck me. I don't know which I prefer; her with an attitude or her innocent and sweet.

"Before you get all angry, let's get going. Can we do that? Just for the night?"

Zariah softens, as I rub a thumb along her bottom lip. Though she mellows, she turns away from my touch and takes my hand instead.

"Well, I feel like this just-for-the-night crap won't stop.

Our night together ended over seven years ago. You Resnovs don't play fair."

I give her hand a little squeeze. "We don't."

"The Red Door? Very exclusive, even by your status. Either you have a gun in your pocket, as a form of persuasion or you booked months in advance," Zariah says.

I hold the door open to my G-class Mercedes truck.

"Months in advance? Nyet, I don't even anticipate what I'll eat for breakfast."

Zariah licks her lips. "All right, but no strong-arming the employees. My father has a new and improved business card."

I chuckle softly. "How could I forget your social ties?"

We start toward the long line of trendy dressed people, waiting to get inside of my first lounge. It's a cover-up for my family's business, legitimized by a good portion of the money from my MMA sponsors. When Zariah heads to the back of the line, I wrap my arm around her waist, bringing her soft body closer to mine.

"Don't insult my connections, Zariah." I nudge her on. "I never wait for shit."

We make it inside the three-story lounge. Bright red streamers hang from the ceiling. Gold plated statues of dogs posted along the walls. I can tell Malich's upscale escorts from the regular beauties. All the men tossing around money are as ugly as shit. The flashiest and wealthiest ones have one of our bitches on both of their arms. Granted, I still keep my distance from the Resnov way, The Red Door has become a peace offering to Anatoly. My father believes that I run the whores around here. In actuality, Malich pockets the cash from connecting girls with willing gentlemen. I collect from our smuggled Russian alcohol. There's virtually no money in the food.

It's too packed in here for my liking. Leaning into Zariah, I speak over the music, "I'll get us a little water."

"Oh, sparkling water would be nice."

I head to the nearest bar while she lingers, people watching. I slap my hand onto the glittery counter. The Russian behind the bar does a double-take as she notices me.

"Wow, Karo, I never see you here. You made me a lucky girl this evening."

I nod. "Good, those side bets always were where the money is. I need a bottle and two shot glass. Tell the chef to head upstairs."

"The whole roof is closed off. It might," she warns.

"A little water never hurt," I reply, not concerned in the least bit.

Zariah leans against a glossy red pillar when I return. She eyes me and the vodka then smirks. "So that's the water?" she says, closing the gap between us. "There was always a very big break in communication between you and me."

"That so?" I smile, recalling the arguments she started when I'd texted her pictures of my cock.

"Where are we going?" Zariah asks as I lead her back toward the elevator.

"You thought I'd share you for the night, Zariah? Fuck, there you go, still underestimating me, girl." I give the up button a little push with the end of the vodka bottle. "What do you think of my place?"

"*Your* place?" she questions, in disbelief.

I watch Zariah's lovely ass. She saunters into the elevator. I step beside her, then override the elevator levels for it to stop at the roof.

"Yes, beautiful. Would you like to try the food first? I

remember something about the freshmen ten when I mentioned your cheeks."

Subconsciously, she rubs a hand over her cheekbones, which are now higher and more defined.

"It's the freshman *fifteen*, asshole. And if you ever say I look like a chipmunk again..." she slugs me in the arm. Instantly, Zariah grumbles under her breath, rubbing her sore knuckles.

"Never miscalculate your opponent's strengths, Zariah. Suck it up." I step out of the elevator. Red fire glass glitters in hearths throughout the area, with seats surrounding them.

She walks across the roof, eyes brightening at the sight. "Wow, this place is beautiful," Zariah mumbles, under her breath.

"The whole objective was to get you alone. Somehow, I had the feeling you'd run if I took you to my house. This is my home away from home."

"Run? I'm not a little girl. Although it's freezing out here." Zariah snaps, stopping short of licking those plush lips. I opt not to toss out one of my typical cocky lines. She knows good and damn well I'll keep her warm. She is, after all, mine.

Letting her irritation cool, I pull out a box of matches and light a cigarette. I drag, then blow the exhaled smoke away from her. Once finished with it, I flick the cigarette into the hearth closest to my selected seats for the two of us. A blazing fire illuminates the night around us. I sit and pat the tiny space next to me. "I only bite when provoked, Zariah."

"Somehow, I find that hard to believe," she sasses back with a slight smile.

With not much room left for her, because of my size, Zariah's curves brush against mine.

I smile and say, "See, gorgeous. You're in good company. Besides, you haven't lived since I last touched you."

"Whatever, Vassili. Matter of fact, I preferred you a thousand miles away, faux dick pics included. And I have lived too," she jokes. "I was in a sorority."

"Glad you approved of my long, fat cock. It's one hundred percent all me, by the way." I reach down between us to grab it. Every inch of my beef was hard and ready, all for her.

"I'm a Russian bull, baby. As far as you living, *nyet*, you haven't lived. You were in the sorority esteemed for their brains. Not the one with the hot, party girls."

Zariah's body sinks close to mine as she laughs. No longer tense, all soft, luscious and sweet. She's slipping into that comfort zone we once had while messaging.

"We still drank, Vassili. Sheesh, I guess you're right. I haven't lived," she says, smile falling for a moment. "You've been keeping tabs on me? By the way, how did you know Rhonda and Taryn were my friends?"

"Yuri. He works for me."

"Which guy? The heavyset one or the tall, slender one. I remember them ready to pounce on me at the gym."

"The slim one is Nestor. Heavyset? That's polite. But *dah*, Yuri is the fat fuck."

"Humph." Zariah turns toward me. "I remember your penchant for sidestepping certain *simple* questions. So, I take it Yuri doesn't work for you in a coaching, sparring regard?"

"Nyet."

She smirks. "I won't do these one-answer convos. Tell me more about your stalking me through Yuri? I guess it pays to be Malich's son?"

Malich—my father? I decide not to correct Zariah. Anatoly is dangling at the tippy-fucking-top of America's Most Wanted list. If she thinks I'm Malich's son and she's 'okay' with it, then we'll leave it at that. It's better for her sanity, anyway. I plan to tell her the truth, once we are more acquainted.

She shudders as a cold wind comes along. This is my saving grace. Zariah Washington will one day make a great attorney. She's never any good at letting me shrug shit off or be too vague.

"Sweetheart, I'm a mudak! You still cold?" I start to pull out of my jacket. "Beautiful, drink, it will warm you well."

She picks up her glass. "I'm all right, Vassili. Please, don't take off your jacket. Here, I'll take a sip."

Zariah tosses the drink back and then wiggles in surprise. "Shit! Did that get stronger since I was eighteen?"

"My family is always trying to improve the product."

She opens her mouth to argue. But I place the jacket over her anyway.

"Thank you," she mumbles. "Why- why didn't you ever come to see me?"

"You weren't ready for me yet, Zar."

"And you knew I wouldn't," she whispers the next part, "give it up to another? Cocky much?"

"I'll agree with you. Yes, I'm cocky, but I believe in you. In you being intelligent enough not to screw any mudak."

Shit, her beautiful body is as malleable as liquid lust. From my viewpoint, the chef is exiting the elevator. He'll fuck up the moment.

Her shoulders jolt as the chef speaks Russian, apologizing for the intrusion. Our connection is shot to hell. I place a protective hand on her leg while he puts three silver domes on the coffee table across from us.

"Dumplings," Zariah recalls. "And what are those? Chicken skewers?"

"It's lamb, shashlik. Say it with me, beautiful."

She does, with a smile.

I open the last silver dome.

"Damn, Vassili! Seriously? Fried drumettes. Oh, and none of those sissy-ass flat wingette pieces. You remembered! Now I feel like crap for not responding to you all those years ago." Though Zariah started off joking, I can tell her punch-line choice of words is regretted.

"Zar, I remember everything about you," is my reply. Once more, those thick lips of hers, curve into a grin.

7

ZARIAH

What am I doing? This man is perfect in a world where legality isn't important. I've tried to tell myself that the few years we spent talking and texting were to save me from loneliness. Those conversations reminded me to have a life, not to be rigid and self-centered like my father. Every semester, another Honor Roll notched on my belt. And every semester I had Vassili to remind me to take a damn breath when needed.

It wasn't that I was consumed with education. My brain is a sponge. Jokes and cock pics aside, I really, really liked Vassili Resnov.

I'm a little tipsy after that one shot. Any more and I'll be wide open. As Vassili and I chat and eat, I see myself wanting to include more nights and days with him in my future. I'd alienate myself from the poison of my father and drink in something as toxic, potent. Vassili.

"This is so good," I tell him, trying one of the shashlik sticks. I bump my shoulder against his. "Dang, I should've tried it sooner."

"There's one left and it's all yours, Zariah."

Wow! He offered his last bit of food. If I recall anything from partying with rich boys as a teen, they inhaled food. What they didn't do is offer much thought to any female counterparts, girlfriend or not. There was no sacrificing their last bite, either.

The firelight glows against his golden skin. With his jacket around me, I'm submerged in power, invincibility and the spice of testosterone. I want to bring it to my face and breathe him in. For a hundred times, I've had to stop myself from looking at the defined muscles in his arms.

Butterflies lift off throughout my stomach, as Vassili gazes at my lips. Though he doesn't smile much, the look in his eye says exactly what he wants. I've never felt so desired in my life. There's something special about a big, muscular guy who can wolf down a pack of food, offering me his last. Again, I'm all smiles as I speak, "No. Thanks, anyway. I don't work out like you do, Karo."

"Ah, don't call me Karo, Zariah," he corrects, gently. "We can work you out, though."

Vassili's hand skims across my thigh and the walls of my pussy spasm like crazy.

It's hard enough to think, let alone find my voice to speak. "*Karo*... I like that. Where'd you get the name?"

"Ana— my father. It's my middle name. But if you like the name and think it sounds hot..."

His voice trails off. He has this way of pushing me toward the edge of insanity. He seems to know how hesitant I am. I swear he has intentions, serious intentions, of breaking me.

"You've got something on your face," he says. Before I can do anything, his knuckles rub along my jaw and lips. It's the roughest texture to ever touch my lips, sending a burning fire over my skin on such a cold night. Then his hand clutches ever so softly at my throat. He leans in and tastes my lips. The fighter is out-of-this-world attentive as his tongue twirls around mine. Fireworks go off in my nether regions, lips swelling and contracting in a way they've never before.

His other hand slips into my collar. Tremors course through my body as he squeezes my nipples while kissing me.

Delectable and slow, Vassili growls against me like a lion ready to devour its prey. I gasp when the arousal to my taut nipples ends. He reaches between my thighs and paws at my intimate place.

"Between those curvy hips is the sweetest, ripest pussy I've waited seven years to taste." His words tickle across my cheek. I'm burning hot for him. Like the sun is scorching my body.

I yelp, as Vassili picks me up and plants me smack dab on top of his lap. Holy shit, his cock seemed so huge before, when I first felt it. Now, it embeds against the length of the inside my thigh. Though his jean material blocks us, I feel the heat.

It takes a moment to find my voice. I lick my lips and sputter, "Vassili, what are you doing?"

"I thought you were cold. Did I warm you up?" There's no need to answer him. The look in his eyes tells me how pleased he is. "Oh, and you've been begging to see my cock, right?"

"I've been begging?" I scoff.

He leans back on the couch, one buff bicep reaching back. He places a hand behind his head. Even with a leisure demeanor, he dominates the entire roof.

I start to move my leg from around his waist. "Boy, I haven't beg—"

Vassili's other hand clamps along my hip. Our eyes lock, as he holds me in place. My head is buzzing, and I haven't had nearly as many drinks as Vassili. In truth, I was still cold before him tasting my mouth. He gives my ass a little squeeze with one hand. His buff bicep clutches my hip while the other reaches for my hand. He places it on his crotch, nodding his chin as if to say I hold all the cards now. Fire twinkles in those devilish eyes. My tongue glides across my lips. I silently pull down his zipper. I reach in, meeting warm, hard silk. My God, this bastard isn't wearing any boxers!

Still leaning back, his stacks of abs before me, he growls the instant I touch him. Looking down at my hand, I notice his dick is ridged and so perfectly veined. My lack of experience proves that I have a lot of exploring to do. He's so thick, my fingers and thumb don't meet. That vision sends a rush of desire pooling in my lower abdomen.

I'm smart enough to know that he could seriously hurt me. But God, I want him to hurt me so good. He finally leans forward to taste my lips again.

"You like that," he acknowledges, helping me stroke his cock.

"Yes," I admit, even though it wasn't a question. I press my teeth into my bottom lip. Vassili continues to work my tiny hand along his cock. While we continue stroking his shaft together, he pulls his face closer, biting my lip, exactly where I did.

"You still tight for me?" Vassili asks. His thick, frowning mouth almost seems to be relaxing in contentment.

"Touch yourself, Zar," he demands before I can answer. "I have to know if you still taste as good as water."

He pulls my hand away from his cock. Should I whimper, beg or cry? But before I can do any of the above, Vassili clasps a hand along my hip. My nether regions swell with desire. He pushes my panties to the side. I gyrate in anticipation along his lap, craving his next move.

"Work your pussy for me," Vassili orders. He clasps my wrist again. "You have tiny little fingers. Mine would fucking break you, baby."

Damn, he's playing me. I want to tell him to stop gaming me up since I can still feel his fingers pleasuring me until I lose it. But the spark in his dark gaze tells me he is aware that I'm still uncomfortable with masturbation. I reach down between my thighs and give my clit a nice little squeeze to alleviate the ache within my tightness.

"Get yourself off," he demands, with a slight frown. His command is more pronounced as if to tell me that my attempt disappointed him. Trying again, I press my fingers inside of my body. It's still a foreign feeling, even after all his attempts to teach me at eighteen. So soft. A sweet, little gushiness too.

Vassili's frown deepens. "You've neglected this beautiful pussy. Shame on you."

"Whatever, Vassili." I snap, in embarrassment.

He places his hand over mine, his thumb kneading the back of my hand. I gulp down the desire to beg him to get me off. Damn, how many times have I headed straight for the shower after dreaming of his touch? His dark gaze latches onto mine. Again, I plunge my fingers into my wetness while he coaxes me to love myself in ways that I never have before.

Catching a rhythm feels good. I stroke my kitty while working my hips and gyrating around his waist. Vassili groans, leaning back and fist his cock.

"*Khorosho, Zariah, Khorosho.*" Though I'm not sure what he saying, he smiles with his eyes.

With a moan, I work my pussy, imagining that it's the fighter. He's so versed on pain, offering me this pleasure.

Vassili leans forward, his head tilts as he catches my dazed pupils. "You did well. Tell me how sweet you are right now, Zariah."

Having concentrated on filling the loneliness Vassili has created within my body, my eyebrow lifts in confusion. "Huh?"

He places a hand around my wrist, thumb gliding over the quickened pulse and holds it up. I glance at my glossed finger. The fire reflects off it. His tongue licks out as does mine. We taste the sugar together from my fingers before our mouths connect.

Our tongues twirl around each other in a feverish hunger. My hands clasp against his strong jaw. My mouth is coated with my taste. The shock hasn't set in because I'm in the presence of my longest craving.

"Condom, condom," I breathe the words, hardly moving my mouth from his.

"I got you." He slips his hand in his pocket while kissing me furiously.

I grab his bicep; its steel strength against my palm. His tongue sends me into a tailspin of delirium. Vassili places a condom on his cock, never taking his lips from my mouth. Damn, the taste of my pussy along my lips has him glued to me. Then before I can scream, my body is tossed into the air. His hands clamp down onto my ass. My thick thighs slide around his neck in one quick, effortless move.

My back arches as his tongue impale my pussy in one fluid motion. His lips crush against my labia as he dives deep into me. Vassili stands with me on his shoulders. I grip his hair and my eyes bug out. The skyline of Los Angeles is all around us.

"Vassili…" I screech. Fuck, it feels so good. But the fencing around the roof no longer shields us from prying eyes.

"Shhhh," he looks up at me, chiseled chin and lips glossed with my honey. "You tell me if any mudaks lay their eyes on you. I'll fucking murder them."

With a quick grunt, Vassili assaults my pussy, one lick and a thick tongue thrust at a time. He comes to his knees, pulling me forward into his seat. My legs clench around him.

Do I want his dick or for him to keep fucking me with his mouth? My indecipherable moan falls on deaf ears because he continues to feast on my pussy. My back slams against the soft pillows, my second set of lips quivering.

"Vassili... fu-fuck me," I groan, pulling my hair. This foreplay is enough to send me to the madhouse. While kneeling before me, the fighter holds onto my ass cheeks. He has no intention of letting me go and he has no use for air. He hasn't come up for a single breath while my lungs are on fire, gulping down too much.

Shit, if someone is looking, I have to appear the crazed fool. I laugh at that. Then I feel a new tingle between my thighs. Mmmm, it's a nice delight as Vassili alternates from licking deep inside of me to coating my labia. I stop tugging at my hair and grin while tooting my ass down to offer him more of my pussy.

Once more, his nose tickles my clit, sending spirals of desire through my body. His tongue—

"Hey!" I screech. Vassili's tongue nudges against my untouched anus. My argument is met by a cocky chuckle.

"Rock that ass on my tongue," Vassili commands. "I am not going to hurt you. Sweetheart, we've got to get that pussy ready for my cock."

When he grabs his heavy shaft, I nod in agreement as reality hits me. He's right. I couldn't fit my fingers fully around him. Following his direction, I work my ass against his tongue. Is this shameful? Yeah, I bet it is.

"Fuck with your clit, Zar. You're almost ready."

"Hmmm," I moan in question, concentrating on his breath against my skin.

"Fuck your clit, I need you wetter. Zar, my cock has never been so hard. So I need you really wet unless you want me to break you." He paws my cheeks, bringing my gaze to his. "You want me to break you?"

I nod like a bobblehead, ready to submit to any of his wishes.

Vassili laughs on key. He pushes my legs up until my heels are on the edge of the chair; it's almost as if I'm squatting before him. He licks out at my labia.

"Zar, work that clit. Fuck it good, so I can get ready to enter you."

As he alternates, going from tonguing my pussy to my ass, I obey his command. I moan while caressing my hard, tiny nub. Damn, my ass is an inch away from falling off the chair. My climax comes quickly. I rub my clit and pump my hips against his face until I'm screaming from deep down in my soul. Shit, if I could sing. I hit Mariah Carey octave. Maybe it's that of a scalded cat, but either way, at least a half-mile radius is aware of how good Vassili gives lady-head.

He finally leans back on his legs, muscular chest taking a deep breath. Vassili's eyes lock onto mine as he fists his cock into his hand. I take a deep gulp, ready for the fighter now.

Out of nowhere, a large drop of water plops on my forehead. With it, comes an onslaught of rain as if I was back down south. It's not supposed to rain in Southern California, damn it. The hearth is doused out in a second flat.

In less time, I'm lifted into Vassili's arms.

"What are you..." I haven't finished arguing before we're beneath the roofing of the elevator. He was faster than lightning.

He sets me down and presses the button. Torrents of water splash against my legs, which aren't shielded from the angled rain. My teeth jar and seconds seem like minutes. The doors swoosh open and we hurry inside.

The lights are bright in the elevator. My mascara is probably streaming down my cheeks. But my gaze is glued to how every well-defined muscle in Vassili's arm is perfectly contoured. The plane of his chest extends almost forever before meeting his broad shoulders. His thick, curly locks are plastered against his head. I smile, thinking how much I've missed grazing my hand through his Mohawk. Damn, I only did that once. That realization makes me smile even more.

I notice then, I'm now hugging his jacket to myself, inhaling more of his power. His bronze skin is cool and wet, begging for my touch.

"Sorry." I start to pull his jacket from over my leather one and hand it over.

"I'll live," he says, refusing to take it.

The elevator opens up and we step out into the lounge. The lights are soft and certain areas that were intimately lit before are now dark.

"What time is it?" My eyebrow arches. How long have we been on the roof?

"A little after three in the morning. I've got to key in the alarm code," he explains, since we aren't headed toward the front door.

"Okay." I tremble in my skin. The water from my dress is dripping down my legs and onto the floor.

Like a lion, ever on the prowl, Vassili moves down the hallway. He pulls his drenched thermal off in one quick swoop. The Kremlin, in Moscow, is meticulously drawn, almost rivaling the exact architecture. But it's arched in the shape of a crown and perched atop of a wolf's head. The design is so lifelike, it almost seems to leap from his skin. With the words: *oderint dum metuant* etched below. I recall the Latin phrase from a slanderous political article about government coercion. They read, "Let them hate, so long as they fear."

The rest of the meticulous muscles of his back are also bathed in ink. Though the tattoos aren't as bold in meaning, each one has a certain level of detail and attention to them. From an X-rated tattoo of a matryoshka doll, also known as a Russian nesting doll. It's open, with a large-breasted woman sticking out of it, to another, that's the depiction of a skull. A cigarette sticking from its mouth. The biggest tattoo of all? A cross with Jesus on it, which seems to have been perfectly airbrushed on his skin. The cross blends into some tattoos and out of others. It extends over his broad shoulders and down along his spine.

He opens the door that has an office sign, tossing his thermal into the darkness. Then Vassili reaches into a pitch room and pulls something from the wall. It's a hoodie.

"Don't worry. It's mine." He hands it over. Before I can argue about him being without a shirt on such a chilly evening, Vassili retorts, "I am still not cold."

"The ladies' room is across the way. Change. If you catch so much as the sniffles, I'll feel like a dick, okay?"

"Okay." I smile my thanks.

The bad thing about leather jackets is their ability to match the temperature. Though my upper half isn't wet, I'm still frozen to the core. I step into the women's restroom. The entire place is very luxurious. I place his hoodie and jacket onto the settee in the powder room and unzip my jacket. Next, I remove my soaked dress, careful not to sit it next to the hoodie.

I shrug into the dry hoodie and a delicious aroma infuses itself into my nostrils. My eyes close. The scent is of him, his slight musk. Damn, I love that smell. The hoodie stops mid-thigh on me. I shake out my leather jacket and then wrap it around my legs. It's almost post-apocalyptic attire, but I'm warmer.

My hair has kinked and frizzed up. No amount of training it with the flat iron could have saved it from this evening. I smirk at myself in the mirror, grab Vassili's jacket and step out of the ladies' room.

The lounge is deathly quiet. With hesitance, I call out his name, "Vassili?"

"I'm almost done, beautiful," his response comes back instantly.

I follow his voice down the hall to a room across from the first office. Staying in the hall, I look in. Vassili is standing on the opposite side of a very expensive desk. His eyebrows are pinched together as he stares at a stack of papers.

"Are you okay?" I ask.

There's evil darkness in his gaze before his eyes lift to glance my way. "Good. Everything's good," he says, too quickly.

No, it's not. You were about ready to commit murder, I think to myself.

"Okay," I reply, as he pushes a few papers around on the desk. Not my business. He has his secrets, I have mine. We have one shared secret that will always be for us. Backing away, I recall the same crappy mantra of mine that helped me stop responding to Vassili, years ago. He is a Resnov and there could never be much between us.

Vassili steps out of the room and locks it. My mind begins to wonder why the other office, where he grabbed the hoodie, wasn't locked. Someone has more secrets than he does. Is this *really* his business?

"So my place or your father's?" he asks, successfully cutting off my curious thoughts.

I sigh. "Mine is best, Vassili."

He glances at me. There's so much more to that statement than the words. *There is no need to prolong the inevitable.*

Instead of challenging me, he punches in a key code near the front door. "Zariah, as soon as I open the door, we run, okay?"

The truck is less than twenty yards out. My feet pound

the pavement. Torrents of ice-cold water slam against the top of the hoodie and my shoulders.

As I get inside, I press the jacket further down my thighs. My brown skin is all glossy and wet. Pushing the damp hoodie from my head, I rub a hand through my hair as Vassili gets into the driver's seat.

The ride home is a short distance due to the prime location of The Red Door Lounge. Not a luxury car is in sight when Vassili's truck zips up to the curb. He turns the truck off and looks at me.

"I've got to go out of town for a few days, Zariah. But we will go to dinner on Thursday." Vassili's tone is definite. "In the meantime, don't lose my number or I might not be able to focus on handling my business."

"About that..." I falter, not daring a glance in his direction. I gulp down a rock. His 'business' is as taboo as the thought of us together. "Dinner and Thursday. Vassili, this was supposed to be one more night."

"And Thursday is another night, all in itself. Okay, beautiful?" His Russian accent is stronger than usual. It leaves no room for miscommunication. I can just about hear his thick accent say, 'We will go to dinner.'

I scoff. "Am I in the clear if I fuck you?"

He laughs, abdominals all sexy and flexed. "Nyet. You're never free of me, Zariah. Seven years ago, I said you were mine. That was a fucking promise and I don't break my promises."

The dark storm in his eyes warns that I am all his. He claimed to be patient in the past. I am seriously stuck in a situation here.

"Vassili, I like you, more than I should. When we're

together, time stops. Something supernatural happens. My mind forgets to comprehend that *you are a RESNOV.* Malich's son! Not just his goon. Or his damn nephew or second cousin or married into the family or something," I argue. *Why can't Vassili be related by marriage?*

"Vassili, I am the daughter of the chief of police. My father is in the process of campaigning for mayor." *And I don't trust you.*

He runs his knuckles along the bristles on his impeccable jawline, unfazed by my remark. "I've got a question for you, Zariah."

I start to tell him that this is the end of the line, but Vassili doesn't ask what I expected him to. He inquires, "Do you think your father is clean, squeaky fucking clean?"

"What?" My eyebrows knit together in confusion. "Okay, this is going left field. Forgive me if I ever gave the impression that I or my father were better than you."

"I'm not asking if you think he's 'better' than me." His brown eyes sweep up and down my body. Not like before, there's no desire here, only interest in the truth.

"He has his faults. My dad has made upwards of 300 grand a year during his seven years as the chief of police— I'm sure that's nickels in your eyes. Look, I always thought joining in on the integrated LAPD Commission crew would be Maxwell's next step. But he has talked of campaigning for mayor this November. He has friends..." *And* I admit, if only to myself, *he is "mildly" crooked.* Licking my lips, I steer clear of airing my father's indiscretions.

"My dad has higher goals to achieve than the Commission. He'll become the mayor. While he's campaigning, how would it look if I am sleeping with a Resnov?"

Vassili is quiet for a moment. "Nobody on the streets backing the Resnov name is afraid of Washington, sweetheart. Fuck his friends. I do not give a damn about his goals. Though I have no intention of stepping on his toes."

I huff. This man listens to nothing! *"Whatever, Vassili."*

"I don't want to get to know Maxwell Washington." His hand skims over my leg. It's rough and sends an earthquake against my pussy walls, but this time fate doesn't push it away. The rain is drumming against the window. Nothing is stopping us... except for me. I push his hand away.

"I won't ever say anything about you, Vassili. But the more we become involved, the deeper our association..." I pause for the oxygen to reach my brain.

"My father won't like this. Regardless of me being a grown-ass woman, Vassili. Maxwell Washington is a man who gets what he wants." *Dad won't touch me, but he might go after you.*

Vassili laughs. "Beautiful, you're tired. Should I walk you to the door or will that piss off your dad? He's been peeking through the window for some time now."

I glance over my shoulder. Damn, I've gotta move. Yet I am aware that Vassili is ignoring my request to part ways.

"You're invincible in the ring, Vassili. I'm positive you've been more engaged in the family business than you *claimed* to be, during our past correspondence. There is nothing for us. This was one night of shooting the breeze for old times' sake."

"Run along, beautiful," is all Vassili says in response.

My mouth tenses. It would have been nice to have one final kiss goodbye. I snatch up my purse and get out. The rain isn't as commanding as it was before. Dampness seeps on to the shoulders and top of the hoodie as I step to the door. It's opened by my father as Vassili pulls out from in front of the house.

"I never took Taryn for a truck kind of girl, Mercedes emblem aside." Maxwell eyes me suspiciously with a thick terry cloth towel in hand.

"Thanks, Dad," I reply, grabbing the towel. "It's not Taryn's."

"Rhonda?"

"Nope." I start toward the vast staircase, without so much as an interest in his inquisitiveness.

"Then who? I know Ronisha isn't driving around in that thing? Zariah, you start at Levine and Levine law firm next week! And I'm sweet talking colleagues about a potential mayoral campaign."

"Doubt I require a reminder, Dad," I toss over my shoulder. "I've been exercising this muscle for a while now."

I tap the crown of my head, disregarding his mention of Levine and Levine law firm. That was his dream for me. Though I'll be in a cubicle bright and early on Monday, I have no intention of working there.

"Are you talking back to me?" His voice is lower. Closer. Harder. Much harder than usual. I turn around and my father is inches away. Does he think I'll cower like my mom? I wish a man would try to hit me. Blood or not. One of us would have to die because I would fight until my last breath.

"First of all, you're my father and older than me, so I'll try being as respectful as possible. Second of all, I was out. I simply choose not to tell you with whom, as I am twenty-five years old. Third, and I implore you to take heed, I will not ruin your campaign for mayor once you begin. My actions will not be a reflection of your capabilities because I know how to handle myself. So do you have any other question that you'd like me to answer—or plead the fifth on, rather?"

His animosity decreases, but I realize that mine is boiling. Though I lived in Northern California for much of the time,

I was previously in my mother's territory. Shit, are her divorcée mannerisms rubbing off on me? Yes, there's underlying resentment I have for my dad since I grew up in a hostile environment. But what has my lips set in a sneer the most, is having my cake and not being allowed to eat it.

I cannot have Vassili Resnov. He isn't a man to be had. I cannot be his. He's a Resnov. Come Monday morning, I'll return to the focused mindset, where my career will be my life. Once I'm established, I'll meet a man of like mind. If he so much as looks at me sideways, I will bite his head off and find a divorce attorney to take, take, take.

"Pleading the fifth isn't necessary." Dad pats my shoulder, with a smile of his own. "You're like me, Zariah. Very convincing speech. You will get what you want..."

The underlying tone is that I will get what I want as he always does. Too bad he isn't aware of exactly what I covet, a man who should never be mine.

"Continue to surround yourself with winners," Dad implores.

"All right, Dad. Are you still apartment shopping with me tomorrow?" I inquire, trying to lighten the mood.

"Yes, I've enlisted an agent."

"Why? I've already checked off a few places on rcnt.com."

"*Rent.com?* Funny," he says, not laughing.

"Dad, you live in a white man's world. My money is funny at the moment. I'll be leasing a studio or perhaps a one-bedroom. And it most definitely won't be in the Hills, or anywhere an agent would garner a commission."

"All right, how about we look at two of your preferred places and two of mine?" he compromises.

No need. I shrug, realizing that this is not a winning battle until the ink is wet on an inexpensive apartment lease. "If you feel like wasting your time, Dad."

"Nonsense. Spending time with my daughter isn't a waste.

I've had alternating Christmases and Thanksgivings with you since you've been up north. I assumed your mother would let up when you moved to Berkeley for law school."

What about you spend time with your son, Martin? The few times my dad made the trip to Atlanta during my undergrad, he never got around to seeing his firstborn.

I meander toward my room, praying to God that my time here would be short-lived.

My phone vibrates in my hand. I glance at it and see that there's a text from Vassili.

See you; 8 pm sharp on Thursday. Though I grumble, a part of me welcomes his dominant demeanor.

8

VASSILI

Ulyanovsk, Russia

I love my country. Having been born after the Berlin Wall collapsed might have had a little something to do with it. But that being said, it hurts me to my core every time I return home. When I'm in Russia, my only thought is how long will it take me to get back out of Russia.

The compound my father owns covers a vast area in the suburb of Rublyovka. It's compared to Beverly Hills in prestige. In a neighborhood of trillionaires and slimy government officials, he fits in perfectly. I pull up to the gates, hands gripping the steering wheel so tight that the color of my knuckles is pallid. The guards on either side of the gate offer glares. Fucking *mudaks*.

They covet my position as Anatoly's firstborn. *Have at it.*

I toss a stiff middle finger, pulling inside of the courtyard. Luxury supercars are scattered around a lengthy lap pool. Before I step one foot out of the SUV, my father saunters down the front steps of his home. He's in a charcoal gray tailor-made suit. Though the sky is cloudy, gold shades cover his eyes, which match the gold loafers on his feet. His skin is darker. Not the ashen color it was the last time I was here a few years back.

He greets me as a father would his son and the shit is awkward. It's the same routine I've completed with Malich a thousand times over, yet I'm numb to Anatoly.

"Come, come." He ushers me past more guards and inside of his home.

The ceilings are high as the sky, all murals lined in gold. My father leads me to a grand dining room. A heavy wood table, fit for a king, is loaded with food. Women, each more beautiful than the last, are at our service.

One languishes over my father, pouring him vodka nonstop. Another one feeds him between kisses. Two are flocking around me. I stop the blonde's attempt to spoon up a bit of my borsch soup with a raised hand. "Girl," I snap. She paws at me instead while I feed myself, and the other one rubs my shoulders.

Anatoly asks, "So what is my brother up to?"

Though I never took my *job* seriously, I'm supposed to keep tabs on Malich. I pause from frowning. This is the reason for my visit. The Red Door is mine, all mine. The criminal activity, which gathers five times as much, well, that's supposed to be my claim to fame.

Little does my father know, I'm too busy to assign whores to the highest bidder at The Red Door. I'm also too busy to ensure those rich guys are tied down with premium drugs and our signature smuggled water. Malich handles it for me.

The other night with Zariah, I went into Malich's office at The Red Door. There were papers on his desk that my father should know about. Malich is embezzling from the alcohol funds. There were two sets of inventory; same dates, but different charge amounts. Telling Anatoly will only amplify the disappointment my father feels for me. It means that I

77

haven't watched Malich. In truth, I don't give a fuck how Anatoly feels. But my uncle lied to my face. That I can't have.

"Malich is good," I reply, surprising myself. Shit, I have more loyalty for my lying uncle than for my father. I fork up a bit of food and shovel it into my mouth. Inside, my veins are on fire. *I'll check into it and then...* I stop analyzing shit because the proof was in my motherfucking face.

"He's good?" Anatoly nods, a mask of uncertainty unveils, and he raises a glass. "My firstborn is at home. Ladies, show him a good time."

"Nyet." I brush my forearm against the blonde bitch again, who's hungrier for affection than she was a minute ago.

"What is this?" Anatoly's eyebrow rises. *"Cht za chert?— what the fuck?* Vassili isn't a whoremonger anymore?"

I have a taste for one woman only. I cannot tell my father that though, or he will want to meet Zariah. I glance away from the bitch that has been begging for attention. On the opposite side of me is a brunette. She's more chill when it comes to pouring my vodka and massaging my neck.

Like Zariah, her hair is a chocolate brown, but thin and blunt instead of strong, thick, and long. The silk robe she's wearing glides across this set of tits that might've been perfect. If I hadn't learned to compare every female trait to Zariah's. I recall the morning after Zariah, and I woke up on her balcony. It took a hot shower, jacking off and a train to get me off.

"Come here," I tell her. She tosses back her shot glass and then her mouth is all over mine. The other woman takes it upon herself to begin unzipping my pants.

"Oh, I must go." Anatoly arises.

He and the other women have hardly made it to the door when the darker one's tongue lodges down my throat. The blonde girl's lips coil along the ridge of my cock.

"Mhmm," the auburn girl moans against my mouth.

I press my hand against the crown of the blonde's head, forcing her deeper. Auburn kisses a trail down my neck, to my chest and meets the blonde in an intimate kiss. They both begin to flick at my cock. Sweet pink tongues slide and glide wet trails across the rigid plains of my stiffness.

Though I haven't been satiated in seven years, ever since Zariah Washington came into my life, my hand clamps onto the blonde's throat. I tug firmly enough to gather her attention.

"Get this bitch wet for me," I order.

The auburn girl grins, bashful eyes glancing up from my erection. Fuck me. She has this coyness about her like Zariah. Though hers is for play. I stand quickly. With one swipe, the food before me goes crashing to the left. The girls jump and giggle. The auburn lifts her ass onto the table. The blonde goes straight for her pussy. Zipping my pants, I exit stage left. There's no way I'll rat out my uncle, not for this life or my closest blood tie.

In the main hallway, I head straight to the door.

"You leaving?" Comes a hard voice from over my shoulder.

I ignore it and keep walking.

"Vassili," the voice nears. From my peripheral vision, I see an arm reach for my shoulder. I grab the goon's wrist, yank it low and bring it down. The man in the expensive suit is flipped over. My foot slams into his chest. I pull out a freshly rolled cigarette and my lighter.

"Walking up behind me is a bad idea…bad motherfucking idea. Got that?"

"Your father would like to see you," another hard voice says.

I turn a dead glare at Semion, my father's most trusted and deadly left hand. Besides, being the Bratva, he's family. My father's sister's son.

"C'mon, *kuzen*, play nice," Semion says, no emotion on his face. He has one dude on his right and two on his left. I hold up my hands in a show of peace. I don't have a gun, but if they keep at it, I will take them all down with my bare hands.

Semion walks beside me. The twins are in front of us. The one in the back helps up the mudak that was dumb enough to try and touch me. We head down toward the west wing. One of the twins opens up the double doors to a cave-like room with shimmering 24-karat gold walls. My eyes narrow since there's no natural lighting. The sound of giggling and Anatoly echoes against the low hanging ceiling. Then we step into a jacuzzi room, where my father is playing with three of his girls.

"*Moy syn*—my son." He starts toward the stairs. "You aren't leaving so soon?"

"Yeah, I am."

"We must talk business." His attention returns to the women. They huff while getting out of the jacuzzi after him and leaving the room.

"I'm watching Malich," I reply. The glare in my gaze tells him this is for show. "What other business do you have that needs my attention?"

"Tomorrow, I attend the council meeting in Monte Carlo. We'll gamble," Anatoly says. What he means is they will be talking about eliminating whoever in the political world is fucking with the heroin trade.

"Nyet, I'm going home. Can't help."

Anatoly rubs the back of his neck and laughs. "Home? That new president of yours rides my cock. You wanna go home? You are my firstborn, Vassili. Don't be a pussy."

I shrug, turning to walk away.

"Every morning I tell myself that my coward of a son is more like Sasha. More and more like Sasha."

I pause, glaring him dead in the eyes. Sasha is his blood, the daughter he didn't care about.

"Or your mother, maybe you're—"

My forearm slams into Anatoly's neck. A vision pulls me under. Sasha was nine. I went into her room and there were three of my father's goons, running a train on her. I picked up a lamp and bashed one in the head. The other two thought that shit was funny. But I fought my first fight. Only to be stopped by my sister because she couldn't stand to see me get my ass kicked. They had already handed it to me before she could even struggle into her clothes and try to stop them. While blood leaked down the side of my face and with one eye swelling by the second, I cleaned her up. Then I let Sasha cry in my arms for a while. She begged me to keep quiet. But I went to my father's home and told him what they'd done to *his daughter*. The mudak rubbed his neck and let my words roll straight through. Then he reached down, gripped my chin and asked me why my eye was swollen shut. When I said those bastards and I fought, he laughed and patted my head. He hit me softly on the chin and told me to keep fighting.

And I kept fighting. Not because Anatoly took an interest in me. But because true to his word, those three mudaks and their families were murdered. Though not for the right reason. They were murdered for touching his firstborn, not for raping his daughter.

The clicks of every man's gun going off safety are instantaneous as Anatoly yelps in shock. He's pressed back against the gold wall, unable to breathe.

"Say something else, Anatoly," I threaten. "I will fucking kill you. Mention Sasha or my mother again. God cannot save you."

Barrel nudges my temple. "C'mon, *kuzen*," Semion says.

"If... if..." My father's face is red and shaking as he tries to catch his breath. These motherfuckers will be all too happy to pull the trigger before my father passes out or gives the signal. But they don't realize it's not necessary to squeeze this mudak's life source. I can snap my father's neck in an instant and he knows it.

Slowly, I let him go.

Anatoly's chin is held high, face a dark frowning mask as he rubs his tender throat. "They could've killed you, Vassili!"

My voice doesn't rise above a whisper. "As long as I take you out too, I don't mind."

I turn toward the door again. The *piz'da* who met me at the exit has his finger on the trigger, still itching to squeeze it. Having no shits to give, I walk right on by.

"One day, you'll have to forgive me, Vassili," I hear my father shouting. The bitch move he pulled by mentioning my little sister, Sasha and my mom reminded me of the cold, hard truth. I'd rather burn in hell than forgive him.

My sparring partner is one of Vadim's up and coming MMA fighters. He's an undercard with a wild knack for flipping the script. With a flurry of left and right fists to his face, I draw first blood. His right eye is red. I concentrate on that.

Vadim is cursing in Russian.

Frown deepening, I pummel the kid. The gash above his eye sends blood running down his nose and chin. His forearms finally come up.

"Block me, bitch," I order, though this is no longer a sparring match.

His attempts to protect his face are for shit. Arms are at my left and right. It's Nestor and one of the gym employees pulling me off of the douche bag.

The fighter jabs toward my chin. He's just shy of his mark before falling on his back again.

"You crazy?" Vadim asks. "I have a potential booking for him in a few days. He's gonna look like a bitch, Vassili."

"Yuri, why didn't you hop your fat ass in the cage?" A very familiar voice speaks up from behind us.

"Ah, Pops, I'm not an idiot." Yuri's heavy body shifts in his seat. His nose is glued to a porn magazine.

I glare at him before turning around to address Malich. My hand goes to the back of my uncle's neck. His goes to mine. He pats me softly.

"We missed you for dinner the other night."

I consider making up a lie, but Malich continues, "So you and Anatoly have a good time this weekend, eh?"

My fucking father! He had to have called his kid brother. Anatoly gave Malich a subtle reminder and warning that I'm here as the enforcer. Keep his brother on the up and up. The smile on Malich's face tells me that he doesn't give a damn. We are good. I didn't swoop in and leave him high and dry. My uncle nods his head toward the stairs.

"I'm hungry, Vassili. You can eat, right?"

"Fuck yeah, I have to hit the showers first."

"All right. Vadim, your wife cook?" Malich asks. "Vassili and I are going to stop by."

"Dah, she cooked. Shit, Vassili can watch you eat. This *mudak* tried to injure my fighter before a big match." He mutters about fucking with his money and Malich laughs.

"C'mon, Vadim, I'm your favorite." My hand goes to the back of his neck. "You fucking love me."

"I cannot stand you. Yeah, I guess I also love you." He pats the back of my neck quickly and then he's back to cussing. This time his wrath is toward his MMA fighter, arguing about him needing to be a bull. It's always 'bull this' or 'bull that' with him.

I head to the locker room, wondering what Anatoly told Malich. *Had to be a simple warning. Or nothing at all because I didn't tell him anything.*

D ressed in a long sleeve shirt and khakis, I saunter down the second level to the first of Vadim's Gym. In the alley, Yuri is leaning against Malich's SUV. The window is down. They're speaking in Russian, low and quick. The squawk of seagulls further obstructs my ability to hear them.

When I step up to the passenger side, Malich is all smiles.

"I tried to get this motherfucker to let me go with you all. I'm hungry, too." Yuri pats his belly. "But Pop gives me another assignment, instead."

"That so," I reply, half-listening, as I open the door and hop inside.

Yuri backs away from the SUV.

"What's troubling you, son," Malich asks. "Your grandfather never fought angry. MMA is different from boxing. However, that's one of the most fundamental parallels. Don't fight angry. Where's your head at?"

These are his normal questions of concern. Had it been Anatoly inquiring, my brain would be in overload with suspicion.

"I'm thinking about a girl." Dah, it's true. Though, at the time, I was concentrating on Sasha. Now, I'm considering the girl I'm obsessed with. Where will I take Zariah tonight? And what the fuck is my father doing telling Malich I visited?

"Shit, you're in love?"

I nod. "First sight."

"Only you, Vassili. What was it, some odd years ago..." Malich pauses in contemplation while stopping at the red light.

"Had to be a year after you went pro. You were moving your way up from not making a dime—fighting for fucks. You were in love at first sight then."

My relationship with my uncle was that close. I told Malich about Zariah and her best friend, Ronisha. He disposed of Sergio's body for me. He was proud of my work, saying it was pure torture. Pure hate. And to tell him I did Sergio in for a woman; *that* he said was priceless.

"The same girl."

"Did you even... Never mind. Vassili, you didn't fuck and tell, even when a bitch stumbled out of your bedroom at age fifteen." Malich chuckles.

"Now that I think about it, I didn't think you did. It's all a woman has over us."

His laughter dims. Malich's mind is on his wife. Contemplating my late aunt. She got sick and died long before I moved to the States. I remember them visiting Moscow during New Year's, which is the biggest deal for us Russians. They were always happy, always in love. I never thought a man so deep into the crime syndicate could have a heart. With my father and younger brothers as my main example, I thought only I was stupid enough to care about the female race. Malich loved his wife in the way my mudak of a father was incapable of giving a damn about my mom or Sasha.

My poor sister...

"So, you were chatting with the girl before you even moved out, Vassili." Malich breaks the silence. Apparently, the years have allowed him to cope with his pain. Whereas I'm accustomed to keeping Sasha from my mind. "That's a long time to know a girl."

"Dah."

"*Dah?* That's all?" He laughs. "Kids these days... Shit, you aren't even a kid any longer, but you stay with your mouth shut. Your grandfather took me to my first whorehouse when I got a bit of fuzz on my balls. He said to put on a rubber. That was the extent to our chat about love life. I'm genuinely interested. You two have been off and on?"

"Zariah's been out of L.A. for a while now," I offer.

"Any plans?"

"Dinner." I huff. Keeping Zariah from my family and *keeping her* won't be easy. "I'm taking her to dinner tonight. Not sure where."

"Well, your first name is golden at most of the ritzy spots on Rodeo Drive. Wherever it isn't, mentioning you're a Resnov will place you on tonight's VIP list, which often takes a year at those crappy places. Shit, The Red Door is better."

"I took her there." I glance out the window, so he doesn't connect my visit to The Red Door with my travel to Russia.

"What did the girl think of your place?"

"She loved it." I shrug. "It's going to be warm tonight. Not that blocking off the roof will force me to go broke..."

"Far from it."

"I want her alone. I don't like to have my woman around others, not now."

"Then cook her a good meal," he says, simply pulling to a stop in front of Vadim's home.

I pat the back of his neck. "I'm going to cook her a good meal!"

"See, your old *dyadya* is good for something."

9

ZARIAH

On Monday morning, I called my father's friend at the Levine and Levine law firm and explained the confusion. Simply put, Maxwell was doing his best to place me where he wanted me the most. He knew good and well I had already wormed my way into his old colleague's law firm.

Instead, I drove to Billingsley Legal. The family-focused firm is much newer and less revered. My plan to work part-time and study my ass off for the impending bar exam this July was set in full swing. Though my father and I went in search of an apartment, the next few days are filled with bar exam material and work. What's even sadder about my current pathetic existence? Ronisha and I have grown apart. We met at Panera Bread on Wednesday evening, but neither of us had much to talk about. I hate that we're drifting like this.

After deep-conditioning my hair in the shower, my tresses have shrunk into a curly Afro. Dressed in silk pajamas shorts set, the wind from the balcony bristles across my dewy brown skin. The sheer drapes bellow into the bedroom. I scan my bookshelf for something old school. My index finger skims across "Flyy Girl," which is sandwiched between two high school favorites, "The Great Gatsby" and "Leaves of Grass." Nothing in this world can persuade me that love exists more than books and certain songs. The songster who introduced me to love was D'Angelo, back in his Angie Stone days. Though I'm not convinced love is attainable, he had a dreamy way of making me crave love.

My fingertips skim over my old romance collection. I search for the book which coupled well with D'Angelo, placing my heart in that fall-in-love state of mind.

"It's 8:20, Zariah," Vassili's hard voice is so very near and tangible.

I spin around on the balls of my feet. "Vassili, have you lost your damn mind!"

"We had a date at eight. You still didn't touch your pussy the way it was meant to be touched in the shower."

"Boy—"

"Do you know what stopped me from stepping into that bathroom and taking what's mine?" he asks, his voice smooth, low and lush. Jeans encase his bulging thighs in a wide-legged stance. A white undershirt strained over his stacks of chest muscles, with a trendy blazer amplifying his sexy, bad-ass persona. Devilish good looks and he has the nerve to have a cross around his neck.

He's seated on the ottoman on the veranda outside of my bedroom. The expensive bottle of whiskey that my father keeps under lock and key dangling in his hand.

"Respect, Zariah. Respect stopped me from stepping into

the bathroom as you showered. Your heavenly cunt drenching wet while you massaged it with brown sugar. Is it brown sugar soap or do you fucking smell as good as brown sugar?"

With a lump lodged in my throat, I mumble, "It's pink Himalayan salt scrub." I shake the cobwebs from my brain. *Why the hell did I answer this deranged man's question?* "Why are you here, Vassili?"

"It's *Thursday*, sweetheart. I've never been a prompt person until I met you." His eyes roam across my body. This is what happens when I call Vassili's bluff. Looking like a hot mess, shame on me. I was going to comb my hair and braid it, after choosing an old book. Yet I underestimated this man once again.

"Oh, good for you." I grin. "When I move from here, it will be into a cheap apartment on the highest floor. No balcony. No damn trees for you to climb, either. Good luck, asshole."

His frown deepens. "You aren't moving anywhere unless it's with me."

"Wow, Vassili. You're so used to having the last word. I know good and damn well you aren't trying to give me the key to your home." I shove a hand through my hair, coifing my coiled afro. "All you are is talk."

"You refuse to give me a chance because your squeaky-clean father will be running for mayor?" He arches a thick, sexy eyebrow.

"Wow, am I that sadiddy?" My mouth tenses.

"In a nutshell, yes. Among an entire list of issues. You know what, Vassili, having you around has helped me brush up on my opening and closing remarks. Although grounded in reality, I'm constantly defending my reasoning."

"You enjoy having me around." At that, Vassili brings the bottle to his lips. His face is still set in a deep frown. A twinkle in his eye tells me he loves screwing with my mind. With each gulp, he drains down even more of my father's most prized alcohol.

He stands up, towering over me. His breath is intoxicating, damn near capable of getting me drunk. I crave a taste from his lips.

"You're my good girl, Zariah." His mouth brushes against the corner of mine. The subtle touch sparks like wildfire. Then Vassili stands to his full height, my heart clenches.

This time I'm in pursuit. His mouth was close, teasingly so. Though he's prompted me to be good, I covet the notion of being bad for him. My tongue dips out and licks the spiced goodness of his mouth. His lips are tender, with notes of whiskey, mint and all man entwined within.

His hand grips my hair tightly, fingers wringing around the ultra-coiled strands. His dark gaze is deadly as he searches mine.

"I'm a bad man, Zariah. Let me be honest about my intentions. I'll never deliberately hurt you, beautiful. The second I touch you, I'll tarnish you. I'll ruin you for the good guy you've always dreamt of."

With the way his hand clamps into my hair, I can't reach up to kiss away his doubt.

"You're wrong, Vassili, I never dreamt of a knight in shining armor as a child. I've always been grounded in reality. Then I met you, and all I ever wanted was you." His mouth crashes down onto mine. I rise to my tippy toes, coveting this feeling, needing it to last forever.

No, needing it to expand, to blossom. Waves of pleasure electrify throughout my body. This is how I imagined it would be to kiss him. Yes, he tasted my mouth until I was speechless on the first night. But me clamping my hands along his face, thumb caressing that jagged scar on his jaw, me kissing him long, hard. I was ready for it to lead to things that grown folks do. I'd been too afraid to be bad for him.

I was in awe, damned teenage awe while he caressed my pussy before. Now, my pussy is crying for the fighter. I'm not a kid anymore. And the way his tongue caresses mine tells me that he is aware that I'm all woman.

His hand clutches the back of my neck. Ownership is freeing. Vassili presses his forehead against mine. His minty breath tingles my nose.

"Mhmmm, Zariah," he groans, "I'm going to feed you, then I'm going to eat you."

I lose all sight of rationale. My entire body is hot, on fire and wet all at the same time. Yet Vassili reels me back down to reality, ordering me to get dressed and pack an overnight bag.

I had opted for my canvas duffle bag when Vassili told me to pack light. I ended up stuffing my old high school backpack to the brim. 'Packing light' was anti-conducive to being prepared for any outing. I wound up on the back of a matte black Harley Davidson with modified chrome finishes and wide back wheels.

Now, we're in the kitchen of his beachfront home in Venice. My head cocks to the side and I lick my lips.

"No water?" I refer to his beloved vodka. Recalling the taste of whiskey on his lips not an hour ago. The twining of whiskey around his tongue took me into a tailspin. I have the inkling that Russian vodka might send me to the point of no return. I'm tipsy off of his mouth.

"Nyet. You are my water."

Heat erupts all over my body. I reminisce on the moment that Vassili licked the glossed juices from my pussy off of his finger. He'd said then I tasted of water. I place my apple juice on the counter and remove the small glass of cranberry and vodka from his large, rough hand. I take it to the head, like a shot.

It's smooth and makes me tingle down below.

Vassili offers a low growl of a laugh. "Sweetheart, I want you sober tonight."

"Mmmm," I moan.

His hand goes to the back of my neck, claiming my mouth with his own. Dizzy butterflies take flight. A delightful fog descends over my brain until I yelp.

"Dang, Vassili must you give me a heart attack?" I ask, cradled in his arms. It's as if every move he makes I am unable to gage. He's forever keeping me on my toes or rather in this instance, picking me up.

He carries me down along a dimly-lit hallway. A few crystal sconces dot the walls as we go. My heart is damn near beating out of my chest cavity. We. Are. Headed. To. His. Bedroom.

I'm as quiet as can be, conscious of every inhale and exhale of breath. I'm gingerly placed onto my feet as Vassili presses open the double doors.

Now, I'm faintly aware that I can barely breathe at all as I take in the sight before me. Half the room is glass walls. The dark ocean rages below. Stars twinkling to the same tune of a sea of scented candles. Not just any candles. Tapered ones. Chunky short ones. Tea candles and more. An array of thoughtfulness that Vassili considered when planning my first time.

Tongue feeling like sandpaper, I inquire, "Aren't you supposed to feed me first?" *Shit, why did I ask that? Fear.*

"We will get to that," is Vassili's only response as he takes my hand. He leads me to the bed.

His wrist flicks and I am turned until my back is to the

edge of the bed. I glance up at him. A million thoughts roam through my mind. I want to please him, but so many women already have. How damn high has the bar been set?

"This is all about *you* tonight." His words seem to tell me that my newness to sex is a jewel that he intends to cherish.

His hand takes hold of my large breasts. Electricity shoots to my core as he squeezes through my silk camisole.

I start to reach for the hem of my shirt.

"Don't fucking think about it, Zariah," Vassili orders. There'll be no undressing for him from me. "I've got everything covered. Tonight, you speak only if I'm doing something wrong. If you don't like the way I lick your pussy lips, by all means, cuss me the fuck out. If I don't dig deep," he says, his other hand slamming down onto my ass. "You'll let me know, won't you?"

Vassili cocks an eyebrow waiting for my reply. I nod swiftly.

"Good girl." His lips brush across my forehead. "You are *my* good girl."

My shirt is pulled over my head by him. And then he unzips my jeans, tantalizingly slow. He lowers his large frame and assists me with removing one pant leg at a time.

Onto the bed he places me. "With your legs closed, we won't ever get anywhere. Besides, we have to work our way up to me fucking you with your legs crossed, Zariah."

"Duly noted." That sharp wit reminds me why I enjoy him so much. My laughter douses me with a dose of confidence. "Maybe I want you naked, too."

"Oh, you want me naked? As you wish." His shirt swoops over his head. That wavy Mohawk of hair, flopping onto his forehead.

My mouth drools with saliva as I glance at his chest. He isn't overly muscular, but I swear before God that days were spent sculpting Vassili. He has an eight pack, with reinforcements on each side. With his other hand, he flicks open the button on his jeans. Shit, Vassili doesn't pull his pants off. I'm left with the tease.

Vassili reaches down to kiss me. His hands work beneath my back to unclasp my bra. I'm sprung free. When his fingers touch my thong, my skin is lit on fire. He doesn't lift or pull down my panties.

There's a twinkle in his eyes as he catches my gaze.

"You know I've waited seven years for my very first taste."

"I'm sorry." The words lurch from my mouth. I've returned to my simpleton state of drool and desire.

"Fucking right, you're going to be sorry. I'm going to eat your beautiful, little pussy until you pass out," he growls.

A shredding sound is so erotically pleasing to my ears, my head kisses the pillow. My thong is no more. Vassili scoots down on the bed. I'm on bated breath as his paws slam down on the inside of my thighs. He spreads my legs wide.

"I'm going to make you cum until you go crazy." Vassili purrs like a lion against my pussy. Shit, I nearly cum from the sound of his voice. His tongue trails out and glides across my second set of lips, slithering around my clit. There's a symphony of loud moaning and I realize that it's mine the instant my legs shake. It's a feat to keep my thighs wide open for him, as I tremble like a leaf while cumming all over his face.

His mouth rocks along my core, tongue edging its way inside of me. Automatically, my hips swivel, twisting upward. Beckoning his tongue to break me apart more and more. His nose nudges against my swollen clit, the stimulation brings my desire to a tailspin.

"Mmmmm, Vassili..." I squeeze my eyes shut, stopping the flow of tears at the notion of how I've saved myself all for this man. My thighs can hardly stay open as I cum over and over.

"Fuck me," I shout, begging for him to screw me with his fingers, his cock! My words might even be Swahili. Vassili doesn't come up for air as stars dance before my eyes.

I grit down on my bottom lip, riding out another orgasm. He eats my pussy like it's a full-stack of hotcakes.

"Oh, my, Lawd, Vassili, Fuck!" I scream, clawing at the headboard.

He grumbles against my labia, alternating from titillating slow tongue movements to spearing his tongue deep inside of me. My pussy is drowning wet. My cheeks are flooded with tears. If I could reach up and look at him. I imagine his chiseled face is rain-soaked from my goods, yet energy fails me. I'm unable to move.

Moans flow from my mouth nonstop as he stiff tongues deep into my ocean. Deliberate and slow, Vassili brings me over the edge. I scream out, face sliding side to side as I grip the sheets. Shit, I groan from frustration and needing him inside of me.

"Vassili! I-I can't cum again."

"Yes, girl, you can cum again. You will," he orders.

He leans up. His body is art, magnificently constructed. My gaze roams all over him as he finally tugs out of his pants and briefs. His shaft is like an ivory elephant's trunk, thick and long, with these beautiful ridges and veins.

I whimper. "Please..." My throat is too heavy to speak. To argue that he's only fucked me with his tongue as of now. To beg for something more because, first, I am in heaven just as much as I am in hell right now. My head kisses the pillow once again as his handsome face disappears between my thighs.

The cocky bastard growls, "You made me wait, Zar. Now, I get to break the pussy."

His wet, stiff tongue glides around my clit in a perfect circle. Slower and slower he goes, focusing on my tiny nub until my legs go rigid. My limbs feel heavy like lead as he catches a rhythm. God, he catches a rhythm that has me bypassing opera vocals. Damn, I could shatter these windows as an orgasm slams through my curvy frame.

This motherfucker wants me committed.

He wants me in a damn straitjacket, rocking back and forth. No wait, my hips are rocking back and forth, coasting over his tongue. He hasn't killed me yet. A psychotic laugh from deep within my body tugs at all the energy I have.

"Pahlezzzz, pahlezzzzzz," I beg, addicted to the fighter. Heat and pressure tighten at my second set of lips until my pussy is twitching like crazy. I twerk on his tongue because that's all the motherfucker is offering. It's enough to get me off a thousand times over.

Out of nowhere, one of his fingers caresses my perineum; that silky soft patch between my ass and pussy. More rivers flow from my cheeks. Vassili is meticulous in the movement of his finger along my swollen lips. He goes gliding across my inner walls. The crackhead in me that got her fix sniffles back tears.

"Ohhhh, Vassili," I scream. More of his fingers begin to sooth my trembling pussy. This time my hips rock along his fingers until a peaceful moan tumbles from my mouth.

He climbs on top of me now. My mouth caresses across his stubble, reassuring him. His hand clamps against my thigh, he pulls it up across his hips. Internally, I tell myself not to hyperventilate. He's going to kill me. I've always feared sex. Not any sex, *his* sex.

My core is wet, my labia heavy from his taste. Yet it twitches as his crown glides against it.

"Mmmm..." My eyes close in delight. His dick is smooth and slides along my moistness so perfectly. His cock head rubs along my arousal and then stops against my shell. I relax

as his mouth descends over mine, stealing away my anxiousness. Vassili's tongue circles around mine.

"You are so fucking beautiful, Zar." His eyes are on mine
as he slowly stretches me.

The pain is enough to bring tears to my eyes, yet I savor
each second.

"You are perfect. Too fucking perfect for me." He leans
back down and kisses me, "But that shit doesn't matter. Now
all of you belongs to all of me."

1 0

VASSILI

Fuck, I was gone over this woman the moment I laid eyes on her. She was that beautiful and she stole my heart while fighting for justice. Now, my cock is gripped inside of her wet, tight pussy. I stroke and I look into her beautiful eyes. She has transformed from a beautiful face and a glorious body to become my possession. I spent seven long years, waiting to get inside of Zariah Washington's panties. All I give a shit about is *her*.

The brown sugar taste of her pussy is coated all over my tongue, my mouth, the stubble along my jaw. I can't stop licking my lips as I stroke deep inside of her body. Her pussy is such a hot glove. Tightest cunt ever. Her slick walls grab my cock in ways that no other girl has been able to do.

Hand clasped against the back of the headboard, I gain leverage. Never taking my eyes off hers. Zariah has to enjoy every single second of this. I cannot hurt her. She feels so good. *Don't be a bitch, Vassili. Don't nut yet.*

My hands run along her body, every touch calms the beast. I'm thrilled by her curves. I kiss her delicate neck while stroking her nipples with one hand.

"Oh, Vassili, baby… damn…" she starts cussing like earlier. I have to control myself.

Her pussy tightens, eliciting more wetness, as my cock glides in and out of her entrance. I fuck her deeply, going all the way into her tight heat. Forcing myself to control my shit no matter how wet, sweet and ultra-tight she is. As I mold in her pussy, I learn how to make her moan. My hand comes down and swats at the dark, sensuous hip. Her innocent mahogany orbs widen and then Zariah is gripping my shoulders begging me to go deeper.

"You are so fucking tight," I growl, grabbing a fist full of her hair.

I lean on my elbows, but Zariah claws at my biceps, pulling me deeper into her soft body.

"Mmmm," she moans. Fuck, her eyes are wet with tears. But I can't stop myself from impaling her slick, fitted folds. It's like I'm addicted to this shit. Though it pains her, it fucking bruises my cock, too. I continue to stroke, hollowing out her pussy. Molding her to my perfect fit.

My tongue dominates her mouth, before working my way over her jaw and down to her breasts. Pounding increasing with the sound of her crying out. This time, I drive my cock so deep inside of her tight pussy. Her cum drenches all over my dick as she cusses, "Lawd, damn, Vassili, baby… oooh … oooh… Vassili."

In less than a second, the tightness from my nuts is instantly relieved. My cum explodes, gushing against the condom, nearly perfect. Would've been better for this shit to soar into her thick, little frame.

A thought hits me like a roundhouse to the chin: *shit, I'm never letting this one go.* This incredible feeling is engraved in my memory forever. Zariah wraps around my large frame, further turning me into her bitch. Concerned for my girl, I lean on my forearms. But Zariah worms her tiny arms along my waist as if her body is screaming for mine. I'm fucking crushing her, yet she holds me there. I move strands of hair from her forehead and kiss the soft, dark skin.

W e trade in the bedroom for the top deck. The hearth casting shadows across her luscious mahogany skin. A few stars dash across the void. I hadn't even noticed until she pointed them out. Zariah is leaning back against me on my old leather couch I couldn't give up during the move here. I rub the back of my neck, comprehending how off the deep end I've gone. All for a taste of Ms. Washington.

"So, Venice Beach," Zariah speaks. The bubble of her ass is nestled against my sore cock.

"Yeah, this place is a few miles from the gym." I pull her closer, she could never get too close while pointing north. "I got tired of fighting for a parking spot. Parked my Harley a few lots up, saw the for sale sign and thought 'fuck it.' I might as well take it off the market."

"Ha, so you purchased a $2 million home on the beach for good parking..." her voice trails off.

"Dah." I agree, waiting for Zariah to finish her train of thought. Yet, she doesn't. "Speak, sweetheart, what else were you going to say?"

"Nothing at all." She starts to arise, thick, kinky strands of hair flying in every which way.

I grasp her wrist and her voluptuous ass slams back against my cock. I wince. She was so tight.

"No need to hold anything back from me," I respond. I hadn't considered the ramifications of my comment. Zariah has turned me into her bitch. *I'm an idiot for that one because she sure as hell isn't ready to know that I'm Anatoly's son.*

Zariah scoots around in her seat to face me. There's

something amiss from her eyes, but she kisses me then says, "Umhmm, Vassili. How about you feed me now."

I huff. A part of me doesn't want to be a selfish mudak. It wants to be truthful and to see if Zariah will still look at me kindly with those big, innocent eyes of hers. Yet she's already sauntering back into the bedroom. She flicks on the lights, as most of the candles have been doused in their wax. I arise, following her ass down the hall.

She pauses, eyes sweeping around the kitchen as if she's viewing it for the first time. Earlier, her nerves were shot. My hand glides across the small of her back as I recall how her legs shook when she came in my mouth.

"Vassili, I can't even think about cooking after *you said* tonight was all about me." She brushes away my hand and glides toward one of the barstools.

I chuckle softly. This woman, I could fall for her even more. I was in love with her from day one, but I could love her the same as MMA, one day. The thought punches into my gut and lingers there. Loving her as much as the cage. Adoring her more than bloodied knuckles. Craving her more than pulses weakening within my grasp while using the art of the submission.

Dah, I could love her that much, one day.

Zariah's stomach growls, and she clears her throat to cover up the sound. "That wasn't a lion in case you're wondering. I am hung-ray."

I rub my hands together. "All right, I will feed my girl. What can I feed you?"

"Boy, I was under the assumption our night was all planned out."

She gets up from the stool and stalks around the island to the subzero refrigerator. Like a prosecutor stepping toward the stand to interrogate an eyewitness. She argues, "What exactly do you mean, 'what can you feed me?' "

I watch in amusement as the first girl to ever enter my home becomes more comfortable in it than I ever could. I wasn't lying about purchasing the home for its location. Besides my Harley, I could give a fuck about material possessions. All my workout gear and the expensive ass weight room down the hall doesn't count. She leans back on her heels to open the heavy, stainless steel doors.

Glancing into the clean refrigerator and back to me, Zariah huffs. "Vassili, you and I were on an accord last week when I had little drumettes for dinner at The Red Door." She lifts a carton of eggs. "I even enjoyed some Russian food. Damn it, I will fight you for some meat. No seafood required, but beef is a must. I see fruit, vegetables, *eggs* for days! Where is my marinated steak?"

Hands coming to rest on my head, I admit the truth. "To be honest, I got caught up purchasing candles. Do you know how many weird looks I got from motherfuckers in Walmart—"

She cackles. "You lost brownie points mentioning that place. Kidding, just kidding."

" . . . I wheeled a cart full of candles out of that bitch. I'll make you eggs any way you like 'em."

"Humph, it's my night. I was going to pass on the shrimp and lobster combo. Maybe I'll have you jump into the ocean and catch me a fish since you're immune to cold weather," she says, leaning into me.

"If that's what you want." I step a few paces backwards toward the sliding glass door, which leads to a deck.

"You're naked." She grasps my hand.

"Does it look like I care? Sweetheart, you gave me something that no other man can have. I'll catch a baby shark between my teeth and put that bitch on a bonfire. You're hungry, I got you."

By now, Zariah is tugging my hand and giggling. "Don't

you dare go outside with your johnson swinging everywhere."

"Why not? I've already shown you how beautiful your pussy is, Zariah. We're two beautiful motherfuckers. My cock is a masterpiece."

She chokes on her laughter and I almost laugh with her. Damn, I could freeze this very moment, rewind it and listen to her chuckles forever.

"Dang you, Vassili. You arrogant bastard."

An hour later, Zariah offers a weak, confused smile. "My hunger has passed. Besides, it's almost one in the morning and what are these, extra fluffy pancakes?"

"Oh, you're no longer hungry, sweetheart? You have to try it." I order. "Yeah, it's like a fried pancake, but say syrniki. You'll eat this tonight, we work out tomorrow morning."

"Work out in the morning? It's morning now." She huffs, picking up the fork, pronouncing syrniki just right.

"Good. Eat. I slaved in the kitchen."

Her mouth hitches up to the right "Thank you," she says before forking up a bite.

11

ZARIAH

Blinding sunlight burns the inside of my eyelids. I rub a hand over my warm, sun-kissed face, roll to my side and expect to be met by hard, steel comfort. Instead, it's all firm, Tempur- Pedic mattress. Damn, how did I ever survive sleeping alone?

There's a note on Vassili's pillow. I breathe in his musk and strength while leaning on an elbow to read it.

Went for a quick run to the pier. I placed workout clothes for you in the bathroom and a smoothie in the fridge. Join me.

"Humph, so sure of yourself. How about Good Morning America with a cup of coffee instead?" I mumble, stifling a yawn. I contemplate crossing paths with Vassili on the way back from the pier. The limestone is temperate against my feet, as I meander toward the bathroom.

A heavy wooden chair next to the balcony catches my eye. A built-in bookshelf is below the armrest. My eyebrow lifts as I glance through Vassili's choice of reading material. Most of the books are about the MMA technique. Then there are a few books by Fyodor Dostoevsky. I wonder if this is Vassili's favorite author. The spine of each book is worn more than the rest of the other fiction books. Bypassing the classic, "Crime and Punishment," I pick up the most tattered one. The damn thing is thicker than a good number of my grad school textbooks. It's called "Idiot," and the cover pulls me in with intrigue.

In college, Vassili would ask me how I was doing. He wasn't shooting the breeze. He'd listen as I told him about my favorite professors. Something about this man blows me away all the time. When I fall in love for good, I want the man to astonish me every day. I don't think I'd be able to fall out of love so easily, like the example I grew up with.

I place the book back between Dostoevsky's 'The Possessed' and another fighter strategist manual.

On the thick chair across from the vanity, there's a bright pink and black shirt. The same skull, with a cigarette sticking out of his gritted teeth and crown on his head that is tattooed on Vassili's neck is on the front.

"King Karo," I mumble the words, which are splayed across the chest area. I pick up the shirt and notice that it's dangerously cropped. The tight shorts, also with King Karo on it, will have my ass cheeks falling out.

"Hell to the no, *Karo!*" I smirk, tossing the outfit back onto the chair.

The Nike box has shoes which would match the outfit and are my size. I pick it up and then opt, instead, for the new toothbrush. Vassili was thoughtful enough to put fresh towels on the vanity too.

My backpack didn't include a single workout item. So, I go in search of something more appropriate in the bedroom. I press against the limestone wall where two slabs come together. It doesn't move. I push at another spot and the wall retracts to a walk-in closet. In the center, drawers are stationed. On top are more spotless designer tennis shoes than one man should be allowed. Vassili's clothing is folded like tight burritos. I find a simple white t-shirt and a pair of black sweats.

Dressed in Vassili's clothing, I tie the pants drawstring while entering the kitchen. I opened the refrigerator and gawk at a glass full of thick green muck that might be a smoothie. Nope, instead, I close the refrigerator, pick up a bottle of water and head to the sliding glass doors.

With a deep breath, I saunter down the hundreds of steps. My new Nikes welcome the padding of the sand. It almost feels good when I catch the groove of running. That is until I realize I'm not a fan of this.

The Pacific Ocean is an ugly muddy brown, not enough visual stimulation to keep me interested. With a huff, I stop, gulping air like a fish out of water.

"Zariah Washington!" My name is carried by the salted breeze from a couple of yards ahead.

"Samuel Billingsley," I call out. Samuel was the district attorney when my father made lead detective. He switched gears and became the owner of Billingsley Legal, the up and coming family-centered firm I work at.

His white teeth pop against skin the color of black licorice. His hair is cut into a taper and more salt than pepper than I remember. He'd attended my graduation from Spelman. He's offered a wealth of information via email and phone calls during my time in law school. But he had a big case and was unable to travel up north to attend my graduation at Berkeley. He appears to have begun jogging. I give him a quick hug.

"I arrived home from D.C. last night," he says, striking up a conversation. "I had plans of taking you to lunch this afternoon. Then my niece texted me to cancel, said you'd taken a very brief sabbatical."

Chewing my bottom lip, I wonder how bad this looks. I'd

messaged my supervisor, Connie, his niece, yesterday evening about skipping town for the weekend.

"Yeah, I uh…"

"Oh, don't tense up on me, Zariah. Maxwell and I have argued about you since you were a bright-eyed young girl, watching me throw down in the courtroom. He said you'd become a cop as *all* Washingtons should." Samuel's tone dips. My entire parentage was cops, my dad disowned Martin for not becoming a cop. Samuel is still disgusted by my father's antics. "My old friend settled for you to join the prosecution team."

"Well, I had a very good mentor who decided to get out of the game." I shrug. Although I would've followed Samuel anywhere, when he chose to leave the DA office, I'd grown fond of family law. "My dad will get over it. Somehow, I'm still his favorite child or the only one he's willing to stomach."

"You're his baby girl, of course. But Maxwell had strong convictions about you choosing my team instead of joining *those* Levines. *They* are the start of greatness in his eyes."

"Sheesh, I'm guessing my dad bragged to you when he took it upon himself to secure a job for me at the Levine firm." I almost smile at the dig. Ephraim Levine is handsome, but I've been told he's more of a wild card than his predecessors. Albeit, the worthier choice in my father's eyes, if I chose not to work my way up to prosecutor.

"Zariah, I believe in work *and play*. Maxwell should've insisted you took a vacation before returning to the workforce. During the lunch we were supposed to have today, I had a few suggestions. Such as, I'd prefer you to study for the bar exam instead of mindlessly filing papers or waiting for a field trip to court. My niece is a pretty good study partner. The exam is fresh in her mind, too."

"You'll pay me to clock in *at work* to study with Connie's help..."

He pats my shoulder. "Call it an investment. I'm a man who gages potential. Pay into you and once you've passed the bar, I've added an indispensable team member. No, an added family member, rather. Maxwell was always like a brother to me, even though he ..." Samuel pauses mid-sentence as he stares up the shore.

His gaze is focused, narrowed somewhat and I turn to follow it. *Vassili.* He's noticed Vassili, who is standing about twenty yards away. Vassili is like a perfectly tagged cement wall. All the tattoos on his chest glisten in the morning light. He's wearing a pair of compression pants that tug at the thick muscles in his thighs, legs, and calves. While I gawk, Samuel eyes him wearily.

My mentor glances away, shakes his head and recaptures his train of thought.

"Maxwell is a greedy old man, but together the firm will explode. We will leave those Levines in our dust."

"Wow!" My admiration returns. "That's very confident of you to say."

"I'll see you on Monday." Samuel backs up, jogging in place. "Make it on Tuesday. Enjoy somewhat of a time off first. We will get you polished up for the bar exam, all right?"

"Yes, sir." I grin.

"Now, do you have some sort of pepper spray," he asks.

My face tilts in confusion. "No."

"Watch yourself. There are some unsavory people in the area." He nudges his chin toward Vassili before jogging on.

My bottom lip drops. I watch Vassili pull a cigarette from behind his ear and grab a lighter from his pocket. He places the cigarette at his beautiful lips and takes a long drag. It's easy to gather my bearings while desiring his gorgeous body. Samuel's morsel of wisdom about awareness of bad guys goes in through one ear and out of the other. Though I doubt he assumed we were together, Samuel always had a father figure stance about him. It came naturally when I'd spent countless hours at the precinct. He spoke with victim's families, empathetically informing them of plea deals given to the criminal who had hurt a beloved family member.

I'll never forget this wailing cry coming from a caregiver/granddaughter. She'd learned that her grandfather's murderer received a lighter sentence. The woes of technicalities. Everyone in the precinct heard her heart shredding in half. Samuel tried to comfort her. He was the best attorney the City of Angels has ever known.

I saunter over to the wolf. Wind mixes the seaweed scent, coupling it with the natural cologne of his muscular body, testosterone, and sweat. It's a delicious fragrance.

"Mr. Billingsley, that mudak," Vassili says under his breath. Giving his cigarette a puff, he blows the air away from my direction.

"Yup." I reach up, pretend to kiss him and grab the cigarette, to put it out.

"Really? Fuck, Zariah, I just rolled that cigarette."

"In your occupation, you shouldn't smoke. Dare I ask how Samuel knows you?"

"Samuel?" His thick brows come together. "Oh, that ublyudok—bastard. My unc—my family lawyers toughened him up when he played the DA. Someone tried to put him on payroll but apparently, he is by the book."

"Well, let's change the subject," I mumble. *Samuel said I needed a vacation before the bar. Vassili has offered that. Everything about him breaks the monotony. We have to keep our everyday lives separate.* Damn, last night I brushed off his comment about how he purchased his beachfront home on a whim. Criminals have it like that.

My gaze falls. It's hard to look up at him, with the truth

slamming into my chest. We have no future together. If our family isn't in the cards, then all we have is memories. And we have the present. With the way he sexes my body, I'll gain thirty, maybe even forty pounds from crying in tubs of Ben and Jerry's ice cream. That is after we crash and burn.

Vassili places his palm on my collarbone, thumbs massaging the pulse at my neck. Then his head lowers. I expect one of those mind-blowing kisses to extract the selfish thoughts from my mind.

No future. Just for fun.

Vassili's breath is on my forehead. His mouth traces across my skin. "You can ask me anything."

"And prepare myself for what?" I chortle. Damn, I've got an attitude for no reason. *We don't have a damn future, Zariah, stop it!*

"The truth, Zariah. It's all I will ever give." Vassili doesn't match the aggressive look in my eye when he can epitomize anger so very well. Tone soothing, he adds, "Only the truth, sweetheart. If you ask."

He's imprinted on my heart, so soon. It's too damn soon to love him. "Vassili, that's unnecessary."

"Unnecessary, Zariah, are you fucking serious? You aren't a bitch I'm screwing. Are you?" His lips that offered an endless amount of pleasure are set in the hardest frown I've ever seen.

I push his chest. "Don't you ever call me a bitch, Vassili!"

"I'd never do that. You place yourself in that category if we can't be honest. I gave you the truth about my association with that motherfucker. But listen to me and listen to me good. I own a lounge, The Red Door. That damn house a half-mile back wasn't paid for with a dollar of dirty-ass money. I have sponsors when I fight, beautiful. I won't be anywhere near as rich as most Resnovs, or even Mr. Billingsley. But *I…*" He pounds a fist at his chest, "I am legit."

"Calm down, Vassili. I'm not placing my hands in your pocket, *but.*" I shove a few strands of flyaway hair from my face. "B*ig ass but,* though. Your family isn't comparable to the Crips or Bloods. Evidently, Samuel knew you without introduction. So, it's not some neighborhood gang that you can disaffiliate yourself from." *How does Samuel know you?* Thoughts whirl in my head. *Don't do it, Zariah, don't ask it!*

He chuckles, "I told you that I'm motherfucking legit. No protocol necessary to leave, Zariah. I've never had my hand in the family business. Mr. Billingsley crossed paths with me when I came to pick up a *kuzen* from the precinct. He was unable to throw the book at 'em. I'm clean." He holds out his hands. "I might look like a dirty motherfucker—with tats everywhere. I can go into a five-star restaurant in another country and I'm either asked if I'm an NFL player or some other damn sport."

"You live for MMA, which is a sport." I shake my head and offer a half-smile. "That's far from making your point."

"The point is, I'm judged by my looks across the nation. And judged by my family when I open my mouth or if I'm around one of 'em who so happened to have a run-in with the cops," he huffs. "I will not be judged by my woman."

My eyes sting with tears. I reach onto my tippy toes, lingering. Because he's so angry, it's scorching hot. Something tells me this isn't a fling before life and career consumes me. I say, "I'm sorry, Vassili."

12

VASSILI

Why the fuck am I already offering to tell her whatever she'd like to know? Zariah apologizes, wrapping her arms around my neck. This time, instead of using that mouth to argue, her mouth is soft against mine.

"I'd love to know more about you, Vassili. I'm a hypocrite. Damn, like I'm part of the group who's stereotyped you."

"Nyet, you aren't a hypocrite. You're slow to warm up and trust. That's why it took us seven years to get to this. You've got to trust me. I swear, I would've never bothered you if I was a bad guy."

I'm legit, I tell myself it's true. The only drug I've ever touched was cocaine and enough to catch a celebratory high. Nothing more. I'd rather vomit than lay a hand on Malich's most esteemed bitch. *I. Am. Legit.*

"I trust you," Zariah utters.

My tongue soars into her mouth, searching for her sweetness. We kiss until our lungs burn for oxygen.

"Mmmm..." She inhales deeply, spinning around before me like she's drunk off the taste, too.

"Now that you see things my way, let's jog to Vadim's." I

paw her ass, offering a hard squeeze. "We'll see how much this ass can lift."

"How far is Vadim's?"

"Did you drink breakfast?"

"*Drink breakfast*? What a very confusing phrase. How about I catch a Lyft to Vadim's?" she asks. "What's with the killer face? I'll even do a light stretch during the ride, get myself all hot and bothered for you."

"Run now or pay later," I order. My growl in her ear prompts her to move. My lips twitch as I follow her. Then, I lead the way to the gym.

"You brought meat!" shouts one of the loyalists at the electronic machines in Vadim's Gym. He's staring at Zariah as she opens the bottle of water I grabbed from the industrial refrigerator in the lobby.

"Don't get your ass handed to you," I snap.

The guys at the weights station all mention how beautiful Zariah is, calling me a lucky fuck.

"Where's Vadim?" I start to ask when Zariah presses her face into my bicep.

Her voice is muffled as she peeks from around me. "Is that the Sergio... Sergy? The guy I came to beat up. Some of those other faces look familiar, too. They were all like wolves, offering him to me. I never apologized to him."

"Yeah, that's Sergy. We call him the Three-Headed Monster. I'd never let you apologize to him, no matter how wrong you were." I place my arm around Zariah's waist, blocking her desire to hide her face. "Don't look in fear. You can beat his ass right now. He's all steroids and salt. We're going to make it so that you can take down any of these cunts on the weights."

113

We make it toward the octagon, where Vadim shouts at sparring partners. He's dressed in a collared shirt and jeans. A golf cap is on his head, to cover his balding spot. He steps down when he notices us, never taking his eyes off Zariah.

"Old man, meet my woman."

"This *mudak* has himself a real gorgeous one. I heard you're a smart young lady, too!" Vadim shakes her hand.

"Thank you." Zariah grins.

"No more eye-fucking. Vadim, you're half-blind until a *krasavitsa*—beauty—comes around."

"Yeah, yeah, Vassili. I can still bring *you* to the canvass," Vadim says.

"He wishes," Nestor steps down out of the cage, in sparring gear. The rookie in the cage glares at me, I glare back. It makes sense. We have a rule of not cutting in on anyone's practice time.

"Zariah, I'll show you the ropes in a few. Rhy has about thirty minutes to go." Vadim eyes me wearily. "You're early."

My coach retreats toward the cage. I stare at the rookie, who will ensure that every second of my interruption is accounted for with Vadim. And then I tune into Nestor as he flirts with Zariah.

"Oh, you know my name already?" His eyes brighten, and she slides her hand away from his grasp.

"Yes, it's very nice to meet you, Nestor."

I grip the soft meat along his shoulder blade, applying hard pressure. Nestor's face contorts, as I speak. "This is my ace! Nestor is always in my corner when I hit the cage."

"Oh? You should be a lot nicer to him, then," Zariah admonishes, eyes twinkling.

"Yeah, well, he didn't catch on to the fact that you're

mine." I let go of his shoulder. Now, he cusses up a storm in his native tongue.

"Shit, Nestor, if I'm not mistaken, you're talking about me!" I waggle my finger at him.

Zariah's eyebrow lifts. "You don't speak Russian?"

"This mudak is *Ukrainian*." I shrug. My voice rises, in order for the undercard to hear me. "All right, Nestor, get back in the cage with Rhy. Teach him to strengthen those lungs. If he makes Vadim look bad in ten weeks, we all look bad."

"Fuck you!" Rhy points a finger at me.

I toss a middle finger over my shoulder and escort Zariah to the mat area.

"Wow, Vassili. It's like pulling teeth to get you to smile. Now, I see you reserve those sexy smiles for mockery." She turns away from Rhy, "What happens in ten weeks?"

"I defend my belt, as usual. Rhy is the undercard. It's his first pro televised fight. Millions of people will see him get slap boxed to the ground and strangled to death. I want you to come. We fight in Vegas." I nudge my head to the rope. "Pick it up, beautiful."

"There are other more appealing workouts we can be doing right n…" Zariah's seductive voice drowns. She tries to pick up the ultra-thick conditioning rope. "I'm not trying out for a triathlon, Mr. Cocky Pants."

"Cocky? You should've stuck around seven years ago. I was the spitting image of Rhy in demeanor, not looks. That face of his is like the rear end of a bitch in heat."

"So, you were out of breath easily." She tosses back exactly what I told Nestor to assist Rhy on while struggling to hold up the rope.

"Fuck, no. I'm a bull, baby." I step behind Zariah. Her ass is so fat against my cock, I have to focus on training her. Make her better. Her best. I can't keep tabs on my woman at all times and I don't believe in defenseless women. My teeth grit at the thought of my father. Anatoly will learn about her in the future. He'll ask to meet her. For all his politeness and my outright denials, he's relentless. It's a good thing we both are.

With my forearms along hers, my hands engulf the back of hers, steadying her hold on the rope. I kiss the nape of Zariah's neck and pray that God always keeps her safe when I'm not around. My voice is surprisingly steady as I continue with our conversation. "But I was all about power, knocking a motherfucker out."

"How much does this weigh?" She grumbles. "TKO's were your main motivation. Hello, isn't that what you're supposed to do unless the judges call it?"

With the flick of my wrist, I help her position the rope to move. "Not entirely. I've never had to win through a decision. However, there's something better than TKO—"

"Really?" Her eyebrows push together in interest.

"A submission. It's ultimate control. TKO is power, nice, quick. Submission is a mentality, setting that shit up, waiting to kill."

ZARIAH

"Watch your hips!" Vadim orders, as Vassili practices with Nestor in the cage. He stands on the ledge outside of the fence, fingers gripped into the fencing. For an old man, he's agile, stepping into the cage whenever he needs to. He has also brought me into the fold. I've learned about Jujitsu when he had Vassili complete a few sets. Vadim also explained a few wrestling moves. I was unaware that Mixed Martial Arts encompassed a wide variety of strategies. Regardless of the obvious, it's "mixed" martial arts, I have been in the dark.

Every move Vassili makes has me caught up in the rapture of him. I squeeze my legs shut as a new feeling of lonely trembles along my lady lips. My panties are moist, and my mouth is agape as I watch.

"Sweetheart," Vadim says to me a while later. One of the workers has brought out a dummy for him. He comes over and shows it to me. "This is a grappling dummy."

Like a nurturing teacher, he tells me about the technique. I watch as Vassili hit the ground and beat the daylights out of the inanimate object. Although Vadim is helping me foster an understanding of the MMA world, I have to tell myself to breathe. Vassili slams into the grappling dummy, making me hotter and hornier by the second.

Enthralled by his raw power, I sit at the edge of my seat. He does a combination of a left hook, followed by a right low kick that seems to be lethal.

My cell phone vibrates in the pocket of my sweats. To stop myself from salivating, I answer the phone.

"Hello?" My eyes lock onto Vassili as he alternates from punching, elbowing and kneeing the dummy.

"Zariah, you've finally answered," I cringe as Phil speaks. "I was beginning to think you were avoiding me."

Not avoidance, I'm not a fan of looking back.

"Hey, I'm settling in. How are you?" I shrug, tearing my gaze away from my one weakness.

"Good. But, I'd be even better if you joined me for drinks."

"Why?" I arise from my chair and walk away from Vadim's shouting.

"Zariah, princess." He stutters for a second. "You're still angry with me?"

"Do I sound angry? No, I don't. You're a very busy man, aren't you? I'm acclimating myself to LA…home." *What* else *is there to say? I don't believe in wasting my time.*

"I can't see an old friend?" he coaxes. "What about coffee?"

Shouting has followed me. Vadim passes by yelling, "Not there! Place the new machine over there, mudak!"

"Hello? Hello, Zariah. Sounds like you're at a brothel?" Phil gasps.

"Gotta go." I hang up, following after Vadim. The fighter is my focus, not Phillip. I feel like a new student with Vadim as my teacher while shadowing Vassili. I want to know more about MMA. Vassili loves it with a passion.

"So, how long have you trained Vassili?" I ask, curious

about the man I can't stop myself from falling for. It's like my first time in court watching Samuel argue a case. I clung to every word. Then I went home and researched on my MacBook until my eyes burned and my brain screamed for rest.

The old man's eyes take on this distant look. "I was born in Iksha, say forty or fifty kilometers from Moscow. Vadim's grandfather and I were good friends. That was before he changed occupations and bullied himself into a small-town boss position. I trained him for boxing. We got 'em a heavy-weight title and he was on his way to fighting Sugar Ray before—"

"Robinson, Sugar Ray Robinson?"

"The one and only. Then with the death of Stalin, Vassili's grandfather decided to use his power in other areas. The Resnovs became the *Resnovs*. A real *Bratva*—brotherhood." Vadim's lips rise in a bittersweet smile. I'm submerged in this story completely. The fear of crossing paths with a Resnov doesn't faze me like usual. Also, hopelessness doesn't weight me down at the concept of Vassili and 'family' in the same construct.

"I came on to the States. Took on a few boxers. Good ones. You know of The Honey Badger or Figueroa?"

"Nope. The extent of my boxing knowledge includes Will Smith when he played Ali."

He chuckles. "Yeah, that's all right, Zariah. In the late 1990s, I fell in love with MMA."

The glimmer of his eyes reminds me of Vassili, further magnetizing me to listen.

"Met Vassili when he was fifteen or sixteen. The boy came into my gym. This little shit was humble to me, which I swear must've been a first for him, back then. Vassili is good at the cold shoulder..." For a while, Vadim goes off on a tangent about how anti-social his fighter is. "Anyway, the boy was alright in my book. Only cocky in the ring. Wanted to take off every opponent's head. I was honored myself, to have the grandson of Anatoly Sr. in my gym."

I nod slowly, pushing past the fact that Vassili is related to Anatoly Resnov. I've convinced myself that he's not Anatoly Resnov Junior's son. Malich is the safer bet. "So Vassili has a match in Vegas coming up?"

"Yeah, look up The Hauser. H-A-U-S-E-R," Vadim starts before I can ask about submission. He cusses at Nestor. "Don't make it easy on him! Vassili, don't drop your fucking right, man!"

R eturning to my spot, I take a deep, cleansing breath. I loved the way that Vassili sported me around earlier. Those tips he offered when we sparred for a few minutes were more than invaluable. He'd given me all his attention, he was so caring while teaching me. Don't stop moving or you become an easy target. My mind transitions to Phil and how life would no doubt play out had I given him a chance. He's an assistant director at the largest financial consultation group in Los Angeles. I could see him showing me off. Unlike Vassili, who coached me and showed me the ropes first. I'd be a trophy, Phil's shadow.

A little while later, I notice the big guy who was with Nestor and Vadim during Vassili's match in Long Beach. He's dressed in a coal suit that's draped as perfectly as it can be over his belly. The cut and fabric are expensive, shedding a good amount of his pounds.

He sits next to me. "You're the girl Vassili went slumming for last week."

"*Slumming?*" I cock my head. "I'm not a little-ass girl. My name is Zariah Washington and—."

"Trust me, I know." He touches my shoulder. "No harm

either. I meant slumming as in my *kuzen* fought in Long Beach. He gave nobody a moment of shine so your girls could get you to attend."

"Oh, Vassili is your cous—"

"The motherfucking champ is what he is, girl," he cuts me off in excitement. He shakes my head. "Yuri Resnov."

It clicks in my head that Yuri's use of "girl" isn't an insulting attempt. Maybe it's a Russian thing? Even Vassili and his coach have done it. "Nice to meet you," I mumble, for lack of a more appropriate response.

"You too, girl. Vassili is a title fighter in UFC. Already got himself a few belts that he isn't ever giving up. He will defend the welterweight belt in Vegas. Then it's off to Brazil, again."

"Vegas. Brazil?" I cock an eyebrow. It's been ages since I've cyber-stalked Vassili. Facebook made the perfect cover in the past, when I missed him. But I would imagine his voice while glancing at his photos. "How big of a champion is he?"

"Big enough not to take any local shit, that's what."

"So, the Long Beach event." I ease my way into the question, though Yuri seems easy enough to chat with. "Does he do matches at small venues to impress women?"

"Nyet. We're blood. He's closer than a brother. But I'd go bat shit crazy if Vassili tried to impress women all the time with these stunts." He laughs so loud that Vassili glances over here. "It was the first time. And it wasn't easy for me to secure that fight. Champ or not, the opponent was ecstatic about the chance and bragging rights, just to lose to Killer Karo. The other guy had trained for months. Mudak probably shitted ten pounds to make weight, then...."

The hair on the nape of my neck prickles. If the other guy practiced anywhere near as hard as Vassili, he didn't want to pull out of the fight. I would've refused. "What happened to the other guy?"

"What the fuck you doing here, Yuri?" Vassili asks. Sweat

drips down every muscle of his delicious body. "You got shit to do."

"Why *you* hounding me? Can't I watch my *kuzen* practice?" Yuri grunts, putting his hands on his knees. Before the big man arises, he whispers to me, "So much for being friendly."

"Did I say you could talk to her?" Vassili stares the shorter, heavier man down.

I'm speechless. When we arrived, even after the catcalling, Vassili didn't treat the gym members anywhere as rude.

"I'm your *kuzen*, Vassili. Nyet, I am your *brat*! Forget your other half-brothers, I'm your *brat*! Closer than any of your siblings! Why are you hounding me like this?" Vassili places a hand on his shoulder. Yuri shrugs him off. "Man, don't touch me!"

Again, Vassili has a stiff arm on his shoulder, this time pulling Yuri closer.

"I should shoot your ass!" Yuri pats his waistband while unable to get away from the grip, as he grimaces in pain.

Are they blood cousins? I glimpsed a nine millimeter in Yuri's blazer as Vassili yanked him a few steps away. Gusts of cool air have come from the air conditioner above until this exact second. It's hot and stuffy. Anger radiates from Vassili. They exchange words in Russian.

Yuri huffs, heading off, not offering another look in my direction.

Vassili glances down at me. The deep frown is erased from his chiseled face. "Are you o—"

"So no introductions?" I arch an eyebrow, standing up.

"That's my cousin, Yuri. No introductions, sweetheart."

"Vassili, you were being an asshole. He was so happy, talking about you. That is all."

"I'm positive that you were. He's a good cousin. My closest. I'm also not that jealous, so I know he wasn't flirting.

Besides, it's an honor when any man looks at you as long as they don't touch what's mine."

"Okay…" I wait for more. So far he's being open about it and it didn't appear he was being an overbearing boyfriend.

"I won't argue with you, Zariah." He kisses me rough on the lips.

Hands slamming against his rock hard chest, I push away. "You're being an asshole. I don't like it."

"I'm being an asshole? To bring you up to speed, I told 'em to stay away from you or I would break his fucking jaw. Then there'd be no talking to you or smiling at you. No Resnov, besides myself, is to address you."

"You said that to your cousin?" I place a hand on my hip and then realize, this isn't just family. Any other man ducking, dodging and keeping his family away from his woman would be suspicious. To add to the equation, Vassili introduced me to so many people. He joked about hurting them, but it was met with equal amounts of humor and fear as we walked through Vadim's Gym. But to threaten his own family? I'm baffled.

Then it dawns on me. Vassili is keeping me *safe* from the Resnovs.

"Look, Zar, I don't need any of my family giving you doubts about us. Let's get out of here. My practice time is almost up."

Vassili's mouth descends onto mine. This time, the kiss is succulent. His teeth tugging at my bottom lip. All my thoughts of pushing him away fade from my brain.

After Vassili wipes down his sweat, we make our way outside. Vassili jokes about forcing me to run back to his house.

"Boy, I will hop on the back of somebody's bicycle. You better be glad I'm willing company." I retort as we pass a sunglass and incense boutique. Ronisha and I used to come to Venice Beach for the knock off Versace glasses. Five dollars goes a long way, out here.

For a moment, I'm melancholic for the past. Then Vassili argues, "You hop on someone's bike, and I'm liable to…" He slams a hand against his thick forearm. "Knock them off and bloody their fucking nose. You can get someone knocked out. It's your choice."

"Whatever, Vassili." I chuckle and bump my shoulder against his. The fighting has gotten me aggressive and hungry. I pat my empty pockets. "Can you buy me a taco?"

Vassili's hand glides into mine as we step into line for a taco cart. I moan in desire. "Mexican corn with mayonnaise, yummy, I can use one of those, too."

He gives me a disgusted look, though I know he's only half-joking.

"Boy, starvation is a form of torture. I've worked out enough. You don't know what you're missing."

"You hardly worked out, Zariah. Every punch came with a complaint. Your back kicks were sloppy."

"Ha! I tried my best. You were checking out my ass anyway—"

"Excuse me," a high-pitched voice calls out.

We turn around, Vassili looking very far down to meet the gaze of a young Latina. Can't be more than nine or ten. Her hair is in two ponytails, baseball cap, and an extra-large Karo Sport tee; typical tomboy.

"Yes, sweetie." I smile

"Hi!" She tells me. All her attention returns to Vassili. "Karo, can I have your autograph?"

She lurches forward, being bumped from behind. My

heart warms as a boy with a handful of curly hair steps from behind her. The toddler has a Mohawk like Vassili.

"That's my *dumb* brother." She glares down at him for bumping into her. "He's always blocking the TV, trying to do your moves."

Their father stands behind them, giving her shoulder a tiny squeeze, as her brother pouts. We step out of the taco cart line.

"Of course, sweetheart." Vassili squats down, resting his bulging forearms onto his knees. He's now closer to eye level with the girl. Little things like this make my heart lurch.

"Aw, thanks, Karo," the father says. His tone fluctuating, with the same excitement as his daughter's.

"It's nothing," Vassili replies.

"I knew we would see you leave the gym today." She thrusts a binder into his face.

He laughs, taking it and her pen.

"That so?" he asks, scrawling a 'K' and then it's all indecipherable chicken scratch from there. He glances up at their father and mouths Vegas.

The guy's eyes pop out. He nods.

Vassili then returns his gaze to the young girl. "Wait, I thought of something awesome. I've got extra tickets for my upcoming match in Nevada. You think your parents can take you?"

"Totally!" She speaks for her dad. "You're going to destroy Hauser! Karo, it's your *house!*"

While Vassili offers the little girl all the smiles I crave, my heart melts.

Then his next words warm my heart to the core. "Sweetheart, I'll give your family tickets if you'll do me a big favor."

"Yeah, yeah! Anything!"

"Good, good. All I ask is that you stop calling your

brother dummy." He hands her back the paper and pen. "One day, he will grow big and strong. He will defend you, girl."

I almost smile so hard I cry. Vassili points to the gym while shaking the man's hand. "Go speak with Nestor. Get yourself tickets for the family, backstage passes, too."

"Oh, man, thanks, Karo, thanks so much," the guy says, hyperventilating. He starts to ramble, "I've been watching you since ... since day one. I saw your first fight in Pasadena. Man, I'm always telling my daughter not to call her brother names. I love you, dude. She's my mini-me and my boy is her mini-me."

I smile at him. The father, his daughter and young son all love Karo.

"You've got yourself two little fighters." Vassili pats the father's shoulder and he finally lets Vassili's hand go.

"Okay, kids, let's go get those tickets!" the dad exclaims.

"Kill me, Karo! *Kill me!*" The toddler finally speaks. Gone is the frown and shame of his sister calling him a bad name. He giggles while turning to catch up with dad. "*See?* I told you I would say it!"

"Ugh! You're wrong, dum...you're wrong, okay?" the little girl squeaks, stressing each word.

"You're doing good, girl," Vassili calls after her.

We move slowly back into the taco line. A giddy beam is on my face as I ask, "Um . . . Did that toddler ask you to kill him?"

"I plead the fifth."

"Good idea. In any other circumstance, I may consider defending you. Not if you implicate yourself."

"The saying is Kill 'em Karo, kill '*em.*" Vassili's fingers strum along my lower back. He whispers the next part, "That idiot line came from a health drink commercial I did as an up and comer. The crew wanted to solidify my Killer Karo

brand. Vadim was the one who said it first. He barks it—
makes it sound hard. They ruined it, though."

"Ruined? That's debatable. No, not with cute, innocent kids
saying it." I laugh. "Honestly, I like your coach and Nestor."

I'm determined that the hard warning he gave Nestor was
nothing compared to the look he had for Yuri. We move up a
pace in the ever-growing line.

W e never did end up eating tacos. Returning to
Vassili's home was filled with sex in the shower, not
food. A first for me and he delighted in my firsts. Then
Vassili being as nosey as he is, asked me about all my bills.
I'm still in a daze that he paid off my student loans. I argued
my way out of him fronting the bill for an apartment.

Now, we've debated about dinner in the most embarrassing situation of all. He rushes us out of a Vietnamese Pho
restaurant in Brea.

"You want soup?" Vassili says, guiding me toward his
Mercedes truck. "I'm from Russia, I'll feed you the best soup."

"No, Vassili. I don't want any damn borsch." I press back
on my heels, but my argument is futile. Though the Pho
didn't rival that of a place I often frequented in Berkeley, it
was good. And it would've filled my belly had I gotten in
more bites before Vassili stood up. With a frown, he placed
more than enough cash on the table to close the tab.

"You'll try rassolnik or schi." He opens the passenger door
for me. "Get in, Zariah."

"I am hungry, Vassili. What the hell is ras… rassol-nick
and sh…"

"Schi is Cabbage soup. Rassolnik is," he offers one of
those rare, sexy smiles, "Kidney-pickle soup."

I reach over and pop his arm. "Dang it, Vassili. If I had consumed real food today, instead of juicing, I'd vomit all over your boots right now!"

His square jaw juts toward the passenger's seat.

"You really are an asshole."

Vassili rubs his middle finger against his eyebrow. Through the dusk of late evening, he subtly offers me the bird while closing the door. I laugh. How have we transformed into an old married couple? We alternate from arguing to nurturing to laughing and deviate back toward arguing again. My arms fold and I offer a scowl while he navigates onto the 101, heading toward the Dodger Stadium. He exits toward Franklin Avenue.

"How much further, before I waste away?"

"I'd never let you go hungry, Zariah. You had your green machine a few hours ago. If you're hungry for anything else . . ." He gestures toward his pants. "I'll satisfy that craving, too."

My teeth press against my bottom lip in thought of pleasing him. The titillating sound of Vassili unzipping his jeans sends a rush of water into my mouth. He cocks his head over. Paranoia and desire bubble up in my chest as I reach down between him and the steering wheel. I'm wet and I haven't even tasted him yet.

I breathe in the heady scent of his dick. Moaning from the slightly salted, woodsy musk. Then my tongue follows a juicy vine along his masterful cock. Pussy percolating instantly. Though it's more than impossible, I attempt to swallow his thick, long, heavy shaft. I could suck him off forever, his cock is hypnotizing. I shiver with drunken anticipation, craving his cum.

"Zariah, suck my cock, baby."

"Mmmm," I twirl my tongue around his cock head, before attempting to gulp it down past my soft tonsils. My lips kiss halfway down his cock. By now, my pussy is screaming, lips quaking. Like a slut, I put all my energy into deepthroating his glorious cock. I concentrate on working all the angles of its slightly curved, extreme fattiness. The length is enough to bring another pool of lust to my mouth. His hardness is all slick.

We're no longer moving. I glance up before ducking my head back down. "Damn it, Vassili. No warning?"

"Nobody's around. Get up, Zar. Jump up on my cock."

With my cheek nudged against the royal crown of his erection, I glare up at him. "No, not outside." *I want to drink you down to the last drop.*

"It's dark, sweetheart."

Though his fingers are already twining through my hair, I resist. "Someone is bound to walk by."

"Let 'em. If they stare, I'll bash their heads in with my fist. Climb on top of me, Zariah." Vassili tugs softly at my tresses, as he groans, "Let me see how good you fuck."

Mesmerized by the heavy look in his dark eyes, I arise from his lap. It's dark outside like he said. The closest street-light is weak. The line of shops parallel to us is all closed.

The driver's seat zips backward. I place a hand on the middle console, measuring where to place my knee to get around him. I then straddle Vassili's thick, taut frame.

"Fuck me, Zariah," he whispers in my ear. His lips press against my earlobe, tongue twining inside of my ear. "Fuck me with that sweet pussy."

With one hand on the leather headrest beside him, I slide my skirt up. Vassili's hands are hot against my cool skin. He moves my thong aside. I position my valley at the pate of his dick. My sex creaming along the way. Slowly, his humongous Russian cock fills me up. Screwing him still hurts, but my pussy accommodates his heavy, golden cock, inch by inch.

"Shit, you are so tight." He clasps a hand along my throat and kisses me hard. "Sweetheart, get wetter for me."

When he thrums my clit, I moan, thighs shaking against his frame. "Vassili…"

"Fuck me, Zariah," he groans, gripping my ass. I stroke up and down his cock, craving an explosion. As my pussy massages up and down his long erection, we hear people outside.

"Don't stop fucking me, Zariah," Vassili growls.

I can't fucking stop. My hips twirl and my pussy rides his dick.

"If they look, I'll kill them." Vassili's hand tightens around my throat, giving it a squeeze. "So, you keep fucking me. Keep fucking me."

"Yesss," I moan. Ass bucking, I focus on how wet I am.

Vassili leans back. Hands behind his head, a cocky grin on his face, Vassili watches. I reach over and taste his pleasing lips. My eyes never leave his as my pussy makes sloppy, slick sounds over his beast of a cock.

Now, only pleasure floods my mind. He's telling me that I belong to him. That he'd kill for me, again. I grip the headrest. My most sensitive parts continuing to explore his cock. Our tongues entwine as Vassili again groans about murdering anyone who dares look my way. He begs me not to stop, as my back arches. Damn, I'm in too much of a daze to stop. Never been wetter, never loved the feel of something so much.

"Vassili…" My legs weaken. His mouth latches onto mine as my cum streams down his cock. His tongue darts into my mouth, stopping me from bucking so loudly. Vassili's hands expertly squeeze my breasts. A pinch to my nipples amplifies the pleasure. I ride my orgasm along his cock. I grind on his shaft, pussy climbing to the head of his shaft before much of his cock fits inside of me. Back to that thick, thick crown and gliding down a mountain of hard, fat erection. My sugar walls are tender from the stretch. There's so much more of him, so much more cock than I am ready to take. He still has a few inches that have yet to explore my insides.

"You're wet for me. All for me." His dark gaze all but has me lost. The entire world can crash and burn around us. I'm breathless, I reach forward. My nipples crushed by his hard chest.

Vassili grips the sides of my thong.

"Ahh, Vassili…" My senses are on overload as the fabric strokes my clit and anus, at the same time as I'm screwing him.

"Don't stop, beautiful," Vassili growls in hunger, continuing to pull the strings of my thong. I climax, showering all over my man's cock. He leans forward and buries his face into my breasts. Kissing and kissing my dark brown skin, coaxing me to cum harder, longer, more.

My drenched pussy engulfs even more of his dick now. He fills me up and I hump him like a rabid animal. The sweet, slushy sound I've created with my juices have Vassili's thick muscles tensing. With each thrust of my hips, my walls stroke the hard contour of his generous cock.

"Fuck, Zariah." Vassili's hands grip my ass. "Tell me if you hurt."

I bite the shit out of my lip. He'll stop if I'm hurt. There's no way in hell I can stop. The pain continues to burst into pleasure. Vassili's vast hands grip onto my hips. He begins to pump me up and down. A whimper transforms into a moan deep down in my throat. Desire rises through my sex and up into my belly as he thrusts up into me. My body weighs less than a feather as Vassili's cock disappears in and out of my body. Each drive sends him deeper, stretching me further, molding my pussy. I cry against his scruffy jaw. He finds my mouth as he buries his cock deep into my body, flooding me with his seed.

High off the fighter, I stay in his lap. He's leaned back

against the headrest. Both of our hearts beating wildly. I bite my lip, the walls of my pussy quivering incessantly. Though he'd stretched me to capacity, and I know his fat cock needed more, I'm sore. Despite this, something in me wants to offer him more.

14

VASSILI

My cock is bruised and I'm loving it. She's the sweetest, tightest fit I've ever had. Did I hurt her? Zariah didn't respond when I asked. Her moans turned me into an animal. Slamming my cock into her tight pussy, shaping it for me.

Holding her in my arms, I remind myself not to squeeze too tight. *Don't fucking hurt her, Vassili, you dick*. Seven years ago I made a promise to God not to screw Zariah if He gave me a sign. Her leaving for Georgia was that sign. I'm too smart to make any more promises to God I can't keep. As selfish as I am, I can't hurt her, and I will kill anyone else who does. There's no way in hell I'll let her go. So, I hug her tighter still. Her thick, curly hair tickles my chin. Heart drumming against mine as she catches her breath.

"Vassili," she murmurs against my chest. "Is it okay if I fall in love with you?"

"What, baby?" I glance down, those large brown eyes of hers were closed.

She moans against my chest in ultimate comfort. "I'm twenty-five years old. Never knew the feeling. Had no anticipation of it, either. Maybe this feeling in my heart, stomach, the haziness in my mind, is all lust. It could be tied to the fact that you're my first."

"Baby, you're analyzing love like it's a potential case to accept or deny." I nudge her chin up, to look into those innocent orbs again.

"Yeah, I am. So far, the cons outweigh the pros. Maybe it's lust—"

"I love you, too, baby. So get that shit out of here. It's not lust." She whimpers as I kiss her mouth.

"You love me too?" Zariah asks, seeming to look at me for the first time. "I do love you, Vassili."

"Fuck yeah. I even love the air you breathe, Zariah, when you get on my last nerve."

"All right, but can you smile at me more?"

"What do you mean?" I grasp my hair, half the damn time she doesn't make sense. "You said something about me smiling earlier, baby. I don't understand what you mean."

"You're always frowning, and *'talking like this'*," she says. Her forced tensed lips dip into an easy smile.

"Sweetheart, you're mimicking some other accent, not mine."

She chuckles at me.

"I didn't think my smiling mattered. Truth be told, I'd murder to see you smile." I pause from sharing that I'm still confused about which I like more, attitude Zariah or happy Zariah.

She laughs harder. "You'd kill for a grin. Whatever, Vassili."

"You came into the gym ready to blow the bitch down. You were drop-dead beautiful. Why wouldn't I want to make you happy? You're even more beautiful years later. You look fucking gorgeous." I plant a kiss along her jawline. Can't be a pussy and tell her it was love at first sight, not just for her looks. Shit, she has those curves from her plush mouth to that sweet cunt and below. But it was all in the way she claimed Vadim's Gym as her own for justice's sake.

As if her smile wasn't already as bright as the stars, Zariah's grin amplifies. "Thank you, Vassili."

She offers one last grin before climbing toward the passenger side. With her pussy puckering up at me from beneath her skirt, I reach out for a touch.

"Tight," I say, enthralled while skimming a thumb against the swollen lips of her cunt. They're thickening ever so beautifully. Her breathing shallows as I stop. She sinks into her spot, almost as if her pussy is in the same pain my cock is in.

I rub my glossed finger along my mouth in thought. The brown sugar scent of her has me licking my lips, now. "Beautiful, your pussy looks so good right now. Good enough to eat, but I have to feed you first."

"Hmmm…" Her eyes beg for another good, hard fuck. Almost trance-like. She can take more of a pounding. But I won't break her yet.

"Before I feed you, love, clean me up." I point at my cock, slick with our cum.

She leans back over, tasting the thick coating of her own pleasure and lapping it up. At the head of my cock, remnants of my cum have her tongue swirling leisurely as if she dare not miss a drop.

"Good girl."

A few minutes later, the weak glow from the visor mirror, encompasses all her attention. She fluffs her thick natural hair and applies more lipstick.

"You ready?" I ask once she's settled back against the seat again.

"Yeah," she nods.

I get out and come around the Mercedes truck. There's no such thing as keeping my hands to myself. The second I open the passenger door for her, she gives a little tug of her skirt, beaming brightly as ever.

We head to the entrance of Urban Kashtan. The place is new era Russia. But the food tastes like somebody's fucking *babushka*—grandma— was slaving away in the kitchen.

A while later, we've settled down, surrounded by so much memorabilia that each table has a level of intimacy. I ask, "All right, Zariah, the *shchi* or pho?"

"You could've taken me to Wienerschnitzel, that's about as Russian as I'm going to get." She twirls her spoon around the cabbage soup while chewing on her bottom lip. I take it as my chance to reach in and bite her lip, too. My mouth skimming over the exact spot she chewed on until I sink my teeth into her plush mouth.

"I love you," I growl the words. "Never saw myself as mushy, then I met you."

Fireworks spark, bursting in Zariah's pupils. "Who you telling?" she jokes. "Kidding, kidding. You are unexpected. That makes it all the better, Vassili. Here's to the man who..." she holds up the vodka, "thugged his way into my life and held my heart under siege."

"And I'll never let it, or you, go." Again, I take to her lips with fierceness. We both toss the drinks back.

"Can I ask you something?" She lingers. Sweet mouth slightly peppered with the pussy juices she licked off me and her gaze is still so innocent, too. Her index finger drawing along my bristled jaw.

"We've already agreed to not having any ..." shit, can't say 'secrets' Anatoly is my only one, "lies."

"Why help?" Zariah sucks her lips into her mouth as if this sole question has been analyzed a thousand times. "I told you my story. Hoping that the bad cards Ronisha was dealt would allow me to leave a Resnov's sight after I cussed you all out. I was sick and tired of her being abused.

But why did you help, Vassili? It couldn't have been to see me smile. As scared as I was after finding out your last name, you could've made me do anything. Smile... anything."

Sasha begins to enter my mind.

"Because . . ." I begin, keeping my sister at bay. "Zar, you were sexy as fuck. You *are* sexy. I told you, the gym that motherfucker was a member of wouldn't take so kindly to your pretty ass mouth. Didn't want to hear about that mouth getting you popped."

"Humph, aside from me, Vassili, why help?"

"Your story compelled me." I crunch on a few shards of ice while Zariah patiently waits. She's already got the mentality of a lawyer. I toss my drink back, then mumble, "Your friend reminded me of a girl I once knew."

"Were you in love with her?" she questions.

I laugh boisterously.

"Were you?" she demands.

"You fucking kidding? We declared how new this shit was for both of us. The girl was my sister."

Zariah gasps. "What happened to her? Did she have a disability or delay similar to—"

"Nyet, nothing like that. Unless you count being female. Where I'm from, the Resnov name means nothing for a girl."

She places her spoon into the bowl. I sink back in the seat. I've got my girl's full attention and no amount of steering clear of the topic will work. Besides, something urges me to tell Zariah. "Sasha, my sister wasn't treated so kindly by the men in her life, like your friend Ronisha."

"Damn, I'm not even that close to Ronisha anymore, which ..." Zariah bites her lip and a grimace pierces her heavenly face. "Oh, no. Your father... Was he her father?"

"Dah. Why?"

"Statistically speaking, stepchildren have a higher chance

of abuse . . ." Her voice drowns out, she shrugs as if further explanation is no longer important.

"Yeah, that mudak treated his only daughter, his blood, like shit. Some of my father's guys were roughing her up one day."

She gasps. "What happened?"

"Got in my first fight, that's what." I shrug. "When I told my dad about it, he didn't give a fuck. He grabbed my face and asked about my black eye. That mudak had those dudes and their families dealt with, for me, not because they abused his daughter."

"What? What happened next?"

"Nothing much," I start. "Sasha, man, was she beautiful. She had dark skin and gold hair...24 karat gold. She got touched, again. I fought harder, started working out more. We moved around."

"You didn't live with your parents?"

"Nyet, every couple of years my dad had a new bitch who brought more minions into this world."

"What about your mom? Did she try to help?"

"Skipped town soon as she got the chance." I glance away. "Sasha always wanted to keep the peace. And I was a kid, getting my ass beat because grown-ass men couldn't keep their hands off her. Sasha was pure goodness through it all. We were moved around from my father's girls. Those *piz'das* never watched us. She made friends with our siblings." I almost laugh. "I wasn't so nice to them. Spent most of my time at the boxing gym after class. Didn't bully them, but people knew when not to test me or talk to me."

Her teary gaze sparkles somewhat. "You have your moments of being very guarded."

"Guess I still do. Sasha could go from fighting one of my father's goons off of her to baking *medovik*. It's a cake that takes forever to make and tastes like honey. She taught me how to make that pancake I forced you to try."

"Awe." Zariah sniffles with a smile.

"One day, Sasha didn't feel like baking or cooking or lighting up the room with her smile anymore. Shit," I whisper, breathing deeply. "I didn't even know she wanted to die until I found her with a needle in her arm. Overdosed with her father's very own product. She was eleven, twelve maybe."

My woman caresses my cheek again. "I'm so sorry, Vassili."

"Let's not fuck up our mood, baby." I grab the drink, pour us more. "You and Ronisha aren't too close? How is she working doubles at Shakey's?"

"I'll pass." She waves away the drink, then her lips twist in thought. "Wait, you're aware Ronisha works at Shakey's Pizza."

"Dah. She has the Resnov name behind her and doesn't even know it. Keeping her safe offered me peace of mind. You go postal. I turn killer again."

Zariah offers a sentimental squeeze to my forearm. "You'd do anything for me. Vassili..."

"Baby, you know me well. But if you start crying, I get angry, believing I've done something wrong." My fingers skim the nape of her neck, as I blink. An image of Sasha crying fades from my mind. She'd cry in my arms but never wanted me to defend her. Failing my little sister is my biggest regret. "Don't cry, Zar."

"Not even happy tears?" She gently tugs her bottom lip with her teeth.

"No tears—period." I grab the bottle, pouring the vodka into her mouth. She gulps some down. I pour more, place the bottle onto the table, and then quickly drink from her lush mouth. Our tongues entwine. My hand slips into the hot juicy apex of her curvy thighs.

Zariah places her palm over mine. A ceasing attempt.

"What you doing, girl?" I nip at her mouth.

"Not here," she murmurs, mahogany skin burning by the second.

"I could fuck you anytime." My tongue glides over her bottom lip, tasting traces of alcohol and sweetness. But I remove my hand, with no desire to stain my respect for her. Though I'm a bull, ready to screw her at the drop of a dime, she isn't like the others. She's *my* woman; the one I love.

"Mmmm, get me home, Vassili." She picks up the bottle. "Is this ours?"

"Dah."

With a quick zip of her hungry, dilated orbs, Zariah smiles at me mischievously. She rubs the bottle against the inside of her breasts. "You can pour this anywhere you'd like, once we get home."

My cock stands to attention. Shit, I can see my balls clenching, as I cum for days all over her.

"Anywhere?" I lean into her. Hand engulfing her much smaller one, until I have the bottle. I grab it and point it between her thighs. "So, I can lap you up like a fucking dog?"

"I said anything, Vassili."

"What about your ass, I can see the liquid rushing over your dark brown skin, into that puckered little hole." I kiss her fervently on the neck. My tongue drags up her cheek. Shit, I can already imagine gliding it over her tiny asshole. "Can I lick it all up?"

"Now you're being nasty Vassili." She chuckles. Although eating up all my words.

I unscrew the top of the drink and guzzle it all down.

"Boy, what was the meaning of that?" Zariah smirks.

"We need a new bottle, baby." Right at that moment, a

waitress is walking by. I quickly ask for the check and another bottle in Russian while Zariah giggles about how crazy I am.

"Yeah, I'm crazy. I've had a few concussions, sweetheart. We need a full bottle for all the curves you have."

I stand, grabbing my wallet from my jean back pocket.

"Um-hmm, long as I drive us home."

"Nyet, baby. You relax and I'll give you instructions on how you can prepare yourself for me."

"By masturbating, right? I'm way ahead of you," she scoffs. "Vassili, I *am* driving."

"Nyet. You can get yourself off." My voice lowers as the waitress returns. She places the bottle and the closing tab onto the table.

"Sorry for you. I won't be capable of any such thing while driving."

I glare at her and pluck up enough of the change to still leave a good tip.

Once outside, Zariah demands, "Cough up the keys, Vassili or you've paid for another bottle in vain."

"You serious?"

"These legs lock."

"Should've ridden the Harley. You couldn't drive us back then."

"I was never one for sitting in the house as a kid. I know all the bus routes, from here to the valley," she scoffs.

I fish for the keys in my jacket. "Zar, I never get drunk, baby and wouldn't drive if I was. You think I'd put your life in danger?"

"But you downed the entire bottle without much help. Should I strap you into the passenger seat as well?"

My teeth grit in response. We get into my Mercedes, then Zariah pulls out from the curb.

"I don't mind driving. Oftentimes, you zip through so many cars, as if this is a sports car. My stomach knots."

"Need directions?" I ask.

"Ha, I'm not a defenseless woman. You're squirming in your seat like I'm the one driving for Grand Prix."

Before I can retort about her being the first to drive my shit, there's a loud blurt sound behind us. The flash of lights on the police cruiser makes me roll my eyes. These bitches...

"Zariah, I'll do the talking."

"What? We haven't broken any laws." She signals, a few yards away from the freeway onramp. Zariah parallel parks next to an ARCO gas station. "I am driving perfectly. This asshole is wasting our time."

Her argument goes through one ear and out the other. Thank God I'm not the target of her wrath. I lean my head against the side window aware of exactly what the cop wants.

Nothing.

No need shitting bricks or losing my cool. I cock an eyebrow. "Zariah, will you let me handle it?"

"No. If he can't justify pulling us over, which he *cannot*, I'll get his badge number. Tomorrow morning, I will—"

I chuckle softly. "Damn, you have a fucking mouth."

"Don't, Vassili." Zariah points a finger at me. "Don't place yourself on my shit list, too."

I turn my head away, kneading the top of my spine. The officer knocks on the driver's window. Stiff lipped, Zariah presses the button and it zips down. The man is black, much lighter than Zariah, with flared nostrils and dark eyes that cut their way from her to me.

"How can I help you, Officer Jackson." She proceeds to read out his badge number.

I smirk.

"Ma'am, can you step out of the car, please?" Jackson asks.

"Nope. I asked how can I assist you in completing your civic duties? What compelled you to stop us?"

Aware that she won't make this easy, I start to unbuckle my seatbelt. The cop places up a hand, gesturing for me to stop.

15

ZARIAH

"Sir, stay put." Officer Jackson holds up his hand while barking to Vassili. "Just Ms. *Washington.*"

Damn, Jackson knows who I am. I grumble as it sinks in that my father is somehow the cause. He dropped crumbs about only mobsters driving Mercedes G class while we toured apartments.

"I'll be back in a second, baby." I glance at Vassili. He doesn't seem amused by the situation.

I unbuckle the seatbelt and get out. There's another cop standing next to the cruiser, as Jackson and I walk over. This one's hand is cradled against his gun, nestled in its holster, as he glares at the vehicle. Hatred targeted on Vassili.

"I'm going to pretend to breathalyze you, Ms. Washington." Jackson's tone has lost its abrasive ring. He offers a soothing hand along the middle of my back.

"No, you won't!" I do a two-step so fast from his touch that the Cha Cha Slide rings in my ear.

"Are you alright, ma'am?" His brows crease in concern, glancing over me.

I glare from him to the cop, who hasn't blinked to keep Vassili in his line of vision.

"Officer Jackson, I've only had one drink," I lie. "So either give me a reason why—."

He cuts me off, eyes warm with concern. "Ma'am, is Mr. Resnov holding you against your will?"

"No. Hell, no!"

"Are you sure, ma'am, you are safe now?" Jackson probes.

The other cop glances over, too, keen gaze not as hard.

"Did you illegally profile us? I'm still waiting for you to *lie between the cracks of your teeth*," I accentuate the words. "Why were we stopped? Your name and badge number are ingrained in my memory, believe that I'm fully aware of how to execute a complaint."

"Your father wouldn't like this," the other cop snaps.

"Ms. Washington," Jackson sighs. "We are merely concerned for your safety."

"Thanks for the *de facto* parent, bullshit." I shrug away from Officer Jackson's attempt to touch my shoulder again. There'll be no building a rapport with me. I saunter toward the truck. A dull ache in my jaw warning me to stop gritting my teeth.

Vassili holds my ringing cell phone in his hand. "It's your father."

"Maxwell was behind this."

His eyebrow rises. If he weren't so sexy in his nonchalance he would be in trouble, too.

"Damn, Vassili, you look like you don't give a damn. I take it you're used to the bullshit?"

The left side of his mouth tips up.

"What?" I ask.

"You're cussing." His defined shoulders shrug slowly. "It's cute."

"Vassili, are you used to unlawful stops."

145

"Unlawful? Baby girl, I'm a motherfucking immigrant," he mumbles.

"Tell me about when they stop you." I glance through the rearview window. "These pricks are going to follow us home."

"They won't. You've never been pulled over before, have you, Zariah? They have to make sure you ease back into traffic."

"Vassili, I asked you a question." I grit out, placing a foot onto the brake and slapping the shift into drive.

"Like what, reasons and dates of the occasions?" He leans back in disinterest.

"Precisely. Dates. Times. Who do you recall stopping you and –"

"Zariah, I have lawyers, when necessary. I won't be adding you to the payroll, sweetheart. Tax attorney is a good look on you, girl."

I scoff. "You're an asshole."

"I'm being an asshole?" He cocks his head somewhat. "Tell me that you'll be a prosecutor instead? That was your dream. Those gorgeous chocolate brown eyes were full of determination on our first night. I recall that shit like yesterday. Beautiful. Naive. Determined. So, you still interested in a career as a blood-sniffing prosecutor?"

He's right. I glare through the side mirror at the police cruiser, before gliding toward the west onramp.

Vassili clears his throat.

"Billingsley Legal is family law," I admit. The childhood dream of becoming a top litigator has slowly faded. A great love for justice in the familial cohort has become so important to me over the years. I owe this love to Vassili and how he took justice into his own hands, for Ronisha. There won't always be good attorneys for every socioeconomic demographic. I promised to display availability to those in need.

Vassili grips my thigh, not full of lust or gloating about being correct as if he understands.

I contemplate on what he told me about Sasha. Their family has more than enough capital at their disposal. Born into wealth, no matter how ill-gotten. Moreover, she was surrounded by men who don't condone disrespect. There was no way Sasha Resnov should have had to endure such a cruel life. She truly was like Ronisha, on the outside looking in.

My phone continues to ring as we're almost in Venice.

"Will you answer it?"

"Why?"

"He's your father, he's concerned."

I chortle. "Maxwell is selfish, like Malich. Not to the same extent, but he tried to play us for puppets back there."

"Dah. In his eyes, I'm a piece of shit. He does it out of love."

"Don't be so sure, Vassili. He had this nasty habit of beating the snot out of my mom, was that love? Before I left for college—"

"Has he hit *you?*" Vassili booms.

My shoulders jar. So far, Vassili has been blasé about the entire event, to the point of siding with my father.

Again he asks, his usually low voice much louder. "Did that motherfucker ever hit *you?*"

"Oh, you refused to answer my questions when we drove off from the cops. Why are you finally so concerned? More importantly, do not yell at me, Vassili."

"I asked a question," he growls.

"What can you do? You don't even represent your family or do you?" I shoot back, still livid over Officer Jackson's audacity. But something in me isn't ready for a broken heart.

"Does it look like I need my family name to get shit done?" Fists clenched, he flexes his forearms and biceps straight before him. "I handled that mudak for *your* friend. What do you think I'd do for *you?*"

The fine hair on my arms prickles. In the days following Sergio's death, I learned more about how his body was tortured and mangled. When Vassili asks how much further he'd go for *my* sake, it's enough to weaken my knees with fear. Man, it wasn't easy to set that aside during Vassili and my many texts and calls.

But Vassili Resnov is my kryptonite. Even feeling his anger radiate, I love and want him. He will never hurt me. The truth is there mingled within the dark, death glare in his eyes.

I realize that in my anger, I didn't notice pulling into the garage. How long had we been sitting here, arguing? I reach over, skimming my hand across the length of his arm. All steel, all powerful. Hot with fury.

I climb deftly across the center console, straddling him. Though my core is recuperating from the mega-size of his cock, I still crave him. Crave decreasing the anger that burns his golden skin. My mouth opens, yet Vassili places his finger over my lips. No kisses. No reassuring words.

"Has your father placed a hand on you?" Vassili's accent has lowered once more. Yet, it has amplified in coldness, chilling me to my core

He removes his finger, the glower in that dark, dark gaze warms me to answer.

"No," I murmur.

"Tell me the truth. You know that I can go from chill to a mill in a second, baby. My father had a way with the ladies. My mother ran from us all to try to save herself. After I told you about Sasha, how could you believe I'd give a fuck for that man?"

Tears sting my eyes. Damn, his story about his sister broke my heart. Add in his mother? I can't tell if there's resentment or also sadness, because his tone doesn't fluctuate. His mother abandoned him and left Sasha in the lion's den. Though I can't fathom being placed in her position.

I shake my head. "No, Maxwell didn't even spank me as a child."

"But you've got your stereotypes. All cops hit their wives. All fighters beat their women." He cocks an eyebrow. "I chose not to take your virginity our first night because you had that mentality. We were supposed to change that."

"But I moved so soon." I nod slowly. "Baby, you've noticed a change in me. Look, I'm pissed off because of those dumbasses back there. I know this has been an underlying issue for us, though. You mentioned earlier. When you told me, you knew I no longer strive to be a litigator," I murmur, coveting his touch, yet too afraid to reach out. "Vassili, I don't have the same convictions."

"Convictions our fathers and motherfuckers like Ronisha's boyfriend have exposed you too. All I can be is me, Zariah. I promise you, on my life, that these hands will never hurt you. This being said, anybody else lays a hand on you, they're dead."

I pull in a deep breath and squeeze my thighs against his waist. "Vassili, calm down. Where is this coming from? I had my beliefs about you when we met. You used your name to your advantage."

His chest is still puffed up as he growls, "I'd do it again."

"I have no doubt. But, Vassili, we declared our love earlier tonight. Don't ruin the moment. *I love you.*" This time, he doesn't stop my mouth from locking onto his.

"I love you, too."

Voice salacious, I ask, "Do you still want to drink vodka off of me, you still game?"

We hardly step foot into the living room, lips fused to each other. My stilettos are kicked off. Vassili has wrapped me in his large arms. It's a feat for him to rip my blouse to shreds, let alone unzip his pants.

Before I can fall to my knees, desiring *his* taste, he swoops me up. My legs clamped around his waist. He leans in, biting the flesh of my breasts as they spill forth from my lace bra. With only my thighs hugging him as support, I reach around and unsnap the back of my bra. In a second, it disappears.

Next thing I know, we're in his bedroom. I have my panties off in a flash and I start to climb into bed.

"Don't." His voice is harsh.

I step away from the bed as if it's been doused in gasoline and set on fire.

"You have these thighs and hips." Vassili grips my curve, "Thick as hell. Let's see how strong they are."

I lick my lips in anticipation of anything he has in mind. He pulls off his jeans and his cock stands tall. It feels like I've waited for an excruciatingly long time. Vassili moves the heavy chair with black-and-silver Chevron signs to the center of the room.

He points the new bottle of vodka at it. "Sit at the edge."

I cock an eyebrow.

"You are my queen, Zariah. May I kneel for you?"

My heart rate rises as my ass claims the edge of the seat. Spine erect, I feel powerful as the fighter drops to his knees before me. The entire sight leaves me breathless. My legs spread wide and I wonder what he meant by having to use the strength of them. Knowing Vassili, he has it all planned out. The chilled bottle moves along my belly, gliding to my breasts, leaving my nipples taut. His body heat between my thighs. I wait in heady anticipation for him to taste my brown skin.

"Please, Vassili, don't tease me," I beg. A sudden surge of cool, wet vodka pours down my left breast. The chill is so cold it pricks at my hard pearl. The precision of his amazing warm tongue soothes the mild ache. Another pour of vodka on my right breast is followed by Vassili's warm breath. His tongue dances around, caressing my stiff nipple. While Vassili repeats the process, my head lingers against the pillowed backing of the chair. Eyes closed, I moan.

My brain begins to register another sensation. Vassili's fingers inside me, he lowers himself more, muscular legs stretched behind him as he sucks at my clit. The vodka flows along the coils of my pubic hair, spilling along my slit. He groans in delight while eating the fuck out of my pussy. He takes me to the stairs of heaven, only to return his attention to my tiny bulb, teeth grazing over it. I almost cum a thousand times, as his fingers work inside of me. The sensation floods back to my clit. I arch my back, ass slipping further from the edge of the chair. I'm damn near riding Vassili's face, as his tongue hungrily probes my pussy.

'Stay there,' I want to tell him. Don't stop eating my pussy, baby. But my eyes are shut tight and I cry out. *Lawd* have mercy.

Heat spreads over my soft skin while I drip down Vassili's finger. He caresses my clit with his tongue over and over again. Back and forth he alternates from lapping me up, eating me, to grazing his tongue and teeth across my crown.

"Damn, Vassili, oh…" I gasp. "Right there. Right there! Don't stop, please! Don't stopppp!"

Instead of returning his attention to my clit, Vassili stiff tongues just the right spot to unlock an endless flow.

Growling like a beast, he drinks his fill, along with my ebb and flows. My legs tremble, the bubble of my ass almost falling out of the seat. He drinks the cum straight from my pussy. My climax leaves me so sensitive that I have my hands planted on my hips, elbows locked in place to help keep me up.

"Fuck, Zariah, we haven't even worked out those thighs, yet." His voice is but a whisper, teasing the entrance of my pleasure.

"You ready to stand?"

"Hmmm," I am so disoriented that my eyes close. I can feel my ass has halfway fallen to the floor by now. Probably looking like a hot mess, but do I give a damn? No, my body is in a state of euphoria.

He repeats himself. "Stand, Zariah."

Vassili offers a hand. I take it and arise in such a daze that my toes clench under.

"Look. So much ass." His hand slams down on my cheek. The tight squeeze sobers me and helps steady my stance.

With a hand to my chin, Vassili brings my gaze to his dark, sinful eyes. "You still with me?"

My tongue darts out along my bottom lip and I nod.

"*Khorosho.*" His thumb caresses over the subtle wetness I just left in my mouth. "Touch your toes."

"I don't think I can," I murmur, brain turned to mush. My tongue is tied, heavy, like I've been drugged. Something highly addictive courses through my veins. And, I'm tipsy off the stacks of muscles on his heavily tattooed body.

He's behind me now, reaching around me with a hug. Caressing my breasts. I expect a bit of sympathy, due to his mouth fucking me so well. But with my breasts filling out his large palm, Vassili offers a little squeeze. "You can, Zar. Touch your toes."

I sway gently back against him, his hands supporting along my belly button as I lean forward.

"Spread your legs."

Widening my stance helps my equilibrium return. My ass arches and my pussy rises, as I reach over to interlock my hands around my ankles. From my position, between the triangle of my sturdy legs, I have an eyeful of his beautiful, large balls and the underside of his manhood.

He lets out a harsh gasp from behind me.

"What, Vassili, what?"

"Most amazing sight ever," he falls to his knees behind me. "Your lips are so tender."

"My lips?" The blood is rushing to my brain by now. Then I groan, "Ohhh…"

More vodka is poured against my backside. The liquid slithers down the tiny opening of my ass. He pours more until the liquid begins to drench from my ass to my pussy, dripping from my clit down my legs.

The first lick is sensual, sliding from my clit and up along my labia. He probes the folds of my soft wetness with a tongue that isn't as stiff as before. It slips into the heat of my core. I douse his tongue with more of my musky sweetness than the vodka had offered.

I remove my grip from around my ankles, finding better leverage by bracing my hands against the floor. I tilt my ass downward. The bristles of his jaw are sharp, painful along the inside of my thighs. Rotating my hips, I continue to toot my ass lower, beckoning him. Damn, Vassili leans back against his calves, working my pussy out with his tongue.

He's moaning and licking me harder, still. Arousal at its highest peak, I warn, "Vassili, I won't—"

In a second, his arm is around my waist. He saddles me down onto his cock so hard I cry out in pain. My pussy takes more of him than it ever has before. My thighs are over his muscular ones, my calves spread along his. With my knees on the floor, I lean forward again, this time it's much easier since we're both kneeling. With me in reverse cowgirl position, he reaches forward. His nose, mouth, and jaw saturated with my juices. Lips locked against each other's, I love the taste of myself on his tongue. There are no more nervous jitters as he pumps in and out of me.

He strokes my ass and hips. Cock buried deep inside of my body, Vassili says, "You are strong, Zariah. Those thighs and hips, so strong."

A beam brightens my face. "I love you, Vassili," I murmur.

He murmurs his love for me while reaching around to toy with my clit. Several times he tapers off his hard thrust, so I can catch my breath. The incredible sensation of his dick pumping in and out has my breasts jiggling with each thrust. Another tailspin of sensation shatters through my body, as we explode together.

16

VASSILI

All weekend long, I became more acquainted with Zariah's gorgeous body. We talked more than I have ever in my entire life. It's Monday night and I finished sparring with Nestor at Vadim's.

With my gym bag over my shoulder, I push along the wet sand. There's not a person in sight this evening. It smells like rain.

My body was pushed to the max tonight, now my muscles feel like shit. Jogging along the dark shore, I'm not ready for my after-workout routine of cooking dinner.

Zariah's smile is ingrained in my brain. I can hear her arguing about eating Russian food. The only cooking of mine she will eat is syrniki.

A quarter of a mile away from my home, my cell phone rings. I pull it out, press the decline button to my father's call, without breaking a sweat. The *piz'da* heard me full well during our last conversation. Anatoly has called nonstop since I left Moscow, which is new for him. Most times I cross paths with him, it's me threatening his life, him threatening mine and guns clicking off their safety.

I was six years old the last time I was scared when a gun was placed to my head. My grandfather, Anatoly Senior, had gone senile. We were all foot soldiers to him. Soon as we came to visit, my grandfather would get confused. He'd cock back the hammer, even pulled the trigger a few times, but my dad had taken all his ammunition by then.

"Don't show fear, Vassili," my grandfather would say—after being reminded of who I was to him. Then he'd place a hand behind my neck and exclaim that I was his right hand. Now, his right hand was rotting away in jail because someone had to take the fall for murdering the head of defense.

My gaze narrows as I notice someone standing beneath the stairs to my place. He's in the shadows of the wooden pillars, blending well with darkness. I pretend not to notice. But in half a second, I've learned that it's one of those "to protect and serve" motherfuckers.

With a hard frown, I play stupid, continuing at my current pace.

There's a baton at his side. In the last second, the cop lifts it. Fog mists from his mouth as he says, "A message from—"

The stick whips against my palms so roughly, it breaks my skin. I grab the baton from his hands.

"You're gonna fucking hit me?" I whack him across the head with the stick, determined to break the damn thing. Then my hand goes to his neck, slamming him against a pillar. His feet dangle, his white face turning red. I'm numb to those feeble attempts of his, punching me in the face and neck.

"Next time you're given an assignment, back your shit up." I squeeze tightly. I've never been so angry in my life that I don't even enjoy the weakening of his pulse. One second I'm holding him up, next he's dead weight. I slide him down to the ground. *Fuck, what have I done?*

I reach down and check his pulse.

Weak.

I glance around. Million-dollar homes are in each direction. Bright lights shining, but nobody is looking out any windows.

Were you here for Maxwell Washington, my father, or Malich?

My father just called so that shit is a little suspicious. I returned from Russia to sell out my favorite uncle to my mudak of a father, so that adds Malich to the fold. Chief Washington is on the list for obvious reasons.

I dig into my phone and dial the only person who'd get his fat ass up at this hour.

Speaking into the phone, I order, "Come over. I'm at the bottom of the stairwell at my place."

Yuri huffs and then hangs up.

Less than thirty minutes later, I hear a creak of the wood steps and heavy breathing. My cousin comes downstairs.

When I step out of the shadows, his gun is to my head in an instant.

"What the fuck, *kuzen*. I owe you a slug to the balls for treating me like shit. There'll come a time when you can pay up." He places the gun back down.

"Is my father fucking with me?" I knead my temple, almost too tired to give a damn.

"Seriously? You had me leave the comfort of my bed for—"

"Look," I growl, not ready to ask him if his father did this!

Yuri peers through the darkness. "Who is it?"

"A cop."

He pulls out his iPhone and turns on the flashlight application. Ducking his head, Yuri moves to where I placed the unconscious cop. He digs in his pocket again. Less than ten seconds later, there's a quiet puff sound. That fool put a silencer on his gun.

Indignant, I whisper, "You fucking killed him?"

157

"Dah," Yuri nods. Stepping from beneath the stairway, he fists the dead cop's badge. "By the top of the hour, we will know who his family is."

"Yuri," I search his gaze. He's closer to me than all my half brothers and sisters. Closer than I ever was to both my parents and Sasha. "Do you know him?"

"Wow! You think?" He points a thumb over his shoulder. "Man, Vassili, you and your father have a dysfunctional crazy relationship, but shit! I've never laid eyes on him. We acquire bigger fish, much better ranking than that. The name doesn't ring a bell. Now, I need to know who you're screwing with before I leave with the stiff. Like I said, give me a few and his entire family—"

"We aren't killing his family, Yuri."

He cocks an eyebrow and then he leans over, hands on his knees to laugh. "I forgot. The girl. This is all because of the girl. She's that cop's daughter from the past, huh?"

"Dah." I rub my tensed face. Relieved that none of my family sicced a dirty cop on me.

"Alright, I'll kill her dad." He offers.

"Nyet."

"Don't worry, Vassili. I'll do it without so much as having a conversation with your precious girl. You said to stay away, I didn't forget." He placed up his palms. "I may be big, but I can get in and out without—"

"Nyet, Yuri. Get rid of the dead fucking cop," I growl through gritted teeth.

The speed-punching bag torpedoes. My fists slam down on it rapidly, as Kendrick Lamar's newest rap blares in my eardrums.

It's been nine weeks since Zariah and I've jumped into the deep end. We've gone from The Griffith Observatory to fucking faces on the "It's a small world" ride at Disneyland. Since she and her father are fans of the Lakers, I got them court-side tickets to the playoffs in April. It wasn't until the second quarter that her dad texted about not being able to make it.

Besides that, there's been no more resistance from her father.

Benny, one of Vadim's Gym's employees catches my eye.

I pull off one earphone while one is handing the bag. "What?"

"You got visitors."

"Who?"

"How should I know?" He cocks his head to the front. "Fans probably. I made them stand at the front desk."

I glare at him.

"Whoever they are, hurry them along. Vadim isn't happy with you."

My eyebrow cocks.

Benny huffs. "You weren't here yesterday to workout. Matter of fact, looks like you've eaten well. Remember how much you hated getting down to weight as a rookie?"

"I'll make weight," I snap.

"Sure, the belt can sit across from you in the sauna as you pedal."

"Fuck off, Benny," I huff, imagining the sauna suit clinging to the sweat on my skin. Duct tape to lock in every entry point while I'm coasting on a bike in the sauna. I shake my head. At least that will be new. I haven't had to shit pounds and shed water in at least a year or two.

This is what love does to you. Makes you soft. Makes you lenient.

Nobody is standing at the front desk. Beachgoers are

159

biking or skating by on the pathway outside, so I step out of the double doors to take a look.

There's a dude in a suit, puffing on a cigarette. He's next to a blond chick in an ultra-tight dress, who is chatting on the phone. They look out of place, with the beach as a backdrop. I start to step back inside when the suit notices me.

"Karo, Karo!" He smashed the cigarette into the steel bike rack.

"Vassili," the blond corrects. She hangs up her phone, without so much as a goodbye to whomever she was speaking to. "Mr. Vassili Resnov, I'm Jennifer Pruitt. This is my business partner, Dale Landry." She has a business card between her fingers in a half-second.

"Talk to my manager." I shrug her off, but the bitch still has her fingers extended. "Ms. Pruitt, please save the card for my manager."

"Have you heard of Power Water?"

I stop dead in my tracks. This newer line is blowing Smart Water out of the motherfucking *water* these days.

"Let's do dinner tonight, Mr. Resnov. Bring your manager. Bring a date." Jennifer's blue orbs lock onto mine as if she's imagining riding my cock.

"All right, I'll do both." I address Dale only. Hopefully, she perceives that my only interest is Power Water. Besides, this past week's training camp, for the Vegas fight, has started. Though Zariah and I are two months solid, I haven't laid eyes on her in almost a week.

Soon as I return to the back of the gym, Vadim shouts from the cage. "Vassili, get your ass in here. I swear, if you can't keep up, I'll be sparring with you myself."

"My takedown is for snow-haired mudaks, too, Vadim," I

shoot back, climbing the steps. "Let me know if you'd like to wake up sooner or later."

I somersault, ending with a stand. My sparring partner shakes his head. These days, I reserve the cockiness to entertain the fans on stage, sometimes it gets the old man to crack a smile.

We rarely ever smile.

"I rarely get to see my favorite *kuzen* these days. With the girl, too? You tell me to stay the fuck away from the girl." Yuri points his cigarette at me. "Now *you* want me to go to dinner with the girl?"

"That's right, *glupyy*—stupid." I lean back in the chair, shot glass in my hand. We are sitting at a card table in his father's home.

"When do I get to meet the girl?" Malich asks, coming into the room. He places the LA Times newspaper under his arm and pulls off his glasses. He's genuinely interested. I recall the day Yuri's old brother, Igor, began to talk about engagement rings. Malich was right there. Ready to meet the girl, telling Igor how the girl reminded him of their mother.

Zariah might like him. Set aside the syndicate, they'd make good friends. But for starters, this week I'm telling her that Anatoly is my father. It's now or never. Then I may or may not introduce her to more family.

Or if I've underestimated our love, then I lose her. So introductions with my uncle are unnecessary anyway.

"You coming to Vegas?" I ask. Malich's only claim to entertainment is my matches. Well, it was before I started fighting out of state and internationally. He does anything for his family. But I'm sure the next time he gets on a plane, a tragedy or celebrating a new life will be the cause.

"Vegas? Ah, how about you bring her for dinner." He rubs the back of his neck, considering it. "Maybe I can, it's not all that far. Should I get Yuri or one of these other knuckleheads to—"

Yuri cuts in, "No way, Pop. If I can break bread with the girl tonight, I'm going to Vegas on Friday. Shit, I'm not going to be able to get that shipment in San Pedro in two days. Vassili has to be in New York for promotions. I go too."

"What about your responsibilities, Yuri? I should fucking..." Malich threatens, his backhand is poised. He's all smiles while doing so.

"Don't talk back to your father, you fat fuck," I argue, shuffling the cards. They both chuckle. How personal of a relationship would I have with my father if I called that motherfucker 'pop' instead of mudak, *piz'da* or, the obvious, Anatoly? All of which I call him to his face, so there's that.

"Shit, had I been more like your dad," Malich says, "Yuri, Igor, all my boys would've shown more respect. There'd be no telling me shit! Just doing."

"C'mon, Pop." Yuri picks up his cards, one at a time. "I'm perfect in every way."

Malich pours us all another round. I hope for Christ's sake, Yuri doesn't scare off my woman. Come Thursday, it's truth time.

1 7

ZARIAH

"Connie, if I never get rewarded with a red vine again, it won't be too soon." I pluck the candy up that she just tossed at the side of my head and shoot it back in her direction.

"Well, we have half a tube left. It's not my fault you excelled in Constitutional law today. Now, we better beat my uncle Samuel to the car, or he will honestly leave without us. He has this habit of being on time to court."

We both rise from our seats. The conference room of Billingsley Legal is cluttered with textbooks. It's become the quintessential hub of my bar exam studies. A few cases that Connie is currently assigned are here, too.

Connie gets to the exit first and opens it. It's refreshing to see a predominantly minority group of lawyers scattered throughout the office.

Samuel is already headed toward the front door. He's in a navy blue business suit, canvas briefcase strapped to his shoulder and phone superglued to his ear.

"Sam," Connie's voice is at a respectable interoffice volume as she calls out.

163

"Oh, sweetie, I almost forgot about the two of you." He pulls the phone from his ear, murmuring to whoever was on the line that he will be there shortly.

"We are a stellar team in the making." He pats my shoulder while allowing us to pass through the door first.

Later in the evening, I attend a birthday dinner for the governor, Taryn's father. I had no intentions of attending. This is the moment where my father planned to 'plant the seed' for his quest to run for mayor. Since I haven't moved out of his house yet and we hardly see each other in passing, I felt obligated to come.

My golden cocktail dress hugs my curves. Glancing around the venue, I notice people are dressed to the nines. Many of them, who my dad swore told him it would be a good idea to run, are in the Republican Party.

Well, at least I straightened my hair tonight. The place is a notch below black-tie until I spot Taryn. With her tight eyes and dark skin, she is an exotic beauty. She's in a tutu skirt that hides the fact that she wasn't blessed from her Somali mother's side, with an ass or hips. Anybody else would look like a young girl, but she'd get a nod from Tyra Banks.

"Hey, where's your dad?" I ask. "I haven't wished him a happy birthday."

She hugs me. "Girl, see him later. My father told me that you should blow this joint, ha, ha."

Her Asian father always thought he was a comedian. We let him tag along when the first 'Hangover' movie came out, during our last year of high school. My eyebrows knit together. "What do you mean?"

"Phil," she mouths. "C'mon, my father is the *Governator*," she jokes in a Terminator franchise voice. "However, my dad can't very well talk badly of his benefactors. Dad knows about my yacht parties and how much 'you know who' was in love with you. *I'm still in love with you.*"

"You can't be serious," I groan.

"Well, my dad, your dad, and Phillip IV, they all had their expectations. So, allow me to be frank," Taryn says. Though, she's never offered anything less than a hard dose of reality. "Maxwell and both the damn Phils are living in the olden days. That's why your dad begged you to come tonight."

I grumble. "Well, they all have another thing coming."

"Hey, where's your fighter?" Before I can answer, Taryn's voice rises as she glances behind me, "Phillip Everly!" Taryn fakes interest while cueing me to look behind me. "Wow, you've traded in Ralph Lauren for custom made."

I'm too irritated to thank her for the heads up. They hug. I glance around the venue, in blatant disinterest. Damn, my father is sauntering up the stage now. From about fifteen yards away, he glances at me. He then glances at Phil, smiling while his gaze pans back toward me, once more.

This is a setup if I ever saw one.

There's a round of applause as my dad starts sweet-talking to the crowd,

"You look stunning," Phil whispers, coming to stand next to me.

"Thank you."

"I saw you the moment you walked in." His arm goes around my back, skimming my opposite shoulder. "Can we go somewhere to talk?"

"About what? Beautiful little mulatto children?" I cackle, shrugging my shoulder. He doesn't remove his hand.

"Why am I still paying for what Landry said?" he speaks through gritted teeth.

"Excuse me, Phil. Maybe I confused you for your father or any other man who has balls enough to correct his friend for speaking ill of your girlfriend. Landry mentioned how cute little *mulatto* kids are. He jokes and acts like an idiot. I was seventeen, dumb too. I thought the best form of defense in responding to his covert racism was *no, we aren't together for gold complexion offspring, but love.*"

"Zariah, will you—"

"No, I never loved you. Albeit, I believed the stupid word you said about *loving* me. And it's not Landry and his mulatto statement or the *other snide* shit he said. It's a simple fact that you being a rich white boy doesn't mean I'm fortunate enough to date you. Oh, and I can't afford your love at the moment because it comes in the expensive, addictive white powder form. Fuck off."

I stalk away, rubbing my skin where he'd touched it. Perhaps, I chewed his head off a tad more than necessary. Hopefully, he'll see this as a learning lesson for the woman who doesn't itch in his presence.

About an hour later, I'm able to inch my way into one of my father's conversations.

"You've stolen every potential vote here, Dad. Come November there'll be no stopping you. They all love you," I whisper. "I'm going to slip out the side door now."

"Oh, why? You have a hot date tonight? Every man here has eyes for you, Princess. Some of which wouldn't have to work too hard for my approval."

Good for you. "It's a group dinner I'm attending." My tone is so blasé he isn't interested in learning any more regarding my dinner with Vassili. He brushed us off at the Laker game. Why bother?

"Sounds like fun. Will you be accompanying Zariah as well?" He asks. I glance over and Taryn is there.

"I sure am." She offers me a wink.

"Damn you," I grumble as Taryn catches my stride, toward the exit. She's always embraced her Japanese side over the black. "What happened to snag rich boys with a pedigree? I swear I saw royal-marriage material here."

"Been there, Booboo." She replies unamused. "You're going to see Vassili, aren't you? And if you're going to see him, that cousin of his, Yuri is there."

"Don't tell me," I quickly respond, aware of her next statement.

"Yuri has a super fat cock, my name is written all over it."

Succoso Pomodoro–Juicy Tomato–is an expensive Italian restaurant on Rodeo Drive. The restaurant has a grand, dramatic environment with marble walls. Touches of oak wood offer a classic Italian-villa style. A to-die-for aroma wafts through the place, as Taryn and I are escorted to Vassili's table. We're already thirty minutes late since I played cordial with my dad before walking out.

Air hitches in my lungs as Vassili comes into view. He's seated at a table, cater-corner from me. The only tattoos visible are the ones creeping up the back of his neck. The works of art disappear into the curly tail end of his Mohawk, and those along the backs of his hands. He's dressed in a black suit, which complements his broad shoulders and thick biceps. There's a blond next to him. The trick does her best to touch him, every chance she gets. Damn, his cold shoulder is fit for that nasty, little fly.

Another Caucasian man is seated on the opposite side of her, with Yuri rounding out the table.

"Good thing you brought me," Taryn grits in a whisper. "That bitch will bow down, one way or another."

I shake my head. Taryn has never had to work. The mean girl mentality from high school still rides deep on occasion.

The hostess parts ways with us as we continue to weave around the tables in the dark-lit atmosphere.

"Ah, you must be Ms. Washington." The man with the perfectly cropped hair stands first.

Vassili's entire demeanor comes alive. The blonde's ambitions fade into oblivion as he arises from his seat to hug me. Vassili hugs me so tightly that my body sways, and I mold to his muscles.

"Zariah, you brought Taryn. Damn, you're family in my book." Yuri raises his snifter, clear liquid sloshing toward me. He slides his arm around Taryn to grope her hip. He's at least a hundred pounds more than her hundred pounds.

"Drinks! We need real drinks," his voice rises.

"Yes, the best wine!" the man says.

"No, wine. Vodka." Yuri snaps his fingers and a waiter rushes over. "Two extra chairs and your best vodka. Don't play me either, your *best.*"

"Baby, here sit." Vassili offers me the chair next to the blond chick. "Oh, this is... Uh... Dale Landry and Mrs.... Yuri, fucking help me out here. *Manage* the situation."

They both laugh. Dale's chuckle starts slow as if getting a feel for whose ass he should kiss. She is clearly his boss.

"Jennifer Pruitt," the blonde reaches out a hand to me. Yuri offers Taryn his seat. Any managing he's supposed to be doing has gone out the window. He's only got eyes for her.

"The conversation has evolved around you for almost twenty minutes," Jennifer shares. Her response causes me to be even more unapologetic to her trifling ass. Either she's attempting to flatter me, or this hoe tried to steal my man while he continued to mention *me.*

I offer a fake smile. "We were late."

"It was all my fault," Taryn chimes in as two chairs are positioned on either side of us.

"So tell us how you plan to make my man rich."

"Direct. I like her." Dale grins.

Yuri scoffs. "Word from the wise, don't like Zariah too much. It isn't safe. The champ is a jealous man."

Vassili places a possessive arm around me.

Yuri offers a smug grin. "See, and this is clearly how I manage the situation."

My man reaches over to whisper in my ear, "I can't eat this fucking food. When I get you home, I'll have you all night long."

A silly grin is slapped on my face. Anyone he stares at should be able to read his intentions.

With his arm around me, Vassili rubs my cheek with his thumb. "Look at that gorgeous, coy smile. So, should I eat you, tonight?"

"The best is here," our waiter says, stepping to the table.

Before cheering with everyone, I murmur, "Vassili, feel free to eat me all night long if you'd like."

18

VASSILI

Z ariah gasps. The silk scarf falling from her silky hair. For the life of me, I don't understand why she wraps her hair around her head into a weird ball when it's straightened. Her long hair falls along her shoulder as she says, "Vassili, baby, what are you still doing here?"

"In my bed?" I ask, throat heavy from sleep.

"Uh, you *know* what I mean. You have another day of boot camp left before your promotions in New York." She cuddles close to me. "I expected to snuggle with your pillow like I did last Saturday morning. Are you okay?"

"Good, good," I caress her cheek. Shit, there's something I should recall. After the night we've had, all I remember is her pussy squirting in my mouth once she mastered the technique.

"Honestly?" She climbs onto my waist. "Don't you need one more day and night of crazy training. I refuse to watch The Hauser slap you around. I don't want to hear it's his *house*." She mimics the fighter's whiny voice from watching a history of Hauser's matches with me.

"Slap me around? That's blasphemy, baby." In one fluid

swoop, she's beneath me again. "I'm going to grab him by the throat." I place my hand across her delicate neck and offering the faintest squeeze. "There's power in feeling a man's pulse fade."

"As long as he doesn't hit you. My heart can't take it," she murmurs as my lips smack down onto hers. The sweetest little moan comes from her mouth. Deepening the kiss, I move my hand toward the back of her neck, kneading the tendons with my thumb. My foot hooks around hers, and once more, Zariah is flipped. Now, her ass is wedged against my hardened cock, my chest against her back. My lips press a few soft kisses at her spine.

"Keep flipping me like your toy." She threatens. In the next breath, Zariah purrs as my hand swims down into her pajama pants. My thumb works its way along the tightest, little hole ever.

"Vassili," she groans.

"Okay, okay," I chuckle. "Tilt that fat ass for me."

She rises to her knees and I lift some in support. My thumb glides between her ass cheeks. Restraining myself, I shove her pants down and continue to glide toward her sweet pussy. I pet those thick petals before plunging inside of her. My dick is swallowed in her tight ocean.

"You sure you don't want my cock in this ass? All that beautiful ass?" I smack her left cheek so hard, it bounces back against my palm.

"Vassili," she growls, gyrating against my cock. My thumb is still playing against her tiny bud and she's angry. "I. Will. Kick. Your. Ass."

"But it's the prettiest, roundest ass." I grip her hips, working her pussy out.

"Fuck you, Vassili . . ." She groans, taking each thrust. Zariah's ass claps back against me, and she matches my drive as I work her like a piston. My thumb roams over the ridged resistance of her asshole. Zariah slams harder against my cock. Her cunt eating my entire dick.

I stop playing with her resistance. She looks back as I bite the tip of my thumb and smile cockily. There's an underlying lust behind her eyes, but I won't push. I then lick her juices from my thumb.

"Grrr..." Zariah's pussy quivers against my cock, holding it siege. Damn, if I don't stop looking at her beautiful body, I'm going to nut.

"I've got more for you, girl. I always do," I say, continuing to fuck her doggy style. An amazing desire washes over me, bringing all the heat to my stiff cock. While ramming into Zariah, I consider how I want to eat her pussy, eat her ass, eat her. I want to totally devour and demolish her juices until she's more malleable in my hands. More willing to allow my cock into those chocolate cheeks. But I let her cunt milk my cock for all it's worth. This might've been a quickie now, but I'll have her later.

I fall into her, with a grunt.

"Good morning," she giggles. Her eyes are a haze of desire and I can tell her mind is good and clear of all thoughts.

"Good morning, beautiful." I move over a little, spooning her, so my wet cock isn't laying on her ass.

Zariah's phone rings on the bedside table. I reach over, ready to smash it into the wall. Anything to stop the sound, but she says, "It's my mom. I have to answer it. After Vegas, no more boot camp."

She sits up, crossing her legs and grabs the phone. "Hey, Momma!"

Fuck me, I could've used a moment of cuddling. But I'd be a pussy to have mentioned that.

"Breakfast?" I mouth.

Zariah quickly shakes her head, lips sneered. She hates

breakfast with me while I'm practicing for a match. "No thanks, baby."

I'll make her a smoothie, anyway. I head to the kitchen, rubbing the back of my neck.

At the cupboard, I pull out the protein and peanut butter wondering, *what did I have to do today?* The thought slams into my mind. My alarm didn't go off and I'm uncertain if Vadim left a voicemail threatening my life for not visiting the gym yet.

Though uncertainty settles in my bones, I grab a few extra ripe bananas Zariah had asked for the last time I made her a smoothie. My eyes narrow, I swear I hear a tiny vibrating sound. Mindlessly, I start the blender. I lean my elbows against the quartz countertop. My dick is still a little sore. Zariah's pussy is now a tight mold in the shape of my cock but creating such a beautiful shape has been work. I yawn, warning myself about discipline and not to fuck her the night before the event.

"Babe? Babe! Please stop making a ruckus," Zariah calls from down the hall.

After I press the pause button, chunks of strawberry and blackberries float to the bottom of the slushed drink. I'm pouring two glasses when Zariah leans against the pantry.

"My mom would like to talk to you."

I arch an eyebrow.

"The phone is on mute. Please, she said I sound like a woman in love. I had to tell her about you."

"Okay." I hand her a glass and she offers over her iPhone. Instead of placing the phone to my ear, I see Mrs. Washington's face on the screen, in real-time. I press the mute button to release it and position the FaceTime screen.

"Hello, Mrs. Washington."

"Ms. Haskins will do fine. That's my maiden name. So you're Vassili. I've heard lots about you."

"All good things?"

"You are very handsome, but what's with all those tattoos." Her neck is craning, wanting to see where the cross tat on the side of my neck ends. Or perhaps it's the top portion of the KILLER KARO on my chest that she'd like to inspect further.

"I can tell you what most of them mean."

Ms. Haskins arches an eyebrow. "Did you get a few of them while inebriated?"

"Nah, nothing like that. The others might not be appropriate to discuss."

"Oh…" Ms. Haskins says. Zariah groans

"Mom, you said you only had one question. Please play nice."

"Or what? I like him. The truth tastes much easier than a lie. She's so much like her father at times." Ms. Haskins makes a clicking sound with her tongue. "Alright, Vassili. All I'd like to know for now is, what are your intentions with my daughter?"

"I love Zariah. My only aim is to place a smile on her face."

Ms. Haskins lingers, her brown eyes narrowing faintly. Then she smiles. "I believe you. I will, of course, have a lot more questions whenever I meet you in person. When do you two plan to visit me?"

"We can come anytime," I reply.

"Mom," Zariah stresses.

"What?" She chortles. "I guess the two of you can figure out when you'll come. Zariah's brother, Martin, is expecting his third baby any day now. It would be nice to have my daughter home sometime soon. I'd love to meet you as well. Then, like I said, the real questions can start."

"Momma, dang!"

"Next week is good," I tell her. "We can head over after my match."

"That's perfect," she says.

"No, sorry, it's not perfect for me," Zariah cuts in. "There's too much on my plate now, Mom. I planned to visit this August after the bar exam and save Martin's baby from all your kisses."

When her mom continues with the small talk, Zariah grabs the phone. "Goodbye, we have a busy day."

She hangs up. "Sorry, my mom promised not to put you on the spot.

"It's okay." I shrug, downing my drink. "Baby, I don't mind meeting your mother if you'd like."

Zariah rubs a vulnerable hand over her forearm. I corner her by the cabinets and skim my lips over her forehead.

She murmurs, "My mom knows you're a Resnov."

"Okay…"

"I think she likes you despite your blood ties. However, due to her relationship with my dad, she has always been a tad overbearing. Sheesh, I think she's still in love with my dad."

I cock a brow. "After what he's done to her?"

"Yeah," Zariah pauses, reluctant for a moment. "My parents split at the beginning of Junior year. I tried to convince myself that I stayed with Dad instead of living with my mom to continue at Presley Prep. But . . . my mom, she kind of begged me to. No matter how close we were, she begged me to stay. It took forever for her to stop asking about my dad's secretary. My poor mom was still tormenting herself with the bitch he left her for. Even when I got to Spelman, she had me check-in just for those reasons."

Zariah huffs. "Anyway, my mom has this way about her. She loves too damn much. But it takes a little to get her there. She's the same way with Martin. Before he married, Momma was a ball of nerves. She worried about him being hit by a woman, about his happiness. My brother chose not to become a cop, but he's far from a sissy." Zariah shakes her head in thought. "She will hound you. All those tattoos will be discussed."

"You said she's concerned about Martin's happiness. Your happiness. Then I answered correctly, right? She asked if I loved you." I play with her breast.

"And you answered perfectly, Vassili," Zariah moans. "Can we take this party into the shower?"

"Yeah, I haven't fucked you in the shower in a whole week."

"Humph, whose fault is that?"

"When we return from Vegas, you'll be locked to the headboard for a month. I'll make it up to you." I hug her tightly. "Now, drink your smoothie. Join me once you've downed it."

"Aw, Vassili," she groans as I place the glass in her hand.

"C'mon, girl, get your strength up. I'll get the water ready. We get to screw like bulls for..." I glance at the wall clock while reaching down to grab her pussy. "Another two hours. That's good. I don't want to break you, baby."

A few minutes later, steam clouds the bathroom mirror. "Zariah," I shout over the sound of shower while stepping over the pile of clothes I took off. "Baby, get your ass in here."

"Coming," her reply is muffled.

I imagine Zariah tossing her smoothie while I grab my toothbrush out of the holder. Zariah's reflection appears in the mirror behind me.

My eyebrows crinkle together. She leans against the wall, fully dressed in jeans, a silk blouse, and boots. She's gripping something in her hand.

"So, I just took an interesting call," Zariah says, holding up my iPhone.

I toss the toothbrush on the counter. Naked as the day is long, I turn around to lean against the ledge. Nudging my chin to the deep scold on her face, I ask, "Babe, what's with the look?"

"I spoke with Malich, your *uncle.*"

Shit, my ears ring as I recall the reason for my impromptu visit with Anatoly two months ago. I had assumed Malich was doctoring numbers for liquor and food, which made no sense. The majority of money flooding in came from his whores. My uncle often fronted the bill for some of the provisions. Come to find out he was tracking money moving around. Then it dawns on me, the uncertainty about what I had to do today. My uncle had left a voicemail, right before the Power Water business dinner. He mentioned coming over this morning to tell me about the cunt that had screwed us both. Because The Red Door isn't something I'm intrinsically motivated by, I forgot.

"Malich wanted to apologize for being late this morning. Eeyore, or Igor, *his son*, apparently has diabetes and was eating a little more than he should. *His son's* wife freaked out. Then *his other son, Mikhail,* had to help. I'm learning all about your family tree, you see, Malich loves to talk. He told me how *his son's* wife just about has a heart attack as well. The baby was crying. Also, he offered to have us over for dinner." Her eyes are glossed as she speaks, though not a single tear falls. "So, you're wrong about Urban Kashtan; it doesn't have the best *shchi*. Malich makes the best *shchi*. Funny how I learned so much from *your uncle. Your uncle* is good conversation. Very open, very friendly by the way. Anyway, Malich apologizes for being late this morning. Vassili, *enter the fucking conversation, anytime! You lied to me.*"

"I..." The sound of the mirror crashing behind me stops me from stepping forward to touch her. A few shards and splints prickle into the back of my legs and neck. My phone clatters, coming to a stop next to my bare feet. The screen is cracked. "Okay, Zariah, you assumed about my father. I didn't correct you."

"You're Anatoly Resnov's son? Not any fucking Resnov, not married in or a third cousin twice removed. Vassili, your father is on America's Most Wanted! Stay away from me!"

"I'm sorry, baby." As I start to walk towards Zariah, she spins around and stalks down the hall. Bits of mirror embed in my feet. "Zar, let me explain!"

I grit my teeth until an even sharper piece of glass digs into the sole of my foot. "Fuck!" I lift my left leg, gripping the shard of mirror. It's at least two inches long. Blood pours from the wound as I pull it out. Using the padding of my left foot, I run toward the door. My left heel slams down, and I almost slip on blood. "Zariah!"

SLAM. She shuts the door.

A trail of smeared blood follows in my wake. I grab a pillow from the couch, placing it over my cock, and rushing outside. By the time I get there, my girl is already inside the backseat of a Corolla, with the LYFT sticker on the rear window.

"Zariah, baby!" I toss the pillow at the car as it zooms along the one-way street.

"Dude!" A bike messenger argues, wheeling by. "Cover up."

"Does it look like I give a fuck?" I toss my middle finger and hurry into the house. Back through the warzone with the driblets of blood and the long trail of it. I head toward the bathroom after grabbing a broom, careful to stay near the door, I begin fishing for my phone.

"Shit, I'm gonna fight with an injury," I grumble, as the iPhone and bits of the mirror are swept toward me. It won't be the first time but being in prime shape is best. I reach down and grab the phone up. The entire front of the screen falls off. Now I'm tossing the phone, and it slams against the toilet, breaking into even more pieces.

I head toward the bedroom to get dressed. I'll call my doc from one of these fucking neighbor's houses, then threaten his ass to get here soon. My heart walked out of the door, and there is no such thing as letting her go.

19

ZARIAH

The television is on when I arrive home. My eyes close tightly. My father is home on a Saturday morning. Usually, Mom and I had the entire house on weekend mornings. We had this tradition of going to IHOP for breakfast. Due to being lazy Saturday morning people, we always got there when the breakfast crowd died down. God knows where Dad would be. Martin is about five years older than me and I hardly recall him choosing home over staying at a friend's house.

I head toward the staircase, rubbing the tears from my cheeks when I hear footsteps.

"Princess?" My dad calls out.

"Yes," I reply, in a muted tone so he is unable to read my voice. My eyes are throbbing from the long cry on the ride home. But I fan my face before heading to the sound of the news. Maxwell is meandering around the kitchen, pouring himself a cup of coffee. He grabs the spoon on the counter, eyes glued to the television.

"Pay attention to your surroundings." My attempt to lighten the air doesn't work as he finally glances over me.

"You usually disappear for the entire weekend." Maxwell's gaze is questioning.

"We both are ghosts on the weekend. Why aren't you at Beatrice's?" It wasn't until I was sixteen and my parents separated that I knew my father wasn't this hero. The good cop who spent all hours of his life advocating for and helping people. I always thought my mom was an anomaly. He'd beat her. Save *other* people. Then I learned he also spent the weekends at his secretary, Beatrice's home.

"Her daughter was sick," he says.

I nod and turn around to leave.

"Will you be gone in the impending weekends?"

"Probably not." I hurry down the hall before more tears can wet my face. I slip into the bathroom to apply a cold towel along my skin and decrease the heat. Walking out, I realize Dad isn't aware that the studio apartment approved me to move at the beginning of the month. "Dad," I call out.

He's leaning against the counter, tone low. "Amp up the cruisers in my neighborhood."

My curiosity piques. Leaning against the wall, I wait for him to speak.

"Yes, rotate each hour," he continues in a hushed tone. "Zariah appears fine. If anyone eyes Resnov around my house, take him in. I don't give a damn if that Russian scum is skipping along the sidewalk, chewing gum."

I head up the stairs, my first instinct is to call Vassili. Yet another sob unsettles my heart. On our first night together, I brought up Malich Resnov at The Red Door. He never denied it. Never even missed a damn beat!

Like a wet rag, my body slams down onto the mattress. I kick off my boots, contemplating both Vassili's father and his uncle. Malich is the lesser of two evils. In the beginning, the surname shook fear into my bones.

Grabbing a pillow into my arms, I squeeze my face into it,

stifling a scream. Why did I fall in love with a man who has Russian Mafia in his genes! With each curse, I'm reminded of how I separated myself from Vassili over the years in college. He was the deepest addiction ever, and like with Phil, I had a reason never to look back. A big reason.

And then our paths collided, again. There was no saving me.

Sounds of arguing perk up my ears. The sun isn't shining into the balcony like before. I must've fallen asleep.

The voices are woven in titanium, each order pristine. I rub a hand across my forehead, pushing back mounds of sweated-out tresses and pull myself off the bed.

"I came to the front door out of respect!"

I gasp, Vassili is at my house. I open the bedroom door and hurry toward the stairs.

"Fuck your respect, Resnov. Step outside. Walk back to your car."

"Or what? Those cops rough me up? I told those mudaks to do their worst. Guess they backed off out of respect for your neighbors?" Vassili argues. Then his hard voice tapers out with feeling. "All I'm asking is to have one single conversation with your daughter, please. We can chat man to man, once you're ready."

My dad's voice is louder now, "I'll never allow—"

"Dad!" Hurrying down the stairs, I glance between them. Outside the open doors, three cruisers line the curb. Damn, I'm the cause of this. I gasp, noticing a bandage around Vassili's ankle and heel. He's wearing Nike slides. "Your foot."

"I'm good." Vassili's weary eyes meet mine. "Zariah, please talk to me. Mr. Washington, you have my word, if I piss her off, I won't be any more trouble."

There's an undercurrent of finality to his statement, offering my father the end of *us*. My father's eyelid twitches. This isn't a good enough bribe.

"Can you?" I point to the staircase. Vassili bites his lip, nods, and heads toward me. The back of his hand grazes across my cheek, his rough knuckles reminding me of home. My eyelids surrender to peace.

He then starts up the stairs. I stay put.

"Dad, you cannot intervene in my life."

"You're my child, Zariah."

"True. For over two months, we've skirted a few issues. I am somewhat to blame. Today is all my fault."

"All your fault?"

I shake my head. "No more involving your friends down at the police station. I apologize you felt the need to bully Vassili. He isn't like—"

"You mean to tell me that those barbarians adopted him?" Maxwell scoffs.

"No, Vassili just doesn't repeat the cycle." I snap. My glare speaks volumes, but I'm livid at the thought of my father using his power to harass Vassili. "He's like Martin, independent, choosing not to follow the mistakes of his father."

The underlying truth hits him hard. The snake isn't quick to strike back. Like him, my grandfather was a *peace* officer and a wife beater.

"Twenty-five and as naïve as the day I first held you close." He sighs. "Resnov manipulated you into believing he isn't in the family business? Independent, you said. Let's add intelligent. Has to have a stellar strategy, mental conditioning and reasoning. UFC champion. Beloved fans for days. But no illegal activity the department or the feds can pin on him."

"Alright, you've analyzed Vassili and me, Dad. Don't you think you're overdue for a self-assessment? Maybe, I've embarrassed you today, I've disappointed myself for overreacting. But if you run and then lose the election, only you are to blame. Not me or whoever the fuck I choose to love."

Two at a time, I hurry up the steps and enter the bedroom. Vassili is seated at the edge of my bed, chewing on the nail of his finger. The despondency in his gaze crumbles my heart.

"I'm a mudak," he says.

"No, you're not. I cried myself to sleep this afternoon." The air between us thickens. He hates when I cry, and my words have made it worse. I step before him, wedging myself between his legs and run my hand along the chocolate curls at his nape.

"While I slept I had time to think. Babe, my mind has turned circles, wishing you were a man of any other name and association. I just finished arguing with my dad. It took all this to realize you are more than a Resnov. You add value to the name, and I love you for who you are."

"You don't hate me for lying?"

"I placed us in this situation by continuing to have reservations, Vassili. All I have now is happiness and my trust in you."

He's quiet for a moment. "Can you see a future with me?"

"Yes."

"Marriage and children, Zariah, I won't continue this …"

I plaster my mouth against his. "I love you, Vassili. I would marry you in a heartbeat. How many children would you like?"

Vassili kisses me longer. "A boy and a girl, that'd be good."

I sit next to him. "We have to be on one accord. No assumptions or confusion."

Vassili clasps my inner thigh. There is power in his touch. It offers strength and consolation. He offers the rundown of Malich. His uncle is the connection for Anatoly's business, delegating "roles." I force myself to heed without judgment.

"The Red Door isn't even a drop in the bucket. Just another avenue for Anatoly to interest me in the family."

"He's paranoid about Malich?"

Vassili scratches the scruff on his jaw. "Yeah. I almost snitched on Malich, but he was looking out for my business. The bartender who served me, the very night I brought you along, was doing more than gambling on my matches. That cunt was scheming at my lounge."

"Has Malich..." my throat clogs.

"Baby, it's the Resnov way. Playing lenient when there's a lesson to be learned can come back and fuck us, the family, in the ass."

"You said, *us*. Be honest." My hands flex in discomfort. "Are you involved? Aside from owning The Red Door, which holds legal repercussions, as well."

"Nyet."

Squirming in my seat, I contemplate how I'd placed Vassili in the position to lie to me about his father. His facial expressions never gave anything away. So I'm beating the dead horse. I ask, "Have you ever engaged in any syndicate activity?"

He's quiet for a moment. Then he looks me in the eye. "Nyet."

"Ronisha's ex aside, have you—"

"That motherfucker is the only one who's died by my hands, Zariah."

Breathing deeply, I nod. "Okay, I feel like crap for what happened to your foot."

"I'm good."

I snuggle myself into his strong arms. The underlying fear I had for the Russian fighter fades into oblivion.

20

ZARIAH

T-Mobile Arena, Las Vegas, One Week Later

This morning, the last conversation I had with Vassili included him laughing at me. And I mean he rewarded me with a killer smile, the one he reserves for key moments.

Cocky bastard didn't respond to my worry for his foot. The cut in his left heel isn't fully mended, though that wasn't reason enough for him to laugh. At least, I don't believe it was a good reason.

The daze I have lived in for much of the undercards leading to the main event evaporates.

The announcer shouts about Karo. My index fingers zip into my ears. The diverse crowd, of all ages, roars while I recall the news segment of Vassili and Hauser's promotional conference. My study textbook had fallen to the floor as my eyes glued to the television. The reporter's questions egged them on, though the two didn't need help. Hauser mocked about Karo's "hurt" ankle. Vadim had him wear a brace to cover the bandage along the bottom of his heel.

My man's response rings in my ear, clear as day. *'I usually put my opponents to sleep, but in Vegas, I'm gonna crush your head in!'*

The two teams had to stop them from blowing up on each other right there.

"Are you ready for WAR?" The announcer screams, bringing me back to the present. Blinding lights shine down on Hauser's bright red curls. His tan chest is full of freckled splotches and jacked muscles.

Taryn leans into me and flicks her hand toward the underdog. "Girl, that Ginger isn't even intimidating. You've got a Russian bull, baby. Hauser is going down."

"Oh," I reply, "I take it Yuri harps 'bull this and bull that,' too?"

She winks.

21

VASSILI

After a quick prayer, I kiss the cross pendant, before placing it with the rest of my gear. Thanking God for strength is always the last, most imperative part of my routine of warming up. I then rise from my knees. Adrenaline surges through my veins.

"*Vy gotovy*—are you ready?" Vadim's eyes lock onto mine.

"Dah!"

He, along with Nestor, who has my belt draped over his arm, and the rest of my crew follow me along the corridor to an entryway, which reads 'main stage.'

The vibrations of my opponent's music bang against the doors as Nestor opens it.

With the change in music, it's my cue to migrate toward the octagon. A camera crew is in front of me. I head out with my people right behind me. The cameraman pacing backward, tracking my every step.

The lighting is dim, my vision is tunneled and targeting the cage. This motherfucker talked his way into this fight. Now it's time to break his neck.

This is personal.

It's always personal when a motherfucker is gunning for what belongs to you.

At the entrance, I hug my team and pull off my pants. Then I stop, standing still for the cutman to place Vaseline on my face before I enter the cage.

While Hauser poses himself to look hard, I place my hands behind my back, head tilted in disinterest. That bitch isn't intimidating anybody but himself.

"Ladies and gentlemen, this is our main event of the evening, sanctioned by the Nevada Athletic Commission." The announcer mentions the three judges and the referee's name.

The announcer broadcasts the undercard's bullshit stats before mentioning mine. I nod, jumping in place. That's right, I'm the champ, bitch!

We touch gloves and a rush of adrenaline pounds through my ears. On my toes, I reach in for a quick jab. He punches my chin as I go for his nose.

My body is on fire, ready to kill him. First, I'll fuck with him. This fight will last all of three minutes— so my fans get a little show. I fake the takedown and come back with a right hook. Hauser kicks my left ribs. Shit, I'll feel that later. But it's all about baiting him now. He reaches in, jabbing my nose.

He extends his arm in a cross. Blood trickles down my mouth, I bait him. My hook claiming the side of his ear.

"Stay on him!" Vadim shouts in Russian.

Then I catch him with a left, right, left. Blood squirts from his nose. My fist hits the cage as Hauser drops to the mat. The referee is on me, but I'd already stepped back.

I gesture for Hauser to get back up. His eyes are spacey. Those dilated pupils catch my taunting while the referee checks on him. Hauser's gaze hardens, connecting with mine again. He clenches the ground. I step back to my corner, not taking my eyes off him. *Get up. So I can bring you the fuck down once more.*

The referee says something inaudible. In a second, he rolls over and scrambles to his toes. The arena applauds this peace offering.

We come to our feet, hands up, chins down. I let him feel me out. Hauser low kicks toward my shin. I toss a cross punch to his face. It's met with air. Then it's all about control again; gauging his strength. Hauser reaches low and punches me in the chin. Looks like he's got his swag back. Once I bring this bitch to the ground again, there'll be no complaining. He's had his chance, but he's going down.

This motherfucker's head gets big. He tosses a cross, then goes in for a shin kick. I reach low and catch his foot. I yank and bring us both onto our backs. We are foot to foot. As we are ascending, Hauser's pupils almost pop out of his eye sockets. Cornered animal. Yeah, he knows the drill. By the time we hit the canvas, I've wrapped my arm around his ankle, securing it at my armpit. My free arm locks down his shin before he can wiggle away. Hauser's free foot kicks at the opposite side of my ribs. The least amount of pressure is applied to his calf—

TAP! TAP!

Either he's totally weak or his Achilles' tendon is. The bitch taps out. I offer a smug smile, getting up and spitting out my mouthguard. The ankle lock submission was a little tit for tat since Hauser had mocked my bandaged ankle the other day.

"Whose house is this, bitch!"

The Sky Villa at Aria is my sanctuary. Yuri and his girl tried to get Zariah and me to come out tonight. Any little bandage on my arm or leg always was a pussy magnet. But I already own the best piece of tail in the entire universe. I promised we wouldn't sleep tomorrow. My legs are kicked up, arms draped over the back of the couch. "Nu, Podogi," a Russian cartoon similar to Tom and Jerry, is on the television.

The door opens and Zariah struts in, hips swaying in her dress, bag in tow. "I found it!"

I clap my hands. "I believed in you!"

"Don't be sarcastic." She drops the wad of cash I gave her onto the coffee table. "Did you have the masseuse come while you're watching that old-ass cartoon?"

Her tone tells me she already knows the answer. So, I position myself more comfortably on the couch.

"Vassili, why get the flashiest room if you aren't using the accommodations?"

I nudge my chin at the cartoon. "Baby, this shit right here, isn't free. And the old episode is done. This one isn't as old. Now, that ass." I reach around her, grabbing her ass cheek as she pulls a black container from a bag. I squeeze the fat meat, saying, "it's all the accommodation I'll ever need."

"Whatever, Vassili. You're crazy. Or am I crazy because I love you?" Zariah places the container in my hand with a spoon.

"Where's your soup, girl?"

Her eyes shift. "I am not hungry."

"You telling me that you searched high and low on the Vegas strip—"

"Off the strip."

"Off the fucking strip? Shit, you did all that to find borsch for me?" I grab her hand. She places the container back on

191

the coffee table and tries to sit down next to me, but I pull her down onto my lap, instead.

"You're sore, Vassili," Zariah, plants her hand against the couch as leverage to get up, but my bicep flexes around her.

"No, I'm good. No babying me, beautiful. What did you eat?"

"Nothing," she says, teeth gleaming in a smile.

I squeeze her waist harder. A bubble of chuckles causes Zariah to place her face against my neck in embarrassment. "Karo, leave me alone."

"Nyet, don't call me Karo."

"You're being a bully, who ironically, likes to watch cartoons." She pulls away from my kisses, and I'm hypnotized by the twinkle in those mahogany eyes.

"This is the funniest cartoon, baby. No shit talking. What did you eat?"

Laughter bubbles from Zariah's lips. "Damn it, Vassili, there's a place downstairs with huge lobster sandwiches."

"So did you get a sandwich on your way out or..."

She points a finger at me. "Who's asking? Judge, jury or executioner?"

"Fuck, I'm all three, baby. Yuri and your friend almost tripped running out of here when I said I was hungry and wanted borscht. You knew I was hungry."

"I'm sorry," she chuckles.

"Sorry, my ass. I have a surprise for you. It depends on if you enjoyed a sandwich on the way out while I rotted away. Or did you scarf the sandwich down while in the elevator back to the room?"

"All these technicalities," she chortles. "Alright, well, my answer depends on what exactly do you have for me?"

"Okay, let me show you." I grimace leaning forward. My ribs are sore as I reach into my pocket.

"Vassili, you're hurt." Zariah again tries to arise from my

lap. My bicep squeezes harder around her waist, enough for her to groan and stay put.

"Ouch, Vassili! Oh… Oh, my God!" Zariah comes face to face with a shiny diamond ring.

I say, "Seven carats, for all those long years you made me wait. Princess cut for the obvious reason."

"Oh, my God!" Zariah's face is shocked and full of tears.

I rub a thumb along her cheek. "No tears, baby. I don't like to see you cry. We are fearless, you and me. I'm in love with your character, Zariah. How you fought for justice for Ronisha. I failed when it came to my sister but feel better because I was able to help your friend. You will continue to fight for justice in the courtroom, and I'll continue to put mudaks to sleep in the cage."

"Are you proposing? Because it sounds more like coaching," she murmurs.

"Dah."

"You haven't even asked the magic question, Vassili. You are so crazy."

Oh. "Will you—"

"Yes! Yes! Yesssss!" She lunges against me. I grit my teeth against the pain.

"Tomorrow? Zariah, marry me tomorrow?"

"Tonight!" she says, "Damn, I don't know where that came from. You make me so excited."

"No, I'm locking you down, tonight." I pull out my phone and call Yuri. "Zariah and I are getting married."

"Fuck, *kuzen*, when?"

"Now."

"Where?"

"That's where you come in, Manager." I pause. Zariah mouths exactly what I say when I order him to 'manage the situation' and hang up

"Oh, my God, we're getting married right now?" Zariah asked.

I softly grip the back of her neck. "Dah and that's the way we will stay. Married forever with God's blessing."

22

ZARIAH

We exchanged vows in a tiny chapel at the entrance to the Strip, with Yuri and Taryn as our wedding party. Vadim grumbled about being awoken in the middle of the night until he saw me dressed in white.

The lace and frill dress was more like porno attire, lacking much in extra material. It was cute though, skimming along my chocolate thighs. The back has more of a puff to it, extending down with white shimmery feathers, comparable to a peacock. I love my dress, it's badass.

Vassili carries me to The Sky Villa. His frame is draped in a suit—a suit that power and money got him after midnight. My thumb plays with the enormous rock on my finger as he gets the Aria villa door open. I glance into the room and gasp.

"Oh, Vassili..." There is a sea of white tulips along the glossy floor. Crystal vases, of every size, filled with them. The bunches are posted on the baby piano, even at the large windows with Las Vegas in the backdrop. It's the wee morning, and the sky is heavy with lilac and the lightest shade of blue. With the coming of dawn, the casino has lost its bright lights. Though, there are still scatters of people below.

"Yuri made sure your favorite flowers were at that chapel, I'm using my accommodations here."

"Yeah, you almost bit his head off about it," I grin. "About everything. We had a lovely wedding, Vassili."

He places me down on my feet.

"You are beautiful, Mrs. Resnov." He nips at the smile on my lips. Then his mouth is against my forehead, whispering across my skin, "I fucking own you."

His erection firmly pressed against my tummy. I moan as his mouth returns to mine. We stay like this for a while, having all the time in the world to love each other.

"You are mine forever." Vassili's voice is luscious, low, with his Russian accent so thick and tasty. His teeth clamp down on my bottom lip. No longer nipping, but sinking in, as if he's going for blood to seal the deal. It hurts, I cling to him, concentrating on how his cock is digging into my abdomen.

I'm in a heady daze as Vassili steps behind me. One at a time, he unlatches the faux pearl buttons of my lace dress. His breath caresses along my shoulder blade as he moves slowly, meticulously. Then he pulls the dress down, careful to remove it from my stiletto adorned feet, one at a time. Next, he unhooks my strapless bra. My tummy flutters, craving sex with *my* husband.

Strong hands that have perfected the art of executing pain, glide along my tiny waistline. Vassili only moves fast as he hastily undoes the top few buttons of his shirt. I want to beg him to undress. Though it's rare to see him in a suit, he is so hot right now. I stop myself from imploring him to remove at least his blazer. The look in his eyes tells me he is consumed by unraveling me, his wife, for the very first time.

Vassili descends to his knees, kissing the contour of my pelvic bone while easing my panties down over my hips.

"I used to be obsessed with this ass." Vassili's voice breaks through the silence. Such a powerful damn voice that he could turn heads if people were watching. "Still am. But it's mine. All of you belongs to all of me, Zariah."

He cups one cheek of chocolate, bulbous flesh as I stand, legs wide. His fingers skimming along my crack. He grabs a good bit of it and squeezes. My pussy milks, trickling sticky wetness between my thick thighs. Now his words are inaudible, stark and tickling against the flesh of my anus. He's declaring his ownership again while nudging his nose against my ass.

The pressure is applied along the inside of my thigh. My stilettos resound against the marble as my stance opens wider. I place my hands along an end table. The floral scent of tulips is forced down my nostrils as a sudden surge of warmth presses against my tight hole.

"Vassili," I speak hesitantly. His ass fetish is my biggest fear.

"I'd never hurt you." His tongue slithers along the smooth, constricted ridges again while pawing a cheek. When he probes, I find my lower back is arching for it. My pussy is sopping wet, lips soaked, sugar trickling even more down my thighs. He strokes the curve of my back, I swivel my hips more. Damn, I've never approached a climax like this, no penetration. My tiny anus is no match for the stiff tip of his tongue.

"Fuck your pussy for me," Vassili tells me.

With one hand still planted on the table, I reach down between my thighs and seek out my treasure. Vassili's tongue slithers along my ass, twirling around the virginal apex. I press my fingers inside my body while nudging my ass against him. A crescendo of moans sweetens my mouth.

Groans come from Vassili. At this exact instant, there is nothing in this world but us. I am Vassili's pleasure, his everything. His voice is a million miles away as he encourages my orgasm.

I don't know it until Vassili is leaning against the table beside me. Large shoulders filling out his suit. Vassili pulls me up into a position that has me straddling his waist.

"My brown sugar," he says, clutching my hip. I swear my pussy juice is drenching into his linen shirt as my curvy legs fold around him.

"Zar, do you know how much fucking restraint I have tonight?" I glance into his eyes, darker than a fallen angel's. He wants to do bad things to my ass. I know he does.

"You can," I murmur. "I'm yours, Vassili. Do anything you like."

My feeble declaration is met with laughter, his large abdominals expanding and contracting against me. But unlike earlier, the fighter isn't laughing at me. I'm hugged tightly, his hard chest crushing against my lungs. A reminder of his strength, of the pain he could bestow on me if he chose to. He gently places me onto the bed.

The faintest sound of my blood pulsates as he starts to undress. First, his blazer that slides over ropy, long arms. When he gets to his button-down, I lick my lips as a plethora of tattoos come into view. My mouth is twisted into a half-smile as I lean back against the pillows. My gaze is glued to his glorious golden muscles. That bulging cock in his pants is finally unwrapped for me. Like a horny primitive animal, he begins to fist his swollen erection. His hungry gaze fucking me senselessly as he climbs into bed.

Vassili grabs my ass, pulling me down below him. The head of him slides along my swollen lips before he lines himself up. His cock spreads me open, impaling me with one long swoop.

"Shit," I growl deep in my throat, back arching. His balls smack against my ass cheeks. His hands dominate my breasts and curves as his hips thrust against me. Plunging all the way in, gliding back out and hitting my clit with his slobbery head. I buck against him, clawing my hands into his shoulder muscles. The stimulation of Vassili working his cock along the walls of my pussy and slamming into me causes wet friction of a sound. It's music to my ears. My Kegel muscles clamp his erection as I cum all over us.

A yelp had hardly exited my mouth when suddenly I'm on top.

"Taste it." Vassili runs his finger down my cheekbone and nudges his chiseled jaw to his awaiting cock.

On hands and knees, I move down his thick frame. My mouth goes straight to his sugar-glazed cock that's twitching in anticipation. He lets out a guttural moan as I suck him hungrily, learning the taste of *us*. I love how sweet my pussy makes his shaft. Kneading his balls, I concentrate on coaxing his hot cum into my mouth.

"Zar." He tilts his head, and I climb back around his waist. Plunging down on him, I lean forward and kiss his lips, allowing our tongues to twirl together. My hips glide slowly and sensually around as I work his cock over with my pussy until I'm on the verge of coming.

Then to my hands and knees I go again. Back and forth, tasting his cock with my mouth and pussy until the sun reflects off the hotel mirrors across from us.

Finally, I feel him stiffening in my mouth. Savoring the milky taste of my honey along his ridges, I suck for dear life. I massage his balls, as cum jets across my lips. I hold it there, savoring it like a connoisseur of the finest wine. The white cream peeks out among my pink lips. I grin before my head tilts back and his precious seed glides down my throat.

"*E*very instant you cum, that pussy is sweeter..." Vassili whispered that to me, on the third or fourth round of my grinding on his cock, rousing me awake.

I'd lick the sweet, sweet taste of our sex from his cock and ride him, again. Eyes closed, mind murky from sleep and desire, I smile. For a second, I'm embarrassed at how vigorously I cleaned my cum from his cock, and then I'm happy for this gift. This beautiful gift of me loving him and him loving *me*.

Even half-asleep, a habit has my arm reaching out for Vassili. I grab for him in a daze of comfort and slumber, addicted to the tang of his dick after sex. Yet I'm met by soothing, woven covers, not my man. *My new husband.* Whimpering, I open my eyes. He isn't on his side of the bed. My wedding ring twinkles even though the curtains are drawn.

"Vassili," I grouse, "this bed is too comfortable."

I start for the living room when I hear Vassili speaking on his phone. The call is on speaker, but he and the male he's talking to are speaking Russian. Vassili's facing away from me. He's in a low seated chair, hand at the back of his neck. He isn't much interested in the call, and the man on the line is carrying much of the conversation. I walk around him to check on him until I hear him say, 'Anatoly.'

I almost trip over my bare feet. He's speaking with his *father*.

Vassili finally snaps. His Russian words issued with such brute force, each one punctuated slow, hard and deadly. Seconds later, he's pressing the phone off and tossing it toward the couch across from us.

"Good morning, baby," I begin, not sure if I should kiss him or keep my distance. "That your dad?"

He grunts. "Dah."

"Is everything alright?" I bite my lip.

"Of course."

"Does he know that we've married? Vassili, talk to me."

The long planes of his shoulders rise. "Dah, Zar, he knows."

"So what was all this about? Do I honestly have to fish for answers from my husband?" I place a hand on my hip, wishing I had the height advantage of looking down on him. Something to intimidate him, because there is no emotion on his face. Vassili has always been virtually unreadable. Uneducated on the Russian language, I have no leads.

"Come, come." Vassili points to his lap, and I sit down on him. "We aren't even man and wife, for twenty-four hours, Zariah. No pouts, no worrying. None of that bullshit about happy tears. No tears."

He clasps my throat and plants his lips onto mine. "You are the only good thing I have in this world, Zariah."

"Mmmm…" I moan in response.

"That mudak is aware we're married. Half the world does. Taryn posted photos everywhere," he says, and I can't tell if her actions have made him angry. Vassili massages my neck with his thumb. "Zar, the only thing you need to know about that mudak is he does *not* need to meet you, so he won't. You have my word."

Vassili and I honeymooned for an extra week in Vegas before heading to Atlanta. We ventured to Madame Tussaud's, where we were almost kicked out of the museum for pretending to be props. Vassili tried to weasel me into skydiving. I agreed only if he would go with me to see Thunder From Down Under. We settled on the Michael

Jackson holographic, followed by sky lining at an old casino off the strip. There were middle school kids in the line, so I couldn't chicken out.

———

The instant I set eyes on my mom as Vassili pulls the rental into the driveway, I've unbuckled. She's like a breath of fresh air, standing in front of Martin's stone and black-shutter home. I jump onto the concrete before he can brake.

"My baby!" My mom and I jump while hugging each other. She screeches. "You're married. My baby girl is married."

"Hi, Momma." I squeeze her tighter.

She pulls away, tears streaming down her face. "You said you have a video."

"Yes, we have a video of the ceremony. Oh, Momma, we can do it all over again for my favorite woman in the world."

She rubs at her cheeks. "No, I'm fine. I'm actually more surprised and so, so very happy. Zariah, you are a very hard thinker, like your father." I start to ask her not to compare me to my dad, but she happily chuckles. "So, either Vassili is the best man in the world, or he has brainwashed you."

Vassili doesn't take offense as he comes around the car. "Momma!"

"Child, I'm kidding." She hugs my husband saying, "My daughter never was one for the banana in the tailpipe. You'll make sure she takes the bar exam this July."

"Dah," he promises.

"Mom, it's only two months away. There's no stopping me now."

"Yesss, I love this confidence. All right, I cannot stop saying how happy I am for the two of you." Mom backs up, watching the two of us stand together. "Alright, we have to watch the video."

"Ma, you and Zariah go start that video while I have a chat with the man," my brother says. Dressed in khaki shorts and a polo, Martin comes around our mom from the doorway.

"Martin," I sigh.

He nudges his chin to the house, then his navy blue framed glasses land on Vassili. My husband kisses my forehead. "Go in."

"Okay..." I follow my mom up as Martin stuffs his hands into his pockets. I mouth, "What the heck did you tell him?"

"The truth," she whispers. We meander inside of the foyer, headed to the kitchen. The scent of my mom's famous chicken enchiladas calms my nerves. The casserole pan is on a woodblock in the center of the island, oozing with cheese and toppings.

I start to turn around, "Let me see what they're talking about."

"Oh, no, you don't." My mom plants her tiny frame at the exit. The bubbly aura surrounding her falters for a moment. "I guess my daughter has grown up and gotten married. Guess I have to stop asking you . . ."

"About Dad?" My face warms with sadness. I've always been a world-class snitch for my mom. She tormented herself by asking me to stay with Maxwell for the last few years in high school.

Mom perks up. "You know what? The two of you have something I never saw in us. Let's eat and watch the video."

I cock my head. My parents have been divorced for years. But I feel like my love life is pushing her in the right direction. "You made guac?"

She grins. "Girl, you don't even have to ask."

We move around the kitchen. Mom grabs sour cream

from the fridge, with other necessary condiments. I head for the plates. Then we both turn around when we hear the front door close. Both men are holding a conversation at a respectable level while headed to the den. Kissing my teeth, I pivot on my heels and head to the granite island. Part of me is tempted to listen to the guys, the other part of me is content that Mom seems over Dad.

My mom laughs. "Zar, I'm sure your brother is doing what brothers do. Stop analyzing it. I had a good first impression of your husband despite his tattoos. I suppose, now, despite how muscular he is in the flesh…"

I grumble under my breath as her imagination runs rampant.

"But," my mom accentuates the word while picking up the tray with a pitcher of iced tea and glasses. "Vassili must know that you have me and Martin to back you up."

"Only you and Martin?" I smirk.

We head into the living room where Martin and Vassili are talking. Both men arise from the leather couches and the conversation shuts down.

As paranoid as my mom is, her gaze ping-pongs between the two. She asks, "Where's my grandbaby?"

"Rochelle went to feed him," Martin answers.

"Hmmm, we need more grandbabies. This house isn't loud enough yet," she chortles. I breathe freely as my brother finally offers a smile that tells me everything will be okay. Of course, I know it will. I love Vassili but having him garner their approval is important to me too.

"Leave it to our mom," Martin shakes his head, "every question segues into babies."

"Well, I have a handsome son and lovely daughter, and your mates are just as attractive. So bring on the children. When can I expect my next one?" she questions, glancing around at all of us.

"I gave you two granddaughters and your first grandson. This conversation can't include me." Martin shrugs.

"Very soon," Vassili speaks up.

My cheeks burn. "Seriously?"

As we all have a seat, Mom claps her hands. "See, that's what I'm talkin' 'bout!"

"Mr. Resnov," Martin speaks up, his tone enough to sober up any drunk man. He asks, "What are your thoughts of a man who hits a woman?"

And here we are, back in left field! "Martin!" I hiss.

"It's okay, baby." Vassili pats my leg.

"No, that's not an appropriate question to ask anyone. It's like accusing and expectancy all wrapped in one shitty-ass bow," I argue. "Bro, you never were the overbearing type when I was a teen."

Martin continues with a steady gaze on my husband, not offering me so much as a glance.

"First, I don't believe a real man would hit a woman," Vassili says. "Secondly, only a mudak who is offended by this question would be the sort to hit women. I am not."

Martin blinks before nodding his head.

Vassili reaches between us to grab my hand.

Later on, I corner my brother in the nursery. He places a stiff finger against his lips. "I just got the baby down."

My mouth grits, I whisper, "I should wake up Junior since you had the audacity to interrogate my husband. You're in HR, dammit, you aren't an asshole. It's not your M.O."

He grabs my arm and yanks me out of the room. "Wrong. Checking on my baby sister *wasn't* my thing when I was home. I can't apologize enough for leaving you and mom with that bastard years ago. Our dad hit mom from day one."

"Mom's better now," I murmur.

"I'm not. I grew up with a tick every time Maxwell's voice rose. I played every sport in the book to get out of that house and have a normal life. Then I had enough." Martin mentions the one time he snapped on our father.

"Vassili wouldn't..." I say, sadness on my face.

"Good. Zar, I interrogated him like he was interviewing for his dream job, but he didn't back down. You did well." My brother hugs me. He apologizes again to me for not having been my protector.

I smile. "Martin, I have all the protection I need."

While visiting my mother's side of the family in Georgia, Vassili learned the shuffle at a family gathering. Their acceptance of him was a pleasant surprise. We returned as newlyweds to Los Angeles. Our first stop is my father's house. Law terms are on my mind, and Vassili helped me study with flashcards on the plane.

Damn, was I wrong about love? My only claim to real romance in the past were music and books. He's more than a book boyfriend or even a multi-platinum R&B song.

He is everything. Through good times and bad. He makes for an awesome ear to hear my issues. My study buddy. I smile, walking up the slate steps in front of my home. Vassili follows me, carrying a few large empty containers in his hands for some of my clothing. As I unlock the frosted glass door, I say, "Um, I'll search out my father. Please drop those off in my room."

I've got to run interference and have a quick chat with my dad. Vassili nods and heads upstairs.

With a huff, I saunter down the sconces-studded hallway. Maxwell was vague during our conversation about my marriage. I want to ensure that he hasn't lost his only daughter, which is exactly what he said. His tone was melancholic while congratulating me.

"Dad," I call out passing the formal sitting room and kitchen.

"In my office," he says.

I place a smile on my face. A respectable smile. It shouldn't be confused with the megawatt grin I've adorned since Vassili and I 'jumped the broom.'

When I step inside the room, my dad is relaxing. His face is tilted upwards to the chandelier, mouth dragging ever so softly on a cigar.

"Hey, Dad," I attempt to gather his attention. He knows full well that I'm not a fan of smoking.

"This was to be my celebratory cigar for winning the election." His gaze never meets mine; O's continue to ascend.

"I'm sure you have an entire box of Cuban's."

"I do. I also had intentions of purchasing a box solely for your wedding. To smoke with the groom and his groomsmen." He sits straight, smashing out the cigar with a frown. I feel Vassili approaching as I lean against the doorframe. I place up a subtle hand to my husband while offering all my attention to my father.

"I'm sorry you weren't invited to the wedding, Dad."

Maybe he doesn't hear me, but Maxwell continues with his story regarding cigars and the groom.

"I'd pat the man's back, congratulate him on the fortune of engaging such a *sophisticated* young lady. But you gave yourself to that communist scum, a *Resnov*."

The sneering makes me cringe. My husband's blood is boiling. He stands outside of Maxwell's line of vision. I hurry to find my voice.

"Dad, do me a favor and get to know Vassili."

"Get to know him?" Maxwell arches an eyebrow, grunting

while rising. "No, thank you, Zariah. You're the one who isn't well versed on the fucking *Bratva*—brotherhood. Hijacking weapons, extortion, drugs, and human trafficking. Sleeping in the bed of the Mexican cartel. I suppose the billion dollars a year in loan sharking might cloud your mind or you haven't even done your homework. They're a secretive family, but this is all common knowledge."

In shock, I blink as my father continues to flay my character.

"Or did he only introduce you to the Resnovs in banking or those who run state companies in Russia? Doesn't matter. The two of you must go. I'll have movers gather the rest of your things. The security system has a new passcode. Word to the wise, the locksmith will be here by evening."

My mouth drops, I stare at him in horror. "Are you serious!"

"I love you, Zariah. It's disconcerting what you've done. I need time for *it* to penetrate that my daughter has spoiled herself for a piece of shit!"

My lips are hardly set for a comeback when Vassili stands before me.

"Take your time, Mr. Washington," Vassili grits. His tone lethal, low. "Evaluate yourself as well. Why exactly did Zariah choose to marry me without so much as calling you first?"

"Baby!" I call after Vassili as he storms away. With a grumble, I turn to my father. "We are in love. It was a spur of the moment. But, dad, don't ever talk negatively about my husband again. There will be no more warnings. Go ahead and change all the locks you'd like."

Maxwell stares straight through me.

Outside, I hear Vassili talking. Who is he speaking to? When angry, he is either mute or beating someone to within an inch of their life.

Not talking.

"Phil was surprised, too," Maxwell mumbles, returning to his cigar.

Damn, I almost slip on the marble, arms out to steady myself in the foyer as I hurry to the door.

"So you're the man fortunate enough to marry Zariah?" Phil's facing me, slimy smile slapped on his mouth. Vassili's back is to me. Muscles stacked purposefully.

"Get the fuck out my face!" Vassili saunters down the curved pathway. His words were literal, Phil almost falls in the grass while moving out of the way. My husband doesn't stop while heading for the Mercedes.

"You refuse to address me? I'm Phillip Everly the fifth!" Phil scoffs. Then he steps toward me as I start down the pathway.

"Stop!" I push away from Phil.

"I'm the man who had her first." Phil's arm is heavy around my shoulders as Vassili comes back up the steps. "Actually, I only had those lips. What? Now, you're interested in a conversation. I tried to shake your hand."

Phil removes his arm from around me as I push at him. "All I strove for was to shake the hand of the man who fucked her first. Or did you sleep with this thug before leaving for college? Was she spoiled already?"

Vassili's hands ball into fists.

"You can't fight him," I argue with my husband as he simmers in silence. He picks me up and sets me aside.

"Hit me, you animal," Phil's voice rises as I beg Vassili not to hit him.

"Bitch," Vassili utters his first word, low, Russian accent thick. "If I hit you, *your fucking spine dislocates.*"

His fist raises. I grab hold of his forearm, my fingers not connecting, not a good grip at all. I'm almost lifted by the sheer strength of his arm. Vassili seems to be in a trance while I try to talk to him. My right heel slips from the slanted steps, wedges into the rolling grass. Losing my grip of his bicep, I start to fall.

"He hit her!" Phil shouts.

The cloud covering Vassili's face wanes as if he hadn't even noticed I was here before. He catches me. "Zariah," he mumbles as Phil shouts about him hitting me.

"No, he didn't!" I screech. There's a look of hurt on Vassili's face that I haven't seen since our first night together. Man, how I had I ever misjudged him.

Something is off about my husband's demeanor. Vassili picks me up. With all my curves, he's always picked me up with ease. This time, he holds me loosely, like he's afraid to hurt me. Almost too careful, as one would be with a newborn.

Maxwell is at the door.

"He hit her!" Phil lies.

My dad sputters, "Place my daughter down!"

My husband turns to glare at him before carrying me to the car.

"Zariah, you are my daughter!" Maxwell starts down the stairs.

"I'm sorry," I tell my husband as he places on my seatbelt. Aware that my dad brought Phil here for this very purpose, I repeat, "I'm sorry."

Vassili doesn't say a word. My body is alight with fear at the thought of him not talking to me.

The drive to Vassili's beachfront home is met with infinite silence. In the past three months, he has become my everything. I'm thrilled with his happiness. The softening of his attractive, carved features brighten my soul. Genuine, good smiles all for me.

Now, we should be completing our honeymoon with him carrying me over the threshold. I expect him to walk away, to leave me in the garage alone. But Vassili gets out. He comes around to open the passenger door. I hold my breath, praying we can return to our raw goodness. We're still on our honeymoon!

He massages the back of his neck. "Why'd you stop me from bashing that man's face in, Zariah?"

"What?" My eyebrows furrow. His speaking was so out of the blue that I hadn't anticipated it. I wrap my mind around how unapproachable Vassili was while Phil aggravated him. He seemed a billion miles away from me.

He keeps his distance, not offering a hand as I get out. He asks, "Why'd you stop me from bashing that *piz'da's* face in?"

"Vassili," I scoff, searching my husband's eyes for some form of sentiment. "What? Do you think I have feelings for him? Was it the bullshit he mentioned about me giving him…"

His thumb nudges against my chin making it impossible to glance away from him. My mind is muddled with thoughts, and I need to think. But our eyes lock.

"*Nyet!* This is about him not respecting my wife. I don't give a fuck what you two have ever done as long as it was consensual. You could never one-up me in that regard, sweetheart. But I'm your husband. You stopped me from handling it. You made me look like I…"

There's an imaginary vice grip over my throat. "You're angry with me?"

My tone is so low that I'm not aware he heard me until Vassili slams a hand down onto the roof of the car.

"Nyet!" His shout vibrates through my chest. And then he steps back from me. "I apologize, Zariah." The fighter's voice lowers to its usual tantalizing accent. "I didn't hear half the words that mudak said. I saw him touching you.

You pulling me away when I should've handled the situation."

"Aww, baby." I reach out to him. There's a fence between us that was never there before. An invisible force field is between myself and the fighter standing less than two feet away from me.

"I apologize, Zar. But where I'm from, a man touches your wife or looks at her oddly, he is handled."

"I think my dad brought Phil over. They expected you to overreact. Your hands are registered. Vassili, your entire body is registered. You can't fight civilians. Why play into their trap? Vassili... Vassili..."

"I did nothing." He hikes his leg over his Harley. "I'll be back."

"Please, don't let the idiotic—" the engine drowns my words out.

"I love you," Vassili mouths. He places the helmet over his head. With that, he pulls out of the garage.

Tears sting my eyes, I reach over for the keys to the Mercedes.

Damn!" I frown, Vassili has them. I pick up my purse, head to the garage door leading into the house and open it. Making quick work of turning off the alarm, I then sink against the wall and onto the floor.

I dial my father. It goes straight to voicemail. "Dad. Grow. Up. I am not your little girl anymore. What did you expect?" I seethe. "I swear, if you do anything to try and ruin my relationship with Vassili, I will never talk to you. And FYI: I married a good man because he is *not* like my father!"

My hands shake as I hang up. *He better listen to this entire voicemail too!*

23

VASSILI

Rarely does my mother cross my mind. My tattered knuckles are white from gripping so hard against the handlebars. Fuck me, only for this girl. Only for Zariah will my stomach become tied into knots over emotions long ago forgotten. And for fuck's sake, I spent so long forcing these memories from my mind. I didn't even have hair on my balls when my mother ran off on me and Sasha. She left us with one of Anatoly's bitches, who was pregnant with his third or fourth son.

I saw images of *her*, and I shut down. It took the grace of God for me not to murder those two mudaks. On the drive from Mr. Washington's, I concentrated on removing the images of my mother from my mind. I tried not to give a damn about the woman who at the very least could've taken six-year-old Sasha with her.

She was too selfish, too fearful of Anatoly. Yet she left Sasha.

The bitch left me too, but I survived. Sasha didn't.

When pulling into my garage, I kept thinking, *Make this*

about Zariah. My beautiful wife had already apologized for the shit she hadn't even slung.

Now, I hit Pacific Coast Highway. The wind slaps against me at top speed. Palm trees blur by. The light turns yellow. I gun the engine and veer around a van which was prepared to stop.

Then there's red and blue flashing behind me. My middle finger itches, but I don't toss it up. Grumbling at myself at allowing silly emotions to dominate, I slow down. My eyes search for a place to pull over.

As I ease the motorcycle to the curb, a cop's commanding voice blares through the speaker. "Take off your helmet. Remove the key from the engine."

I do as told. As an immigrant, it's a safe way to go about things.

"Now, hands up and get off the bike. Don't turn around."

I've gotten speeding tickets before. Something tells me these pussies haven't stopped me for doubling the speeding limit.

———

Not one single ticket was given to me. I asked for my phone call, one single call. No response. I asked for a lawyer. The mudak eyed me like another species. Now, I'm sitting in the middle of the precinct. I expect to see the chief strolling in, but another black man in a power suit eyes me. He's on the opposite side of the partition, he'd just been walking by. He stops and speaks with the idiot cop. Then he's buzzed and the short door opens.

"Mr. Resnov."

"Billingsley," I glance at Samuel Billingsley, the man my wife admires. While we were on a flight from Las Vegas to

Georgia she spoke of Samuel. She told me the motherfucker was the reason she chose law.

"Why're you here?"

I shrug. "Because I'm Russian."

"Shouldn't you be honeymooning with Zariah?"

"You found out we were married?" I shake my head, I'll be blamed for everything.

"She called me the morning after speaking with her mom. Zariah has very nice things to say about you."

"Same for you," I counter.

"So, why aren't you at home? I spoke with her this morning. She said her flight landed safely and that she'd return to the office at the beginning of next week. I expected you two to be holed up for another few days."

My frown deepens. I'm not speaking of my relationship with him.

"Listen, Mr. Resnov, you're more than aware of who I am." He speaks as if this should have me wide open like a cunt, telling him everything. After an uncomfortable moment of silence, Billingsley asks, "Have you gotten your call?"

"Nyet."

"One of those stellar Resnov lawyers on his way?"

"What's it to you?"

Billingsley paws at his goatee in contemplation. We will get nowhere because I don't trust him. "Zariah, that's what. I love her like a daughter."

"Well, her pops is doing a good enough job advocating for her."

He laughs. "I see, Maxwell is the reason you are here."

"I was speeding, too," I add for the obvious reason.

"Give me a second." He walks toward the uniform cop who brought me in. They speak, yet he leads the conversation.

The cop and Samuel Billingsley step over to me. The cop pulls his tab from his front pocket and mumbles.

"You'll still have to get the bike from the impound."

"Well, if I wasn't in family law, I'd tell him to sue as well," Billingsley argues as he follows me and the uniform cop to the exit.

Once outside, I pause and nod my thanks.

"You're very broody," Samuel says. "I can't fathom what Zariah sees in you, but she's smart."

I lift a brow, my body language enough to ask why Samuel followed me out.

"I'll drop you off at the tow yard and give them a piece of my mind as well."

"Nyet," I back away. This is a situation I got myself into by thinking of my mother. Hurts me to my core, when I mumble, "Thanks."

"Vassili," he says, "Call me Samuel. I'm positive we will run into each other on various holidays. You'll have to give Zariah a party for passing the bar. Connie will want to help."

I nod. "She will this July."

His head bobs in enlightenment, then he points at me with a smile. "It must be the confidence, what she sees in you. Good luck with her father. Maxwell is a snake."

I place two fingers to my temple and salute him in response.

At home, a strange aroma wafts through the air. I hold a bunch of white tulips for my wife. Zariah is in an apron, her eyes widen as she sees me. She doesn't run to me as usual, no hug. There's hesitancy in her gaze as she points to a recipe on her cell phone screen. "I'm making stroganoff for the first time.

Vassili, I'm sorry for my dad and Phil's actions."

"Please don't apologize." I huff. *Keep that woman from your mind, Vassili. You'll cherish Zariah and you'll be a good man.*

Sounding fake as fuck, I add, "I brought flowers."

"My favorites."

She places the flowers down. Her demeanor is questioning, asking me why I reacted the way I did. "There's never been a brick wall between us before, Vassili. The only thing that I'm in fear of, is you not touching me."

Brushing my lips across her forehead, I silently warn myself, *be a good husband.*

"Touch me, Vassili. Please…" her murmur is tiny and filled with the innocence I've loved about her since day one.

She pleads again. I scoop her up into my arms and turn off the pot. She's imploring me to fuck her body as I carry her to the bedroom.

I'm good at this shit. Fucking her until her throat has this sexy rasp to it.

But at being a husband?

Maybe I'm more than confident in the octagon, but I've got fears, too…

24

VASSILI

July

"This is your office," Zariah says, all that ass strutting left to right as she steps inside of the room at The Red Door. "Now, I see why you reached inside, grabbed a hoodie for me and came right out. Boy, there is nothing in this room to distinguish it from belonging to *the boss* to an oversized janitor's closet."

Biting the inside of my lip, I nod. What the fuck can I say? There's a desk, a very comfortable chair that still has the fresh leather scent. Nothing else.

"Zariah, your bar exam is at the end of the week." *Let me handle my shit.*

"Do you care about your business?" She places a hand on her hip. A few beats pass. "Vassili, baby, you've gotten rid of Malich's ladies and the illegal activity that occurs at the bar. Do you want to keep The Red Door or sell it?"

218

"Nyet, I'm not selling it." *This was Sasha's place. May not have been a lounge in her dreams, but this is all I have of my sister.*

"Then will you start giving a damn about it?" she reaches up to stroke my face.

"I have a fight I'm practicing for. Maybe," I begin, planting kisses on her face between every word. "You can review everything once you've returned from Sacramento."

"Nope. You're a master at persuasion. However, while I'm away taking the exam, it's crunch time for you, as well. Besides, you haven't even agreed to the match. But, as your wife, I'd love to help read over a few of your documents until you hire a manager."

"Yuri?' I cock an eyebrow.

"Allow me to disregard your last remark. How about this, you tell me what you love about this place. If you love it, I'll love it and we can team up to get everything in working order."

We've already chatted enough about Sasha at Urban Kashtan. It took everything in me to speak, and I won't do it again.

I reach around, hands owning every inch of her ass and place her onto the empty desk.

"I love how beautiful you look in..."

"Stay on topic—"

Her mouth is sweet, lips pillow-soft as my tongue goes deep. *Yeah, that's right, shut up, beautiful.* How can I explain to Zariah that The Red Door is sentimental to me without sounding like a bitch?

Nothing comes to mind.

I tease the left side of her mouth, recalling how sweet her brown skin tastes. Then I kiss the corner of the right side of her mouth, enjoying the sheer act of fucking with her. Beneath me, Zariah's trembling body motivates my cock to grow harder.

I reach down and grab my dick. Her chocolate brown orbs brighten with desire, and she licks her lips.

"We can stray now, Vassili. Mark my words—"

Again, I kissed her mouth. A symphony of moaning and sighing comes from Zariah's lips as our tongues slither around. I work my buckle with one hand. She yanks me closer with her legs around my waist.

KNOCK. KNOCK.

"Damn," I curse against her lips.

"*Plemyannik*—nephew?" Malich calls. "Everything is finished," he says in Russian.

"*Khorosho*," I reply. Shit, the door opens fully before I can tell him that I will step out.

Zariah has already hopped down from the desk and pulled at her tight skirt. Though she's decent, I stand in front of her.

"Oh, is that your wife?" he speaks in our native tongue and then corrects himself with an apology to her for doing so.

"Dah," I reply.

With a soft touch to my back, Zariah comes around me. "I'm okay, Vassili."

Malich smiles at her. "A blind man can see why Vassili keeps you all to himself."

"Oh, thank you!" She shakes his hand. "You must be the infamous Malich Resnov."

My lungs fill with air. Aside from Yuri, Zariah hasn't met a single person in my family. I planned on keeping it that way, for her peace of mind.

He nods. "Can I invite you to dinner? Vassili, will you spare her for the night to visit with your cousins, their families and me? Zariah, it's a loud place, but I promise the food is good."

I reply, "Nyet. Tonight won't work."

"Yes, of course," Zariah speaks up.

"Okay," Malich backs toward the door. "Vassili, you should take my office. The computer is *clean* of anything other than the lounge business, okay?"

"That's sounds great. Baby, now you can learn how to review files and all that good stuff," Zariah says.

I'll have a general manager by the end of the week. The office door closes, and my wife turns toward me. Hands clasped together before her, she says, "Okay, game plan. Dinner with your family, tonight. Tomorrow night, I'll return to studying. While it's crunch time for me. Vassili, you can dedicate a couple of hours to reviewing the dynamics of your business."

"You'll eat dinner with my family?" Folding my arms, I lean back against the desk, my mind stuck on the basics. I threatened Anatoly's life for asking to meet her the morning after our wedding. He hasn't called since.

"Your uncle sounds charming. Nevertheless, I'm not an idiot, Vassili. I'm sure he's got blood on his hands, but I've married you."

"You haven't married into my family, Zariah." *I won't let Anatoly anywhere near you, no matter what.*

Now my wife is in the position to shut me up. She paws my jaw. "I have the feeling that you and your uncle have a very good relationship. Malich speaks highly of you. When you're ready, you can tell me about your last conversation with Anatoly."

My lips spread into a thin line. Shit, my wife is smart, *but I won't be talking to her about Anatoly.*

"You want to go through with this?" I ask, removing the extra helmet softly from her head. I place it down and smooth over her freshly ironed hair.

"It's too late to turn back." She glances around at the clay water fountain and tropical plants in Malich's driveway. The entire lot is so filled with vehicles that the wrought iron gates wouldn't even close.

I eye her to make sure.

"The ride helped, too, but I love you and despite how disparate our individual families are, it's only right that I acquaint myself with yours."

"Okay, Zar." I place my fingers through her silky tiny ones. Her head kisses my shoulder as we walk toward the door.

It bursts open. Malich is holding my fat baby niece in one arm. He kisses the chubby bundle and says, "Albina, your *dyadya* came."

"Dy..." Zariah begins to pronounce the word.

"It means uncle. Come, come," he ushers us in. "I've made soup. The best you'll ever eat."

"Soup? Zariah hates Russian soup." I pull Albina into my arms while murmuring how beautiful she is.

"You hate our soup?" Malich clutches his chest. "Fuck, that hurts."

"I don't." Zariah gives me the evil eye.

He locks elbows with hers. "Come smell *my* soup and tell me your thoughts. No tasting unless you approve, okay?"

She stutters, "I..."

Malich carries the conversation, claiming the embarrassment I caused by telling the truth, which I knew he would. He brags about being the best chef while we start inside. People sit in overstuffed chairs, drinking vodka. Kids are all over the vast floor, playing games with each other. He introduces her to each one.

"I need a bigger house for all the family," he harps. Some raise their drinks as Zariah mentions how big and beautiful the house is.

"Yeah, we're on the good side of the street. Too bad it hasn't had new furniture since my wife died."

Malich has more money to burn these days. He'd rather fatten his family and friends' birthday cards. Little Albina's first holiday card made her a millionaire. The old man does nothing entertaining without the people he loves. After this party, he'll ensure our family, down to the youngest ones, have what they need and desire. He steers her into the kitchen. Since she's in good hands, I stop to chat with a few cousins.

I'm on my third shot by the time I search for my wife. More family are on stools around the marble island, but there's a crowd around the breakfast nook.

My wife is smack dab in the middle of women. Igor's wife, Anna and her sisters surround her. Malich eats up all the praise they have for his soup, from his position, leaning against the marble island. They down their shot glasses of vodka.

"Zariah, baby, I guess you're okay," I mumble.

"Yeah, this food is so good," she says of the mozzarella meatball soup.

"Get outta here, Vassili. You too, Malich!" Anna tosses a cloth in my direction.

"Drink! Drink! Drink!" They pound the table.

I've made it past the archway of the kitchen when I'm bulldozed. Igor's head slams into my ribs, arms around my waist as he tackles me.

"My *kuzen* is a *piz'da!*" He shouts as I'm slammed into the wall on the opposite side.

I slam my fists down onto his back and he lets up.

"You drunk enough, you dumb bastard?" I cuss him in Russian.

"Nyet, never." He shakes his fat head with a laugh. Igor is about fifty pounds smaller than his kid brother, Yuri. But shorter, so his pasty face is soft like a baby's.

He grabs the back of my neck. "You finally bring the girl around. She's hot as fuck."

My fist slams into his jaw before he can blink. He rubs it and clicks it back into place. Grabbing his crouch, he asks, "Vassili, why you afraid the girl would leave you for a real man?"

"Don't let Anna hear you, *glupyy*," another cousin shouts to him in a warning.

Igor tosses his hand as if he doesn't care, but Anna would beat the shit out of him had she heard. We head toward the wet bar. "So, everybody loves the girl."

"Dah." I nod, pulling out a shot glass for myself. This drunk idiot grabs one, and I shake my head. It's nothing though, he could be drunker.

"You know there's only one person that would hate the girl. And not Anatoly. Yuri told me all about how you thought Anatoly had a cop. Don't worry, I know you and Yuri keep secrets."

He leans into me and laughs. I shove him off. "I was up that night. My brat tried to keep your secret, and I hounded him. Stop worrying about Anatoly, your only problem would be Danushka."

"I'll break that cunt's neck if she ever came around my wife."

"Chill out, Vassili. Danushka is your sister." He pats my shoulder.

His brother, Mikhail, who stays out of family business

cuts in. "Danushka has not been a problem in years, Vassili. Don't listen to my brat."

Though Yuri is halfway joking about my half-sister, my frown increases a notch. Mikhail is the voice of reason, but he doesn't know Danushka like the rest of us. The bitch is a few days younger than me. The bitch thought my sister and I would disappear after my mother left. Doing so would've placed her in the position as firstborn. No matter how many times I've told her she can have the throne and shove it up her ass. She's missing one vital key. Anatoly isn't in the business of allowing any female to rule, regardless of how ruthless she is.

An hour later, my stomach is full, and I've played *durak* with my cousins Yuri and Igor and one of their friends. I decided to search out Zariah.

I'm halfway down the hall and get one glimpse of her smiling and talking before Igor shouts, "Come here, cousin. I want to win my money back!"

"Nyet."

"You afraid I'll win and take you for all you got?" He pours himself more.

"Brat, you will lose," Yuri yells at him.

"I've got little Albina," Igor argued, "the boys and Anna is pregnant. I gotta recoup my money…"

"Igor, no more for you," I point a finger at him. "Your ass is drunk enough to believe he'll be the victor. You forgot you're a diabetic."

"*Dah,* stop, Igor," Yuri add. The idiot should've stopped his brother a while back.

It takes a tussle for me to pry the vodka from his hands. And then I search out my wife again.

This time, her laughter isn't brightening the kitchen.

"Where is she?" I ask Anna.

"On the patio," she nods her head. "She's talking to Malich. Don't worry, Vassili."

I open the French doors nearest me and step out.

My uncle is mentioning how he used to be a physician before Anatoly pulled him in. Our grandfather was a dictator, telling all who was blood that they had to take part in the syndicate.

I start to speak up but realize Zariah wants to know more about me, *us*. In an attempt to keep her safe, I have alienated her from my entire family, even the ones who wouldn't wish her any harm.

"My big brother pulled me out of the hospital from saving lives. I stopped healing people to work for him," Malich tells her.

I lean against the wall and listen as she learns more about Igor, his wife and their children. Malich's other sons and then Sasha and I are mentioned, too. This is the part that breaks my heart.

"My wife and I never had daughters. My wife begged and begged Anatoly to allow us to bring Sasha to The States. We even promised to leave Vassili with him. Sasha was a good child, and my brother wanted nothing to do with her. My wife cried to him, but Anatoly said no. To this day, I regret not saying anything, but my brother isn't persuadable. He's a crazed mudak on a power trip. He could never love his daughter. He can never love a woman."

Zariah asks, "That's why their mom abandoned them?"

"Abandonment? No, sweetheart. Their poor mother never had a chance."

The pain of having her snatched from my hands is still there. I was seven. She had me in one hand, Sasha in the other. Tears so strong they stained the collar of her dress.

Anatoly said the bitch had to go.

She should've tried harder.

25

ZARIAH

"I apologize. But where I'm from, a man touches your wife or looks at her funny, he is handled." Vassili's words from our first big argument ring in my ears. He loves me and wants to protect me in the only way he can. He redirected his family from me until Malich knocked on his office door. And then I recall the look on his face after Phil showed his ass in front of my father's house. He must've believed Phil was humiliating me. Not goading *him* but shaming me.

My heart crumbles as Malich speaks of Vassili's mother. Her husband never laid a hand on her. He had his ways of embarrassing and shaming her in front of crowds. Tying her to a post in the middle of the street. The disgraceful sign that hung around her neck was abuse enough.

He had her head shaved until it bled. His crew *touched* her. That's what Malich says. Anatoly never laid a hand on her, too repulsed by his wife after she'd given him two kids.

Every one of his goons that hurt her, Malich's people retaliated against. Though it was met by amusement from his older brother. Plus, Anatoly had more thugs to spare when it came to roughing up people, so nothing helped.

I sat in disbelief as Malich spoke. I almost asked why he didn't take out Anatoly himself. Then Vassili had come out and said, "That's enough."

We left the get-together shortly thereafter. Now, hot torrents soothe my bruised ego as I wash my hair in the shower and reflect on the ride home. Though I rode on the back of Vassili's motorcycle, I was hugging a cement wall. All those muscles weren't my haven.

My fingers began to graze the knob when Vassili steps into the bathroom, fully naked. He opens the glass door and gets in. Though the shower offers plenty of room, his thick frame presses against my ass and back. His touch allows me to breathe for the first time in hours.

Vassili's hand glides across my tiny waist. His chin nestles in my thick, wet, coils of hair.

"Ask whatever you'd like to know about them, later."

"Okay."

His fingers skim up my breasts, squeezing my hardened nipples then trailing higher for my jaw. The slight pressure from his fingertips guides my face, so he can reach around and taste my mouth. "These fucking lips. I love these lips, Zar."

Vassili turns me around. While kissing me, his thumb sneaks into my mouth. Instead of caressing his tongue with mine, I suck at the ridges in his thumb. The vigorous way my mouth works is like I'm attempting to draw out his seed. The strands of my hair are tugged downward, and I kneel before my husband.

I work him sloppy, sucking him so good that his toes curl and those sturdy legs of his lock. I grip his ass cheeks, letting the crown of his cock bang and bruise my tonsils. Damn, I've never sucked a cock with this much ambition before. Now, I'm sucking for dear life like Vassili's seed is my sustenance. A jet of warm semen erupts, coating the roof of my mouth, my tongue and soaring down my throat. I drink him down to the last drop.

Vassili moves down to the travertine seat, water drumming against his skin. The mist shielding much of his contoured muscles.

"You next," he tells me, dark eyes filled with lust. I stand before him, placing my leg onto the shower seat, next to his hip. His fingers skim up the inside of my thigh. Damn, I'm dripping wet. The flush of water on my skin masks the lust drenched from my pussy as he reaches out to lick the swollen folds. I angle my hip, he digs in, chopping softly at my clit and spearing my G-spot with his tongue.

Vassili squeezes my bulbous ass, his nose nudging my clit while he laps up my pussy like a rabid dog. My leg begins to shake.

His hand slams down onto it. "Steady, beautiful. Work those nipples, for me."

I bite my lip and tweak at my erect nipples. The action is like asking someone to rub their stomach, jump while reciting their ABCs backward. Vassili is a pro at screwing me with his mouth. He's fisting his cock. The miraculous shaft expands in length by the second. He groans in my nether regions. Then Vassili stands up, helping me place my leg back onto the floor. He presses me against the travertine wall. The cool tile soothes my hard nipples. A hard slap against my ass smacks with the sound of water as Vassili grips my ass cheek. My back arches and he squats somewhat before entering my pussy from behind. I clutched frantically at the wall.

"Fuck, shit, damn…" I scream, stars in my eyes at how perfectly he fills me up.

"Keep steady," he growls once more, hammering in and out of my body like a piston.

"Fuck me, Vassili!" I cry out, begging for more. His cock goes deeper, my moaning becomes raw.

He screws me until I'm spent, only to send a jet of cum inside of me before my body caves to weakness. Tonight, Vassili holds me in his arms, his ebony jewel. Gone is the feeling between us that he's unreachable as my hands skim over his tattoos. Sleep beckons me, and I forgot to ask about his mother and Sasha. Something tells me that it will be a while before he's willing to speak of them again...

October

I kick off my stilettos while sifting through the envelopes. My heart clutches as I read "The State Bar of California." Ice frosts my veins.

"Babe, it's—" I stop shouting and shriek. "Damn it, Vassili!"

I clutch the mail to my chest. He's upside down in the doorway of his gym room, completing curl-ups. "I'll never get used to this," I tell him.

"Stop being so scared, Zariah. Open up the—"

The envelopes go falling as I smack my hands over my lips while sprinting to the restroom.

"Baby, what the fuck?" He says, his large frame goes landing onto the floor.

He's on my heels before I even make it to the toilet. I release every bit of lunch into the porcelain bowl. My hair is gently pulled from my face. While I toss-up sushi, Vassili softly rubs my back.

When it's all completely expelled, my body weighs so

much that all I can do is settle onto the floor. My arm flops toward Vassili, as I beg, "Go away. I look like shit."

"Nyet, I can't do that." He grabs a face towel from the rack, wets it and wipes my face. "Zariah, what's wrong, baby?"

"Bad poki," I mumble, head in hands.

"Make a doctor's appointment."

"For what?" I ask, stirring into a seated position.

"Because I told you to." He scoops me up while I complain about my bad breath.

"Okay, okay." Vassili sits me onto the counter, then grabs a toothbrush and paste.

"Thanks. My test, go get it," I murmur before starting to brush.

He returns while my mouth is foamy and clean. I gesture for him to open it up. Vassili does as I ask. His dark eyes scanning the paper. He puts it down, mouth taut.

"Aw, no… I can't fail," I grumble. "You won your last match. I was supposed to pass, but I'm a fail—"

"Don't say that shit, Zar. No, baby, you aren't a failure," he says.

I'm half-listening, spitting out the paste and quickly pooling enough water to wash my mouth out. That damn test is right before my eyes. I grab up the paper, fingers poised to rip it into shreds. From the corner of my eyes, I notice that Vassili is offering one of those rare, gorgeous, devilish smiles.

"Damn it, Vassili," I pout. "We've only been married for half a precious year and you already get on my last nerve!"

He hugs me, "Congrats, Zariah."

231

26

ZARIAH

It's the first Friday in November. The last day for my
father to formally declare his intent to run for mayor. I
bite my lip, considering calling to remind him that he has
until noon to complete the process.

"Worried about your first tango in the courtroom?"
Connie inquires while stepping into my new office. The
tiniest one. Nevertheless, I am blessed.

I shake my head. "No, my client is a great father. It was a
shame I had to convince him that judges don't automatically
award children to mothers."

"Sheesh, that child's mother ..." she shakes her head.
"There are some awful black men out there, why try to ruin a
good one."

"Yeah, there are," I smile at a photo of Martin and his
junior on my desk. The background is neutral. It was the
only 5 by 7 left. My mom hogged all the Thanksgiving-style
photos in preparation for the babies' first turkey day.

Hey, did you ever make yourself a doctor's appointment
last month? Our accounting manager called in this morning,

saying something about Pokilicious. And here I had hoped you were pregnant."

"Ha!" I rise, gathering a few briefs for court. "Wouldn't that be my luck? At the commencement of my career?"

"Well, babies are cute."

"No, thank you," I reply. "Vassili added another submission under his belt and signed to Power Water. We are too busy."

T his evening, I have a celebratory bottle of wine in my hand. Though Vassili has offered to cook, I've learned that not all Russian food must have cabbage or a sour taste. Unfortunately, those are the two staples he lives by. He's put a frozen lasagna in the oven and is on the phone with his new restaurant manager when I come into the kitchen.

He rubs my hair away and kisses my forehead before returning to the conversation. I grimace as he talks into the phone. Vassili has the most *sensuous* voice with me. With others, his tone is concrete, scary.

In the bedroom, I sit on the accent chair and undo my stilettos. Then I grab my iPhone from my slacks and dial my father on FaceTime.

My thumb is already poised over the 'off' button. He pops up on the screen, releasing the cuff from the top button of his sharp linen shirt.

"Y ou didn't run for mayor?"

"No. It is nice though, to hear from my daughter other than the brief, token calls on the weekend."

"Well, once you're prepared to respect my choices you and I can return to more time. Besides, my husband wants

New Year's, Mom is a stickler for Christmas, so Thanksgiving is up for grabs."

"Will you attend alone?"

"The fuck she will," Vassili cuts in from behind me.

"Goodbye, Dad," I cut the call. After tossing the phone onto the bed, I glower at my husband. He leans in the doorway, muscles on display.

Something in me is itching to argue, so I snap, "When there's no testosterone involved I'm a relatively good debater. Just won my first case. So, let me toss this out into the universe. How about you having faith in my ability to deescalate an argument?"

"Have you ever considered distancing yourself from Maxwell?" He paws at the scruff along his chiseled jaw. "Zariah, you don't know your father, do you?"

"He has his faults."

"Have we had this conversation before?" His gaze narrows in thought, though I know damn well, Vassili is angry. He is more direct in our conversations than this.

"Whatever, Vassili. I'm sorry you distanced yourself from your father. You don't have to on my account. But I have this gut feeling. You wish I didn't talk to my dad. Hell, no!"

"Sweetheart, Anatoly is a very bad man. Before you, I've gone years without seeing him and couldn't give a fuck. We never had much of a relationship from the start. Sasha and I lived with one of his cunts. I mean we were fucking orphan squatters while the girl raised our half-siblings. Anatoly will never cross paths with you—just so we are clear. That being said, you need to reevaluate your relationship with your father."

I repeat his words about reevaluating in a sardonic tone. Yes, that sounds petty, but my hormones are working overtime.

"Our fathers are the same type of people, different businesses, Zariah."

My face contorts as I feel a sharp pain.

"What's wrong?"

"You, starting an argument for…" I pause, grimacing. "My father is annoying. You were ready to match him—Ouch!" My abdomen sinks in, I double over in the chair, "Vassili!"

———

Dark eyes sparkling with worry, he'd scooped me up and took me straight to the car. On the way to Kaiser hospital, I'd encouraged Vassili to calm down. The pain had subsided, but he wouldn't hear of it. I finally weaseled my way out of ER for Urgent Care. I'm seated on the examination table, dressed in those robes that show all your ass. My legs are dangling. Vassili is at my side. He already argued with the nurse about having to wait for a doctor when she took my vitals and a urine sample.

Now, my head kisses his shoulder and he says, "Zar, how are you feeling?"

"Baby, I already told you, I'm all right. Just a few cramps. Stop being so extra." I smile up at him.

A few minutes later, the door opens. In comes, Dr. Washburn, who has built rapport with me since I needed birth control to regulate acne. Her snow-white bob pops against her rich, dark complexion.

"Hello, Ms. Washington. Oh, forgive me, *Mrs. Resnov.* You're married and moving so swiftly, I love it."

"Yes, this is my husband, Vassili," I make introductions. "It was a spur of the moment."

She shakes his hand. "Well, congratulations, Vassili. Marriage, a new baby on the way. Some families wait years to welcome bundles of joy. I like your style."

"Fuck! She's *pregnant?*" Vassili asks. He then apologizes for cussing while pulling me into a bear hug. My body becomes numb.

"You two were unaware?" Dr. Washburn sighs.

I gasp for air. "I'm pregnant?"

"Yes, you are," my doctor grins. "You're most likely feeling mild tummy cramps which are a totally normal part of early pregnancy. Have you bled any?"

"Yes, yes!" I place my arms around my belly. *This is too soon.*

"Still, it may be nothing to worry about. Some women cramp, with a little bleeding when the embryo implants itself to the walls of their womb. But we will schedule you with an OB/GYN who can assist a lot more than I can."

"And prenatal vitamins?" Vassili speaks up.

"Yes, Vassili, I can write up a prescription for those, folic acid as well." Dr. Washburn mentions how 'eager' we must be to view our first ultrasound. She chats a few more minutes before excusing herself from the room.

Vassili stands up from the examination table by my side, he stands before me. I open my legs to welcome him closer. His hand clasps the back of my neck, kneading it, ever so softly. My eyes close on key.

"Look at me, baby," his low growl is soothing.

"But this feels so good." I sigh, complying with his request.

"Through every moment of pregnancy, Zariah, I will be there." He touches my womb. "You'll keep him safe—"

"Her," I correct. "Vassili, I was literally eating your words until then."

"*Him.* Every man needs a son first; to help keep his daughter safe. You'll keep him healthy. But I'll be there beside you."

"I know you will." My eyes brimming with tears. I laugh, "You sound like you're coaching me."

"I am. We have created a life, Zariah Resnov. Our children must be ten times better than us. That's where you and I come in."

My mouth seeks his. Our lips lock, tongues tasting and loving each other.

27

VASSILI

Christmas
Atlanta, Georgia

"Step past this imaginary line, I'll take you out," Zariah emphasizes each word. She points a stiff finger to the floor where the tile meets plush carpet in her brother's home. There's mistletoe hanging before us, but her gorgeous eyes rival mine when I'm in the cage.

"Why, I can't cook?" I raise my hands, my eyes smile for me. "Martin is making his famous peach cobbler. Everyone in your family is cooking. We're supposed to be a team, Zariah."

"Unh-uhn, you and I are a team when it involves this," she points to her still flat abdomen. "The kitchen is your haven for juicing. Not cooking."

"Okay, okay," I retrace my steps.

Martin is seated on his couch watching the basketball game. He chuckles. "I heard you yesterday morning working out at the crack of dawn. You should've cooked with me. My dish is already complete. It's safe to steer clear from these women. They're known to throw down in the kitchen and *throw out* anybody they don't deem worthy."

"She likes my breakfast, not the smoothies, but my syrniki's she can't get enough of." I shrug.

"That pancake thing? I think she mentioned it. She bragged about your uncle's cooking. I'd take one of your pancakes, but..." He gestures toward the women, "Every Christmas morning, I go hungry waiting for dinner."

"They're like wardens." I shake my head.

He nods. "The baby and my nephews will be up soon. The women won't bully us while opening gifts."

I rub my hands together in anticipation of watching Zariah's face as she opens what I bought her for Christmas.

A while later, a stampede comes down the stairs. Martin's wife's family bull-rush into their lavish living room, down the hall.

"If they break something, you have my permission to break a few necks." Martin grunts while getting up from his La-Z-Boy.

We all head into the room. As an Orthodox Christian, I celebrate Christmas on January 7th. So, today is all for my woman. We stand toward the edge of the all-white living room watching kids snatch from each other. Zariah subtly presses her ass against my groin. I plant my chin to the top of her head, wrapping my arms around her.

"Vassili, don't get too comfortable, I'm almost as spoiled as these children," she murmurs.

"I didn't have time between Vadim's to gift wrap your matryoshka dolls."

"Humph, dolls are for babies. I prefer favors, which sparkle in the sunlight. Besides, you opened your gift. The better I'm treated now, the more you'll love Ms. Claus *again* later." She winks.

"Okay. Let me see if there's anything left under the tree." I slap her ass, then head into the war zone.

"Girl," I gesture to one of the kids, seated on the floor closes to the tree. "Hand me the silver box."

"The tiny one?" the little girl sneers.

"Yeah, sweetheart, the *tiny* one with the bow on it." When she hands it over, I glower at her enough to send her shoulders jerking.

"Vassili," Zariah reprimands.

"Don't hate, sis. That's what she gets for having that mouth," Martin says. He and the girl's parents laugh as she settles down with another big box.

I step back over to Zariah.

"You aren't a nice person," she murmurs, lips spread in a smile.

"I am to you."

"Leave him alone, Zariah. Vassili will be broken soon." Martin pats his own daughter's shoulder. "Lord knows, my daughter tied me around her tiny finger. Vassili, you're in for some real trouble. Sons remind you to *live*. Daughters humble you."

"Yup." Zariah pats her slightly curved belly. "This is my gift to Vassili this year. A sweet slice of humble pie."

As they laugh at her joke, she settles down with the box. Her mom brags about it being the best size for jewelry while winking at me.

"Solitaire diamond earrings would be nice," Zariah says, pulling off the bow.

It's been years since I gave a fuck what someone else got for a holiday, let alone offer a gift. I recall how coy Sasha was opening a present I bought her one New Year's. Her big, gray eyes kept glancing at me.

"Big Brother, what did you do, what did you do?" Rings in my ears. She was too afraid to open the gift for fear that I'd joined the family business. Adamant that she'd rather have nothing at all than a gift bought in blood, she tried to shove it back into my hands.

"Keys!" Zariah murmurs in curiosity. Shit, I missed her initial reaction when she opened the lid.

"To our house," I reply.

"What? We have a *new* house! When? How? Where—"

"Child, your husband is a wise one," her mother says.

"Remember a month back when Taryn and Yuri dragged you around to those new homes."

Her hand fans at tears. "Oh, my God, Oh, my God…"

By now, silence engulfs the entire living room. Even the children have stopped terrorizing wrapping paper to watch us. My thumb strokes along a tear, gliding down her soft mahogany skin to catch it from falling. "Don't hyperventilate, Zariah."

"But Taryn," Zariah gasps, hardly able to speak. "Taryn was bragging about her dad *upgrading her!* Taryn's ass is always bragging. She kept asking me which room I'd make a nursery. Damn it, that girl elbowed Yuri something fierce when he mentioned a man cave that you'd like. Vassili, all the houses we saw were huge. Did you pick the one with the man cave?"

"Was that your favorite one?"

"Vassili!" Her hands tug at my bicep. "Tell me, please!"

"All right, all right. Taryn had it down to two homes."

"The one on Rivera Avenue and the one on Cherry Blossom Drive?" She crosses her fingers.

"*Yes!*" Her mom grins. "And *I* chose between the two."

"Which," Zariah clutches her chest. When I tell her, her

hips sway, lips in a sexy pout while dancing.

"Stop with all that twerking," Martin gags.

Zariah is in my arms in seconds. Planting kisses all over my face and declaring how much she loves me. In this instant, my world is consumed with her goodness. Sasha fades to the back of my mind.

———————

W e flew into Helsinki, Finland three days before the New Year. Since my father's hand is in the government, I chose not to get Zariah a visa to Russia. Man, I love my country, but I also don't need to be on his radar when we visit.

After checking into a hotel for the night, we wake up the next morning and catch a taxi to the docks.

"Baby, you see that ferry," I tell her as the taxi travels parallel to the port. Zariah nods, snuggling close to me. "We'll catch that to St. Petersburg and arrive late tonight."

My wife is only aware that this was a last-minute trip. This route is how we will get into Russia without her having a visa or my father becoming aware. However, sneaking her in does have its perks.

"Then it's the night train to Moscow?" She arches an eyebrow, recalling our previous conversation.

"Dah." I hold her close, hoping this isn't too much on her at fourteen weeks pregnant. As strong as Zariah lets on she is, she considers it an insult when I ask.

———————

S now falls outside of the train window at the station in Moscow. Zariah is transfixed by the view while holding a mug of coffee to her lips. Before taking a sip, she mumbles,

"Vassili, I'm freezing, and the heater is on 100. How many degrees is it out there?"

It's negative Celsius, and I'm not dumb enough to admit that. I rub my hands along her arms, which are covered in a thick thermal. "You don't want to see where your husband grew up?"

With a groan, her head falls back. "I keep psyching myself up to it. But I'm from LA, I was born wearing Uggs while it was a *freezing* 65 degrees."

I pick up the new goose puffer coat with fur-trim I bought her for this trip. "So you won't be wearing this?"

"Hell, yes! I haven't had anything from Saks Fifth since I left for college." She takes it and strokes at the fur, which matches the mahogany of her eyes.

I put on my navy pea coat, then tug at the strings of Zariah's ear flapped beanie. My forehead kisses hers. "Beautiful, tell me if you get too cold, we'll race back to the train. My baby is always first." I reach between us and caress her flat abdomen, before zipping up her coat.

With Zariah's head cuddled against my shoulder, we walk along the Luzhkov Bridge. The fencing spans the canal of the Moscow River.

"Babe, are those padlocks?" Zariah's breath puffs out in front of her. My girl was looking miserable and cold a minute ago. Every time I offered for us to return to the train, she'd shake her head. I was on the verge of forcing her back. Now, her eyes brighten as we near a special section of the bridge. Colorful padlocks are linked along the railing.

"Newlyweds do this." I try to sound interested in the act while explaining, "They put their names on padlocks. Then they secure them, and throw the keys into the water . . ."

"Let's do it! We've only been married a little over six months. Vassili, we're still new."

"As I was saying, they throw the key into the water. That's the only memory left after the city comes and cuts the padlocks off the next morning. Babe, not necessary."

"Pah-lezzzz, Vassili!" She tugs my arm.

"Okay, okay," I huff. At the Luzhkov Bridge, stalls are along the streets. The city has designated steel trees for padlocking. I point to one vendor cart and tell her, "Choose a lock, sweetheart. I'll see what good vodka the man has."

We stop at a stall. A rainbow of locks is on display for her to choose from. I turn to speak with the seller. He compliments my coat in Russian and won't shut the fuck up. For a few minutes, the old man chats me up.

"Zariah, choose one already." I turn around. My eyes scan the area. On my toes, I survey hordes of travelers and tourists.

"Vassili? Vassili!" Someone calls my name, in a vaguely familiar tone. I ignore it, searching toward the metal shrubbery of lock trees. Did she already scope out where she'd like to place the lock?

A hand comes down onto my arm. I grab the man's wrist, turn around, twisting his arm backward.

"Bol'shoy Brat—Big Brother?" He questions me, offering a confused smile as I frown. He's much younger, and a lot lighter. Pale like his cunt of a mother. Twenty-something, fresh-faced and not even filling out the tailored suit over his thin shoulders. Anatoly ordered his feminine sons to gain a higher education. They were to work their way into 'good' Russian government jobs. This is one of Anatoly's weasels.

Where the fuck is she? Is this a setup? Did our dad send my half-brother? My heart rate slams through the roof. As a professional sportsman, that shit never rises much. And the little bitch won't stop following me.

He asks, "How are you?"

Does that mudak have my wife?

I stop myself from attacking the simpleton. Anatoly is aware that I don't value most of my younger siblings' lives because of how he treated my mom. He wouldn't put his son's life in jeopardy. Yet, with each passing second, I'm paranoid that he's stalling. While moving down the next line of trees, with this motherfucker at my heels, I recall his name. "Grigor, *brat,* how are you?"

He grins. "Good—"

"Good? Okay, okay." Hardly addressing him face on, I shrug. "We get together soon, eh?"

The smile on Grigor's face fades. Has he realized that I'm seconds from backhanding him into the river? Shock and sadness mar his eyes. I'm not sure why he's surprised by my disinterest. As children, Sasha and I were tossed around like a sack of potatoes. We lived with his bitch of a mother a few times. She could hardly wait for us to trudge along.

He must've forgot that I never had the same good heart Sasha. I was never nice to him. Though I wasn't a bully, he should learn to read people's demeanor.

"Vassili, Dad would like to see you," Grigor stresses.

"The fuck should I care?"

"He's sick."

I shrug. Anatoly mustn't have been bluffing when harping about his illness the morning after my wedding. He'd asked to meet my wife. I threatened to crush his throat. Come to think of it, when I choked him last year, Anatoly didn't fight back. We always go blow for blow.

"*Ukhodi*—go away—Grigor," I shout as worry consumes me about Zariah. "I don't give a fuck about Anatoly. So, what does that tell you about how I feel about you?"

His pace falters. "Brother, why are you acting so..."

I stop searching, giving this mudak my attention. "You

stalling, Grigor? You fucking with me? Is Anatoly fucking with me?" I grip his collar and yank him so hard that my fists at his throat constrict his breathing. "Where is my wife—"

There's a shrill of screaming behind us.

ZARIAH

Have you ever been put in a situation where you know you should react? Like you've cussed at the bimbo on the movie for falling or seeking danger or some other idiotic act.

Smack dab in the middle of the pathway, my body locks down. Eyes widening, I scream to high heaven. Someone snatches my waist and I slam back into a body made of steel.

The taste of copper floods my mouth. I bit my damn tongue. My hands are held out to steady myself, though I desperately need to sit down. I turn around. "Thank…"

"You have a death wish?" A blonde says, with a deep Russian accent. Shades cover her eyes. She's the only one close enough to me. Though super tall in high heel boots, she is slender. I glance around. *Damn, was she that strong to yank me back?*

"Thank you." My mumble is almost posed as a question.

Her thin lips push into a smile. "You gotta be safe. No thanks needed."

I glance before us. The horse that came galloping down the passageway was so unexpected. A woman had screamed.

Now, a crowd is surrounding her. The horse's hooves had smacked her chest so hard she went flying back. And then the startled beast came toward *me*.

"Do you think she'll be okay?" I ask. When I glance back over, the blonde is no longer there.

Vassili is storming toward me from the opposite direction.

He grips my forearms. "Don't walk away without me acknowledging you, Zariah."

Still a little shaky, I push at his hands. "Don't manhandle me! I almost got run over by a horse!"

"What? That horse?" He glares down the street. Since he came from the opposite side, I assume he hasn't seen it.

"Yes, so I could use some concern, dammit. I was pulled to safety from..." I shake my head. Doesn't matter, the blond disappeared.

He rubs my cheek. "Sweetheart, I didn't know you'd left. You have to tell me. I can't worry about you. That shit kills me."

Clinging to him, I murmur, "I'm sorry. I'm okay now. But I told you that I wanted a better padlock. The woman next to us took me to another vendor. You grunted in response."

"I don't grunt."

"You do." I lift my shoulders and mimic his sound. His damn muscles look like they weigh a thousand pounds when he grunts.

"Okay, Zar, we are in a different country. Unless I say yes or no, you cannot go off with anyone."

"The lady had a Southerner accent, Vassili, a stroller and two other kids. I had no idea I'd be in danger." I stop trying to argue, aware that it's hormones. "I love you. Can we symbolize the permanency of our union now?"

Reaching up on my toes, I kiss him. He's still so intense.

His arms wrap around me, and he takes a long taste of my lips. Moments like this remind me of how loved I am.

———

A s the day passes, we head to lunch. Vassili's frown has dimmed. Besides the cold, I'm enjoying myself.

"You're too serious, Vassili." I glance at him as we meander through the Red Square. "The Kremlin is such a wonderful sight. But, *this is how you look.*"

"Oh, you're attempting that awful accent again?" He almost smiles.

I'm about to tease him about it when I gasp. There's a statue behind him of a man bound in chains. "That's at The Red Door."

"Dah." He nods.

Vassili is slow to open up to me. Unsure what to do, I burrow my head next to his neck, take a hopeful inhale of his intoxicating scent. Saying a silent prayer that he'll tell me more, I weave my fingers through his larger ones as we walk.

After a while he says, "The statue was Sasha's idea."

"Hmmm…" I glance up, curiosity in my gaze. How can I coax more out of him?

"Sasha always thought she'd own a restaurant. She had a vivid imagination. She declared this exact statue would be in the center of her restaurant. Being that I can't cook, I tried to do the next best thing with the lounge."

Vassili and I continue to walk around. The sun had long ago descended, the air is crisp; soft snow falling as he tells me about his sister. I never knew such humility existed. I laugh as he talks about her saving a kitten. He'd explained that the furry ball turned out to be a baby Eurasian lynx, an endangered species that poachers had kept for shows.

"Can you tell me a little about your mom, Vassili?" I ask.

His body tenses at my side. He mumbles, "I never needed to remember her."

"Maybe she's thinking of you?"

"That's impossible."

I cradle my arm around my abdomen. "Vassili, I'm having your baby. You said she abandoned you. Malich said Anatoly forced her away. Give me something."

"She's dead, Zariah." Vassili stops walking. "My father didn't just drop her off at Motel 6. He forced her to her knees and placed two slugs into her dome."

"Oh…"

"He thought she'd moved on. She isn't running around Russia searching for her boy and girl like she had in the past. No need mentioning her again, Zar. We have kids to raise. I will not be my father and you will not be anywhere as… anything like her."

I offer a bittersweet smile. Somewhere deep down Vassili can't get over his perceived abandonment. He has years of pain, and I have years to wash it all away. I rise on my tippy toes, wrapping my arms around his neck. I sigh while kissing him until he leaves me breathless.

29

ZARIAH

April

Vassili and I are a month shy of married for a year. We're content making up for time lost. Once in a while, I contemplate our calls and texts while I attended college. Why hadn't I given him the time of day sooner? Shame on me for not cultivating this love.

I'd been young, focused and sadly, afraid of love. My parents as models might as well have blown my depiction of love to smithereens. Now, my belly has grown large, at seven months, and there is nothing that can stop our love.

Aside from this juicy cheeseburger from Fatburger that I'm currently inhaling. It ain't the baby fat size either. I can hardly breathe from the physical torment I endured while running upstairs. At the sound of Vassili's motorcycle entering the garage, I hightailed it. He's home way too soon. I hobble into the Jacuzzi tub of our master bathroom.

Please God, let Vassili stay downstairs. I feel like a dirty little cheat. My prayer fades. I eye the cheeseburger, contemplating how to shove the rest into my mouth. Enjoying calories is the ultimate form of disloyalty when my husband needs to make weight.

"Mmmm..." I giggle and moan. A spurt of kicking goes off in my tummy. "Enjoy your food, Natasha."

"Zariah," Vassili calls from down the hall.

"Um-hmmm, be right there." I down a big, juicy bite and grab a few Rally's French fries. The delicious coating of crisp salt, got kind of cold while waiting in the Fat Burger line.

"Zariah, baby, we've got a problem." His voice nears.

"Alright, I'm on the toilet. It's scary—I wouldn't advise you to come in." I frown in disgust at my choice of words. The French fries go behind a large candle. Then I shove the cheeseburger into a tiny wicker basket for bath salts and oils. Grabbing the marble ledge, I start to get up. "I'm com—"

"You are full of shit," he says, thick muscular body in the doorway. "You're in trouble."

"No, I'm not." I freeze, eyes wide. Are specks of salt on my face? Daring not to touch my mouth, I sink back into the tub. "I love this bathtub. Do you know how many times I've bragged that my husband bought me a house for Christmas? The bathtub is the best!"

He folds his beefy arms, it's no longer intimidating to me. I know his secret. All those muscles were meant to love and protect me. "Okay, Zariah, you got into the bathtub. With no water in it?"

I nod.

"While fully clothed?" He cocks an eyebrow.

"Natasha loves it when I sit in here and read her a book."

"What book?"

I grab the ledge. "Damned this pregnancy brain!"

"Allow me," he walks over. "Yeah right, 'pregnancy brain.'

You chew my head off if I say you've forgotten something. But this is cute."

Eyebrow cocked, I ask, "Shouldn't you be sweating pounds?"

"Dah. However, I've texted and texted asking how the painting is coming along in the nursery. Intuition warned me to drop by. I don't trust my wife."

"You think I'm cheating?" Though joking, I exaggerate the words while pointing at all this belly!

"Eating cheeseburgers and fries, a day before my weigh-in. You had better luck having a man in the tub."

"I'll keep that in mind," I grunt, finally hefting my leg over the bathtub wall. Vassili offers a hand. I burst with laughter. "Now, I feel bad. You help me out of the tub, and I cheat. Do you still love me? I saved the cheeseburger wrapper. I'll let you lick it. Can't be any more than twenty calories. It's all yours."

"Oh, you'll let me lick it," his voice lowers into a delicious growl. In an instant, my sex drive is revved. His eyes devour my ripe skin, zeroing in on my breasts, which have increased in size over the span of this pregnancy. My nipples rub harshly against my cotton shirt, eager for attention. Excitement consumes me as he pulls the t-shirt from over my head. I've gained so much weight, mostly in my belly. It's astonishing as Vassili hefts me up with ease and places me on the counter between the double sinks.

Vassili grabs my tits while nipping at my earlobe. His warm breath titillating across my skin as his mouth works its way to mine. He bites my jaw, continuing to descend. A slick warm trail reaches my swollen breasts. He hefts up one tit, licks the curve of it and twirls his tongue around the stiff flesh at the tip. My hands roam through his wavy hair, softly tugging at his Mohawk as his teeth sink into my nipple.

"Shit," I breathe against the top of his hair. Orgasms come so easily for me, these days.

While offering the other nipple a rough nibbling, Vassili's hand sneaks beneath my skirt. His fingers graze against the lace of my thong. I bite the taut muscle of his shoulder. My pussy offers a sweet stamp of approval before his fingers arrive at my swollen lips. I moan deep and throaty as his fingers pump inside of me.

Not a minute later, a release funnels out of me in a torrent of never-ending spasms that squeeze at his fingers.

"You're so horny," he murmurs, kissing my mouth again. Then something slick glides across my cheek. It's his saturated fingers. He groans into my mouth. "Your pussy has never tasted so good. Can I lick it?"

"Yessss."

"Good, I would love to. You have the sweetest fucking lips, Zariah." He rubs the juicy gloss of his fingers along my mouth and then proceeds to lick it off.

Vassili moves to his knees, and his tongue dives straight into my kitty. As easy as I am these days, my legs spasm on contact. I lean my head back against the mirror and grip the cool marble ledge.

"Don't tense, baby."

"Okay," I hiss, toes curled as he sucks up my juices.

"Zar," he leans back on his calves, looking me in the eye. "Don't tense. You want me to taste this pussy, don't you?"

I nod vigorously, throat clogged. Tears of ecstasy cloud my gaze.

"Then don't tense." After the command, he softens it up with one of those rare smiles before going back in. As soon as his lips touch my swollen ones, I start to pant. Fuck a G-spot, throwing his lips to my pussy is the code to bring on another orgasm.

At this moment, I've forgotten about my never-ending

hunger. My puffy nose and fat belly no longer mean a thing. My husband's mouth is my all.

He stands and places my legs around his waist. "See, no tensing, sweetheart."

While leaning back against the mirror, I wish I had the strength and the ability to push up and rub his abs. All this tummy is in the way.

Vassili fills me up, the thick ridges in his cock massaging my insides. It's so good I have to bite my lip.

"Best pussy I ever had," he declares in that succulent, slow Russian accent.

"Kiss me," I beg.

He continues to slide in and out, filling me to the brink, then he leans into tastes my lips.

"Mmmm," I groan. My mini orgasm coats his cock with more cum.

"You like that?" He cocks an eyebrow, rubbing my stomach and pushing in and out. He looks down at it. Damn, I wish I could see his cock.

"It's pretty, Zar. Your pussy is eating my cock. It's so pretty…"

I whimper with longing, another flow of tears falling down my cheeks.

"Fuck, beautiful, I hate it when you cry."

My voice breaks as I reply, "I can't help it."

"You. Can't. Help. It?" His voice is low, pearly white teeth digging into his bottom lip, and he slams into me with each word. Cocky ass. He's gorgeous. I never knew how much until this moment. Vassili slows down the rhythm again. "Do you know how hard it is for me not to cum right now, Zar? Every time you cum, I have to stop myself from following you."

I love it when he talks to me as we make love. It's beautiful. I sniffle more tears.

"I keep thinking... please her. Please, my wife."

I eat every word as my body percolates for him. "Cum with me, Vassili."

"You ready?" He arches a brow.

"Yes!" I scream as he thrusts into me. Harder, and harder. Each time his balls clap against my ass, my pussy becomes so wet it sings.

An hour later, we've showered and made it to bed. It's late evening, and I won't move from the spot, can't move. My heartbeat has slowed, breasts splayed across his bicep. I lay on my side, leg wrapped between his. In a daze of ultimate comfort, I nudge my nose into Vassili's neck.

"You breathing me in?" he asks.

Silence. Utter embarrassing silence.

"I've been told that I have that super athletic funk," he laughs. "Make sure you aren't made delirious from breathing me in."

I laugh so hard my side aches. Vassili has taught me the true definition of love and marriage. I flutter my eyelashes to stop the burning tears from falling.

30

VASSILI

My usual sweats and workout attire were traded in for a black suit and coal gray lapel. Zariah chose my outfit, saying it brought out my eyes, whatever the fuck that means. She says they're gray; I counter they're black, she says I'm colorblind—and gets the last word. I chose the black square diamonds in my ear and even got a fresh line up for ESPN.

I'm seated next to the popular MMA newscaster, Alex Brown. A light indicating that we're 'On Air' shines. Cameras line along the perimeter. Zariah is seated, her arms flopped over her belly.

In an energetic voice, Alex says, "This man needs no introduction. But if you've been living under a rock or are new to the UFC world, check out this craziness."

Alex mentions a few current fight statistics. Then another screen shows a segment of my last match. We both turn in our chairs to watch a combination of clips from my latest power moves.

"Karo, you hit the ground running, offering TKO's to every fighter brave enough to step into the octagon with you," Alex addresses me. "Only one loss, early in your career. And I swear, your maturity level has elevated beautifully. Almost as beautiful as your 'rear-naked choke' you kill with that! Oh, and the 'Triangle Choke.' What's that saying about you killing 'em?"

"Killing 'em softly." I nod slowly. "I'm a big fan of putting my opponents to sleep."

"Yes! You're quite versatile though, offering many brute force TKO's, as well. I've got a theory." He holds up a hand. "Care to indulge me?"

"Dah."

"Some of these fighters you obliterate are the ones with the biggest mouths. Can I say that you used to have a big mouth? I won't get attacked will I?" he jokes.

"Not at all. I'll admit to being cocky."

"Karo, you have an anaconda grip on the welterweight belt."

"Until I retire, if God allows it."

"Back to my theory, you butcher so many fighters who 'talk' their way into a card. Except for the one instance with The *House*. Hauser had mad words for your ankle when you were in New York promoting that match last May. He 'bad talked' your ankle, you stepped into the cage and, man, you strategized. You took hits. He got cocky. You went for the kill. That ankle of his," Alex laughs.

The hot lights are beaming down on me as I half-smile. "Yeah, was I petty?"

"Nah, man. But speaking of fighters who love to bring attention to themselves by 'verbally' attempting to bully the champ," he says. Shit, I know exactly where he's headed. "There's talk of a certain somebody wanting to fight you, Karo. You're pretty good at allowing fighters to challenge your belt when they've shown real grit. But a certain someone who boasts Mother Russia doesn't believe you deserve the throne."

"Everyone wants a piece of me." I try to show interest, but right now I can give a fuck. Zariah does a thumbs up, catching my rising anger.

"Twitter's blowing up since you've been here, Karo."

"I don't tweet. But what's this Twitter saying?" I arch a brow.

"You've got loyal fans. A good following except for one person." Alex leans forward in his chair to address the camera.

"Let me see what the boy is tweeting," I respond before the red light cuts.

We turn toward the large screen along the wall, what I was told the viewers would see when we aren't live. There are scrolls of Tweets. Mostly positive, from fans begging me to put some mudak named 'Juggernaut' out of his misery. Then the screen stops on a tweet from the bitch himself. My lips set into a firm line as I read what he wrote. Seriously, that *piz'da* can come for my head, but to include my wife?

The bright lights shine back down on us again, and Alex addresses me.

"Wow!" he feigns surprise. "Juggernaut's threatened to gift wrap your balls and send them home to *your wife* as an anniversary gift."

"Really?" My mouth perches up to one side, and I do my best to be engaging. This is why I don't do interviews unless it's after a match. After a win, I've gotten out my aggression. I keep having to remind myself not to cuss.

"Those are fighting words," Alex eggs.

I rub my knuckles along my clean-shaven jaw. "What's the boy's stats?"

"Juggernaut isn't the most consistent."

"So, bad, then? He must use his mouth to rise into certain

places and positions." *The bitch is about to get knocked down to size.*

Alex winces. "It's my job to put it all on the table."

"Okay, tell 'em congratulations. He gets ten seconds of fame."

The newscaster's eyes pop out. Since it's rare for me to go on television, Alex believes I played into his desires. Well, the bitch mentioned my wife, so he's got another thing coming.

Alex's voice amplifies with excitement. "Can we confirm that you're going to enter the octagon with none other than Nikolai Ukhtomsky, Juggernaut? Three five minute rounds of pure..."

"No, *ten* seconds. He gets less than a minute of fame. He will be the quickest knockout I've ever done." I stare at the camera. "Whoever wants to see me knock that (bleep) out that quick, do the tweet thing or whatever?" I yank the microphone from my collar.

"Cut to commercial," a producer says in the background.

Zariah comes from the sideline, waddling over.

"Aw, Vassili you're so cute. You don't know much about Twitter, do you?"

"Nyet, Yuri—"

"Manages everything," she sighs. "So, you'll knock him out in less than a minute?"

"Ten motherfucking seconds, baby. That's all this little bitch gets."

"Good, I hate to see you hit. Lay him out on one hit."

"When I'm done with that bitch, the coroner will have to scrape him up off the canvass."

"Can we get some of that—nix the cussing— once we return from commercial?" Alex speaks up.

Head tilted, I glare at him. Good, he backs away, reading me well.

Zariah softly pushes her belly against me. "Play nice.

Fighters like Juggernaut can say stupid shit. Vassili, you're the champ. People fear you very easily."

———

"Y ou're scheduled to go toe-to-toe with Cordova next. In three weeks, Vassili!" Yuri growls, pacing around the den of my home. The evening sunlight streams in on him. His eyebrows knitted together in thought.

Even Vadim has joined, he's seated on the couch nursing a double of vodka.

Yuri argues, "Now, we are going to look scared. Why did you agree to that little bitch? Mother Russian, fuck off, with that bullshit. He's from Pasadena."

"Calm down." I grab his arms, stopping his tracking over Zariah's Oriental rug. The anxiety gets on my nerves. "I'll fight Cordova in June as anticipated. Make Juggernaut my first summer fight."

"You mean the end of summer!"

"No, the beginning."

"You fight Cordova on June 2nd. So you'll hop your ass back into the cage a few weeks later then?" My cousin gasps.

"Dah!"

"Nyet," Vadim orders, placing the empty glass onto the table beside the couch. "Too soon, Vassili. What will your wife think?"

I almost glance down the hall. Zariah's in our bedroom, consulting on a case she transferred to another member at Billingsley Law. Her maternity leave was days ago. The only secret I had from her these days was working with Samuel and Connie for her baby shower. We're a team. I have Cordova before my leave. I glare at Yuri and Vadim to stop their loud ranting.

"Oh, should I shut up, kuzen? My niece—your daughter—

261

is due at the end of June." Yuri pokes me. "One month between a match is too soon. You're not a rookie anymore, Vassili. You're the motherfucking champ."

"I'll train for Cordova. The very next week I will break Nikolai Ukhtomsky's neck! No training required, I won't even sweat." I issue a forearm punch, then use the other hand to slam into the hard bone. "Easy."

"Make it August," Vadim says.

"And hear that bitch talk? Vadim, I say we cancel it. Blame it on me, the manager." Yuri shakes his head. He places a hand at the back of my neck and looks me in the eye. "Vassili, you are Anatoly's son. Fuck what you're going through. We cannot have that *mudak* insulting you on social media. Juggernaut keeps mentioning Russia, people will forget that this is all promo talk."

"Anatoly could give a shit about me right now," I mumble. Grigor's comment about our father's illness worms its way into my thoughts.

"But you're blood," Vadim cuts in. "Anatoly may hear of it and shut Juggernaut up the good ole fashion way. No refs. No rules and regulations. I'm with you, Yuri, canceling would be best. Sooner if . . ."

"Okay, the end of June it is," I tell them.

Vadim sniggers. "Hopefully, he has to close his cunt long enough to practice."

We all laugh.

ZARIAH

"Each day, it becomes harder and harder to breathe. I'm a grouchy, swollen mess," I whimper while shoveling a spoonful of cookie dough frozen yogurt into my mouth. Connie sits across from me at Yogurtland, which is situated in the center of the mall. There's a Soma's intimates store to my left that I keep cutting my eyes at.

"Preggo, you are as hopeless as the day is long." She shakes her head. "How is Vassili?"

"Suffering."

"Why?"

"Because I am a bitch sometimes and I don't care. Connie, I've jumped, danced, wiggled everything but this belly off! I swear I won't make it."

"Girl, you're almost at the home front," she murmurs. "What happened to being extra horny?"

"Tsk, got that covered, too." I tilt my head back and laugh. "The moment my husband arrives home, he has to get past all of this tummy and ass to survive. And then he has to hear me arguing about not being able to breathe. Natasha is karate chopping my ribs. Or should I say, Nickolas!"

"Nickolas? Oh, hell no," she chortles.

"I swear we are having a son. We've had a 3D ultrasound completed. However, I am not convinced that this *is*," I point to my belly, "Natasha."

After a few moments of laughing, Connie asks, "Do you know what your problem is?"

I arch an eyebrow.

"You're spoiled. Uncle Samuel says there is no such thing as being spoiled but damn it, you are! Your dad spoiled you. Then you married a *fighter*, with big money, and I'm sure something else even bigger in his pants."

We both giggle.

"Zariah?" A familiar voice perks my ears.

"Dad?" I glance across the floral plants, separating Yogurtland from the mall.

His gaze sweeps down to my belly in shock.

Connie arises. "I have a mediation meeting. I'll see you later."

My father comes around, slipping past children and strollers to get to me. We haven't seen each other in person in months. Not since the fiasco with Phil.

Either he was going on a two-week Canadian cruise with Beatrice or I simply avoided him. The last chat we had, he did *try it*. He's tried to blame my husband for everything. And Samuel informed me about the cop stopping Vassili for no reason.

"My baby is having a baby," he mumbles. His eyes are glossed. This is the closest I've ever seen him come to tears. For all the tears my mother has shed in the past, leave it to me to cause him heartache.

I stand and offer him a hug.

"Are you having a boy or a girl?" he asks as we let go.

"A girl or so we've been told. Her name is Natasha."

"That Russian?"

I nod.

"Well, can you just keep in touch with me if anything ever—"

"C'mon, let's refrain from the negativity, Daddy, damn. Keep in touch? We've both been busy."

"I haven't been busy."

"Canada for Thanksgiving. Beatrice's family for Christmas? Not even a note for Valentine's Day. You once claimed I was your very first Valentine as a child." I settle down and eat. Food keeps me grounded.

"Sheesh, Zariah, every day you're becoming more and more like *your mother*," he hisses.

I spear the spoon into the frozen yogurt.

"Funny, Mom says I become more like you. I asked her about a month ago, out of annoyance and hormones. She said that it was because you're a strategist, thinking before moving chess pieces. She apologized if it offended me for making such a statement." I shrug. "But I'm confident your comparison of me to my mom is not one from positivity. *So how do I remind you of Mom?* She got hit and got back up!"

"Zariah," he gasps.

Blood burns in my veins. "What? Mom strove to keep quiet, not muddle the water. Her biggest wish was to have her children grow up in an unbroken home. How weak of her to take beating after beating. Somehow, I believe verbal abuse is worse, though. Some of my previous clients, you could see their demeanor shrinking by the second. Feel free to jump in, enlighten me."

"Zariah," he seethes. "There are children around."

"I have never disrespected Beatrice. But if you need clarification, she is a stupid bitch. That bit of truth aside, when I mentioned the two of you, I wasn't taking my mother's side."

"Zariah, I asked—"

"I was merely stating the facts. You were busy. I was in the courtroom or at the gym or one of Vassili's matches, supporting him because this is marriage! Uplifting each other." In my anger, I continue with my monologue. "Samuel and Vassili are good now. They got together and told me when I had to go on maternity leave. I expected to work until I popped. But they got together, in unity. *People do that for those they love.*"

"Well, I don't love you any less," Maxwell cuts in.

"Could've fooled me. You and I are two busy for each other. So up until now, I've had a hectic schedule. Now, I'm telling the painters that the teddy bears on the walls are a little too scary, asking them to repaint. That started a very comical argument. Side note, I never knew that a man and wife could argue and laugh and still love." By now I don't even see my father before me. Somewhere along the lines, I must've lost consciousness.

<hr>

My first line of vision is Vassili. That strong jaw, his fighter nose, and the most sinful, dark eyes. The vision clears more, and I see that he's in a sauna suit that's been duct-taped at the wrist and to his shoes. He also has on a hoodie beneath the suit. The wide-legged stance he has chosen sets my heart on fire.

Before I can ask him what happened, an EMT steps in the way.

"Your blood pressure was through the roof."

I start to speak. But there's something over my mouth, forcing cool air into my nostrils. Annoyed, I pull at the mask.

"Let's get you breathing." She smiles, adjusting the oxygen mask back into place.

"Let me talk to you, Mr. Washington," I hear Vassili say. His tone is lethal.

"My daughter and I were having a simple..." Maxwell's voice drowns out.

It's all pressure against my chest as I try to sit up. My head kisses the pillow with ease.

Later that evening, Vassili corners me in the bedroom, prepared to have a debate when I'd rather he touch my body. He sits in the chair across from the bed, wide-legged, elbows on his knees, and head in hands. I rub cocoa butter into my skin. The tension he exudes rolls over my shoulder as my hands glide along my thighs. I glance at my feet, the lotion and then at him. His glower tells me I have to wait.

"Connie told me that you were fine when she left you at Yogurtland. You, tell me what happened?" He says through gritted teeth.

I hold out the lotion. He shakes his head. Huffing, I begin to explain, "My dad ran into me at the mall. I tried to have a simple conversation with him, but he got under my skin."

Vassili's hand glides along my calf, he lifts my leg and plants it on his knee. Then gestures for the cocoa butter. His tone has lost its edge. "How?"

"In retrospect, I snapped. I got on him because of how he treats you and–"

Massaging the lotion into my foot, Vassili replies, "Baby, forget about me. I can't have you putting our child in harm's way. Maxwell can't touch what we've built."

"I know, Vassili. But you didn't let me finish, I was going to add that I argued with him about my childhood." I pause, glancing toward the ground.

"Talk."

"You've had a hard life as a kid. In the beginning, I assumed you had the world handed to you or..."

"Or I strong-armed that shit?" he cracks a smile.

"Exactly," I grin. "The Resnov name implies that any asset is at your disposal, willing or not. Remember when I told you about my dad hitting my mom?"

"Dah. He's your dad and you love him. So, he's still breathing."

"After I learned more about you, Sasha, the awful things Anatoly has done to your mother, I tried to keep my emotions in. The crap I've seen while I was being raised didn't compare."

"What?"

"Because you had a worse life," I shrug. "I don't know. My mom always told me I tried to compensate for Ronisha's life. With us, I worry about Natasha. I know without a doubt that you'll be a good dad because you're strong."

He clasps my face in his hands. "And you will be a good, good mother, Zariah."

When Vassili zeros in on the hot tears on my cheeks, kissing each one, I cry harder.

"We are fearless people, Zariah. Ronisha had a fucked-up life. Sasha did, too. No life is perfect. Our experiences make us stronger."

"Okay," I murmur.

"Now, I've got something to tell you, Zariah."

He rubs a thumb over his eyebrow. "I don't want you to come to Kentucky when I fight Cordova. I'd pull out if you'd prefer since it's near Natasha's birth, but—"

"But we have bills and you'll take a loss."

"Fuck a loss. Can't bring a baby into the world with debt."

While pouting, my swollen face feels extra fat as I do. "Since we've been together I haven't missed a fight."

"Zar, you hate when I fight, though."

Ain't that the truth. "What if I go into premature labor?"

"You won't."

"If I did?"

"I'd race the sun to get to you, Zariah. There's no way you'll have Natasha all alone. I will be there."

32

ZARIAH

Louisville, Kentucky

There's not a single seat left at The Kentucky 'Yum!' Center. A slinky champagne-colored maxi delicately hugs my swollen stomach and breasts. I'd applied makeup while the hotel air conditioner blasted at a temperature that rivaled the crisp coldness of Moscow.

I contemplate Connie's words about how spoiled I am. She was spot on. Vassili rented a large luxury tour bus for me to attend this event. During the long ride, Vassili and I watched countless videos of his opponent, Jose Cordova's previous matches. Now, I'm wishing Vassili had enforced his request for me to stay in Los Angeles. A smug smile crosses my face, in consideration of my head game. Then my lips tremble as another contraction breaks my concentration.

Yuri is seated next to me. Thick jaws puffed out like he might blow a gasket.

"How many undercards left?" I grit out the words,

speaking up over the sound of fans cheering for the current favorite in the cage.

He chokes on his bottle of beer. *"Dva!"*

"Two! Did you say two?" So far I've been confident in learning up to twenty in Russian to teach to Natasha, but I must be—

"Dah. Should I go, Zariah?"

"No!" I grab his arm before he can snitch. Another contraction slams into me. They're getting closer.

"Please, Zariah. My *kuzen* is gonna murder me."

I sink back into the comfortable seat so close to the cage. My tensed frame loosening by the moment. "I'm okay. Now."

Yuri glances at me in confusion. "What is this, a fucking exorcism?"

"No, a contraction. It passed. I can't go to the hospital until they occur closer together, which won't happen anytime soon."

He settles back in his seat, grumbling in Russian.

Reminding myself not to grit my teeth and relax, I practice the breathing exercises from the Lamaze class Vassili and I attended. Then I ask Yuri to time my contractions. Music blares through the speaker, marking one more fight before Vassili slaughters Cordova.

A while later, Linkin Park tears through the speakers. I search through the crowd for where Vassili and his crew will enter. A calmness slithers over my bones. Sensing her father, Natasha simmers down in my belly. I begin to wonder if I was having another case of Braxton Hicks when my gaze latches onto Vassili. He moves along the crowd, like a lion in feeding season. He rips the Killer Karo shirt from his sexy chest, exposing a wealth of glorious tattoos and muscles. After he's all lubed up, Vassili somersaults onto the canvass.

Every ounce of my energy is used to cheer him on. *Vassili hurry up and beat his ass*! I meditate on that while squirming in the chair.

The announcer hypes up the crowd when another searing pain courses through my tummy.

"Fuck, Fuck!" I hear over the shouting.

The screaming isn't from me. Yuri yelps! His hand is balled into a fist, as I tear the flesh in his forearm. Teeth gritted, I ride out the pain while exerting all of my energy on him. He lunges from the chair as Cordova has Vassili pinned to the cage.

"Wait, I'm sorry," I call out.

Yuri fumbles with the backstage pass on his chest, gesturing for Nestor in my husband's corner.

They exchange words. Yuri points at me. Then Vadim is in the mix. My husband's cousin returns, frown on his face. *"We go to doctor now!"*

"What about Vassili?"

"They tell him during the first seat."

"No!" I stand, all the strength has burned from my legs. I almost fall into him. "You go tell them to let him finish."

Yuri breathes deeply, helping me steady myself.

Since he hasn't responded, I continue to argue, "You can take me to the hospital now. Don't have them stop the match. If Cordova ends up with Vassili's belt—"

"Okay, okay!" He holds out his palms. "I'll text Nestor. We go, Zariah."

With one arm supporting me, Yuri pulls out his phone. The sunlight is funneling into the dark arena from ahead of us.

The first round is being called. If I was in my right mind, I'd say that Cordova led this one. We make it toward the concession area. The perimeter isn't teeming with hungry fans like it was when we arrived. There are a few people in line for Dippin' Dots when warmth trickles down my leg.

"Oh, fuck, *kuzen,* you-you will have this baby soon," His eyes widen in horror. He mumbles about Vassili killing him now while shouting for help.

33

VASSILI

"Karo, Karo, Karo!" the crowd screams my name. Like I've done since we first reconnected, I search for Zariah's spot. My muscles ache and an ice bath is flashing before my eyes. *Where is she?* My fat-ass cousin should be beside Zariah; there's no missing him. Arms raised, shouting my victory at the top of my lungs, I glare at their empty spaces.

"Hey, where the fuck is she?" I shout down to my corner.

"*Bol'nitsa,*" Vadim mouths hospital. I've jumped from the top of the cage to the canvas. My teeth grit from the pain.

The announcer shoves a camera into my face. I speak first, "I've got to get to the hospital."

"You were a little worse for wear this time, Karo—"

"No! My wife is in labor." I'm already scoping out how to get off this stage through the massive crowd.

"Oh, congratulations," he turns off the microphone but pushes something into his ear. I'm already scrambling toward the octagon door.

"Karo," the announcer speaks up, I glance back. "Exit through the south entrance. We have a police escort for you."

"Thanks," I reply, and then shout over to my crew. "Nestor, did you bring your chopper?"

"Fuck yeah!" He nods. In his personal time, Nestor restores old motorcycles. He added the modifications to my Harley. When we're traveling, at times he prefers to ride one of his motorcycles.

As Nestor navigates the beginning of the crowd with me, I growl, "Give me your keys and shoes."

"What? They have an escort."

"Those cruisers won't be able to get past all the traffic. I need to get to Zariah, now!"

He tosses the keys toward me as I hurry along, shouting about the parking location of the chopper. Instead of bombarding me for pictures and autographs, the fans are now chanting, "Go, Karo, Go!"

That mudak Cordova almost bested me today. The double doors are held open for me. With every muscle scorching, and on the heaviest legs, I hurry through the exit.

"Karo!" Two police in uniform call out to me. "We have a cruiser, Karo."

"I have a chopper."

About five minutes later, I notice Nestor's chopper. In a sea of other stock or custom motorcycles, The Black Widow shines. Touches of red and webbing are accented throughout.

"Shit," I growl, pushing my left leg over. I almost tapped out in submission, and now my tendons are screaming. Yet it's much easier navigating to the exits with this. So I concentrate on my promise to be there for Zariah and not the meat grinder beating I survived. I shift gears while picking up speed to jump a sidewalk and then my right foot presses the concrete.

Mouth tensed, I twist around a tight curve.

As soon as I rev this bitch up, to accelerate on the street, the volcanic heat of June amps up the aches in my muscles.

Loud whirling sounds cause my frown to set harder. Fucking cops. But instead of signaling me to slow down, a cruiser and a motorcycle speed up in front of me. Both drivers eagerly wave their arm.

Soon I see a crowd of people and a blue cross sign. We pull over in front of the Emergency room entrance.

With not a minute to spare, I'm off the bike.

"Congratulations, Karo," I hear as I rush through the sliding glass doors.

"My wife is in labor," I try to scale down my loud, urgent voice. The nurse glances at my appearance, then my hands, which are still weighted down. "Zariah Resnov, please tell me she didn't give birth yet."

"Um," she glances at the rooster, "Mrs. Resnov's in room—"

"Hurry," Yuri shouts, from down the hall. "I'm traumatized!"

I rush down, hearing a doctor order for Zariah to push. Silently I thank God, and in the next second, cuss Yuri for not stopping the match.

"Zariah threatened . . ."

I pop him in the mouth. "Shut the fuck up."

"I'll go get you a clean pair of clothing because that's what a *manager* would do. But don't hit me again, Vassili." He mumbles, stomping off.

My entire demeanor softens as I enter the room.

"You made it," Zariah's eyes are wet. Her beautiful brown skin is aglow with perspiration.

"And you are?" The doctor, who is sitting on a stool between the stirrup contraption, offers a peculiar look. Two nurses are at her sides.

"Her husband." I offer the faintest smile while heading toward my wife.

"You must be the reason she won't open her legs and push," one of the nurses quips.

"Zariah, we need you to push hard," the doctor focuses.

I stand beside her. Zariah takes my arm. She squeezes the blood from my fingers.

"Push, baby," I coach.

———

There's yellow ducky wallpaper all around. Zariah is sound asleep, she'd asked about my match after a nurse took our baby to clean and feed her. The moment I assured her that I won, Zariah couldn't get to sleep fast enough. I rub my hands together, ready for our daughter to return. Yuri peeks his head into the room.

The idiot slinks inside, navy suit crinkled.

"Did you see my wife's…" I gesture.

He shakes his head.

"You sure?" My eyes narrow.

"Fuck, Vassili! I'm her *kuzen* now!"

"No cussing. Look." I hold my hands out as the sleeping baby is brought into the room in a clear hospital bassinet.

"She's beautiful," Yuri says. "Can I hold her?"

"Fuck no, stupid." I mouth the words.

The nurse whispers that Natasha will be hungry when she awakens and that she'd refused the bottle. I must've asked her a hundred questions about my baby going hungry because Yuri clears his throats. The nurse hits the road.

I step over to the beautiful child I've made with my loving wife. Natasha is so tiny. Damn, I'm afraid for the first time in my life. How do I pick her up? I've played with a thousand babies and held as many newborns. But this one belongs to me.

"You have to support her head, Vassili. Igor has a bunch of kids, I know these things."

"Okay," I growl. Her skin is the color of the sweetest butterscotch. I carefully place my hand along her back.

"Aw look, she has a Mohawk like her pop," Yuri says.

Indeed her dark hair has slicked at the sides. In the front, one curly cue sticks up. With fighter hands, I cradle her up onto my shoulder.

"Get the diaper cloth, *use it!*" Yuri quietly reprimands.

"Okay, okay." He's right.

Perceptive of my fear of crushing her. Yuri places the white hospital cloth over my shoulder as I hold Natasha out before me. I then nudge my nose against her. She smells weird. But her skin is the softest silk I've ever touched. *God, I will do right by this gift.*

At this moment, MMA no longer exists. Love consumes me.

34

ZARIAH

A yellow, frilly dress brings out the spark in Natasha's dark eyes. The three-week-old coos up at me.

"You want Daddy, I know, baby." My voice is a saccharine melody. Natasha's reflex is to suck harder on the inside of her lips.

"Aw, this baby is truly my heart," My mother swoons. "I didn't fly all the way from Atlanta for you to hog up my newest grandbaby."

"Give me a few more minutes with her." I place mittens on Natasha's hands and scoop her up to my shoulder, supporting the back of her head.

Mom follows me from the nursery, making funny faces at Natasha every step of the way. At the center of our California King bed are clothes that my mom was in the process of folding. I start to chide her for all she's doing to help.

"Child, this is not a vacation. You are tired. I didn't expect to see your husband gone so soon. A match so quickly after you all returned from Kentucky."

"Yeah, I know." I gently hand over Natasha and glance toward the muted television. When Vassili told me about the

279

match between him and that idiot, Juggernaut, I was surprised. But he said it was normal to get back into the cage so quickly…

Grabbing the remote, I turn up the Pay-Per-View event to a low level. He is oceans away at the Singapore Indoor Stadium.

"Oh, look, it's daddy," my voice rises in feigned happiness. Although the thought of Vassili entering the ring always causes anxiety to clutch my heart.

There's a short documentary, with commentary about Nikolai Ukhtomsky, the Juggernaut. The undercard's stats are comedic since the price for viewing this fight is much higher than some of the others. It shows him working out in a small town, presumably in Russia. Lord knows he harped on about Vassili not representing their country enough. My jaw sets as he makes Vassili seem like he's been 'Americanized.'

Next, the screen shows Karo throwing punches and combinations on the Venice walkway. Vadim's Gym has become a dominating brand behind him. He's mentioned as the favorite while talking briefly about his regimen used to beat his opponent.

My mom settles down in a rocking chair. Samuel came by last week with it and more clothing that he swore Connie picked out. Something tells me the widower is happy about the new addition to our small family. I'm folding and putting away clothes when I hear LL Cool J's "Mama Said Knock You Out…"

Mom chuckles softly while softly rubbing Natasha's back. She leans forward in the rocking chair. "Oh, my Lord, he didn't?"

"Humph, he did. Vassili is cocky." I place my hands on my curvaceous hips and stare at the large screen. My husband came out to old school rap! He's also donning navy-blue

Adidas with the stripes on the side! His shoulders fill out the jogger suit to perfection. The camera frames him.

"Tsk, *I am scarrrred of him*," she jokes. "And he better knock the boy out in ten seconds."

Pausing mid-fold on a 'My dad can beat your dad' onesie, I glance sideways at her. "What do you know about ten seconds?"

"Martin. That brother of yours loves to brag on his brother-in-law. So believe it, I know all about this ten seconds. I'm sure it has something to do with your husband's haste to fight so soon."

I settle down at the edge of the bed, too mesmerized to tear my gaze from the screen. My top teeth work at the fullness of my lip.

The bell chimes. Juggernaut reaches out to tap gloves. Vassili waves him off, meanest glower I have ever seen. Damn, I feel myself getting hot at all his rugged sexiness. My heart clenches as Juggernaut offers a vicious kick. But he doesn't shed first blood. Vassili catches him with a left hook. The punch sends Juggernaut's legs into a noodle-like dance. The idiot reaches in for an errant punch. Does he even touch my man?

Vassili reacts so fast. I don't catch the TKO because of blinking. All I see is Juggernaut's powerful legs knotting up. He slams to the ground.

The replay is instant. Juggernaut's feeble attempt to punch Vassili moves at a snail pace straight up the middle. Catching all air. Vassili strikes with a forearm punch to the nose. He left Juggernaut wilted against the floor like a prostitute after disrespecting her pimp.

"LIGHTS OUT IN SINGAPORE," the commentator shouts.

The ref jumps over Juggernaut's frozen body, ending the fight. Vassili spits out his mouthguard. He raises a hand to heaven and looks up. Then his chest is flared as he punches against his forearm. The tattoo posted across chiseled rock is that of a machine gun. Damn, I gulp down my lust.

Vassili climbs the fence and jumps to the other side. Dominating the ledge. Head back, he growls. Then he walks around the perimeter like a tiger on the prowl.

"How long was that, huh!" His shouting is inaudible. Words display at the bottom of the screen. "How long was that?"

Someone holds up eight fingers.

"Eight seconds!" Vassili's voice is muffled by the microphone attempting to keep up. He heads toward the cage door. The screen switches to Juggernaut. Blood masks his nose and mouth, dripping down his chest. He stands on legs fit for a toddler, leaning against the referee. His head is hung low. The referee stands between them, lifting Vassili's fist as he's declared the winner by knockout.

Yes! I silently scream.

"Wow," my mom's tone is low as Natasha is snoozing again.

Vassili does a few more jumps before smooching his steel forearm.

A sports reporter catches up to him. "You prepared for your card, as always, Karo. But as you look back at all your fights, we know you're a favorite of submission. How did you prepare for this knockout?"

"I fake it low, *throw it high,*" he tells the reporter.

"This will go down in history as one of the quickest UFC matches. Only one second away from being the quickest. That being said, the fans are eager to know how *quickly* you'll return to the octagon?"

"Depends on who else has something to say! No, really," he pauses, offering a humble smile. "I don't always fight the contender who has the loudest mouth. My next opponent must have some heart."

───────────

A round 10 am the next morning, I cling to Vassili's pillow and give him a call. He has an overnight eighteen-hour flight to LAX. My time configuring skills might be off, but I have to assume he's left the hotel after a couple of hours of sleep. As aggressive as he is, he only needs a few winks. But when my husband answers, he sounds a bit worse for wear.

"Hey, Zar."

"You sound like you're asleep? Did you miss your flight? Are you at the airport?"

"Easy with the questions, baby,"

I hug the pillow tighter, my breasts pads are flooded with milk. "Oh, God, you're still at the hotel. You overslept."

His tone holds more urgency now, "Sweetheart, is Natasha okay?"

"Yes, fine. She misses her father though. And instead of you being on a flight from Singapore you're still in the hotel sleeping." I can't stop myself from nagging. He's missed five precious days of our baby's life.

"I'm not…"

I feel my eyes watering, they are as leaky as my tits these days. "So you're at the airport!"

"Babe stop cross-examining me. I'm in an Uber. Nestor took the hotel. The car is turning on Arlington Way. Beautiful, I spent a few hours sitting at the airport praying some motherfucker would miss their flight, so I could get home earlier."

"Arlington Way? You're around the corner." I smile through the tears. "I love you so much."

"Yeah, you better love me. No crying when I see you, Zariah."

I climb out of the tall bed and make a mad dash to my treasure chest. "Vassili, as soon as you get into this house I want you to screw me."

"Nyet. We wait for two weeks, after your checkup, sweetheart."

While massaging a silk negligee through my fingers, I order him, "You will sex me as soon as you get home."

35

VASSILI

CLICK. My wife hung up on my ass. Nervously, I tap the phone against my leg. I've had blue balls since Kentucky. I'd bent Zariah over and fucked her real good the night before the fight.

The day I fell for Zariah I knew I was doomed. That girl walks all over me and I couldn't give a fuck, I love it. While in Singapore, I was eye fucked by one bitch after another, sometimes a few at a time. As with the cage, I kept my chin down, craving what's waiting for me at home. I'd marked the calendar for when I can love her well again. My cock twitches. I lean back in the seat feeling precum leak from the tip of my junk while palm trees zip by. The driver is only a few blocks away from home. I continue to tap the iPhone against my leg, endeavoring not to focus on my knee.

I didn't even use my left knee on Juggernaut.

'You aren't ready to return so soon. Cordova worked you harder than...' Vadim's argument with me after hopping into the cage fades as my house comes into view. Ms. Haskins holds Natasha. My baby has a little fluffy hat on top of her curly hair. They're at the top of the flagstone steps, beneath one of

the many curved arches of the house. Hefting my duffel bag over my shoulder, I get out.

"Where's Zariah," I ask while giving her mother a half hug and kissing my baby's forehead.

"My child told me she was cleaning up something in y'all's room." She smirks as I read between the lines. "Natasha needs to be changed."

I hold my hands out.

"No worries. Vassili, there will definitely be more diapers. I got this one," she says, as we all go into the house.

I hustle up the stairs favoring my right knee. The dull ache is slaughtered by the sight of my wife propped up in bed. A crimson bra brings out the undertones of red in her rich dark skin. The matching pair of strappy panties cling to her juicy pussy. Without taking my eyes off her, I close the double doors behind me.

"I had a new teddy but wanted to show off some improvements."

My eyebrow cocks. *What the fuck is a teddy?* My tone is guttural. "You. Look. Gorgeous."

"Do I?" she teases, coming to her hands and knees. She climbs over toward the edge of the bed, hips flowing from left to right.

The duffel bag on my shoulder hits the floor. I pull off my shirt. While unbuckling my pants, I stare at how her large breasts strain and almost spill out of her new bra. She comes up to her knees. I step over, reach down and press my mouth fiercely against her thick lips. The precum slicked against my boxers seeps even more. Zariah's tiny hand weaves down my abdominals, and she reaches into my briefs. Her fingers glide up and down my erection, thumb dabbling in my cum before gliding it around the head.

"You're even more huge than I remembered, Vassili." She nips hard on my lip.

"Fuck." I sigh as she removes her hand from my briefs. I pull them down while her hands caress across my abs and massage my shoulders.

My cock stands heavy between us. Her fingers glide through mine, and I stop myself from sounding like a bitch to beg her return to my cock. She leads me onto the bed. My frame dominating the center of it. Zariah drags her nails over my abs while licking the salty flesh at my inner thighs. She wraps her hand around my erection, stroking up and down while caressing my balls with her tongue.

Next Zariah frees her breasts from her bra. When those large brown tits spill forth, I reach up to grab one.

"Tsk, tsk..." She presses a tiny hand at the center of my chest, pushing me back against the sheets. She caresses her nipples with her fingers before reaching down and placing those heavenly tits around my cock. Her breasts are so warm and soft against my rock hard length. She scoots down, once again sucking my cock, her mouth is sloppy and exciting. Then she licks around my balls before pressing those tits around my piece again.

"Fuck..." I mouth.

"Nut for me," Zariah murmurs, "Where do you want to cum, Vassili? My breasts, my mouth, my..." She grins, stroking my cock with her tits.

"Sweetheart," my voice is deep and low. Damn, I'm not going to make it. She's eye-fucking me as well, and probably reading my mind.

"You can cum on my tits, I'll lick it all off." She reaches down and her tongue flicks against the thick veins in my shaft.

"Shittttt," I grit out.

"If you don't cum, I will jump on this dick, Vassili," she warns, before her mouth slides down the length of me.

36

VASSILI

Four months later

It's hard to fathom how something so beautiful *was* such a big shitting machine and now *is* the reason for my smile. I recall one day before I'd mastered how to change a diaper. Zariah was nursing Natasha, and our baby grunted. Shit torpedoed from the side of her diaper. I had put the thing on backward. The baby continued to eat like nothing was the matter while Zariah silently freaked out.

Now, Natasha is five and a half months old. She no longer has the one curl at the top of her head that Yuri and my cousins joke is a Mohawk like mine. She's seated in her crib, with a halo of black curls. She leans back to laugh and lands on one of her stuffed elephants. My tensed lips smile, delighted in the way she cracks up.

"God, what did I do for Your blessing?" I mumble.

"Why?" Zariah leans her head on my shoulder.

"All the shit Anatoly, my younger brothers... my whole

family, even Malich does, some of the bullshit from my past. How does God pardon it? How could God give me her, you?"

"You're a good man, Vassili. We serve an even greater God." She glances up at me. The moonlight from the open balcony of Natasha's nursery lights against her eyes. "Now, granted, I worry, too. But only when you step into the cage."

I start to hug my wife for her encouragement until I get a good look at her. "Zar, you worried?"

She shrugs, "You know how I am the night before a match."

"What happened the last time I was in the cage?" I cock an eyebrow.

She bubbles in laughter, it rivals the beauty of our daughter's cooing and chuckles. "You beat a man in less than ten seconds. Don't be cocky, Vassili."

"You stated a fact. How am I being cocky?"

"God blessed you with super hands. All I can say is, Kill 'em, Karo." She kisses me, lips spread into a smile.

Honda Center, Anaheim

"You good?" Vadim asks

"Good, good," I nod, fists slicing through the air so fast it swooshes. Right, hook, uppercut...Skin warm, I mentally review the signature moves of Louie Gotti, The Legion, the next person gunning for my belt.

"Look, son, you fought Juggernaut too damn soon. You promised you'd lay him out. Good..."

"Vadim, get to the point."

He clasps the back of my neck and stares me in the eye.

"You went from hopping into the cage too soon and now, you've been out of the cage for four months."

"That's standard."

His glare is harder. "Don't fuck with me, Vassili. These past 120 days ain't been the same. Not to say you're past your prime. You've got a wife and kid who commandeer much of your days. Are you good?"

"Yes, Vadim," I growl.

"I'm not so sure, Son. I fought with you to visit the doctors. Shit, you were supposed to go after fighting Cordova, not wait till fucking off with Juggernaut. The scan of your knee came back normal. But I'm not convinced." Vadim glowers at me. "*So, are you good?*"

"I'm good," I glare harder, repeating myself for emphasis, "Vadim, I'm good. Okay?"

"Yeah, you barely got that submission with Cordova. Then you go gallivanting around Louisville before the medic clears—"

"To witness the birth of my daughter?" I laugh. "You're going senile, old man. Every time I speak, I come through, don't I? Didn't I say the little bitch would be knocked out in seconds? Did I disappoint? I will murder The Legion—*like I said*. Do you want to shut your cunt or pray?"

Vadim shakes his head, laughing. "That's my line, Vassili. I tell you and all those up-and-comers at my gym to shut your cunts."

"Can I pray? Get my head in the game; or are you trying to hold my dick?"

He steps away mumbling about my choice of words, using prayer and dick in the same sentence. I pull off my cross pendant and place it onto the counter before me. This is a ritual I've done so many times, except when I left the cross with Zariah while in Singapore a few months ago.

In hindsight, I felt as ready as I'd ever been. My father

always told me that I'd have to choose one love. The syndicate or MMA. There was no question as to what I'd choose. But with my family and my love for pounding flesh, I thought I'd found a balance between the two.

Contrary to Vadim's hard questions, I did well. I'd learned how to change a diaper after Natasha's first shitting warzone. I'd baby-proofed the house, and she wasn't even crawling yet. And I split my time, with my rigorous training schedule because Zariah helped me tag-team our child.

Thus, this fight with Louie Gotti, The Legion, starts like any other. I go out, guns blazing. And by that, I mean my fists spray like bullets against his face, neck, and ribs. Gotti slams into the fencing. He's unable to ball up, get to the clinch. All he can do is take it.

The referee steps in. Like a dance, I hustle to the opposite corner. One foot before the other, Gotti catches his bearings. People are fist-pumping the air. The surrounding arena is in chaos. With a nod, I beckon this bitch to me.

He fakes right and goes for a shin kick. Every attempt is blocked. Though his face is a bloodied pulp, I'm tiring him out. When I get him to the floor, I want my signature move to be flawless.

Gotti jabs my chin. I issue a low kick. Soon as he comes alive, I slam him into the cage. My hand behind his neck and a knee to his abs. Now, for the takedown.

Ding. Ding. Dingggg! I navigate to my corner.

Nestor grabs my chin, grinning. "You killing him!"

"Finish him!" Vadim pats my shoulder.

I toss back a bottle of water, crunch it into my hands, then press it into Nestor's chest.

This time Gotti leaps from his seat as if a few moments have revived him. His cross lands against my ear. Sending a long drumming wave through it. I step back. Feeling comfortable, Gotti comes at me again. This time I move to the side. As he's side by side with me, my opposite palm pressed against his forehead. Timber!

With the Italian on the mat before me, I position myself for my signature move. My bicep applies pressure to his esophagus. The greedy feeling of squeezing until he can no longer breathe takes over. His throat is tightened between the steel of my forearm and bicep. Gotti's eyes flutter up and then lock onto mine. The vessels in his gaze pop. What I see next breaks my concentration... Sergio.

My boots stepped over piss, water and vomit. My eyes adjusted to the darkness of the room. Sergio's arms were tied above his head to a beam along the ceiling. One of Malich's goons apparently thought that water torture would be a good starter. His stomach was extremely bloated. Weights were strapped to his dangling feet, stretched his body further. The guys did just enough to break his spirit, leaving the big motherfucker in tears.

I took a drag from my cigarette and released the smoke through my nose. "I've been told you enjoy hitting women. Big piz'da like you can't find someone your own size to fight?"

"Please! Please!"

"Listen." I clasped my hand against the back of his neck, bringing his tear swollen gaze to mine. "I believe in God, too. Maybe I'll pray for your soul later. But tonight, you'll either go..." My cigarette pointed up and then down. "I can't see further than your death, but your death is inevitable."

I tuned out his cries, burning the cigarette into his chest. My eyes locked onto Sergio as my powerful left hook slammed into his jaw. His chin instantly flopped to his chest.

"You killing him with one punch, Vassili," the doctor Yuri had requested to be here spoke up in Russian.

"Nyet, but you can bring him back to consciousness." I nudged my head toward Sergio. The big mudak was knocked out with one hit.

The doctor stepped forward. He stabbed the syringe of adrenaline into Sergio's heart.

"Gaaahhh!" Sergio gulped, like a fish out of water.

I clasped his jaw. "Stay awake, I'm not ready for you to die yet. And if you stop breathing, my doc will bring your ass back to life. You think you can hit girls and go out easy, eh?"

He made a noise that sounded like he's drowning, before spitting up blood.

I chuckled. This time my hands slammed against his ribs like my fists were never-ending fireworks. The doctor readied another syringe. The goons joked about me not killing him too soon. I beat Sergio until his fucking eyes dimmed for the last time...

One second, the Italian's gaze had faltered, and the next, he's pinned his elbow into my ribs. Though I'm conditioned to this pain, I keep fucking seeing Sergio through Gotti's gaze. He twists his arm around. Then he flips his body backward until his legs are positioned around my left leg. He locks my leg forward against my chest, calf twisted sideways.

My mind continues to see Sergio dying before me. Until the crowd is hushed. A searing pain roars through my left leg as my team cusses in Russian.

"Otpustit! Sdavat'sya!" Vadim and Nestor shout. I no longer see them, but their voices are blaring through some imaginary speakers.

They're telling me to tap out. Let go.

Why the fuck are they telling me to tap out? Why the fuck is Sergio praying so loudly?

POP! The sound of my knee joint cracking is heard throughout the quiet arena...

My entire body is desensitized while sitting on the examination table. The cast around my leg might as well be customized by aliens. It's foreign to me. Hot sweat against my skin has salted, cooling over. The pain drugs coursing through my veins have numbed the hurt, but this shit is still in my brain. Feels like I'm sinking. I'm a fucking failure

I'm a failure. There's a second L to my name and my belt.

"Your patella is fractured," the doctor shares.

"For how long?"

"Six to eight—"

"What the fuck do you mean, how long, babe?" Zariah cuts, tossing my question at me. "Vassili, baby, stop. We have a good life! We have a beautiful baby girl, who your doctor hasn't cleared you to hold without you having to be in a seated position! And your only question is *for how long.*"

"Zar—"

"What's next? *How long* until you get back into that cage and . . ." Zariah stops speaking abruptly and steps out of the room. The blinds along the window of the door bounce back and forth as the door is harshly closed.

Heat prickles across my skin as I rub a hand along my face. Vadim's arms are folded. He has no words for me either.

Every time I blink, my belt is being snatched away from me.

"Unfortunately, holding your daughter is off-limits, unless you're seated," the doctor reiterates. He'd explained the 'how to' bullshit. "For now, you'll use a wheelchair."

I gotta get back in the cage! "When do I get physical therapy?"

"We will talk about crutches next month. But I'll see you on Tuesday. Nevertheless, we have a few things to verse your wife on, concerning proper care."

I gesture toward the door, and the doctor flees.

"What happened?" Vadim groans.

"I lost."

"You didn't think to *tap out*, Vassili? I screamed that shit to you, man!" My coach's voice strangles as he shouts. "You didn't even shout because of the excruciating pain. Just held your gaze and your gritted teeth as if you're so fearless. As if you are invincible. The crowd was silent. Don't tell me you didn't hear me shouting: Tap out. Tap out. Tap. The. Fuck. Out. How many times has Nestor—"

"I AM THINKING!"

"— placed you in a 'kneebar,'" he continues right along. "Just for you to get the picture and A, fix the situation or B, tap the fuck out."

My finger points to the door. I shout, "I looked like a bitch! Give me a fucking moment."

"You need a moment? You're an idiot." He pokes me in the forehead. "Tell me what happened? Vassili, you gotta tell me what happened. One way or another, I'm your coach. We have to work on this. Was it all a show of balls?"

"I was..." I stop talking as Zariah returns to the room.

"Where's Natasha?" I ask.

Her tear-stained eyes turn toward me. "I drove here, Taryn and Yuri met me in the parking lot when I called. They're sitting in the car with our child...our child that *you cannot even pick up!*"

"I'm sorry."

"Vassili, it's a game," she softens. "I know how much it means to you, baby. Life goes on, outside of the cage. I am in utter shock, so expect me to be a bitch until this crap sinks in."

Vadim quietly steps out of the room now.

Another image of my belt passes before my eyes. I slam my palm into my forehead. "Fuck!"

Zariah leans against the wall, next to a poster of the human body. Eyes red, her cheeks are a river.

I can't even stand up and go to her. There's nothing for me to say that will soothe the hurt I've caused her.

"You chose not to tap out. I watched every second on Pay-Per-View," she murmurs, with her head to the ceiling. "The scariest thing I've ever watched, but I didn't even have the power to look away. Gotti told you to tap out. I could see his lips moving. I screamed so loud, Natasha started crying. I swear she cried herself to sleep during the hour drive here. Gotti told you to tap out," she whimpers. "Did Nestor? Did Vadim? Were they shouting in your corner?"

Lips set in a line, I nod.

"Then why?" she asks the question that the entire MMA world would like to know.

I rub a hand across my mouth. "Remember that mudak who touched Ronisha?"

Fresh tears wet her eyes. "No amount of trying can stop me from thinking about what I asked of you. That was over nine years ago, baby."

I glance down at my hands, my hands that have failed me. "I was winning the fight. I had that cunt pinned to the ground."

"You did. Talk to me, Vassili. What happened?" Zariah steps before the examination table, stroking my hair.

"I had Louie, The Legion, Gotti right where I wanted him. Fear in his eyes. I was lining that bitch up for the triangle choke. He'd become my next submission—fucking easy."

"Easy," Zariah murmurs, doing wonderful things to my hair. She coaxes the fence around my emotions to fall. The instant I lost my belt, I broke.

I huff, "Yeah, easy. Then I saw Sergio through him. Never did I give a fuck about Sergio. I would *kill* him again. A few years ago, his mother passed. I sent the family a check. I'd been too bitter, didn't give a fuck about him when he died. When I heard of his mother's death, I learned that she lived in a bad neighborhood, she'd been going blind. The mother-fucker was the woman's only kid. Sergio might've been a good son, a bad fucking son. I don't know. But on the chance that he had been there for his mother, I'd taken him from her, Zariah. Not to say that I would go back on my actions, there are few things in this life that I regret. But, I've never been a murderer, baby, not until that day."

37

ZARIAH

My heart is ripped to shreds. The words are lodged in my throat to tell Vassili that it's time to retire. To change his occupation. To become someone safer for our child's sake. For us.

The second he mentioned Sergio, shame clings to me as I move closer toward the examination table. My body is weak, and I hardly have the strength but know I must. I have to be the strength for him. Mentally, as he copes with Sergio. Physically, like the doctor told me. He talks of attending Sergio's mother's funeral, and my heart crumbles.

My hands glide through his slick waves. Placing my fingers along his jaw, I'm careful not to touch one of his bruises. "No, you're not a murderer, Vassili."

I want to place the blame on me. Say I pushed him to it, however, my husband isn't the type to sidestep his role in things. A thick silence ensues, and I pull the hair along his nape.

"Vassili, look at me."

His hardened features soften as his dark gaze seeks mine.

"You are a good man. I love you for it. Oh, baby, we'll always have each other."

Those years before Vassili and I came back together during my undergrad prepared us. He was my rock, catapulting my confidence when I began at Spelman. Pressley Prep prepared me. But sinking my teeth into education, in a college setting, was still different. And for those first few years, I had Vassili.

When we head home, I'm right at his side. It doesn't appear that the situation's sunk into Vassili's mind until I pull into the driveway. Our sleeping baby is in the convertible car seat. Never in my husband's company have I had to strap in Natasha or heft around the heavy contraption. Yet, when I get out to help her, his jaw clenches.

He rubs the back of his neck saying, "Wish I could help."

"It's okay," I mumble. It would be easier to take Natasha from the car seat. But wake her when she sleeps, and heads will roll.

Over the next couple of weeks, we have our highs and lows. The good times are marked with me cleaning the house. I'd laugh at Vassili as he wheels Natasha around to E40's "Tell Me When To Go" on Spotify. The old rap song blares through the speakers that were installed in every room of our house. The way Natasha likes it. Our five-month-old sits in Vassili's lap. With one arm around her, he tilts the wheelchair, popping wheelies in the hallway as I straighten the kitchen after breakfast.

Lord, as bougie as I was, I messed around and married a ghetto ass white boy. "Vassili, if you 'ghost ride the whip' with my baby, I will kill you! Turn that old ass song off." I shake my head, laughing but not nearly as hard as our baby is. There's drool dribbling down her chubby jaw.

The music cuts. I grab the copper skillet from the island and place it into the foamy dishwater. Just as D'Angelo's "Brown Sugar" comes on. I screech, "Heyyyy!"

My hips sway as I step toward the hall again. He had to have changed the station.

"What is this song?" Vassili's sexy Russian accent feigns disgusted while placing his hand over Natasha's ears. "My baby can't listen to this."

She wiggles and squirms, loving the music. She loves *all* music.

"Humph, all the uncensored rap and she can't listen to one of my old favs? Whatever, Vassili, sounds like Natasha likes it. And your other baby loves it." I walk over to them and kiss her forehead before smooching his lips. "I prefer this to gangster rap and rock music, FYI."

The moment I start to sashay into the kitchen, the song cuts as D'Angelo croons about his eyes being the shade of blood burgundy.

"You know what?" I turn around, placing my hand on my hip. Vassili smiles through his eyes as I point a stiff finger at him. "I could have *you* load the dishwasher, boy. You talk all that teamwork and act like you're my coach. So this would be a good time to assert my coaching skills, but I'll play nice."

That was a good day. There are many of those, which ultimately outweighed the bad. Natasha transitions from the army crawl to hustling around like she's training for the baby Olympics. I help Vassili get around. At least, I argue to him. "You can't—"

"That word's not in my vocabulary, sweetheart," he retorts, ready to slide from the wheelchair to the plush carpet in Natasha's playroom.

"So you'd rather fall onto your ass." My toe snaps the wheel into a locked position.

He grunts his appreciation.

"Hey, we're running low on food." I shoot a thumb over my shoulder. "I'll go stock up on groceries."

Our subzero refrigerator and pantry were stock full before the fight. The two of us did big grocery shopping together, when not having a taste for this ice cream or that glass of wine.

He glances around, the hopeless feeling weighs down his broad shoulders.

"I'll get Natasha tired out for the night."

I nod and smile. We haven't screwed since Louie Gotti became champ. I've tried to give Vassili head and he would have just taken his pain medication, which causes drowsiness. Or I'm running after Natasha, which causes an equal amount of drowsiness.

At Whole Foods, I speak with a representative about the grocery delivery service. The prices are ridiculous. Though we have more than enough money in the bank, and The Red Door is a consistent stream of income, I wouldn't feel comfortable paying for such a luxury. At least, not until I start working again.

While meandering down each aisle, I slurp a green smoothie. I chat with rich, old white ladies who either visit the grocery store, donning every sparkling diamond they own. They're here, either out of loneliness or for the samples. After learning about a pink-haired woman's villa in Italy, where she plans to spend Christmas, I notice towers of cranberry sauce. Everyone's preparing for the holidays besides us. I head up the wine aisle. *Damn, I don't wanna go home yet.* The only time I leave the house these days is to transport Vassili to rehab and a few 'mommy and me' classes.

While scanning the red wines, I notice a pale blond. We hardly glance each other's way, but this is Beverly Hills. Everyone is a tad nicer than the rest of the Los Angelenos. Her smile is pathetic, mine is as well. She places a bottle into a cart.

"Are those on sale?" I ask since the cart is full to the brim with bottles. We have a wine pantry that needs filling.

"No," she says in a thick Russian accent. "Still worth it though," she adds, thin lips rising in a wry grin.

"You look familiar." The words creep out of my mouth just as I think of them. Vivid images of a horse galloping down the passageway in Moscow control my mind for a second. "Are you Russian?"

"Yes."

"Were you in Moscow about a year ago? Um, I'm sorry." I run my fingers through my kinky hair. "The last time I was in Russia, I was almost run down by a horse. And a woman, who I swear looks like the spitting image of you, pulled me to safety." *Shit, now I know some folks say 'all black people look alike' but damn.* I wait for her to confirm my notion.

The lady huffs. "Couldn't have been me. I haven't gone home in years. There's nothing in Russia for me. Albeit, there's nothing at my current home for me. Hence, all the wine. Helps me cope with marriage."

A lump of embarrassment slides down my throat. I glance at the sorrow on her face, it makes me want to bow out of this entire aisle.

"My name is Danushka Molotov." We shake hands.

"Zariah, Zariah Resnov. I'm married to a Russian."

"Well, good luck with that. Shit, was that too blunt?" Danushka sighs. "I've got one foot out of the door in my marriage. I could leave my husband, the money. I-I shouldn't be telling you all of this. This isn't your problem."

I start to dig into my purse. "No, I came over and bothered you. Danush…"

"Danny, call me Danny."

"Okay, Danny. I'd like to give you my card. I'm on baby bonding at the moment. But If you ever need an attorney." I hand it over. "Look, you're dressed for the cover of Vogue magazine. I'm confident you can afford the best Beverly Hills has to offer. But if you need genuine help, Billingsley Law will do everything they can. I might not be in if or when you call, but I work with a stellar team."

"Thank you." She clutches the card close.

I grab a bottle of Pinot Noir and head toward the checkout line. I've been gone long enough. When I glance back toward the wine section, Danushka is gone. My eyebrows crinkle in confusion. She'd left the cart, which had thousands of dollars' worth of wine in it.

VASSILI

W hile Zariah is at the grocery store, I tire Natasha out as much as I can for an afternoon nap. She has a colorful play mat gym, with toy compartments hanging from a dome-like structure in the shape of a turtle. While she plays, I wheel out of the room, place up the fencing so she can't crawl out. Then I navigate as fast as I can to the master suite. There are a few piles of clean clothes on the bed. I fold the mountain of clothing for Natasha. Finished with that I pause, looking at the time. The baby monitor registers that Natasha's laughing at something. Good. I start with Zariah's undergarments which are next, fold those and put them away. Then I glance at the clock. *Shit, I want this room chill, but the time is moving too fast.*

I shove my mixed-matched socks into the bottom dresser drawer. Grab a few candles off the top while listening to the baby monitor. It's silent. *Matches, where are matches.*

There used to be a pack of matches in my pocket, with my freshly rolled cigarettes. Zariah wouldn't have it. Putting the candles back, I turn the radio on to my wife's favorite R&B station, isolating the surround sound to this room. Hopefully, she'll be surprised when she comes upstairs. By now, I'm wheeling around like crazy, drawing a steamy bath. My biceps are warmly conditioned as I return to the tub and turn off the water before the suds can overflow.

Then I head to the playroom. First thing I see amongst the play-mats is Natasha's bubble-shaped pamper in the air. Shit, I should have changed her diaper first. I wheel over as close as I can get to the mat without dragging the wheelchair. I reach down and scoop her up as slowly as possible. She coos against my chest while I hold her with one hand and wheel out of her playroom and to her nursery.

Inside, I head toward the cherry wood baby changing table. My mouth tenses as I glance up at how high it is. *There's no way I can do this while seated.*

Downstairs, we have a convertible station, which isn't nearly as tall. These days, Zariah has changed most of the diapers. I feel like shit for it. *I'm a man, no bitching out.* Cradling her in the football position, I kick up the footrest and favor my right foot. *Don't apply pressure to the left, you idiot!*

I arise slowly, placing Natasha onto the changing mat. The moment she's freed from my hand, I accidentally press onto my left leg. Fire shoots through my knee.

"FUCK!"

Natasha's plump arms and legs jerk, stiffening and she cries.

"I'm sorry, beautiful." I stay standing, taking the excruciating pain. No teeth, all lungs, she cries her little heart out. "I'm a mudak, baby, I'm sorry. Let Daddy change your diaper."

No amount of coaxing or blowing raspberries against her belly will stop her. By now I take the pain like the dick I am, changing her as swiftly as possible. "Natasha, sweetheart, you gotta stop crying. You're making my head hurt. You're making your head hurt." *Can babies get headaches?*

I grit my teeth, sinking to the wheelchair with her in my arms. In a fresh diaper and a Thanksgiving onesie, Natasha cries. I hold her out before me cradled in my forearms.

"Listen, sweetheart, Daddy screwed up. But you are my world, I would never hurt you or scare you intentionally." Her eyes are so innocent. I proceed to have a conversation with Natasha about the bullshit reason why I'm not walking.

"Damn, sweetheart, I used to be the life of your party. I'd do bar lifts and you'd be seated on the floor laughing your little ass off until you fell back into scattered pillows. About a month ago, I made the biggest mistake of my life, Natasha."

Her crying wanes, big brown gaze locked onto mine.

"You still mad at me? Because your mom is angry with me. Zar tries not to let it show—and nobody in this world takes care of you as she does. But I fucked up. All because I love to fight. Now, I love you and your mom the most." she smiles, and I nod. "That's right, sweetheart. You and mommy are untouchable, my favorite people in the whole world."

Natasha coos.

I nod, agreeing with her. "Okay, so Daddy doesn't like too many people. But the two of you are at the tippy top of the people I like and love. Then there's MMA. I told you about it before, do you remember."

With my hand at the back of Natasha's head, I make her nod a little, though she appears to be listening intently. "So last month I messed up. I had this guy right where I wanted him, beating the snot outta him. Baby, I had it set up to annihilate him, no sweat off my back. Then I screwed up."

"Cooo."

"Yeah, you're right. I'll get my belt back. When I do, I'm gonna sweep Mommy off her feet, plant kisses on her face and do things that you are never to learn about. Got that?" I grin. She laughs. "Then I'll be back at the top. The king of the cage—welterweight class, but the king, baby, nonetheless."

"Cooo... gaaa. Dadaaaa..."

"You are so smart, Natasha. You are right, again. Dada will get into the octagon. I'll do a few TKOs first, to get into the swing of things, then back to my submissions. Killing 'em softly, I always say. There's a delicacy about it, not everybody can place someone into submission. Shit, not everybody can knock a fighter out in one hit, either. It was 2014 and the man's nose was big, so I had to correct that shit, baby."

Natasha laughs. I start to tell her about another fight. "Seems to me you prefer a good knock out to submission. One day, I'll teach you. Yeah, you're young. Everyone your age loves the brutal, cocky way. There's something about that damn cage, sweetheart..."

"Are you serious?" My wife snaps.

I slowly edge the wheelchair around.

Zariah stands at the nursery door, hands on her thick hips. "You're glorifying and telling our daughter how awesome the UFC world is, right now? At this instant while sitting in a wheelchair."

"Zariah—"

"Forget you, Vassili! My shoulders hurt, my feet hurt. And to top it all off, I met a woman about an hour ago. Her name was Dana... Danas... Danny!" She grumbles. "She made me realize how much I miss working."

"Okay, then you should go back to work." My tone is calming as Natasha turns her head and wiggles around in my lap to see her mom. Our baby is all smiles, but Zariah is seething.

"Go back to work? How? I have to help you, Vassili."

I laugh softly. "Nyet, sweetheart. I'm not an invalid."

"Humph! Whatever, Vassili. Whatever you say. I bet the

moment you finish rehab, it's back to the ring. Is it back to the ring?"

"Nyet, it's the *cage*. And yes, I'll return."

"Good for you." She turns in her heels and struts away.

"Come back here. We need to talk," I call out. Venom courses through my veins. I can't stand up, grab her, and take her over my knee! With Natasha in my lap, I wheel like crazy to our room. "We need to talk, Zariah!"

She's turning up the music and changing it to a more upbeat pop song.

My pupils almost pop out of my motherfucking eyes. "Zar, Zariah…"

She starts for the bathroom, kicking off her shoes and unbuttoning her blouse.

"Guess I should thank you for drawing me a bath. I dragged in a thousand bags while you're chatting happily about MMA! I could understand if you got into an accident, Vassili. But you're going to be in a wheelchair during Natasha's first portraits for Christmas, all because of a game. It's a game!"

I push forward before she can step inside the bathroom and shut the double doors. My right toe swipes inside of her calf, making her pace falter. That's good enough. She stops and turns around.

"What the fuck is your problem?" I mouth quietly. "When it's that time of the month—I take that shit, because … because you cop an attitude once a month. But, you need to calm down."

"Or what," she reaches forward and places her hands over Natasha's ears. Our baby wiggles and tries to paw her away. "Will you screw the anger out of me? We haven't screwed in a month, Vassili. It would've been nice. Thanks for the bath, but after hearing you so jovial in your talk about fighting, I can't. Not tonight."

I grab her wrist. "I am going to return to the cage, Zariah. Maybe not tomorrow, but that shit is inevitable. I know that you know that."

"Vassili, I have sat back and taken you to the doctors. I know you're preparing for rehab, but … but I can't. I swear to you, I can't. Yuri had to stop me the other day from getting onto social media because of your name being on some list. Later on, I went back, and I looked at the damn list. It was of fighters with the top ten worst MMA leg injuries. The sight was gruesome. I know you break a finger and a damn toe after every other damn fight, but… that list. Vassili, you made the top eight. The worst ones, I can't see that happen to you. I refuse."

"Oh, don't give me that shit. So, you saw some dude with a broken fibula or tabula or something."

"Yes! And I won't see it happen to you."

I grit out, "And it won't! Zar. You are too sheltered, sweetheart. Shit is gonna happen, but I won't top that list, okay?"

She straightens up. "How about this. *It's Natasha and me or the cage. You choose.*"

"Don't fucking do that." I glance down at our baby, who is excitedly eyeing us both. "I can't even believe you'd say these things while I'm holding Natasha! *Natasha is my princess. You're my queen, so you know that the answer will always be the two of you!*"

"Somehow," she mumbles. "I doubt it."

Zariah walks into the bathroom and pushes both doors closed in our faces. My eyes are burning.

"Baabaa, daadaadaaaa."

I can't even offer my child a smile. "Listen, Mommy is angry with Daddy. I won't let her go, sweetheart. I was brought up in a broken home. That shit won't happen to you. I will not allow it."

ZARIAH

That must have been the worst night of my life. In truth, I went off. It was a combination of menstruation cramps, not living my dream career and the 'Top Ten worst MMA leg injuries' list. I'd almost puked while watching each one because I was too damn dumb not to watch. The love for fighting was blinding them.

I spoke with Samuel about it, as I value the love he and his late-wife modeled. He told me that people oftentimes argue in their marriage. It's all about coming back together after a fight, not allowing those feelings to propel us further apart. So, I must've wallowed and apologized. Vassili didn't use the shit I slung at him in our argument at all, as I've seen occur in other people's relationships. He simply accepted my apology.

Over the next couple of months, my husband completes rehabilitation. Every increase in his strength, he equates to his queen and his princess. We have arguments, but none of them parallel in comparison to that night.

When Vassili returns to Vadim's Gym, Natasha is nine months old. I silently pray that God keeps my husband safe as he spars with Nestor. Yuri is shouting about how good of a fighter his cousin is, in that accent. All I want to do is laugh about how he says cousin, but I'm too nervous.

Taryn bumps her shoulder against mine. "Girl, everything is good. Now, give me that baby so you can go cheer your man."

I chuckle. When I grab Natasha by the underarms to hold her out, she pulls against me. "No!"

"Oh, hell no," Taryn says. "How many times have I snuck you candy when I watched you while your mom and dad went on a date. I have blown off many Friday nights for your little cute self."

Natasha shakes her head.

"Oh, Natasha," Yuri turns to her. "Taryn and I took you to Disneyland—"

"You took my baby to Disneyland?!" I snap.

Taryn grumbles under her breath. She gives him an incredulous look as she groans. "Yuri, why?"

He shrugs. "It was a few hours while you guys were at that concert. But… uh…"

"Vassili and I haven't taken her yet," I pout.

"Look on the bright side." Taryn grins, "You aren't worried about Vassili now. You can take out all that rage on Yuri." She sinks back into the foldable chair and laughs her ass off.

Yuri says something in Russian. Natasha's eyes widen. Somehow, I believe my baby understands. Her dad says certain things in Russian, too, that shit pisses me off.

"Good, Good," Vadim shouts as they work on a few standard routines. I glance toward the cage. "Tell Nestor if you feel any pain."

Vassili speaks in Russian. *Here we go again.* I narrow my eyes at him, and he winks at me.

"Zar, your husband said he's a pussy," Nestor laughs while blocking another hit.

Vassili fires on him, crosses and hooks. "Don't say that word in front of my baby!"

"Okay!" Nestor does his best to block most hits, and although he's wearing headgear, he stumbles around.

"That is good!" Vadim grips the cage while ordering from the outside, "Now, no horsing around, Vassili."

Natasha climbs down my leg. She's started to stand on her own. She holds onto the edge of my skirt and begins to move around to see her father.

"Vassili!" I shout. She starts to walk.

"Vassili!" Taryn and I screech in unison.

"Oh, shit, oh, shit," Yuri says. "My God baby!"

"She's walking. Go, Natasha," Vassili says, as he and Nestor pump a fist in the air.

"Next year, I want you in my cage, girl," Vadim declares.

"No, she won't," I quickly say while laughing and cheering. She falls. I hurry to catch her, and Vassili picks her up before I can. Damn, he got out of the cage and down here in a second.

"Taryn did you get this on camera," I ask her.

Her eyes brighten. She gives this idiot look. I shake my head. My friend still doesn't have a job, she still lives off her father and Yuri as well. I glance at him. He shrugs. Damn, these two are a match made in heaven.

"Oh, no, we didn't take a picture or anything." I pout.

"Don't worry, I got it." We all glance toward the weight section.

Sergy, the three-headed monster adds, "I got video."

He hands over his phone. Within an album full of selfies, there is a short clip of Natasha walking.

I mutter, "Way to go, Yuri. When I send this to my mom, all she will hear is your cussing 'Oh, shit.'"

Sergy nods. "I didn't get it when she first started, but I got a couple of steps. The way you were all shouting about it, I thought I should. Vassili, I'll text it to you."

My husband nudges me softly as I thank him. Vassili knows damn well that every time I cross paths with Sergy, I'm still a little embarrassed about how I cussed him out. I've never cussed anyone out so badly besides my husband, but that's a part of marriage.

VASSILI

Three months later...

I fractured my patella 215 days ago. Who am I kidding? Getting back in the cage is in the cards, but I'm not quite ready. Yuri asked me if I was sure a million times before securing the battle in Brazil. The current 'favorite' is Tiago. He's got the right stats for eyes to follow. But who the fuck am I kidding? Everyone wants to see the ex-welterweight champ gun for his belt. Anywhere I choose to start would work.

I'm not ready. My knee hurts. But that shit will stay between my new doctor and I. The Doc is paid well to meet me before training. He injects cortisone into my knee. One day, I'll be good without it.

Today, Zariah is in one of her bitch moods. Natasha's first birthday is around the corner. We all know I love my baby, with all my heart. But c'mon. Zariah's recorded these old shows from this dude, who is a celebrity party planner. Taryn said the guy gave her a party once, a party that she and Zariah couldn't shut the fuck up about when they talked.

Now, Zariah's auditioned teenybopper singers and a chef who makes gourmet kiddie food.

"Oh, I have to invite my friend, Danny," Zariah says scanning over the birthday list while we sit at the kitchen table. Taryn and Yuri just left, they'd stuffed these bags that Zariah said were for favors.

"Who?"

"Danash… after half a year, I still can't pronounce her name. Danny hasn't decided to divorce, but we meet for coffee sometime."

I'm halfheartedly listening to her because she keeps cramming people onto the list. The party will be at Samuel's home. We have a big enough backyard, but Zariah said he has a larger yard and less of a pool. The way she's going at it, Samuel's place won't work soon. There's one person she can take off the list. That motherfucking dad of hers. But I choose my battles. We've both been choosing well these days. I squeeze the 'Captains of Crush' trainer in my hand, letting my forearms flex and relax rapidly. *Don't start shit, Zariah...* We've been good for the last few months, but the stress of Natasha's first birthday has me flexing swiftly.

"Vassili, not everyone is highlighted." Zariah's eyebrows crunch together.

"We ran out of invitation cards, Zar, be easy."

Her gaze zeros in on my rapid movement. "Why didn't *you order more?*"

"Don't start, girl. I don't need the Q and A. Have a little faith and assume I attempted."

I sat on the phone, passed around from worker to worker at a special printing place to request more invitations. Now she mentions someone named Danny when I would rather she be a tax attorney. It's much safer than a family attorney, but I won't argue with her on that, as she only works three days out of the week.

"Did you? Or have you been isolating various parts of your anatomy all day? I spent all day searching for the plush elephants to add to the favors. There are a hundred favors..."

I glare. Fuck favors. I don't understand the necessity.

She continues to prattle, "Which means I went to twenty-something stores to get enough of them. Then I come home, Natasha's laughing her ass off while you work out."

My eyebrows knit in thought. That was yesterday. She just got home. Oh, I got it. "You worried about my fight with Tiago?"

"No." Her response is too quick.

Don't lie. "Beautiful, you went postal on me. Are you worried?" I'm sympathetic because I feel guilty for lying. I haven't misled Zariah since she thought Malich was my father. Now, she asks me how my leg is every morning, and I offer the response she craves.

"Vassili, I'm preparing for our child's first birthday party. Hello, Vassili! It's a few weeks away," she says, through gritted teeth.

BAM.

I place the grip strengthener on the table. There's no need arguing with Zariah about how this is teamwork. For every move she's made to make Natasha's party a success, I have checked off something on her 'to-do list.' And my wife has a colorful, highlighted motherfucking 'to-do list.'

My tone is nurturing as I focus on what counts, "I will fight in two days, sweetheart. Only God can stop me. Don't be mistaken, you and Natasha are my everything. I've said that all along. Every morning before I train, haven't I said that? When the fight is complete, I'll pick up our little growing tumbleweed and hug her tightly. After that, I'll fuck her mother until all those stress kinks disappear."

She licks her lips, kneading the back of her neck. I stand

up and go to her. Pulling out her chair, I kneel. My wife watches every move I make, worry sparked in her eyes.

I love her, so I will do my best not to show weakness or pain. But there's no way in hell I'm not getting into that cage this weekend.

"After I sex you senseless tonight, I'll beat Tiago Saturday night. We finish the weekend out in Brazil with family. Once we return, we meet with that mudak party planner of yours, and choose a clown for Natasha's birthday, right?"

"Yes."

"Tomorrow morning, we leave bright and early. In seventy-two hours, all the hard work we both have done will pay off." My forehead nestles against hers, and I caress her cheek. The anxious lioness no longer seems caged.

"I'm being awful," she mumbles.

Instead of agreeing, my hand clamps the inside of her thigh, kneading the thick meat of it. Then I reach beneath her skirt, my fingers push aside her thong, plunging into her wet core. Her lower back curves on contact, craving more penetration.

"Wet and tight," I growl, nipping her bottom lip.

My fingers work her pussy.

"Vassili, no more play. I'm a grown-ass woman."

My abdominals flex against the inside of her thighs as I laugh. "Maybe I'm fucking with you for being so mean?"

"You know how I get." She moans, leaning into me.

"Yeah. After all you did for elephants and fucking favors, you know I haven't been home sitting on my ass or sparring all afternoon."

"I know. I'm soooooorrrrrrryyyyyy." She smiles.

"You sorry?" My eyebrow cocks. "That's not enough."

She gasps and in a nanosecond, Zariah is off the chair. I've positioned her into my lap as I sit on the floor, with her legs straddling me. Shit, the dull ache in my left knee. "You want me to fuck that succulent cunt, don't you?"

She leans in to kiss me.

"Nyet, not so fast, you are in trouble." I hold up my fingers, all glossy and wet. Zariah licks the pussy juices clean off. Her lips pull me into her mouth. "I will let you do that to my dick first, suck it all in your mouth tonight. I'll beat that pussy until you cry. You want that?"

"Please." She sighs.

"Undress first." I hold out my hand, and we both stand.

Zariah pulls out of her sleeveless blouse. I watch her every move, as she pulls out of her skirt and panties. All those dark brown curves surrounding a cleanly shaved pussy. In this instant, I decided to be an asshole, a little. She deserves it and she knows damn well that she does.

"Vassili..." Zariah sinks back down to the floor, glancing up at me, "please, can I suck your cock?"

"You eat this cock and guzzle down my cum," I order. "Maybe you'll be forgiven, and I will beat that pussy for you."

She reaches out a hand. I slap it down. "No touching unless it's with that pretty-ass mouth, beautiful."

Flushed pink lips glide across my shaft. I brace my legs for her. Zariah sucks my dick like no other woman ever has. Her mouth is warm, cozy, as it pulls the tip of my cock in. Zariah takes me in further, sliding me to the back of her throat. About seven inches and the base of my dick is chilled, yet her eagerness is amazing. And then Zariah glances up at me. Ebony eyes searching for forgiveness. My knuckles graze across her cheek.

"Wider, open wider," I command. Though, there's no doubt I'll be slaughtering her cunt, tonight. "You want me to beat the pussy, you'll open wider."

Her moan vibrates against my steel shaft. This takes me

to heaven. I tighten my hand into her thick, curly hair. Helping speed her pace.

Slurping sounds send my balls tightening up against my cock. "You can touch me now, Zariah. Rub my balls, beautiful."

Her mouth fucks me sloppy. All wet goodness. With her handwork, I've arched down her throat now. My cock slides out of her mouth. Her tongue glides over my balls. She does her best to get the baseball-sized globes into her mouth, then settles on sucking and licking. Her throat hums as she alternates from showing each an equal amount of attention.

With those innocent brown eyes on me, Zariah leaves a wet trail from under each ball, to the base of my cock. Then her tongue travels up to my tip, before traveling back down again. She does this sequence until my cock is seeping with precum. My cock pushes against the back of her throat again as she moans along with me. Then she takes my cock to the head once more. Alternating from attending to each of my balls and sucking the life out of my head.

"I'm gonna cum," I growl, toes gripping. I swear her body shivers in anticipation while she works at my straining cock. She sucks harder. Her tonsils massage the head of my shaft while her tongue swirls around the middle. I aim down her throat, shooting a flow of cum straight to her stomach.

ZARIAH

O kay, so I went hard on him today. But my mind is consumed with Natasha's first birthday, and Vassili returning to the ring in less than two days. He picks me up into his arm and tells me how well I sucked his cock. Since my mom is visiting from Atlanta and she took out Natasha, we hurry upstairs on the chance that she returns to the house, as she has a key.

Damn, I didn't quite consider that while begging for Vassili's seed a second ago. In our bedroom, my hands squeeze against the underpart of the headboard. Vassili chomps down on my pussy. His tongue is licks and wags along my throbbing pussy lips. He sucks at my clit, skimming his teeth across it. It hurts so good. Then he sucks deep inside of me, slithering his tongue along my core.

"Damn," I scream, "Shit, *Vassili!*"

He squeezes my thighs in response but doesn't dare come up for air. My back is arched, ass scooted forward as he fingers my anus and drinks more of my cum. He gives such good head that I sniffle tears, screaming and crying while my legs shake.

Once I'm weak, Vassili's muscular frame climbs on top of me. He slaps his cock against the inside of my thigh.

"Best water I ever had." His intoxicating Russian accent is so low, the sound of my heart beating in my ears dominates my hearing. He wipes the gloss from his lips with the back of his hand.

I'm wetter than my wildest dreams when Vassili's thick, veined cock slides into my body. The length of him stretches me out so good. Now his hand slams down onto the top of the headboard, and I suck in a breath and grin. Then he clutches my calves over his shoulders. He kisses the softness of my thighs while slamming into me. In and out, he fucks me so hard that the headboard slams against the wall with each thrust.

"Yes… Lord… Yesss…. Vassili…" I scream until we're slick with sweat and my voice cracks. With each thrust, my walls tremble around his thick cock. My screaming drowns out. He explodes inside of me. I love the feeling of the never-ending squirt of his warm cum. It's like he's doped me up with his dose of endorphins. Vassili sinks onto me. I hold his steel frame for a few seconds without feeling crushed. When he rolls over, I flop over too, pressing my hip and leg over him.

"I love you," he murmurs into my forehead, kissing it.

Warmth spreads across my mahogany skin and I smile. "I love you, Vassili."

He squeezes my waist.

"Can you promise me something?" My breath brushes across taut chest muscles.

Vassili nudges my chin. "Sweetheart, I've already promised you. You've got to believe me. When I get into the cage, if shit goes left, I'll pull out. You and Natasha are first."

He speaks of my biggest worry. Vassili squeezes my waist again. This time I nestle into him and believe it.

321

M om travels with us to Brazil to watch Natasha at the
hotel during the match. Natasha receives her first
passport stamp. Vassili had reclaimed his confidence during
the weigh-in, the day before the match. For the most part, I
enjoyed the scenery and a surprise trip to the spa that Vassili
planned for my mother and I. Then I focused all my energy
on praying for my husband before he steps into the cage. All
I could do was place him in God's hands.

Now, my heart is lodged in my throat. I play with the
cross pendant of Vassili's necklace that he placed on me
before I left him to warm up. Taryn is seated next to me, Yuri
on the opposite side of her. To my other side is a Brazilian
man. Natives dominated the entire area, sending a wave of
cheers for their people and 'booing' the hell out of us.

Squeezing the cross in my palm, I breathe heavily.

"Zariah, Yuri says everything is going well," Taryn tells me
rubbing her hand along my arm.

Like a bobblehead, attempting to convince myself, I nod
vigorously. The referee stopped the fight in the first round
due to a gash in Vassili's forehead. A practitioner cleared him
to continue. However, the blood flowing in his face triggers
the hopelessness I felt when he'd fought Gotti.

"Yuri says heads are meant to leak."

"I know," I murmur, eyes glued to the cage.

"Well, if you keep looking like a ball of nerves, I'm going
to make your ass sit in the middle. Then Yuri can give you a
play-by-play like this is your first fight." Taryn smiles, but her
attempt at a joke doesn't help. "Stop worrying."

In round two, I've rubbed my hand over my face so much
that the little makeup I wear is on my palms. Vassili's forehead is dribbling with blood again.

White noise fuzzes in my ears, dominating the ruckus of

the crowd. The third round has commenced, and I won't make it. I feel her hands weave through mine and we meander through the crowded walkway toward the exit. Yet it's like I'm on the outside looking in as we pass through the doors.

"What are you doing, girl? Get back into the arena and support your man," she chides.

I stalk back and forth near the entrance to the ladies' room. Should've gone in there to hide.

Taryn snaps, "Zariah! How would Vassili feel if he looks over and you're not there?"

My head hangs. "He's in the zone, so he won't even notice I'm gone."

"Yes, he will!"

When I almost bump into two teen girls leaving the restroom, I stop the restless pace, hands atop of my head. "He's getting tired, I can feel it. He's hurt. I feel every bit of his pain, Taryn. I can't watch. It. Kills. Me."

My ears perk up. A rush of tears well in my eyes. The referee is questioning him yet again! The interpreter repeating each word. *Karo, would you like to stop?* Rings out over the loudspeaker.

"Oh, God, Oh, God, I left for a reason, I can't do this." My stilettos falter, I grab onto my friend's skinny frame, surprised that she supports me so well.

Taryn glares straight into my eyes. "Forget doubts, girl! Win or lose, you're returning to that match, Zariah. *If* you love him, support him."

My lips tense as she tosses the last dig, but she's right. Patting my tears with my fingertips, I follow her into the darkened arena. The lights are shining down on one spot. Vassili and Tiago. I beg for a quick takedown, but they're trading punches. Each hit meets its mark.

Jesus, give him strength. My husband jumps to his dominate leg. His left leg is forced forward, crushing against Tiago's mouth.

There's a blanket of booing as the Brazilian falls to his knees. In the flash of an eye, Vassili is choking him out, and Tiago slides down to the canvas in a dreamless sleep. I run toward the octagon, shouting like a crazed lunatic as my husband straddles the cage. He's tired and using every ounce of strength he has left. Happy tears warm my lashes as I place a hand over my mouth.

He's searching for me. A look of anger darkens his face as I push toward the security blocking the perimeter. I've gotta get to him and soothe away his disappointment.

Damn, I shouldn't have left. Why didn't I have the courage to stay!

"Your badge!" Taryn shouts from my side. We're both pushed left to right by those who'd like to congratulate Vassili.

"KILLER KARO IS BACK!" An English announcer shouts.

"Let her through!" Taryn screams at the man as I fumble with the pocket of my pantsuit for the badge.

Nestor helps me up the stairs, we are the last of his crew to enter his cage. Vassili's hugging everyone with a hard glare. My stepping hesitates when he notices me. The dark cloud over his eyes dissipates. His shoulders sag.

"Fuck, Zariah, I swear I wouldn't have continued if I didn't think..." My husband's shouting is almost a whisper to my ear. The background noise attempts to wash out his promises. The large cage decreases in size as more people step into it.

"No, baby." I kiss his mouth as he rubs the blood from his eyes. "You did great, Vassili. I love you. Nevertheless, I left for a moment, I'm sorry."

"Don't be sorry, Zar."

"We've only been married for a short while. I'll learn to do better. For a moment, I forgot that I had to be *fearless* for you."

Consider joining my newsletter to stay up to date on new releases and super discounts (especially during these holiday times). You'll also receive a free book for subscribing.

AUTHOR'S NOTE:

I hope you enjoyed the beginning of Vassili and Zariah's story. They've had a good number of ups and downs during this installment. Trust me, this is only the beginning.

Would you do me the biggest favor?

Please leave a review, I would be crazy happy about it. I read them all. Sometimes, the reviews can inspire me to continue on with a certain side character that people love ;)

Fearless III The Finale is on Pre-Order and launches on New Years Eve!!

Turn the page to sample Fearless II . . . or dive right in on Kindle Unlimited!

CONTACT ME

Before we get to Fearless II, I wanted to cover a few things.

The best way to chat with me is in my Facebook Group. I'm a bit on the shy side, but I'll open up there the most. The readers give me so much good insight. Often, I'll get ideas about what to write next from my group. They get to see all the sexy ideas I come up with first! And I'll be sharing some new Fearless news with them first . . .

But check out the various buttons below, and feel free to connect with me on whatever platform you prefer.

Give a few of my buttons a click and say hi! Then, turn the page for a sample of Fearless II, or grab it now on Kindle Unlimited!

Blessings,
 Amarie Nicole

#FEARLESS II

Prologue
Vassili Karo Resnov

Never get angry. Never get...too angry. And keep my fucking chill when outside of the octagon. I agreed to be a softy to make my marriage work.

I'm wide-legged on a leather chair, so fucking big and plush, it was made for me. A massive flat-screen is before me. I'm on display, slaughtering my opponent with a roundhouse kick. The other fighter is knocked out in midair and fell onto the blood-painted canvas like a rock. The KO segues into another one of my Killer Karo approved highlights. This time, my tactic is a raw submission. I had Hauser in an ankle hold that broke his shit clear in half almost two years ago.

While I stare at my first love, I fist my iPhone in my hand, waiting for my greatest love to answer. The images keep flickering of me in beast mode, going for the kill. I'm too good at this. Too good at being bad.

She finally answers.

"Hey, baby," Zariah says, breathing a tad heavy.

Her intake of air causes me to pull some into my lungs too. Damn, I realize my body was overdue for oxygen during the wait for her to answer. Last month, my wife was pressing the "away" button repeatedly and disregarding my calls.

My greatest matches fade from before my eyes, as I speak to my slice of heaven on earth. I ask, "Zariah, beautiful, you on your way?"

"I'm trying. Your child refuses to walk." Zariah's voice sounds muffled. "I opened the garage. Forgot something. Now I'm headed back to the garage with Natasha on one hip, her favorite juice spilling on me."

Tilting my head to the shiny chandeliers above, I silently thank God she forgave me. "That's Natasha, mayhem with apple juice."

From my peripheral, I notice my cousin, Yuri, has dropped his cane and is leaning against the doorframe. This fat, *mudak*—asshole—is eye fucking the pin-up doll for a maid. So far, she's done more bending over in my face because some idiot blabbed about my impending match.

"Send me a pic, Zar." I chuckle a little. "I don't mind a wet t-shirt contest—with you, girl. Even if you're soaked through with her juice."

"Whatever, Vassili. I don't have time to be abused by your mini-me."

"Oh, you don't?" I break into a grin. Our one-year-old is part of the reason I'm forgiven now.

Yuri turns around. "See, *kuzen* I told you Zariah is all talk. You two are good."

My wife continues with, "I'm all sticky, and we have less than an hour to..."

My eyebrows knit as I focus on the background noise with my wife.

Yuri winks. He thinks all is good. That I'm out of the doghouse.

But something changed in a split second. Zariah's tone is stricken with fear, and her voice lowers, "We —we have…"

My head tilts, facial expression darkening as Yuri stops leaning against the doorframe. He turns his attention from the slutty maid to me.

I ask, "Zariah, girl. What's wrong—"

"Mrs. Resnov, you've taken everything from me…" I hear a Latino male voice in the background.

Zariah scoffs, "Mr. Noriega… wh-what are you doing at my house? How do you know where I live?"

"Zariah," I shout into the phone. "Who is that!"

"Oh, is your husband on the phone?"

There are muffled noises. Yuri silently asks me what's going on. He mouths Zariah, and I nod.

"Mikhail will be at your house in a few minutes, kuzen," Yuri whispers.

I yell into the receiver, "ZARIAH, WHO IS—"

"Tell him."

She's trembling. Fuck, I can feel it light-years away.

Zariah begins to speak into the receiver, "It's Juan Noriega. He-he is—he's a Loco Dios. I'm representing his wife in their divorce," her voice scales down. And then she's pleading with him. Begging him to allow her to put our child in the house so they can talk. And I'm… useless.

Juan motherfucking Noriega? A knife has slid into my bones. Without fail, I've always forced Zariah to provide me with a rundown of every case she picks up. Regardless of it being family law, I refuse to have my wife in a dangerous situation. There was no mention of this mudak, Noriega. I'd have refused her request to take on any case that had anything to do with the infamous Loco Dios gang member. Shit, shit, shit. Whomever she represented against Noriega was more than deserving of justice. Instinct slams into me and churns sour.

This is revenge...

"Does he have a gun?" My voice is tapered. Her fucking answer, 'yes' is enough to feel two slugs piercing into my heart. But I continue to stay calm as Yuri sends out a message.

"Put him on the phone," I command, lips growing tauter with each word.

"Okay," Zariah says, her voice wrapped in terror that I've never known.

"The infamous Vassili Resnov," the man's voice is callous to the core.

"Who. The. Fuck. Are. You?"

"*Ay Dios Mio,* you sound scary," he laughs. "But I know you, mi amigo. You can knock my fucking spine lose, eh? Make me go goodnight."

I glare at the television screen. There's so much fucking blood. I'm massacring my opponent. My gaze fixates on the fighter's eyes, which cloud as he taps out in my arms. I glower so hard that the visual blurs before me.

"Nyet, I won't dislocate your spine. Not at first, piz'da," I grit out. My voice is calm and collected. Too calm for the fighter in me. "Keep talking to me, so that you don't have to die a slow, painful death, Noriega. You let my wife and daughter go. You can keep fucking talking to me about whatever Zariah has done to piss you off. We're both men," I pause for a beat. Fuck, he's not a man. A real man would've brought his grievance to the woman's husband in the first place.

"Sounds like I'm talking to the motherfucking Terminator. You scare me, Karo. I dunno if I want to talk to you . . . or your wife. Mrs. Resnov is so pretty. It's easier to speak to pretty people. Your daughter too."

"Don't," I growl.

"Aye, all I meant to say is I'm Juan Noriega. I take it you

338

know of me. But no worries, mi amigo, I'm a nobody these days. I know all about you, though," Noriega says. "Ex Welterweight UFC champ. Loved by the masses. I also know you're a fucking Resnov. Your family isn't to be fucked with."

The luxurious hotel had faded into oblivion. All I see myself doing is tearing this man limb from limb, killing him with my bare hands. His bones will fracture, turn into powder, to dust and then become nothing. Painting my hands with his blood until my knuckles break.

I gulp down the lump in my throat. "Then I don't need to inform you of my capabilities. My family's capabilities?"

"No, hombre. I'm dead already," his voice sours. "My parental rights were terminated for my ninos because of *your bitch.* My bitch upped and took my house, my cars, every-thing I have, also because of *your* bitch. At this precise moment, I've got a nine to *your bitch's* head. But don't worry, like I said, the bitch took my wife and my two kids. I heard *your bitch* is pregnant. I prayed to God the two of you *were* having a boy. So, the little nina and the baby in her tummy will meet the same ending."

"Noriega." My blood slows to a freezing point. I know that Yuri's in the background compelling me to keep this cunt open. To keep him talking. But I'm not that person. I'm not the fighter who has words for someone because my mind goes straight to how they're dealt with. All I can do is keep sight of my heaven. My Zariah, my Natasha, my baby in her belly! My fucking family that I'd go to hell for.

I beg God for sanity, hands balled into tight fists. It's the moment I need for composure. "Listen to me, if you touch my wife or my daughter, you will die a thousand deaths. I will beat you with my bare hands. That's already in the motherfucking cards. You've already consigned yourself to that. But do you want me to fucking murder you and revive

339

you a thousand times, all to have me tortured and murder you again?"

"You're capable of that, Mr. Resnov. The only problem is, I no longer have a heart. Adios, mi amigo."

Click!

My 190 pounds of muscle are shot. I stand, on limbs that want to fail me. But sheer drive keeps me going as I storm through the suite. "Where are my keys? Yuri, where the fuck are my keys?"

My cousin starts arguing with me. A lamp goes crashing. I toss a chair against the wall to get toward the front door of the suite. Finally, he halts my bulldozing through the room by grabbing my shoulders.

There's pain behind his eyes. Yuri's still favoring his one leg. But he grits through it and says, "*Nyet*—no! Vassili, *brat*. Everything will be good."

My world has tilted on a spindle. My head is chaotic, crazed. I'm seeing red. And I'm about to serve him the left hook he got when we went to jail a little while back. My bark is hard, "Yuri, move. I will fucking murder you to get to my wife, blood or no blood, bitch!"

He flinches, holding his palms out. "I can't. You can't. We can't fucking do anything for them no matter how much we—"

My forearm slams against his neck. Yuri is no longer my cousin. No longer family. He's part of the problem.

Fat cheeks reddening, Yuri bites out the words, "Va-Vassili, we are in Australia."

My eyebrows crinkled. I. Am. In. Australia. My title match is tomorrow. I'm a world away from my fucking heart! I let him go and grip at the top of my head. There's no more Mohawk to tug. My shit is all buzzed down. "Fuck the belt, Yuri. I don't want it."

Yuri rubs at his neck. "Okay, *kuzen*, but—"

"I need to get home!" I punch the wall next to him. It's all marble. My knuckles crush against the glossed stone. The skin has pulled back and blood smears, leaving a trail.

"That's impossible, Vassili. We are too far away. We're in fucking Australia! I have a crew on the way..." My cousin is speaking, though I can't understand the words. All I see is myself becoming a monster.

"You'll have a heart attack. We will handle this. Mikhail promised to keep them safe. He is on the way to your home right now," he argues through gritted teeth. But Yuri's words hardly penetrate. I concentrate on God. Over the years, having faith hasn't been easy. I toss up a promise. This day will mark the end of my relationship with Him if the worst occurs.

Please leave your review and grab book two now!!